James Follet

THE DOOMSDAY ULTIMATUM

CAGE OF EAGLES

ARROW

This edition published by Arrow in 2002
an imprint of The Random House Group
20 Vauxhall Bridge Road, London SW1V 2SA

Copyright © James Follet 2002

The right of James Follet to be identified as the
author of this work has been asserted by him in
accordance with the Copyright Designs and
Patents Act 1988

The Doomsday Ultimatum copyright ©
James Follet 1976
Cage of Eagles copyright © James Follet 1989

Papers used by Random House UK Ltd are natural recyclable products made from wood grown
in sustainable forests. The manufacturing process
conform to the environment regulations of the
country of origin.

A catalogue record for this book is available from
the British Library

Printed and bound in Germany by Elsnerdruck,
Berlin

ISBN 0 09 188545 0

The
Doomsday
Ultimatum

*To JL who hid the manuscript
and lied convincingly*

Contents

Prologue

The army escort in the car park suspected nothing.

Suddenly a nerve-gas grenade exploded in their midst but they never saw the figure that fired it. Choking, they collapsed as the paralysing fumes swirled round them.

And inside the 'Westward Ho' transport café the staff and the handful of late-night customers lay unconscious.

The attack by the armed group had taken only thirty seconds.

Thirty seconds is a long time in the application of chemical weapons. The CIX nerve-gas grenades, shattering and scattering fragile capsules in all directions, completed their task within five seconds. Inside the café the Special Air Service's captain who commanded the escort had tried to stagger to the door and shout a warning to his soldiers in the car park guarding the olive drab army transporter, but he collapsed before he could croak a single word.

His NCO, a Royal Artillery sergeant, had tried to pick up a hissing capsule from the floor and throw it out of an open window, but he too had passed out.

The tray of coffee cups for the escort lay on the floor, the cups broken. All was silent.

Two men entered the café. They wore NCB protective hoods with integral breathing sets, and held smoking grenade guns. They walked through air thick with nerve-gas fumes. The hooded men glanced casually around the confusion. The taller man checked the time against the information stored on his Psion Organiser pocket computer and pressed the 'enter' key.

'We're four seconds behind. Go on Phase Two,' he ordered. His voice sounded flat and indistinct behind his faceplate.

The second man went to the mains switch. He knew exactly where it was.

The café lights flashed three times. The taller man checked his Psion again. They had to work fast; every twenty minutes the army mobile unit was required to enter a status green security code into their radio facsimile unit.

At a signal a petrol tanker drove into the car park. It stopped beside the army transporter.

'Everything okay?' asked a woman's voice from the driver's cab.

The tall man was cutting the lashings of the tarpaulins that covered the army transporter's cargo. 'Tell him to hurry up in there,' he commanded.

The woman vaulted down from the tanker's cab and ran into the café. She too was hooded, and wore a brown jumpsuit.

A mobile crane, parked under the trees, burst into life and rumbled across the moonlit car park towards the tall man, who was now standing on top of the army transporter, guiding the approaching jib with arm gestures.

'Get the tanker opened,' he yelled.

His manner was military. He was used to giving orders and the others obeyed without hesitation.

The woman and the other hooded man came running from the café.

'Help him,' ordered the tall man nodding at the crane driver. He looked at his Psion Organiser again.

'You've got five minutes.' He was wearing a headset hooked up to a portable AR1000 scanning receiver clipped to his waist. It was programmed to all Thames Valley Police C Division repeater output radio channels. Right now most of the mobile channels were taken up with a serious RTA on the nearby M4. So far everything was going according to plan.

It took longer than five minutes but finally the first tanker was loaded and the two halves of the dummy petrol container were snapped shut, The woman started the engine. The tanker moved away to block the entrance to the car park.

The tall man's scanner hung on a channel. He checked the receiver's display. It was reading 451.475 megaHertz. End stop signal strength. 'For God's sake get a move on!' He hissed. 'We've got a unit working Burnham's channel 13 and he's nearly on top of us!'

Working silently, every move planned ahead, every detail rehearsed, they loaded the second tanker.

The captain who commanded the escort was the first to regain consciousness. His head felt as if an asteroid had fallen on it. He staggered out of the café. The army transporter and escort vehicles were still there. The soldiers lay bundled inside. The canvas covers of the transporter trailed on the ground. There was no sign of the vehicle's cargo. The weapons had been old stock, on their way to a Royal Ordnance Factory for dismantling and junking. Nevertheless they were no less deadly.

The transporter had been carrying two surface-to-surface Honest John missiles.

Sunday

1

At 08:34 hours precisely General Conrad Pyne's black official Rover 800 stopped outside the ugly wrought iron barrier that guarded the entrance into Downing Street. He sat perfectly still, barely acknowledging the polite salute of the police officers who checked his driver's credentials. There was a three-minute delay as a truckle mirror and an ion discharge explosives detector was passed under the vehicle.

Even at this hour on a hot Sunday morning there was a gaggle of sightseers and tourists clustered along the pavement hoping to catch a glimpse of the famous. They ducked their heads and tried to peer through the Austin-Rover's black-tinted glass. Japanese tourists clicked Canons in polite salute as Corporal Ian Garnet drove through the gates and into Downing Street. He did something unusual; instead of first dropping his passenger, he turned the car around in the narrow cul-de-sac and eased it alongside the kerb. The wing-mounted pennants of the Royal Army Ordnance Corps furled dejectedly in the oppressive heat around their silver stems.

Pyne made no attempt to move when the officer on duty opened the rear passenger door. The policeman was about to speak when he encountered the hard grey eyes.

Pyne pressed the airmail envelope into his hand. 'See that the Prime Minister's secretary gets that,' he ordered.

Pyne jerked the door shut and tapped on Garnet's shoulder. There was a click as the automatic transmission engaged. The big car pulled briskly away and swept through the gates, much to the surprise of the police officers who had been told that Pyne's visit would last at least fifteen to twenty minutes.

It was done.

The Doomsday Ultimatum had been delivered.

Pyne felt the constriction across his chest relax. He eased himself back into the soft cushions and glanced at his watch.

08:40. So far, so good.

So far . . .

He looked back through the rear window; a police officer was staring after him and another was yacking into his two-way radio. The scene behind the black-lacquered door of 10 Downing Street ran through Pyne's mind: using his official car would ensure the letter went directly to Simpson and not down to the sorting-office. The lightweight airmail envelope, containing a single sheet of closely typewritten paper, was hardly likely to arouse suspicion as a possible letter-bomb. Simpson would be told who had delivered the letter, and was probably opening it at this moment.

Corporal Garnet looked up at the frozen hands of Big Ben as he turned on to Westminster Bridge. From where he was sitting Pyne could see in the driver's mirror the ugly scar that transversed Garnet's left cheek. It was like a ragged furrow created by a drunken ploughman. A lucky escape from an Armalite bullet when Garnet had been serving in Northern Ireland.

'Still stuck at half past three, sir.'

Pyne made no reply. A handful of striking maintenance workers had achieved more than wartime bombs: the stationary hands were a symbol of the anarchy that now gripped the country – schools working a three-day week; water and electricity supplies frequently interrupted; sewage overflowing into the streets; and a government hamstrung by the reluctance of privatised public utilities to use what powers they had against the trade unions.

In the 1980s the power of the trade unions had been broken by a combination of high unemployment and punitive legislation. In the zeal of social reform that had followed the repressive government of the previous decade, many of the trade unions had regained their traditional powers by shifting their headquarters to the Netherlands and Belgium where they were beyond the direct jurisdiction of British courts. The will of national governments was thwarted by fax machines and international credit transfers. Adding to the government's problems was a plethora of militant social unions: patients unions; telephone users' unions; the Green Warriors; Poll Tax protesters. Even more worrying was the wave of fundamentalist Moslem movements that wanted to establish Moslem governed enclaves throughout the United Kingdom – states within a state.

08:43. The Rover was hissing over Westminster Bridge and away from the stench of a rotting refuse mountain in Trafalgar Square guarded by thousands of strikers.

Corporal Garnet slowed to pass a ragged demonstration. The marchers were not holding their banners properly, making it impossible to read what they said. The odd word unfolded briefly as the protestors swayed and chanted.

'INFLATION . . . FOOD PRICES . . . POLL TAX . . . SAVE BILLIONS WITH THE EUROPEAN DEFENCE FORCE . . .'

The last phrase held Pyne's attention. He studied the marchers more closely as the car crept past them. They looked like respectable middle-class clerks with their wives and children – not the type who would normally take to the streets. A woman was carrying the EC flag. She waved the blue banner with its circle of stars angrily at Pyne's car.

The tightness across his chest returned. He closed his eyes on the symbol and pictured the events taking place in Downing Street. Simpson would now be rereading the letter. Perhaps he was already reaching for his telephone to ring the Prime Minister. No. Simpson was much too cautious: he would call the police and make doubly certain it was Pyne who had delivered the ultimatum:

As from 10:30 hours today, Vulcan Hall nuclear power station on Canvey Island is now under the control of the recently formed United Kingdom Policy Control Group. The purpose of this group is to advise and co-ordinate the activities of Her Majesty's Government.

How we will carry out this task and our specific long-term and short-term objectives will be communicated to you later today. For the time being, it is sufficient for you to know that we are in possession of two MGR-1B Honest John surface-to-surface ballistic missiles in addition to the large quantity of tactical hardware supplied to the Oil Platform Defence Force which, as from today, is also under our command. One of the Honest Johns is now trained on the East End of London and any attempt to interfere with our operations on Canvey Island will result in the immediate discharge of the missile.

Our first directive is that our ultimatum should not be made public until our terms have been implemented by Parliament, and have received the Royal Assent . . .

There were certain conditions in the ultimatum that Keller was unaware of. Pyne frowned. Keller had proved himself during the raid on the Westward Ho transport café three months earlier; he had obeyed orders without question, and had always shown respect for Pyne. But there was something about him that Pyne disliked. His unsmiling politeness at the planning meetings and insistence that only extreme right-wing measures would cure the country's problems, had forced Pyne to supply Keller with a phoney draft of the ultimatum to keep him quiet. Pyne disliked having to do it —

15

the success of the power station takeover depended on mutual trust between the four members of the group. Had there been time, Pyne would have looked around for an alternative to Keller. But there was no-one – Keller had been responsible for the installation of the emergency radioactive waste silos at the Vulcan Hall nuclear power station – he knew exactly where to position the high-explosive and how to shutdown the power station's two gas-cooled nuclear reactors.

For the time being Keller would have to be tolerated.

Pyne was pushed gently into the cushions as the Rover accelerated through the quiet Sunday morning streets. Occasional wisps of smoke drifted across the road as householders ignored clean air regulations in their efforts to dispose of rubbish. Traffic lights obligingly winked to green at the car's approach –their solid state relays triggered by the sonic beam from a PATH (Priority Alert Traffic Hold) transmitter concealed behind the Rover's grille; a useful device fitted to all official cars used by government ministers and high-ranking service officers.

By 08:55 the car was nearing Woolwich, and at 09:00 hours precisely it was cleared by the civilian police and allowed to pass through the ornate gates of the Royal College of Artillery. The smartly turned-out sentries checked the documents Garnet handed them and accorded Pyne smart salutes before raising the steel barrier arm. Although Pyne never wore a uniform, he always received a salute.

Pyne walked across the sprawling, close-clipped lawn with Corporal Garnet one step behind carrying the briefcase. Someone had wiped the dew off his Westland Scout helicopter so that it gleamed damply in the early sun. It was the last Scout still in service with the army; Pyne had fought several battles with MoD Procurement to keep the machine in service. The faint circular scratch marks on the Perspex windows – the result of carelessness with a hard rag – annoyed him. He checked his irritation.

Did it matter any more?

'Back to Weybridge, sir?' inquired Garnet, unlocking the Scout's door.

Pyne shook his head. 'I'll fly her, corporal. I've not logged enough hours this year. I ought to keep my hand in.'

'Yes, sir.' Garnet held the door open as the general climbed into the pilot's seat. Pyne waved away the offered briefcase.

'I don't need it any more.'

The corporal looked uncertain. 'Do you want me to come with you, sir?'

'No. Take the car back to the MT depot. Tell them I've finished with it.' Pyne avoided his NCO's eyes – the savage scar seemed to glow in the harsh light.

'Garnet, would you do something for me?'

'Sir?'

'Not as an order – I can't give orders now, but as a favour.'

'I don't understand, sir.'

'There's a buff envelope in the briefcase which contains your discharge papers. You've been a civilian since midnight. That's why I can't give you orders.'

Garnet looked astounded. The briefcase nearly slipped from his grasp.

'I'm going away on an important mission – possibly for a long time. It's not fair to expect my daughter to look after the house, so I'd like you to do it.' Pyne paused and flipped the Scout's power switches. The toggle switches closed with soft clicks and the instruments came to life. 'There's a copy of a letter in the briefcase instructing the Midland Bank at Weybridge to make you monthly payments as my caretaker. You'll also find a cheque in there payable to you so you can have some plastic surgery for that scar, and there's some cash for civilian clothes. Will you do it?'

Garnet stood transfixed.

'Well?' snapped Pyne.

The corporal nodded dumbly.

'If you see Maggie at the house, tell her I'm sorry to have missed the birthday party she was planning for me.' Pyne paused to operate the Scout's controls. The rotors turned slowly. 'You can sell the boat for whatever you can get.' Pyne wondered why he was telling Garnet this. He gazed at the unreal red-brick facade of the college. It looked like a film set dropped amid the disciplined flowerbeds.

'One last thing: don't think too badly of Maggie. She's young and thoughtless,; and doesn't mean to be cruel. She still hasn't got over her mother's death,'

Corporal Garnet stared at his general.

'And you're to tell no one what has happened to me,' said Pyne. 'Absolutely no one. Understand?'

Garnet found his voice:

'How long will you be gone, sir?'

Pyne hesitated. 'Not more than twelve months if all goes according to plan. But it could be five years.'

Pyne slammed the helicopter door shut before Garnet could reply. The rotors became an iridescent disc that bit into the hot morning air until their downward thrust cancelled the Scout's weight. The machine lifted, and dwindled towards the Thames, watched by the bewildered upturned face of Corporal Garnet as he clutched the black leather briefcase with its gold E11R crest.

2

Simpson moved quickly after he had finished reading the ultimatum. He knew exactly what he had to do. He notified the valet to wake the Prime Minister immediately and then called the duty air traffic control officer at West Drayton to establish the whereabouts of General Pyne's helicopter.

Simpson was certain he knew the answer, but with so much at stake there was no room for mistakes – the call had to be made. The officer returned his call two minutes later, confirming what Simpson already knew.

Simpson opened a desk drawer and studied a computer print-out which listed data on every helicopter pilot in the armed services. He crossed the office and pulled a wall map of southern England down by its tassel. His finger traced the winding path of the Thames and stopped at Chatham. He smiled to himself and put a priority call through to the officer in charge of helicopter air-sea rescue operations at Chatham naval base. He kept his finger on the red button so that the alarm would sound continuously in the commanding officer's office until the telephone was answered. He gave his emergency number and pressed the cradle to cut the line. He remained impassive for some seconds with his outstretched finger holding the line closed until the telephone warbled. He removed his finger and issued instructions in his curt, matter-of fact voice and requested them to be read back to him. He listened attentively and carefully replaced the receiver.

The conversation was safely recorded on tape in case the Prime Minister's enemies later accused the department of not trying.

The door opened Simpson looked up at the thickset figure standing in the doorway.

'Good morning, sir. I trust you slept well?'

It was a courteous greeting rather than an inquiry.

The Prime Minister always slept soundly. But the week ahead would change all that.

3

Pyne cleared his routing with West Drayton and passed over Woolwich at a thousand feet. He altered course above the Thames to follow its molten silver path towards the estuary. The free ferry was ploughing across the current on its new restricted service. Pyne felt a pang of regret at the passing of the old paddle steamers. His greatest joy as a cadet from a poor background had been the daily free trip across the river and back on the pounding old side-wheelers.

To the north towering office blocks stood like brooding memorials to the prosperity of a bygone era. Once the angular steel and concrete stakes, driven indiscriminately into the docklands clay, had pinned down fat profits for their owners; now they scarcely acted as windbreaks against the chill draught of depression that seeped and spilled across the country.

Pyne settled more comfortably into his seat.

There was so much to be done.

And undone.

He glanced at his watch. 09:15 hours,

The Thames yawned wider in its lazy, indifferent sweep to the North Sea. The helicopter's grounded shadow chased vainly after its owner – occasionally racing up the sides of slab-sided refuse barges now manned by the Royal Marines – fleeting across cargoes of rotting vegetable waste and plunging back to the gleaming, hammer-beaten water.

So much to be done.

Pyne squinted into the sun as the Thames Haven oil refinery came into view thirty kilometres ahead. Beyond the lacework of pipes and distillation columns, and ten kilometres further eastward down-river, he could just discern the salt-cellar cooling towers of the Vulcan Hall nuclear power station on Canvey Island. The pale structures shimmered in the haze that was being sucked off the water by the strengthening sun and smeared across the horizon like a ghostly shroud.

The power station could wait. First, the refinery.

09:22 hours.

Pyne took the handheld Icom transceiver from its mounting clip and pressed it to his ear. The two-way radio was already set to the correct frequency. He pressed the talk key.

'Pine Needle to Victor Hotel control. Do you copy? Over.'

The direct, line-of-sight reply from the visible power station, ten kilometres beyond the refinery, was loud and clear. 'Victor Hotel control to Pine Needle,' said a voice in the headphones. 'Go ahead.'

It was Keller. The polite nasal accent with the faint American twang he had acquired when working in Michigan for the US Atomic Energy Commission was unmistakable. At least the man was alert.

'I'm thirty kilometres west of the target,' said Pyne. 'I'll remain in this area until after 09:45 hours. I don't want to be too close. Over.'

'Correction, Pine Needle, we have you positioned at twenty-nine point two kilometres west of the target according to our radar display,' Keller answered with his customary politeness.

Pyne frowned. He was never certain with Keller whether the man was being supercilious or subordinate.

'Are you all set? Over.' asked Pyne.

'All set,' affirmed Keller. 'You should have a grandstand view. Did the delivery go as planned?'

Always so bloody polite, thought Pyne. 'Affirmative. Any messages? Over.'

'Negative, Pine Needle, but we picked up Captain Stacy trying to contact you. It looks as if the camp is ready for inspection.'

'I'll call him direct,' said Pyne. There was nothing more to be said. He cut Keller off and set the tranceiver to scanning the 451 megaHertz band. There were the usual police reports in jargon from mobiles and the occasional clear-language directive from their controls. Nothing about Pyne or the Scout helicopter. He checked the air band with the same result. It was only to be expected. He anticipated that the ultimatum would take at least an hour to sink in, especially Article Two in the covering instructions:

As a demonstration of our determination, we will destroy the Thames Haven oil refinery with one of the Honest John missiles at 09:45 hours. Be warned: Canvey Island is now equipped with the latest

21

horizon surveillance radar; the surrounding countryside is flat, giving us two minutes' warning of any missile or low-level aircraft attack, and we require only one minute to launch the second Honest John.

Any attempt to employ radar jamming or any form of ECM (Electronic Countermeasures) against us will be regarded by us as a hostile move and we will act accordingly. Should you decide to sacrifice the lives of many Londoners by forcing us to fire the missile, it would be best if you considered the implications of an explosion from the hundred tonnes of Cyclonite high explosive we have placed round Vulcan Hall's radioactive-waste storage silos.

(signed)
Conrad Pyne OBE
(Major-General)

Pyne remembered deleting his rank and the letters after his name before signing the document.

4

Lieutenant Steven Thorne, RN, had been trained to do everything with a helicopter except how to bring down another helicopter.

He debated the problem with himself as his Mark 10 Lynx, the fastest rotary-wing machine in the world, thrashed westward above the Thames from Chatham.

His one crewman was not much help either.

Marine-Sergeant Hopkins, secured to the floor of the open helicopter bay by a harness and clutching a floor-mounted machine-gun, had no experience of aerial combat.

Thorne scanned the expanse of brilliant blue sky. The sun was behind him, so this terrorist, whoever he was, flying an old Army Scout helicopter, should be easy to detect. That's all they had told him: a terrorist flying a stolen machine who was to be stopped at all costs.

'There he is sir!' Hopkins' voice suddenly shouted in Thorne's headset.

Thorne spotted the whirling splinter of sunlight immediately. It was a Scout helicopter. 'Okay Hopkins. I've got him!'

Thorne pulled his machine upwards to put himself into the sun.

It was a mistake.

In the Scout, Pyne squinted up as the shadow of the Lynx flitted across the Perspex windows. He cursed Keller for not warning him, and pushed the cyclic pitch yoke forward.

Thorne slewed his tail-boom around and aimed his machine at Pyne's Scout that was now windmilling low across the Thames leaving a wake of flattened water in the downwash from its rotors.

The distance between the two machines closed rapidly. The Lynx's airframe shook violently as the screaming rotors sliced into the haze-laden air. Even if Thorne had lost the advantage of surprise his Lynx was the fastest helicopter in the world – Pyne was finished – when he got close enough.

And then Pyne did something completely unexpected – he swung his Scout around like a cornered cat turning on a pursuing dog. Thorne was forced to bank sharply to avoid a mid-air collision. Pyne deftly leapt the Scout over Thorne's plunging Lynx, and stole the larger machine's lift. Thorne frantically increased pitch as the Lynx's rotors failed to bite on the air already being forced downward by the wash from the Scout. For a sickening moment Thorne thought his machine was going to plunge into the river. The Lynx's wheels actually dipped into the water before the flailing rotors jerked the helicopter upwards.

Pyne spun the Scout around and flew backwards away from the Lynx – a move which cost Thorne several seconds as he went plunging after Pyne in the wrong direction. Pyne continued to fly backwards, watching the spinning ellipse of Thorne's rotors harden to a fine line as the powerful Navy machine came roaring after him. Pyne glanced over his shoulder; the main building of the Ford Motor Company was racing towards him.

Pyne felt trapped. Attempting to climb out of trouble would cost too much in ground speed. The distance between the helicopters narrowed as they flew towards the giant car parks where Ford's stored their thousands of unsold cars.

Pyne reached under his seat for the Verey signal pistol, slid a fat parachute flare into the breech, and pulled back the hammer. It was the only armament the Scout carried.

By now, Thorne had a healthy respect for Pyne's flying skill and approached cautiously.

'Try now sir!' said Hopkins urgently. 'I'm in range!'

Thorne brought the open bay to bear, but Pyne thwarted the move by twisting his more manoeuvrable machine within the Lynx's turning circle.

The two helicopters were like cats circling each other as a preliminary to battle. Thorne broke the rhythm. The Scout slipped out of sight down the starboard side of the Lynx towards Hopkins' field of fire. Pyne did not hear the machine-gun, but saw darts of light flicker from the barrel and felt bullets slam into the aluminium skin behind his head.

On the ground Ford drivers pointed excitedly up at the sparring machines.

There was no second burst of fire. Hopkins swore and released his safety harness to kick the jammed gun. Pyne aimed the Verey pistol at the big Navy machine, bracing his arm against the down-wash from the Scout's rotors. His finger tensed on the trigger.

Another burst of fire as Hopkins freed the jammed ammunition belt. The flare arched gracefully towards the Lynx, but it was too high. Pyne cursed his mistake.

Thorne made another mistake: he saw the trail of the flare against the sky and, thinking that it was coming straight for him, banked sharply. It was over in a matter of seconds. The wash from the Lynx's rotors deflected the flare downward. It blasted past Hopkins and exploded like a miniature sun against the far bulkhead. Hopkins screamed to Thorne and actually tried to pick the flare up. He was too late. The fireball melted through the bulkhead and dissolved the fuel line from the armoured tank beneath the floor. Blazing fuel sprayed on Hopkins as he rolled screaming on the floor.

The Ford drivers scattered as the blazing machine came skimming towards them above the rooftops of the unwanted cars. The last thing that registered on Thorne's mind before it ceased to exist, was the kaleidoscope of brightly coloured metal boxes racing towards him.

One wheel of the Lynx struck an Escort. The impact sent the helicopter somersaulting through the air. The burning body of Marine-Sergeant Hopkins was ejected fifty-metres through the air. He landed on the roof of a white Sierra and etched his outline in the blistering acrylic paint.

The Lynx ploughed upside down through the ranks of ownerless cars, its still flailing rotors scything saloons to instant mangled convertibles.

The bewildered drivers, crouching behind tape-shrouded bumpers, cautiously emerged and surveyed the blazing wreckage. Two drivers tried to approach the helicopter but were driven back by the heat. More drivers stood up, then immediately dived for cover as heat-fired bullets from Hopkins' machine-gun whacked into unscathed cars. Windshields shattered and tyres collapsed with reproving hisses at the random onslaught from Lieutenant Steven Thorne's spiteful funeral pyre.

Pyne wasted no time on regret for the unknown crew of the Lynx. He turned the Scout back towards the Thames.

A corner of his mind noted what a beautiful day it was.

5

The shockwave from the exploding oil refinery which rocked the Scout helicopter a hundred seconds after the

25

flash was felt as far away as Chelmsford in the north and Maidstone in the south. Holidaymakers on the Kent beaches scanned the sky for a glimpse of the aircraft that had caused the sonic boom. A ten-tonne slab of metal shaped like a segment of orange peel – part of a propane gas pressure vessel – developed sufficient lift under its curved surface to demolish a row of houses twenty kilometres away. The intense heat fused sixty caravans on a site near the refinery to neat rectangular blobs of solder. The pulverizing shockwave, destroying everything in its path, originated from a single, catastrophic explosion, but the squat containers spread out on the vast tank farm adjoining the refinery site eliminated themselves one by one with their own individual explosions.

One hundred and forty-five refinery workers were flashed to steam before the sound of the blast reached them. A colliery vessel capsized, sank, poured a thousand tonnes of coal on to the river bed and surfaced bottom-up. A two metre tidal wave raced upriver. It was destined to reach Teddington Lock after a journey of appalling destruction where it would sweep away most of the vehicles parked round the television studios, smash down the lock gates and dissipate its energy against the unleashed flood of water raging through the ruptured gates.

Pyne flew cautiously towards the devastated refinery. Apart from the blazing containers on the tank farms round the site, there was no fire amid the twisted, flattened remains of the distillation columns and hydro-cracking towers; everything inflammable had been swept away or vaporised by the blast. The giant globular LPG tanks were no more – they had been pricked out of existence like balloons. The approach roads were empty of traffic. Despite the whine of the gas turbine above Pyne's head, an atmosphere of stunned silence and stillness pervaded the site.

A flash below caught his eye. Seagulls were swooping down and settling on agitated water round the sinking colliery vessel – even the few fish in the Thames Estuary had been stunned by the blast. Pyne watched the birds screaming and fighting. Perhaps it wasn't fish they were interested in.

He switched on the radio to listen to any official announcements, turned the Scout towards the four distant cooling towers of the Vulcan Hall nuclear power station, and felt in his pocket for a cigar. His fingers encountered a piece of paper: 'St Georges Hill New Golf Club. Annual subscription. Received with thanks.'

He crumpled the link with the past and tossed it out of the window.

His watch said 10:00 hours.

The Doomsday Ultimatum was now in force.

6

There was one seat empty when the Cromwell Two Committee sat to finalize details of their plan to seize power and install a temporary military government.

'Where's Pyne?' asked the chairman, a cabinet minister.

Sir Michael Powell, head of the Civil Service, looked up from his notes. 'An apology for absence, Mr Chairman. Pyne called me yesterday and said he wasn't able to make himself available today.'

The chairman nodded and glanced round at the ten faces. 'Shall we start, gentlemen?'

There was a murmur of assent.

The first item on the agenda was the list of two hundred names prepared by the head of the Civil Service of people to fill the top administrative posts in the new government. Several of those present, such as the head of the Special Branch, and the chairman of the Governors of the BBC, General Sir Richard Markham and Sir Oswald Fox, were to retain their existing jobs.

'Supposing the Prime Minister recalls Parliament if Selkirk does call a general strike?' asked the chairman of the Independent Broadcasting Commission.

The man at the head of the table shook his head. 'He won't do anything to risk another defeat. He's playing a wait-and-see game. He daren't even declare a state of emergency for fear of the palace turning it down.'

'Surely he'll resign?' said a voice.

The chairman smiled. 'Only when he really knows he's lost. And that may take another month. By which time our gold and dollar reserves will be exhausted and it will be too late. Right now, the old bastard's praying for a fairy godmother.' The expletive did not raise an eyebrow in the select gathering.

'Very well then,' said the chairman at the close of the meeting. 'We move one week from today.'

A bottle was opened and the company of distinguished conspirators drank a toast to the Queen.

7

There were times when Howard Mitchell regretted the self-indulgent impulse which had prompted him to import a Mustang from the United States. The left-hand drive car was often at a disadvantage when he was trying to overtake on Great Britain's crazy, twisting roads that seemed to go nowhere once and everywhere twice.

Mitchell shifted to a lower gear and crawled patiently behind an electric milk float, grinding painfully up the hill leading to the golf club. At one point he was tempted to pass but was immediately deterred by an XJS which appeared from nowhere and boomed throatily past in the opposite direction.

The milk float glided past the turning to St Georges Hill New Golf Club, which belonged to one of the most exclusive housing estates in the country. There was no sign of the black Austin-Rover when Mitchell parked near the clubhouse and went in.

'Where's General Pyne, Harry?' Mitchell asked the barman.

'I've no idea, Mr Mitchell,' he replied. 'I don't understand it. Hardly anyone here. I wondered if it was Sunday when I unlocked this morning. Only three games out on the course.' The barman gloomily surveyed the deserted lounge. Sunday-morning tips were the only thing that gave him a decent standard of living.

Mitchell ordered a lager and sipped it slowly. 'Did he leave a message for me?'

The barman glanced at the shelf behind the bar. 'No. Nothing, Mr Mitchell. Had you arranged to play a round with him?'

'That's right. The loser to vacuum both swimming pools.'

The barman smiled politely. God, how he hated these bastards with money. Nothing the government did seemed to strip them of their fat. Even with the country in its present state they still had more than anyone else.

Mitchell finished his drink and left the clubhouse. He paused by his Mustang. It was a fine morning, so he decided to walk to Pyne's place.

Pyne's house was one of the older, more conservative homes on the expensive estate. It had the traditional curved drive so that the house could not be seen from the road.

He rang the doorbell and waited.

Mitchell was a shy, thirty-seven-year-old New Yorker who owned a small but thriving shipping and forwarding agency. The success of his business sprang from his knowledge of the North Sea oil-exploration programme rather than a shrewd business brain. People tended to think his easy-going nature disguised a degree of ruthlessness. They accepted his prices and delivery dates because his prices were reasonable, and his dates always met. Howard Mitchell was not ruthless – he was efficient.

Pyne's daughter, Maggie, answered the door.

Mitchell had met her on a number of occasions when Pyne used to invite him back to the house for a drink after their Sunday game of golf. The invitations had ceased with the death of Pyne's wife six months previously. The only times he had met the girl since then was in Weybridge shopping. She always seemed to have Corporal Garnet in tow carrying her purchases.

Maggie gave the American a warm smile and pulled the door open.

'Hallo, Mitch. I thought you'd forgotten me.'

Mitchell almost laughed aloud at the spectacle before him. Maggie Pyne's elfin face was streaked with flour.

'I'm sorry to disturb you, Maggie. But I'm supposed to be having a game of golf with your father.' He looked at the girl with amusement. 'You seem to have had a slight disaster.'

Maggie smiled, and held the door open. 'I've just lost an argument with the food-mixer,' she explained, leading the way to the kitchen. 'Would you like some coffee?'

'Only if you promise to make me four cups.'

The kitchen was in a mess; every available square centimetre of working space was piled high with evil-looking sandwiches, a chocolate éclair was floating in a bowl of punch and the floor was gritty with sugar.

'What happened, Maggie?' said Mitchell as the girl held the kettle under a trickle of water from a tap that was turned full on.

'It's to be a party for Daddy,' said Maggie apologetically. 'It's his birthday today – his forty-fifth I think – so I thought I'd try making some cakes.' She spooned ground coffee into an espresso machine's strainer and latched it into place. 'I did everything by the book and was getting along fine until I tried using the mixer.'

Mitchell glanced at the food-mixer, and tried not to laugh.

'You used that glass jar?'

Maggie looked at the machine in concern.

'Yes.'

Mitchell looked round the kitchen. Everything was covered with a fine film of flour. 'Without the lid?' he inquired.

Maggie frowned at the gadget. 'Is there a lid?'

30

'Honey, that's the liquidizer attachment. Anything you try mixing in that without a lid immediately gets out.'

'Maybe I should just stick to drink,' said Maggie sadly. 'I can manage a corkscrew. I wish Corporal Garnet was here – he's good at these things.'

'Isn't your father around?'

The girl shook her head, and brushed cake ingredients from her T-shirt and jeans.

'He and Corporal Garnet went off yesterday. I haven't seen them yet. I hope Daddy comes home. I want all this to be a surprise.'

She saw Mitchell hiding his face behind his hands. 'It's not funny,' she snapped. 'You try cooking in this weather.'

Mitchell nodded soberly and made a strange noise in his throat.

He watched Maggie as she operated the espresso machine's pump and wondered what she would look like in a dress. She had a figure that was made to be expensively dressed: tall, slim with long dark hair. Mitchell wondered why she didn't spend some of the money her mother had left her on clothes. Her first purchase with her newly acquired wealth had been an MG sports car. Mitchell remembered how Pyne had complained during a game of golf.

'There's too many people with too much money,' Pyne had said, 'and far too many with far too little.'

Mitchell had laughed. 'A car, general? You can't blame her. It's what every kid wants.'

'The latest thing is a house,' Pyne had grumbled.

'You can't say she's wasting it.'

'Well, perhaps not. But it's made her independent. When Helen died I thought we'd get to know each other. I've never had much time for family life – and now, when I've decided to adjust to it, I've got no family left.'

'You should make a clean break,' Mitchell had replied. 'Change your whole way of life before you discover you're too old to change.'

31

Pyne had nodded. 'That wouldn't be difficult. I've considered throwing up everything to do something really positive with my life.' He had dropped the ball neatly into the seventh hole.

Mitchell had looked puzzled. 'I would've thought being a major-general was pretty positive.'

Pyne had laughed. 'My entire army career has been spent in an office. I'm an admin man -" flying a desk" my RAF colleagues in Whitehall call it. I've never seen any form of active service, and I can't remember when I last wore a uniform. I'm not even certain if I've got one.'

'But you're going to command this new oil platform defence unit?'

'Oh yes,' Pyne had said lightly. 'One advantage of working in Whitehall is that you're in the best place for a spot of wheeling and dealing when a plum new job is in the offing.'

Maggie's voice suddenly intruded on Mitchell's thoughts. 'Don't you want your coffee?'

Mitchell sipped cautiously. Even with an espresso machine, Maggie managed to louse things up; it was the worst coffee he had ever tasted. He struggled to keep a straight face.

'If you laugh . . .' Maggie said warningly.

Mitchell replaced the cup on the saucer

'Believe me, Maggie – your coffee's no laughing matter.'

She stared at him for a moment and then laughed. Mitchell joined in when he felt he was on safe ground.

'If only you could've seen your face,' said Maggie.

Mitchell nodded to the plates of sandwiches. 'What will happen to those if your father doesn't show up?'

'Feed them to the birds, I suppose. It'll be a nuisance if he doesn't come home. I've spent a fortune on food and drink. And I got the corporal to clean and refill the pool.'

'I bet he loved you for that,' said Mitchell, 'with temperatures hitting eighty in the shade.'

Maggie shrugged. 'It's what he's for.'

The casual way in which she said it reinforced Mitchell's belief that the British class system still had a firm hold.

A dull boom rattled the windows.

'At least the RAF can still afford to make sonic booms,' commented Mitchell. 'What time are you holding this party?'

'Eight,' said Maggie.'If you can drink the rest of that coffee without pulling a face, I might add you to the twenty I've already invited.'

'Sure I'll come, sweetheart. A party in the dark sounds like fun.'

Maggie stared at the American.

'What do you mean?'

'The power cut for this area starts at nine.'

Maggie looked alarmed. 'But it's this afternoon, surely?'

Mitchell shook his head. 'The electricity rotas are one thing I make a point of knowing. Today's Sunday. The new rota started at midnight. Check it out on the radio if you don't believe me'

Maggie tuned the portable radio to a local London station. A newsreader was describing the latest government talks to avert the impending general strike.

'I'm surprised you haven't gone home, with the state the country's in,' said Maggie. 'It's just like the Seventies all over again.'

'Well North Sea oil isn't in a state,' replied Mitchell. 'The new Hebrides field means that it's the fastest growth industry in Europe. Anyway, I'm one of the few who's keeping quiet about Britain. Back home, they're all writing epitaphs. Dangerous when the corpse isn't dead. They have a habit of suddenly getting better.'

'What does your business do? You don't smell of oil.'

'An oil rig needs a piece of equipment in a hurry, and I usually know where I can lay my hands on it.'

The newsreader interrupted an interview with a trade-union leader.

'News is just coming in of a large explosion at the Thames Haven oil refinery on the Thames near London,' he said.

'Turn up the sound please, Maggie,' Mitchell requested.

The girl did so. 'What's the matter?'

Mitchell gestured her to silence.

'The explosion was heard all over the London area,' continued the newsreader. 'Eye-witness reports say the entire refinery was devastated in one catastrophic explosion. The Thames Barrage was raised for routine testing with the result that a two metre tidal wave is now racing up the Thames through London . . .'

The newsreader broke off. Mitchell's attention was riveted on the radio.

'Mike Bowden is on the phone from near the site,' said the newsreader. 'Can you hear me, Mike?'

'Hallo, Ted,' squawked a distorted voice from the speaker. 'The scene here at Thames Haven is unbelievable. The entire refinery has been flattened out of existence. There's nothing left but a great mass of smouldering wreckage. Police are just about to evacuate the area in case there are more explosions, but it's hard to believe there's anything left to explode . . . About one hundred and forty-five workers are believed to have been . . .'

Mitchell swore, and jumped to his feet.

'What's the matter?' asked Maggie.

'Oh, shit. My car's at the golf club. Maggie, will you do me a big favour and drive me to the Fairoaks Flying Club?'

Thirty minutes later they were airborne in Mitchell's pale-blue Bonanza and heading east at five thousand feet. West Drayton ATC refused Mitchell's flight plan to approach the refinery from London. He studied the charts spread out on his knee and decided to follow the M25 orbital motorway before turning north to intersect the Thames a few kilometres downstream from the refinery.

Maggie watched him covertly. He had ignored her questions during the short car ride, preferring to hunt for news reports on her car radio.

34

There was a faint smell of rotting refuse in the aircraft.

'You can even smell it up here,' said Maggie. She stretched out in the bucket seat and planted her feet on the instrument panel. 'People like you are morbid.'

'Why?' asked Mitchell, looking up from a chart.

Maggie looked at him in mock surprise. 'Good heavens, it's alive.'

'Any more of your bitchy comments and I'll push you out so you can walk home. Why am I morbid?'

'Flying off to look at a blown-up refinery.'

'It just so happens,' replied Mitchell evenly, 'that I've got a brand new drill-string at Thames Haven waiting for shipment to Nordic Queen platform tomorrow – when its UK insurance comes into force.'

'What's a drill-string?'

'The lengths of steel that fit together to make a drill.'

'Isn't that careless? Not insuring it?'

'There was a shipping delay,' said Mitchell. 'Your dockers at Southampton refused to unload it. A prefabricated import, they called it – so I had to pay to have it sent on to the unloading facilities at Thames Haven.'

'How will you know from the air if it's okay?' Maggie asked.

'I'll know sure enough. It's two hundred tonnes of steel in three stacks.'

Maggie looked down at the main roads radiating from London. The heat was tempting the unemployed to find money for petrol to drive to the beaches.

'Are you better at loading cameras than blenders?' asked Mitchell.

'Sure.'

Mitchell jerked his head at the rear seats. 'There should be a camera in that bag behind, and some rolls of film. Maybe you'd load one for me?'

'Say please.'

'Will I hell. You can earn the extra gas your weight is costing me.'

35

Maggie sighed and eased her feet off the instrument panel. Her heel knocked against the toggle switch on the radiotelephone.

London Airport tried several times to contact the light aircraft that was approaching the zone prohibited to all air traffic since 09:45 that morning. The green blip crawling across their radar screens was either ignoring their calls or did not have its radio switched on. Provided it maintained its present eastward course, it would pass through the outer periphery of the zone. A computer was set to monitor the aircraft's progress, and the Air Traffic Control officers returned to their task of diverting incoming London flights to Manchester and Luton.

Thirty minutes later the computer drew their attention to the blip, which had altered course and was now on a heading which would take it right over the Thames Haven prohibited zone.

Simpson had told London Airport that the Prime Minister was taking a personal interest in the Thames Haven disaster and wished to be kept informed of all developments – no matter how minor.

At twelve noon the ATC Officer at West Drayton telephoned Simpson on the special number and told him that an unidentified aircraft was approaching the refinery.

Simpson sat at his desk pondering this unexpected turn of events. He decided to take no chances and reached for his telephone.

At 12:10 an RAF Tornado screamed down the runway at Manston and lifted its graceful nose to the deep blue sky. At two thousand feet its attack radar locked on to the unauthorized blip, and the pilot flipped the switches that primed the ignition circuits in the twelve air-to-air missiles slung beneath the Tornado's wings.

Mitchell's navigation was better than he expected. Straight ahead were the giant cooling towers of the Vulcan Hall nuclear power station standing like sole remaining rooks in a chess game of the gods. To the left, ten kilometres from the power station, were the scorched, still-smouldering remains of the Thames Haven oil refinery. As Mitchell banked to turn upstream towards the refinery Maggie grabbed his arm and pointed back at the power station.

'Look! Those two helicopters! One of them belongs to my father! The olive green one!'

Mitchell turned in his seat and looked back at the power station. On the concrete apron that separated the main building from the waterfront stood two helicopters, a Bell JetRanger and a Westland Scout. Mitchell throttled back.

'Are you certain?'

'That's his registration. And I think the other helicopter belongs to Hugh Patterson.' Mitchell swung the machine round in a wide circle. The Bonanza was about six kilometres from the power station – halfway between it and the remains of Thames Haven. He wasn't particularly interested in the machines at the power station, but they seemed to worry Maggie. A little way from the helicopters two gasoline tankers were parked. He could see figures near them. Maggie was right about the JetRanger. It was definitely the one owned by Patterson – he had often seen it dropping into the dense trees that surrounded the industrialist's house on St Georges Hill. JetRangers were common enough in the United States, but quite rare in England.

'Doesn't Patterson's company make nuclear waste containers?' asked Mitchell. 'Maybe he's showing your father his products that are used in that power station?'

It wasn't a convincing explanation, but he was anxious to fly on to the oil refinery.

He pulled the Bonanza out of the turn and flew on upstream towards Thames Haven.

'There's a holiday camp or something beyond the power station,' said Maggie, craning her neck round to look back.

'The whole of Canvey looks like a holiday camp,' commented Mitchell. 'One big shanty town of factories, beach huts and caravans.'

They flew on upstream.

When the Bonanza was two kilometres from the refinery Mitchell took his first picture and wondered why the site wasn't swarming with rescue workers.

'Can you see anything?' Maggie asked.

Mitchell took another picture. 'Not yet.'

The Bonanza swept over the devastated site. There was no sign of his drill-string amid the twisted, blackened wreckage. It was all very worrying.

He clicked the camera shutter four times and was about to take another picture when Maggie touched him on the shoulder.

'Look.' She pointed to the north.

A Tornado jet fighter was about six kilometres away. Mitchell recognised it by the wing configuration as it banked sharply, turning towards the Bonanza as if closing in to attack.

8

Fifteen minutes after the explosion Pyne flew over the Vulcan Hall power station for an aerial inspection of his new Oil Platform Defence Force camp, which had been established the day before on Canvey Island.

His hands were still trembling as they rested on the Scout's controls. Partly because of his recent encounter with the Lynx helicopter, but mostly with anger at the heavy casualties and devastation caused by the Honest John. Keller had assured him at the final planning meeting held the week before that there would be no more than five of six maintenance workers at the refinery on a Sunday morning. The first urgent police signals picked up on the radio suggested that nearer one hundred and fifty men were in the refinery at the time of the explosion and that several people whose houses were near the tank farm had been killed.

Pyne looked down at the dazzling glass facade of the power station's administrative offices, which presented a burnished face to the Thames. Keller, Patterson and Louise Campion were probably watching him through binoculars from the control room which covered the entire top floor of the main building.

The power station's fifty-acre site was now enclosed by the horns of the new camp that reached to the river on either side.

Operation Oilguard, launched the previous day to establish the camp, had been used by the Royal Engineers, at General Pyne's suggestion, as an exercise in speed. Work had begun in the early morning with the arrival of a convoy of Pickford transporters carrying six kilometres of chain-link fencing with concrete posts already attached. More trucks had arrived ten minutes later, each one laden with fifteen tonnes of barbed wire — enough to make an entanglement over ten kilometres long.

By 11:00 the fences had been complete.

The inner fence encircled the power station at a distance of a hundred yards and the outer fence had been erected two hundred yards away. Two barriers had been constructed where the access road to the power station intersected the two fences. A number of caravan owners whose trailers would have been trapped within the new camp had watched helplessly as soldiers had hitched their holiday homes to Land Rovers and towed them away. A fork-lift truck had shifted a row of beach huts.

By 11:45 bulldozers had been levelling uneven ground, followed by soldiers spraying the earth with quick-drying asphalt. One of the army's cherished machines for making white lines had marked out the positions of roads, crossings and buildings.

The real hardware which makes an army had waited for the afternoon – after Pyne's second in command, Captain Peter Stacy, had inspected the fences.

It had arrived in several trucks: Clansman communications equipment from the Signals Research and Design Establishment; one tonne of night optical and intruder surveillance equipment from the Central Inventory Control Point; armoured cars from the Fighting Vehicles Establishment; and two ex-army Hueycobra helicopter gunships, which had arrived in two huge containers together with their grenade launchers and missile armament from RAF Harrogate.

There had been a moment of confusion when two petrol tankers arrived which were not included on the duty officer's list. Fuel for the camp had already arrived. The tanker drivers had explained that their loads were for the power station, and shown the soldiers their delivery notes. The two tankers had been allowed to pass through the camp and into the power-station compound.

The work had proceeded at an urgent pace through the hot afternoon. The soldiers had been too busy to wonder why the powerstation decommissioning staff showed no interest in the developments going on round them.

At 16:00 hours water purification equipment had arrived from the General Stores Depot, followed by a long convoy of trucks laden with two hundred tonnes of food and clothing – enough to last the camp five years.

Captain Stacy had walked methodically round the camp at 17:30, holding his indispensable clipboard. He had been well pleased with what he saw: the huts were in straight lines, the roads were neatly marked and the flowerbeds were being dug.

He had telephoned Pyne's quarters at the artillery school and told him everything was in order.

Pyne had thanked him and continued playing patience. The airmail envelope had stood on the mantelpiece. He could hear Garnet moving about in the next room. Pyne had

moved the telephone on to the card table at 20:00 hours —
thirty minutes before he expected another unscheduled call
from Stacy. The telephone had rung as he was laying the
cards out for the twentieth time. It was Stacy sounding
slightly agitated.

'I'm sorry to trouble you, sir, but we've got a problem.'

'Nothing serious, I hope, captain?'

Stacy had paused:'Well, I'm not sure,sir. But a convoy has
just turned up from the Royal Ordnance Factory with a load
of Cyclonite HE which isn't on our procurement lists.'

'Tell them to take it back,' Pyne had snapped, wondering
if his acting was good enough. Apparently it was, for Stacy's
reply had sounded hurt: 'The drivers can't take it back, sir,
because police escorts haven't been arranged with county
constabularies for the return journey. They were expecting
to return with empty trucks.'

'How much is there?'

Stacy had hesitated before answering. 'Twelve trucks.'

'Fully loaded?'

'Yes, sir,' Stacy had said miserably. The complex operation had gone so well until now. 'There's a hundred tonnes
of the stuff and a dozen cases of detonators.'

Pyne had erupted: 'Good God, man, who the devil signed
the LPOs?'

'It looks like your signature, sir.'

Pyne had thought a pause would be just right at this point.
'I see,' he had said slowly. 'So it doesn't look as if you
checked them before releasing them?'

'I suppose not,' Stacy had said.

Pyne had noticed a trace of insolence in the man's voice,
for which he couldn't really blame him.

'Have you signed the delivery notes?'

'No, sir. I thought I'd better contact you first.'

Another pause had been required before Pyne had said:
'Well? What do you propose doing with all this high
explosive?'

41

'I don't know, sir. I don't like having the stuff on the camp.' Stacy had sounded hopeful, as if Pyne would have the answer.

Pyne had allowed himself a faint smile. The conversation was going extremely well.

'All right, Stacy,' he had said at length. 'Leave it with me. I'll call you back in ten minutes.'

'Thank you, sir,' Stacy had said with relief.

Pyne had replaced the receiver, waited seven minutes and dialled a number.

'Keller? Pyne. The explosive will be delivered in about thirty minutes. Captain Stacy will be asking you where he can store it. I suggest you get him to put it as near the access tunnels as possible . . . And Keller did anyone get a good look at you when you drove the tankers through the camp?'

Keller's answer had been satisfactory. Pyne had cut the line and called Stacy.

'I've been onto National Power and they say you can store the HE in the power station until I arrange transport to have it moved. The superintendent will show you where to put it.'

Thirty minutes after the call the army had shifted five-thousand cases of Cyclonite high explosive into the Vulcan Hall nuclear power station, and so enabled Captain Stacy to enjoy a comfortable night, secure in the knowledge that he had done his best. He hadn't even considered it odd that National Power should agree to storing a huge quantity of high explosive at a nuclear power station.

As Pyne looked down from his Scout he admitted to himself that Stacy had done an excellent job establishing the camp. The U-shaped hundred-acre site was a model of what an army camp should look like.

Pyne set the Scout down in the exact centre of the landing pad and studiously avoided the anxious face of Stacy standing back from the downwash of the slowing rotors. He held the door open as Pyne stepped on to the compressed soil bearing the marks of yesterday's assault by the bull-dozers. Pyne looked curiously about.

'You seem to have done extremely well, Stacy,' he said after Stacy had welcomed him.

Stacy's worried face eased slightly. 'It's been a hectic twenty-four hours, sir.'

'I can imagine,' said Pyne, climbing into the waiting Land Rover.

Stacy hesitated before starting the engine. 'You must've seen the explosion, sir?'

'Yes,' replied Pyne noncommittally.

'We had a request from the police for assistance.'

'Of course,' said Pyne coldly. He wanted to change the subject. He pointed. 'What are these men doing?'

'Testing the soil with pH meters, sir. To see what sorts of plants and shrubs will do well here.'

Christ, thought Pyne.

The tour of inspection ended at the camp's nerve centre – the operations room lined with radar screens and dominated by a floor-to-ceiling glass map of the North sea.

Stacy fingered his clipboard and nervously cleared his throat. 'Sir, you may remember I rang you last night about a quantity of HE that arrived from Blackburn?'

Pyne regarded the captain coldly. 'So?'

'I'm afraid some more supplies arrived at midnight,' Stacy confessed, as if it was all his fault. 'It was four large containers from private contractors. The drivers said it was more than their jobs were worth to take the stuff back without a senior officer's signature on the six-forty forms.'

Pyne held out his hand for the sheaf of papers Stacy had removed from his clipboard.

The first list covered a wide variety of tinned food, dried food, clothing and personal effects. The second list authorized the supply of radar equipment, intruder surveillance equipment and a quantity of small arms – all in addition to the stores already supplied from Central Inventory Control Points.

'The superintendent at the power station is a decent sort,' said Stacy, wondering if Pyne was about to explode. 'He said I could store the stuff in the power station along with the HE.'

Pyne thrust the papers in his pocket. 'Very well, Stacy. I'll sort everything out tomorrow with the procurement people. And now I'd like to address the men.'

'There's another thing you should know,' said Stacy, avoiding Pyne's eye.

Pyne sighed.

Stacy pressed on: 'None of the power station staff has come through the camp. We haven't had to issue a single pass.'

'That's right, Captain. I didn't want them coming through the camp. They were taken off by boat. They won't be coming back because there's still some construction work to be done and the engineers have gone on strike. The power station is being closed down. That's why I've decided to use the superintendent's quarters until my trailer arrives.'

Pyne addressed the soldiers for ten minutes. He stressed the secrecy concerning the camp's true function. Although their job was to go to the aid of any platform threatened by terrorists, it was anticipated that the force would eventually become the long-debated third force similar to the French CRS. For the time being the camp was under the direct control of the Cabinet Office and could act only on their orders. At a nod from Pyne, Stacy produced an example of the new uniform and outlined the pay structure; most of the men could expect a fifty percent pay increase. There were smiles all round by the time Stacy had finished speaking.

'One last thing,' said Pyne. 'In view of the civil unrest in the country, you may be called upon to act at any moment. The camp is now on a twenty-four-hour alert, so I'm afraid leave is out of the question, and you won't be able to telephone home.' Pyne smiled. 'The weather is somewhat hot at the moment. If you care to examine supply item fifty-two in Hut . . .' he broke off and glanced at Stacy's clipboard, '. . . in Hut Fifteen, you'll find it's a large portable swimming pool complete with filtration and purification equipment.'

9

Only when he had reached Waterloo Station and locked himself in a toilet cubicle did Corporal Garnet dare open General Pyne's briefcase. Inside he found, as the general had said, his discharge papers and a letter to the Midland Bank. There was also a generous cheque, a letter to the Thames Water Authority notifying them of the transfer of ownership of Pyne's seven-metre Freeman cabin cruiser to Ian Garnet, a bunch of keys and a wallet containing several credit cards, which were useless to him, and £500 in cash.

Dazed, the former corporal stuffed the papers back into the briefcase, pushed the money into his hip pocket and left the cubicle without pulling the grubby piece of string that served as a chain.

He drifted aimlessly round the station, uncertain what to do. Blackboards outside the platform barriers announced British Rail's regret at their failure to provide normal service owing to continuing industrial action. Even their electronic arrivals and departures boards weren't working.

The general had mentioned his daughter, Maggie. Even thinking about her made Garnet's toes curl in embarrassment at the way she used to treat him – always taking it for granted he was her personal servant, making him carry her shopping, clean out the swimming pool in blistering sun.

Bitch, thought Garnet savagely. Stinking, cock-teasing little bitch.

There were no trains to Weybridge until tomorrow.

Garnet decided to spend the night in London, He would find a woman – a special woman who would do all the things they usually demanded extra money for. He touched the money in his pocket, savouring the characteristic banknote texture.

He could afford that special woman now.

The general's daughter would have to wait.

10

Pyne's flight from the camp to the Vulcan Hall power station was only a matter of lifting the Scout to two hundred feet, skirting the cooling towers and landing between Hugh Patterson's JetRanger and the two petrol tankers on the wide concrete apron that separated the power station from the river.

He remained in his seat as the rotors slowed, and decided on an immediate confrontation with Keller. The nuclear physicist was in charge in the control room: he should have warned Pyne about the Royal Navy helicopter. It would have to be now; there was no point in letting the man undermine his authority over a period of several days and then acting.

Louise Campion came out of the glazed front entrance to the power station and walked across to the Scout helicopter. Pyne watched her approach while he thought about what he would say to Keller.

Louise Campion was the country's top radiation biologist. She was a few years younger than Pyne. She was always immaculately dressed in well-cut clothes that disguised her slightly overweight figure. The long battle throughout her career to establish her supremacy in a man's world had left her with a brittle personality and an aloof nature. Pyne felt that even after the many meetings when the takeover was being planned he still knew very little about her.

'We were worried in case you were too near the blast,' she said as Pyne climbed out of the Scout.

'Thank you, Louise. But I was even nearer a Navy helicopter,' Pyne replied sarcastically. 'The damn thing tried to blast me out of the sky.'

'Didn't Ralph warn you?' She sounded genuinely surprised.

'I'm not prepared to discuss it now. Tell Hugh and Keller that I want to hold an immediate progress meeting.'

The floor-to ceiling glass walls of the power station's control room afforded a panoramic view of the Thames to the south, the four film cooling towers to the east and the entire power-station complex to the north with the new army camp just beyond. In the days when the power station was fully operational, every function could be controlled from the curved consoles grouped round the main console near the table where the four terrorists were sitting. A radar repeater stood on a tubular trolley beside the table. The beam of light sweeping round the screen created a glowing out line of the Thames Estuary.

Pyne looked up from his check-list and met Keller's blue-flecked eyes.

'And the closed-circuit television is working satisfactorily?'

Keller smiled. 'Perfectly, general.'

'And the radar?'

Keller nodded to the repeater. 'You can see for yourself,' he said.

'If Mr Patterson and Miss Campion can answer questions properly, there's no reason why you shouldn't.'

Keller glanced at Hugh Patterson and Louise Campion. 'The radar is working, general.'

'Then why the hell didn't you warn me about the Lynx?' Pyne demanded.

'Is that what it was? I tried to identify it from Jane's. Keller pointed to an open book on the table. He smiled at Pyne. 'We couldn't see it very well as you were too far off, but you seemed to be giving it some trouble.'

47

Keller's tone was infuriatingly smooth.

'You could've called me on the radio!'snapped Pyne.

Keller looked hurt. 'I'm terribly sorry for what happened, general. But how was I to know it would attack you? I thought it was a routine flight – it was so soon after your delivery, and too soon for the government to close the zone to air traffic. Which they have now done, of course.'

Keller's mannered behaviour angered Pyne. He checked an impulse to reach across the table and hit him. 'I suppose you've heard about the refinery?' he said icily.

'Only that our aim was good. You can see what's left from the fuelling machine roof.'

'One hundred and forty-five maintenance workers killed,' said Pyne icily.

Hugh Patterson looked shocked. Louise Campion's face went pale.

'It's terrible,' said Keller before anyone could speak.'But at least they didn't die in vain. Their deaths will prove to the government that we mean business.' Keller looked down at the table, avoiding the three pairs of eyes on him. 'We agreed a gesture was essential to demonstrate our determination. We couldn't afford for the government to think we might be bluffing. And besides, if you look at the inspection tunnels, you'll see we've prepared to kill millions.'

Pyne closed his eyes.

'Are you all right, general?' asked Keller.

Pyne opened his eyes. Keller was looking at him in genuine concern. Pyne wished he could understand him. He turned his attention to Hugh Patterson, who had been waiting patiently to speak. Patterson was a large, power-fully-built man with a ready sense of humour. His small factory outside London had struggled to survive during the fifties until Patterson had decided to switch to the design and production of radioactive waste containers. Since then his business had steadily grown and now was one of the largest suppliers to the world's nuclear-energy authorities. When Keller had returned from the United States Patterson had offered him the post of technical director – a task Keller performed well, apart from his refusal to return to America.

'Hugh?' invited Pyne.

Patterson cleared his throat. 'Everything went according to plan, Conrad. The explosive is all in place and the supplies are stowed away – including all that bloody corned beef. The supplies turned up just as you said they would. Captain Stacy was anxious to get rid of them. I must congratulate you on your choice of executive officer,' Patterson grinned at Pyne.

'Where are the hostages?' asked Pyne.

Patterson hesitated and glanced at Keller.

'I let them go,' said Keller.

Stacy told me they hadn't been through the camp'.

'By boat,' Keller replied, meeting Pyne's stare.

'Louise?'

'Radiation levels throughout the station are normal,' said Louise Campion. 'I've installed the extra hazard monitors round the reactors. But I'd like to check all of us in two weeks when we've had a chance to settle down and I've ironed the bugs out of my X-ray equipment.' She smiled. 'I'll be pestering you all for urine, Blood and lung tissue samples.'

Pyne smiled, and looked down at his check-list. 'You've all covered your absence?'

Louise Campion grimaced. 'I've taken a job with CERN. I heard someone in my department say at my presentation that I was probably off to look for a husband.'

Everyone laughed.

'Mind you, I could be tempted by the man who's rented my house.'

'Ralph and I are on a round-the-world trip to seek new markets,' said Hugh Patterson. ' My ex-wife is acting chairman while I'm gone.'

Pyne nodded. He looked carefully at the three faces before speaking:

'We've discussed this several times already, but now we're actually in the power station, have any of you got any doubts about what we're doing? Now is the time to say if you have.'

No one spoke.

'And the length of time we might have to remain here?'

Again silence.

'God forbid that it should be five years,' said Pyne. 'If all goes well, we'll be out in a year, but if you're not prepared to accept five years, then say so now.'

Silence.

Pyne folded his check-list and stood up. 'Hugh, I'd like you to take me on a tour of inspection, please.'

'We found everything laid out exactly as per my plans,' said Patterson, leading Pyne down the stairs beneath the concrete apron. He set the knurled wheel combination lock on the massive door at the bottom of the rough-cast steps. Both men grasped the spoked hand-wheel and heaved backwards.

The circular, tapered door which fitted into its corresponding hole like a giant plug swung open. The opening was just large enough for one man to climb through. It reminded Pyne of a bank vault door. Patterson went through first and helped Pyne to scramble in after him.

'There's a safety interlock that prevents the door being locked on the outside if anyone is in here,' said Patterson as he pulled the heavy door shut.

They were in a concrete-lined tunnel about two-metres high. Wall-lights in wire cages extended into the distance along each side of the tunnel. Armoured power cables snaked along the walls. The footsteps of the two men sounded curiously muffled in the claustrophobic surroundings.

'How does air get down here?'

Patterson pointed up. An opening in the ceiling disappeared into the darkness. 'Ventilator shafts,' he said.

'Did you use the hostages to shift the Cyclonite as we planned?' asked Pyne.

'Yes,' Patterson's voice sounded strained. 'Over here we have the—'

'Were they co-operative?'

Patterson hesitated. 'Yes. Keller made certain they would be.'

Pyne saw the fear in Patterson's eyes. 'What did he do?'

'Conrad, I—'

'What did he do?'

Patterson looked down at the concrete floor. 'He shot one of them.'

'Jesus Christ,' Pyne muttered. 'Why?'

'A girl . . . Just here. Look.' Patterson pointed to the floor.

There was a large brown stain that had spread over a wide area due to the capillary action of the unsealed concrete. Footprints, the same colour were etched into the surrounding floor. They led away and disappeared where the tunnel branched to the right.

Pyne picked up some spent nine-millimetre shell cases. 'Why?' he repeated quietly.

Patterson looked away, refusing to meet Pyne's eyes. 'I came down when I heard the shooting. According to the staff, she dropped a case and caused a pile-up in the chain. Keller said she tried to rush him.'

'Who do you believe?'

'Keller. I can't imagine him hurting anyone unless he was forced to.'

Pyne took in the bloodstains splattered on the walls and ceiling. 'Can't you, Hugh? In that case you're a worse judge of character than I imagined.'

Neither man spoke for a moment.

'I'll show you the charges.' said Patterson at length, moving to a branch in the tunnel.

The radioactive waste was stored in stainless-steel flasks housed in three triple-lined containers whose total capacity was 100,000 cubic metres. Each container was encapsulated in thick biological shields of concrete and lead. A system of high-pressure water pumps removed the heat from the vicious liquid that seethed and boiled in their own primitive energies. A period ten times longer than the day since the laying of the first stone of the Great Pyramid would have to pass before the deadly plutonium and strontium isotopes could be released into the environment.

'This is far more than was shown on the plans,' said Pyne.

'I did warn you,' said Patterson. 'The Green Warriors stopped half this lot being dumped in its repositories. It was moved here for interim storage while the courts tried to sort out the mess.'

Pyne nodded. The previous month five Green Warriors had been killed in a demonstration at a repository site in the Midlands. As a result the truck drivers handling the waste flasks had refused to deliver their cargoes.

The inspection tunnel which skirted the periphery of the silos was lined with hazard monitors which maintained a continuous check on background radiation levels – a task they and their descendants would have to carry out for the next forty-five thousand years.

Pyne followed Patterson down the sloping access tunnel beneath the silos. The faint noise he had noticed when he first entered the tunnel was now much louder. He asked Patterson what it was.

'It's the cooling water passing through the outer jackets,' Patterson explained. 'Electricity for the pumps is on an uninterruptable supply line with backups. They won't risk cutting us off therefore we've tapped into them for all our other supply needs.'

'Odd that we should be occupying a power station and worried about our electricity being cut off,' Pyne observed wryly.

Patterson waved his hand round. 'So what do you think of our arrangements?'

Pyne was impressed. The cartons of Cyclonite high explosive were stacked in neat rows along the inspection tunnel's inner wall. The gap between each carton was bridged by a short length of wire connected to a detonator on the side of each of the cartons. Each case was marked with an ICI batch number and the chemical formula for nitrated hexamethlenetetramine: one of most powerful explosives in the world.

The line of grey cardboard cases extended to the far end of the tunnel, where it turned through ninety degrees.

Pyne noticed more of the bloodstains round a steel hatchway set into the wall. 'What's in there, Hugh?'

'It's just a thousand mill pipe we've filled with Cyclonite.'

The urgency in his voice alerted Pyne. He placed his hand on the hatch. Patterson stepped forward and grasped him by the arm.

'It would be best not to, Conrad.'

Pyne brushed Patterson's arm away, opened the hatch and peered into the dark pipe. He could see nothing.

'A torch please, Hugh.'

Patterson reluctantly passed Pyne his torch. The narrow beam of light revealed a chain of the grey cartons disappearing into the darkness. There were more of the bloodstains. They were still wet and glistened when the feeble light flashed on them. Pyne crawled a little way into the pipe and shone the light ahead. Ten yards from the hatch the cartons changed colour. Something had been placed on top of them. It was a girl, lying face down. Naked, with a line of nine-millimetre perforations across her shoulder blades. Pyne tried to turn her over but she seemed to be stuck to the cartons. He pushed hard. Her body came free with a sickly tearing sound. There was nothing left of the front of her body: the nine-millimetre shells had left a gaping hole where her rib-cage and breasts had been. She looked about Maggie's age.

Pyne felt the waves of exhaustion drain his vitality. The shattered body of the girl had, more than anything else, impressed upon him the sheer magnitude of the irrevocable step he had taken. He backed down the pipe. Patterson watched him with concern as he emerged.

'Is she there?'

'Yes – she's there all right.' Pyne handed the torch back to Patterson. 'Why is she naked?'

'One of them complained about the heat. I think Keller made them all strip.'

Pyne clenched his teeth. He had a vivid picture of the scene in the tunnel the previous night: the silent, sweating power-station decommissioning staff passing the heavy cartons from hand to hand; the girl who let one case slip from her exhausted hands and the thunderous roar of Keller's Sterling in the confined space. She weighed only about eight stone – the impact would have slammed her against the side of the tunnel.

Pyne sat on one of the cartons. 'How long have you employed Keller?'

'Five years.'

'And in that time, you never realized–'

'He's a first-class physicist,' Patterson interrupted defensively. 'We needed him.' He paused and looked at the hatch. 'Keller said the girl rushed him.'

'She was shot in the back.'

'Don't be absurd, Conrad.'

'Take a close look. Her chest is a mass of exit wounds.'

Patterson sat beside Pyne and stared at the opposite wall. He could think of nothing to say.

'He's mad,' said Pyne shortly. 'A fucking psycho.'

Patterson turned to look at Pyne. It was rare for the army officer to swear. 'Aren't we all?' he said quietly.

Pyne stood. 'Let's get the inspection over and done with,' he said brusquely.

The two men spent the next five minutes examining the IRIS (Infra-Red Intruder System) detectors that had been deactivated for the inspection tour. The sensors were positioned at regular intervals along the tunnels. It would be impossible for anyone to enter the galleries without their body heat sounding the alarms in the control room.

They were about to enter the last tunnel when a nearby public address speaker clicked and hummed.

'There are two aircraft in the vicinity,' Keller's voice grated metallically. 'One is fifteen kilometres away and closing in fast, the other is much nearer. I can see it through binoculars. It's a Beechcraft Bonanza, flying straight towards us. It seems our instructions are being ignored, so I'm proposing to launch the second Honest John within five minutes.'

11

Now that sex was beyond him, one of the few pleasures Arnold Cox-Spender had left was the ritual morning in bed reading the Sunday papers, looking for his name.

He always read the colour supplements first in the way that a child will always turn to the brightest pebble. Maybe it was a blessing that the Sunday papers were getting thinner each week – there was less to search through. But once again, his name appeared nowhere.

The smell of cooking wafted up the stairs. He would get up in time for lunch and remind his housekeeper to use the extractor fan.

A sudden dull boom shook the windows.

He was mentally composing a complaining memorandum to the Marshall of the Royal Air Force when his bedside telephone rang.

It was a fast journey to London in the Downing Street car sent by the despicable Simpson; all the traffic lights on the route changed to green at their approach. Cox-Spender reflected that it must be urgent for the PM's private secretary to send a ministerial car.

He perched on the edge of his seat to prevent his suit sticking to him in the heat. He had been unable to have a bath because his housekeeper had filled both baths to the brim to provide a drinking water supply during the cuts. He opened the window, but the stench from uncollected refuse simmering in the sun was appalling. He noticed that the fool of a driver was taking him to the Trafalgar Square end of Whitehall. He tapped on the glass in annoyance several times before he noticed the microphone.

'Downing Street's the other way,' he said three times, remembering to press the button only the third time, 'opposite Richmond Terrace.' The driver was obviously a Sunday standby who didn't know his London.

'Yes, sir,' replied the driver, who knew London better than Cox-Spender. 'But I was instructed to take you to this end.'

The car stopped outside the Old Admiralty Building – a four-hundred metre walk from Downing Street. Simpson came out to meet him.

'Good morning, Spender.'

Cox-Spender bristled. He detested Simpson, if only because he never used his full name, certainly never deigned to call anyone 'sir' except the Prime Minister.

'What's all this about, dragging me up here on a Sunday?' demanded Cox-Spender, trying to shake off Simpson's grip on his arm as he was led into the building.

'I'm afraid we'll have to use the tunnel,' said Simpson apologetically. 'All the corridors are locked. These new security precautions you know.'

Cox-Spender wondered if Simpson's mother had loved her son.

Halfway along the tunnel was a spur which branched under St James's Park to Buckingham Palace. Nobody could remember if it had ever been used, and in any case it was sealed by a massive iron door whose key had been lost in the days of empire.

After two hundred metres Cox-Spender's legs were aching, but he strode on grimly, determined not to show weakness in front of the disagreeable Simpson.

'You've heard about the Thames Haven oil refinery?' asked Simpson.

'No. What about it?'

'It was blown up about forty-five minutes ago. By terrorists.'

Simpson smiled at Cox-Spender's horror-struck expression.

Ten minutes later Cox-Spender was shown into the Prime Minister's private office. The politician was sitting at his desk. He made no attempt to rise to greet the Government's Assistant Scientific Adviser.

'I thought there was to be a meeting,' began Cox-Spender, sitting suddenly as Simpson pushed a chair into the back of his knees.

'There is,' said the Prime Minister. 'Right now. Between the three of us.' He smiled at Cox-Spender. Simpson was right, he thought. Just the manageable sort we need.

There was an opened airmail envelope on the politician's desk and a single typewritten sheet of paper. He pushed the document across the desk to Cox-Spender. 'Read. Digest,' he invited. 'And then bubble over with brilliant suggestions.'

Cox-Spender picked up the document and started to read:

POLITICAL MEASURES
1 Government to commit UK to the setting up of a single defence force for the European Community by the end of the century.
2 Capital punishment to be re-introduced for murder and illegal possession of hard drugs.
3 Capital punishment to be introduced for possession of all firearms after a one month amnesty period for handing over of firearms to police.
4 Trial by jury for terrorist offences to be suspended. Indictable terrorist offenses to be heard by tribunals and right of appeal to be abolished.

5 Immediate withdrawal of armed forces from Northern Ireland. Administration of Ulster to be transferred to Irish Republic.

6 Overseas aid to be suspended until further notice.

7 Public transport to be free and financed from central government.

8 500,000 hectares of land to be made available immediately and sold in quarter hectare plots to enable people to build their own homes.

Cox-Spender reached the foot of the page and looked up at Simpson and the Prime Minister.

'Where've you got up to?' demanded the Prime Minister.

Cox-Spender's eyes scrabbled wildly over the sheet of paper. 'Number Eight,' he said, barely able to choke the words out. 'Now turn over and read the economic measures,' the Prime Minister suggested.

Cox-Spender's near lifeless fingers fumbled turning the document over.

ECONOMIC MEASURES

9 Government to participate in the negotiations for the setting up of a central European reserve bank and the introduction of a common EC currency before 31st December 1999.

10 Credit card and charge card purchases to be limited to £50.

11 100% luxury duty to be levied on all manufactured goods imported from outside EC.

12 Poll Tax and business rates to be scrapped. All local government funding to be from central government.

13 VAT to be raised to 25%.

14 Scope of VAT to be extended to include all retail goods including insurance, domestic energy supplies and agricultural supplies.

15 Draft emergency bill embracing all these provisions to be submitted to us for approval

within a hundred hours of the time given on the envelope.

(Signed)

*Conrad Pyne, formerly of
'Sand Hills', St Georges Hill*

*Ralph Keller, formerly of
'High Pine', Ashley Park*

*Hugh Patterson, formerly of
'Brunel Hall', St Georges Hill*

*Louise Campion, formerly of
'Badger Place', St Georges Hill*

Cox-Spender finished reading and looked up in bewilderment at the two men who were watching him carefully.

'I don't understand it,' he said. 'What is it? A list of the government's future plans?'

'It will be unless you come up with something,' replied the Prime Minister sourly. 'Read the last condition again.'

Cox-Spender's eyes skated over Article 15. It still didn't make sense.

The Prime Minister sighed. 'Those four signatories have seized the Vulcan Hall nuclear power station on Canvey Island. The power station is about to be decommissioned and by some administrative cock-up, the nuclear police unit had been withdrawn. The signatories claim to have placed a large quantity of high explosives round the radioactive-waste silos and have threatened to blow them up unless we introduce those measures. Now do you understand?'

Cox-Spender stared at the Prime Minister and Simpson in turn. His eyes dropped to the sheet of paper that had slipped from his hand and was lying on the table.

'But there's no radioactive waste stored at Vulcan Hall,' he protested. 'Only empty silos. The Cheshire repository—'

The Prime Minister sighed. 'It was agreed that the Cheshire repository wouldn't be used until the report into

59

the riots was published. The waste was moved to Vulcan Hall for temporary storage

'But . . . it's impossible to blow-up those silos!'

'Why?' demanded the Prime Minister.

'They're deep underground. The sides, if they're to specification, must be at least three-metres of stainless steel, lead and concrete. They've been designed to withstand a major earthquake.'

'They couldn't blow them up?' inquired the Prime Minister. 'You'd stake your professional reputation on that?'

Cox-Spender saw the trap. 'How much explosive have they got?'

Simpson smiled. 'A hundred tonnes of Cyclonite, whatever that is.'

Cox-Spender began to sweat and wondered why it had to be him. Why hadn't they called in the Chief Scientific Adviser? It wasn't fair.

The Prime Minister noticed the beads of perspiration with satisfaction. They had chosen well. 'I don't know what this Cyclonite is,' he said smoothly. 'But if it's placed under the silos, would I be right in assuming that a hundred tonnes is enough to blow not only them up, but most of Canvey Island as well?'

Cox-Spender could only nod. For a wild, escapist moment, he could considered resigning on the spot, but his pension . . .'

'Maybe they're bluffing,' he blurted out.

'It's possible,' agreed the Prime Minister. 'But they certainly weren't bluffing about Thames Haven.'

'How did they do it?'

'With an Honest John missile.'

There was total silence in the room apart from the refined tick of an eighteenth-century clock over the Adam fireplace.

'We'd have another Cheynobel on our hands,' the Prime Minister commented.

'It would be worse than Cheynobel,' said Cox-Spender. 'There would be the fallout from the waste and the power station's reactors.'

'If only they were asking for something sensible,' complained the Prime Minister. 'A million pounds would be much more convenient. I could call the governor of the Bank of England and get him to produce it here. That's if we've got a million pounds,' he added as an afterthought.

'Perhaps they *could* be bought,' said Cox-Spender hopefully.

'Take another look at those who signed,' invited the Prime Minister. 'Hugh Patterson's got more money in Swiss numbered accounts than we've got in gold and dollar reserves. Also, one of his companies designed and built the silos, so he probably knows the best place to position the explosive for the best, or rather worst, effect.'

'Conrad Pyne,' said Cox-Spender, looking at the ultimatum. 'I've heard of him.'

Simpson intervened: 'He's in charge of the new oil platform defence force which was set up at your suggestion, Mr Spender.'

'Oh, now look. I only suggested it. The idea was approved by the Policy Review Committee and the chiefs of staff. You can't blame me–'

'Nobody's blaming you for anything,' said the Prime Minister soothingly. 'All we want you to do is to take a look at the Thames Haven site and make plausible pronouncements on the possible cause. I've had the area sealed off. After all, we don't want DTI and health and safety inspectors tramping all over the place picking up bits of Honest Johns, do we?'

'I'll go first thing in the morning, Prime Minister,' said Cox-Spender.

'First thing now, Cox-Spender. After that, I want you to take a look at the Vulcan Hall set-up and see how strong they are.'

Cox-Spender was appalled. 'Go to Vulcan Hall? But . . . but how do I get in?'

The Prime Minister looked blankly at Simpson before turning to Cox-Spender. 'Try the front door,' he suggested. 'That is, if power stations have front doors.'

Cox-Spender had the feeling that powerful forces were being aligned against him. The ground was being sucked from under his feet, Simpson and the PM were smiling at him as if he could save the situation. He decided to show them the sort of person he really was. He would be like Harry Truman and rise to the task. With a firm jaw he asked: 'How do I contact them?'

'Try the telephone,' said Simpson. 'You'll probably find them listed under Power Gen, or the Central Electricity Generating Board if your phone directory's out-of-date.'

'Are they armed?' The question made him sound scared – which he was.

Simpson glanced at a paper on his desk. 'They've got command of two hundred soldiers with full combat kit, several armoured personnel carriers, God knows what in the way of small arms. Oh yes – and a couple of Apache gunships.'

Cox-Spender blinked. The Harry Truman resolve melted. 'How did they–'

'The new base depot and headquarters of the Oil Rig Defence under the command of General Pyne were established yesterday by the Royal Engineers,' said Simpson. 'They're located on Canvey Island because Pyne assured us it would be the best place for training purposes and launching offensives against oil rigs that have been taken over by terrorists.'

All the fight went out of Cox-Spender. 'Don't you think the Chief Scientific Adviser would be better able to deal with the situation, Prime Minister?'

'He's in hospital,' pointed out Simpson.

This was news to Cox-Spender. 'I didn't know. Is he . . .?'

'It was a road accident. Hit-and-run when he was crossing the Mall. Nasty business, but he's expected to be up and about next month.'

Cox-Spender felt the two pairs of speculative eyes boring into him. 'Well, I'd better be off then,' he said lamely. 'May I use the front door please? It's rather a long walk to the Admiralty—'

'I'm sorry ,' said the Prime Minister. 'But your car will be waiting for you there. So perhaps . . .'

'Yes, of course, Prime Minister.'

Simpson opened the door.

'One thing,' said the Prime Minister as Cox-Spender turned to leave. 'Don't try any heroics will you? We don't want you attempting James Bond stunts on this job?' He smiled at Cox-Spender and continued. 'I'm the only one round here who's got the sort of licence he was supposed to have, and if you mess things up, I might be tempted to use it.'

Cox-Spender had never read a James Bond book but the Prime Minister's words carried an ominous impact.

After Cox-Spender had left on his long walk back to the Old Admiralty Building the Prime Minister sat at his desk and toyed with the massive amber paperweight presented to him by Welsh miners . . . what was left of them. Simpson watched him carefully.

'Do you think we've picked the right man?' said the Prime Minister.

'Personally, I think he's ideal.' replied Simpson evenly.

The Prime Minister allowed the paperweight to slide from one hand to the other. 'Too bad if we're wrong,' he said.

'Disastrous. But I don't think we are.'

The paperweight spun on the blotter. Yellow light flashed round the walls.

'Let's hope so, Simpson.'

12

Pyne was the first to leave the inspection tunnel and race across the apron towards the two petrol tankers. Then he hesitated, uncertain which tanker still contained an Honest John. Patterson followed only a few paces behind.

'Which one?' yelled Pyne.

Patterson pointed to the tanker facing the Thames.

Pyne could hear the electric servo motors start as he dived into the driver's cab. 'How do I shut it off?' he shouted desperately at Patterson.

'You can't!' croaked Patterson, gesturing up at the power station. 'It's radio-controlled. Keller has the control transmitter!'

Pyne cursed and jumped down.

In a few seconds the dummy five thousand-litre tank would be separating into two halves and opening to the sky like a giant clam. Pyne experienced a wave of panic as a new sound was added to the steady whine from the servo motors – the harsh growl of powerful motors building up hydraulic pressure for the rams to thrust the Honest John to its launch elevation. The tanker had been parked with its tyres positioned on carefully drawn chalk marks so that its concealed cargo, when exposed, would be pointing at the densely populated East End of London.

'A Sterling!' Pyne yelled to Patterson. 'For Christ's sake hurry!'

Patterson disappeared into the power station.

Pyne stood staring helplessly at the tanker. He could hear the piston engine of the approaching aircraft. Then there was another sound – the metallic snap of the electric latches that held the two halves of the dummy tanker closed. The long, oval container began to shudder.

Patterson appeared carrying a Sterling submarine-gun. Pyne snatched it out of his hands and raced towards the tanker.

A widening gap had appeared along the top of the tanker as Pyne threw himself flat on the concrete and released the Sterling's safety-catch.

The tankers's only source of power when its engine wasn't running was a large lead-acid battery hanging in a cradle beneath the chassis. Pyne took careful aim and fired. The battery exploded into shards of bituminous compound that clanged against the underside of the petrol container.

Pyne held the stream of fire steady his eyes tightly shut and face turned away from the jets of acid spraying from the shattered battery. Bullets tore into the battery cradle. It fell. The unrecognizable bulk of the accumulator swayed drunkenly back and forth for a few seconds before the remains of it's black casing fell to the ground leaving only a cluster of riddled power cells hanging by the two heavy power cables.

Pyne stopped firing. His ears were ringing in the sudden silence and his hands were burning painfully from the splashes of sulphuric acid.

The tanker was now impotent, as was the missile. The second Honest John could never be launched.

The pale-blue Bonanza flashed past above the river – heading towards London.

13

Simpson read the telex from RAF Manston at 13:15 – fifteen minutes after Cox-Spender's departure to examine the devastated Thames Haven oil refinery. For the first time that Sunday, he felt slightly uneasy. He crossed the carpeted corridor and tapped on the door to the Prime Minister's office. He entered without waiting for an invitation – a system devised many years before to let the Prime Minister know he had an urgent message.

The Prime Minister looked up expectantly from the Sunday papers as Simpson entered the room.

'I'm afraid an aircraft has penetrated the prohibited zone, sir,' said Simpson, without preamble. 'A Beechcraft Bonanza.'

The Prime Minister's face showed a fleeting trace of alarm. 'When was this?'

'About forty-five minutes ago. I don't think it's anything to worry about, sir. Not now, anyway. Manston scrambled a Tornado to intercept it, but they were too late. The aircraft was too near the power station—'

'But Simpson,' interrupted the Prime Minister. 'You issued strict orders that no aircraft was to be allowed in the vicinity of the Thames Estuary – correct?'

Simpson fumed inwardly. He detested mistakes. 'There was a breakdown in communications, sir. Manston said the Bonanza wasn't interested in Vulcan Hall – it flew straight past.'

'They didn't harass it, did they?'

'No, sir. They told the Tornado to break off – on my orders.'

The Prime Minister relaxed.

'Just as well. Probably a Sunday joyrider. Chase one with a Tornado in a prohibited zone and it'll be all over the flying clubs in southern England before nightfall.' The Prime Minister looked sharply at his secretary. 'Did the RAF get its registration?'

'Yes, sir. I'll see if I can get onto someone at the Air Registration Board. I'll have the owner's name and address on your desk in sixty minutes.'

'Thirty minutes please, Simpson.'

14

Cox-Spender was hungry, thirsty, sweating profusely and feeling very much aggrieved at having to spend his Sunday afternoon stumbling round the wreckage of the Thames Haven oil refinery. The only consolation was that it took his mind off his coming visit to the Vulcan Hall nuclear power station.

He sat on a section of smashed pipe and wondered what sort of statement he could issue that would convince everyone that the area was too dangerous to allow rescue teams to start work.

As he gloomily surveyed the devastation he could hear the distant arguments between the police and families of missing refinery workers who were protesting because a search and rescue operation was not allowed to start. The strident voice of the chief constable of Essex was telling the crowd over a loudhailer that work would start as soon as the government's Assistant Scientific Adviser had declared the area safe. Fighting had broken out as the crowd tried to break through the police cordon.

On the river, what was left of the Thames Division fleet of police launches battled to head off an armada of small craft crowded with sightseers whose boats had not been swamped by the tidal wave.

Cox-Spender climbed to his feet and stood forlornly amid the nightmare of twisted pipes and flattened distillation columns. Chemical engineering had not been his subject, and he suspected that whatever he said would be torn to shreds by engineers and designers who knew the refinery.

He walked slowly along an avenue that seemed reasonably clear of debris – probably a road originally, but there was no way of being certain, so total was the appalling destruction.

There was a sickening smell hanging in the still air. Cox-Spender shivered despite the heat. Perhaps it was the smell of death. Cox-Spender did not know what death smelt like, but he was sure if it smelt of anything it would be the suffocating stench that was now clinging to the refinery.

A pale-blue Beechcraft Bonanza light aircraft circled above, drowning the notes he was dictating into a pocket tape recorder. He tried not to look at the far-off cooling towers of Vulcan Hall standing to pale attention ten kilometres away in the heat-warped distance. His scalp crawled at the prospect of the forthcoming visit and the people he would be talking to there. In his mind was a

67

picture of ruthless terrorists with hard eyes staring through slits in black hoods.

Half an hour later he returned to what had been the refinery's main gate.

The chief constable came forward anxiously to greet him. 'We were getting worried about you, sir,' he said, relieved that Cox-Spender appeared to be intact.

'I'm, quite capable of looking after myself, thank you,' Cox-Spender replied acidly. He enjoyed exercising authority over important officials. The Prime Minister had given him sweeping powers and he intended making full use of them.

The chief constable ignored the childish jibe. 'There's a Mr Maynard wants to see you urgently,' he said. 'He's waiting in the trailer.'

Ivor Maynard was a small, dapper man who came straight to the point.

'Thank Christ you've allowed no one on to the site,' he said breathlessly to Cox-Spender.

Cox-Spender blinked.

'We'd cleared out one of those fractional distillers to process some special liquid rocket fuel, and now it's leaking out of the underground storage tank. If it combines with—'

'How do you know it's leaking?' demanded Cox-Spender, determined to remain master of the situation.

The little engineer stared at the Assistant Scientific Adviser.

'Christ man! Can't you smell it? We've got to get all these policeman and people back another hundred yards!'

Cox-Spender beamed at Maynard and wondered if his visit to the power station would be as successful.

15

'There's one thing you should know about me, Mitch,' said Maggie, setting the eight by ten prints on the general's

68

dining-room table. 'In case you ever decide to propose to me, I'm warning you that I'm better in a darkroom that I am in a kitchen.'

'Don't worry, honey. I'm a gifted cook. It's just that I'm too modest to boast about it.'

Mitchell picked up the damp prints. There was no sign of the drill-string. Nothing had survived that terrible explosion.

'Well?' said Maggie.

Mitchell swore softly. 'Sabotage.'

'How do you know?'

Mitchell jabbed at one of the photographs. 'I can't be absolutely certain, but it looks as if that's the point where the explosion took place. Right at that hub. One explosion – not the whole series of explosions you'd expect when a place like that goes up.'

Maggie studied the photograph closely. Mitchell was right: most of the wrecked, flattened columns radiated outwards from a central focal point at one end of the refinery.

'Perhaps they had something special there which would've caused the explosion?'

Mitchell shook his head. 'I know that refinery. It looks as if the explosion took place in the employees' carpark. That can only mean sabotage.

There was silence for a few moments. 'Perhaps there's some more news on the radio,' Maggie suggested.

She went into the kitchen and returned with the portable radio. The news was still scant. The government's Assistant Scientific Adviser had just issued a statement saying there was a danger of further explosions. An interview followed with a senior engineer who emphatically denied that further explosions would be as serious as the first explosion. No, he didn't know what had caused it. No, he would not comment until the Assistant Scientific Adviser had completed his preliminary inquiries.

The newsreader promised more information as it became available.

Maggie switched off the radio and picked up one of the prints. 'It doesn't look as if there's anything left to explode,' she commented.

Mitchell took the photograph and looked at it for some seconds. 'Exactly the same thought was going through my head.' he said.

She picked up another picture. It was one of the first photographs Mitchell had taken just before they reached the refinery to clear possible fogged film at the start of the roll. In the foreground were the Vulcan Hall nuclear cooling towers.

'I wonder what my father is doing there,' she said.

Mitchell looked at the print over her shoulder. At the edge were the two helicopters standing near the petrol tankers. The registration letters on the American-built JetRanger were clearly visible. The figure of a man seemed to be running towards the tankers.

'Is he friendly with Patterson?' asked Mitchell disinterestedly.

'Much more so lately. I came home one evening a few weeks ago and there were several cars parked outside. One of them was Hugh Patterson's. I went away. It's unusual for my father to entertain.'

'Are you sure the JetRanger belongs to Patterson? I know they're rare over here, but it's just possible that it could belong to someone else.'

'I can easily check,' said Maggie. She crossed to a sideboard and returned with a photograph album. She placed it on the table and leafed through the pages. Some of the prints were not properly mounted and spilled out. She picked up one of the loose prints, compared it with one of the pictured taken that morning, and pushed it in front of Mitchell.

'Look.'

The picture from the album showed a small crowd holding drinks, posing beside a helicopter parked on the lawn before a magnificent Moorish-style house: a St Georges Hill scene.

'I took that picture last year at one of Hugh Patterson's barbecues,' Maggie explained. 'You see? The chopper's registration letters in your photo and mine are the same.'

Mitchell's mind was on the problem of his lost drill-string, but he was sufficiently interested in Maggie to go along with her concern about the whereabouts of her father. He looked at the party photograph.

'Who's the guy sitting in the chopper's door?'

'Oh, that's Ralph Keller – Hugh Patterson's chief physicist or something. He's rather nice. He lives alone and is terribly shy with girls. The woman is Louise Campion. She lives on the other side of the estate. I think there's something between her and Patterson – she's often been over here with him for drinks.'

The girl's voice washed over Mitchell as he stared at the pictures of the devastated refinery.

'Am I boring you, Mitch . . . Mitch?' She put her arm round the American and stood beside him looking down at the pictures.

'Was it worth a lot of money?' she asked gently.

Mitchell nodded. 'It could be the end of my business.'

'I'm sorry. I should have realised. There's me going on about my father while you're–'

'It doesn't matter, honey. I guess I'll sort something out.' He slipped his arm round her shoulder. It was almost an unconscious gesture.

'Are you hungry?' Maggie asked.

Mitchell suddenly realized that he had not eaten that day. 'Yes, I'm starving.'

'Would you like me to cook you something?'

'That would be–' He broke off and grinned. 'Hell, no. I need to keep fit if I'm to tackle this problem.'

71

He propelled Maggie towards the french windows. 'I wouldn't be a gentleman to let you cook in that mess. You sit yourself down by the pool, and *I'll* cook.'

Maggie laughed. 'That's the sort of proposition I like.'

Mitchell returned to the dining-room. He gathered up the photographs and thrust them into a yellow Kodak print envelope.

16

'Mitchell, Howard Steven, US citizen,' began the Aliens' Register report. 'Born Lower East Side, New York City. No material advantages as a child. Parents deceased, formerly garment workers. PS education. Showed early abilities in engineering. Studied chemical engineering at MIT'.

The Prime Minister skipped the biographical details and turned the page to study the résumé of Mitchell's recent activities while Simpson watched him unhappily.

'Sole stockholder of Oil and Natural Gas Engineering Supplies Ltd. Address: The Centre, Walton-on-Thames, Surrey. According to the Articles of Association (appendix 3), this firm is a shipping and forwarding agent specializing in the supply of engineering materials to oil companies operating in the North Sea. Private address: 'Berrylands,' St Georges Hill, Weybridge, Surrey. Telephone number: Weybridge—'

The Prime Minister stopped reading and looked slowly up at Simpson. Their eyes met.

'This Michell lives at St Georges Hill,' said the Prime Minister evenly.

'It could be a coincidence.'

'Coincidence,' snorted the Prime Minister, and returned to the report.

Simpson wondered if he was going to read the last page.

The Prime Minister read the last page.

'Unmarried. Lives alone. Plays an occasional Sunday morning game of golf with General Conrad Pyne. CR:

Several traffic offenses (Appendix 6). Believed to be friendly with Paul Weiner, Industrial Liaison Controller at the American Embassy'.

The Prime Minister read no further. He dropped the report on his desk and unwrapped a cigar. 'Mitchell appears to have a US Embassy contact,' he observed. 'Paul Weiner.'

'There's nothing unusual about that, sir. The nature of Mitchell's business means that he's certain to have an industrial liaison contact in the embassy and we've no evidence that they've been regularly meeting.'

'Where does this Weiner live?' the Prime Minister interrupted.

'Cumberland Mansions in Seymour Place.' Simpson's fingers drummed lightly on the desk.

The Prime Minister watched him carefully through the flame of his table lighter. He knew Simpson well enough to guess that the report had shaken him too. It was an overlooked detail – perhaps more than a detail. Simpson did not like overlooked details and was usually efficient enough not to have to worry about them. The Prime Minister inhaled on the cigar. 'Has Weiner been kept under normal surveillance?'

'Yes, sir.'

The Prime Minister considered. 'Selective surveillance I suppose?'

Simpson nodded. There were times when he resented the politician's knowledge of security procedures. A neat little trap had been laid; he saw it coming.

The Prime Minister examined the glowing end of his cigar. 'In that case, Simpson, if Weiner has not been watched full time, we cannot be certain that he and Mitchell have not been meeting regularly . . . can we?'

'No, sir.'

'And if I remember correctly, the Industrial Liaison Department at the American Embassy covers a multitude of sins and sinners- CIA sins and sinners especially. Am I right?'

Simpson did not enjoy hot seats, even when they were only moderately warm.

'We believe its function is to monitor the behaviour of overseas American firms — to ensure they don't supply strategic materials to the Middle East. It's a negative activity which has suited our book.' Simpson's voice was edged with irritation.

'This fellow flying over Vulcan Hall power station is hardly a negative activity, Simpson.'

'He flew past it, sir.'

The Prime Minister looked faintly contemptuous.

Simpson began to get annoyed. 'It could be merely a coincidence, sir. We don't know for certain—'

'Quite right,' cut in the Prime Minister. 'We don't know for certain. But we will know if we keep a close watch on him. I needn't remind you of the consequences if this business blows up in our faces. So I suggest we keep an eye on him for the time being.'

'Yes, sir.' Simpson reached for the telephone.

'Who are you calling?'

Simpson hesitated. 'Well, I thought the Special Branch.'

'I see. You think we can trust Sir Gordon Clement?'

Simpson considered for a moment and took his hand away from the telephone.

'The only people we can trust,' said the Prime Minister scathingly, 'are one another. There's far too much at stake to involve anyone who has an axe to grind against me. It's going to be a damned nuisance having you out of the office, but Weybridge isn't too far from London, and I only want you to find out what Mitchell knows and what he's passed on.'

Simpson sat alone reading the file on Howard Mitchell for the umpteenth time and decided that he had no intention of being out of London during the crucial hours ahead. On the other hand the Prime Minister was right — Howard Mitchell was a problem: he was obviously working for the CIA, but how much did he really know about the conspiracy? And if he did know anything, how much had he passed on? Simpson sighed. There were so many imponderables. Maybe it was merely bad luck that the CIA had an agent on St Georges Hill where the terrorists had their homes but it seemed unlikely.

Simpson glanced through Howard Mitchell's company returns. It must have taken them a long time to set him up. The thought gave him an idea. Supposing Mitchell was just nibbling round the edge and knew only little of what was going on? There was nothing that could be done about the information already passed, but it would be possible to stop him sniffing out any more. If he was 'deactivated' or otherwise dealt with, it would arouse CIA suspicions, but it would take them months to set up a replacement. Time was the one thing that was vital now.

Time . . . Time . . .

Simpson stared straight ahead, his shrewd brain turning over the problem and possible solutions.

It made sense. Removing Mitchell would kill two birds: it would stop the CIA finding out more than they knew already, and it would mean that Simpson wouldn't have to be out of London to watch him.

Simpson smiled. He was wrong – his plan would kill three birds – one of them being Mitchell. He wondered how it could be made to look like an accident.

17

The afternoon was suffocatingly hot. The fifteen kilometre drive, in what was nothing more than a perambulating oven, from Thames Haven to Canvey Island was enough to make Cox-Spender forget the terrors awaiting him at the power station. The sweat rolled down the inside of his unlaundered collar. The car's air-conditioning couldn't cope. Opening a window didn't help: a vengeful horsefly was sucked into the car and bit him on the back of the neck.

The car crossed the road bridge on to Canvey Island. The army waved it through the checkpoints. Its registration number was on their lists. The barrier puzzled the driver, but he had been trained not to talk to his passengers unless they spoke to him. Holidaymakers and caravan owners were arguing with the soldiers. The troops were indifferent; all traffic trying to get on to the island was ordered into a field for a detailed examination.

The black government car drove across the island towing a cloud of dust. The driver followed the signs that indicated the way to Vulcan Hall power station. The signs were unnecessary because the four cooling towers were visible from every part of the island.

The car stopped before a high steel-framed chainlink gate that stretched across the road. Two soldiers emerged from the guardhouse and checked Cox-Spender's pass. The gate swung open. The soldiers told the driver to park beside an amphibious assault craft, and wait. No one was to leave the car.

Cox-Spender waited as the dark car soaked up solar radiation. A Land Rover driven by General Conrad Pyne arrived just as Cox-Spender was about to tell the driver to leave. Cox-Spender remembered Pyne from meetings when the Oil Rig Defence Force was in the early planning stage. He appeared to have aged considerably since he had last seen him.

'Good day, Mr Cox-Spender,' said Pyne opening the car door. 'Please come with me.' His voice was tired. Neither friendly nor unfriendly. Just very tired.

'I expect you know who sent me,' said Cox-Spender, sitting beside Pyne in the open Land Rover.

Pyne let in the clutch. Cox-Spender had to grab the top of the windscreen to avoid falling out.

'There are several things I should like to see,' said Cox-Spender, opting for the direct approach. 'But first, I wish to examine the reactors to ensure that are safe. Then I should like to see the power-station staff. And then take a look at this high explosive you claim to have placed round the waste silos.' Despite the knot of fear in Cox-Spender's stomach, he felt it was necessary to assert his authority from the beginning and show these people who they were dealing with. The fact that no one had pointed a gun at him gave him confidence.

Pyne drove through the inner camp gate and into the power-station compound. He turned angrily to Cox-Spender. 'The reactor decommissioning programme was started last week,' he snapped. 'You'll see what we've decided you should see. No more, and no less.'

All the fight finally went out of Cox-Spender. He remained silent for the rest of the brief journey.

The Land Rover drove across the shadow of the aluminium containment dome that housed the nuclear fuelling machine perched on top of the twenty-metre-high prestressed concrete reactor building.

Cox-Spender remembered that Pyne used to have considerable dealings with the Prime Minister in the days when the politician had been Minister of Defence. There had been rumours at the time that this had something to do with Pyne's rapid promotion. The two men had much in common – they had come from relatively poor backgrounds and had risen in their respective careers thanks to a combination of logic applied to uncompromising ruthlessness. They were men who liked to get things done.

Pyne swung the Land Rover on to the concrete apron and parked near the two petrol tankers.

A man and a woman emerged from the power station and walked towards them. Cox-Spender guessed that they were Hugh Patterson and Louise Campion. He swallowed nervously. From the way the Sterling submachine-guns were slung casually from their shoulders, it looked as if they knew how to use them.

One of the most beautiful sights man has ever seen is the heavenly blue glow of Cerenkov radiation which occurs when high-energy particles pass through water.

Whenever Cox-Spender had witnessed the strange, ethereal light he felt he was witnessing the hand of God. It was easy to believe that the hypnotic glow suffusing the water in the fuel-element tank beneath the high catwalk held the key to the secret of the creation.

But now Cox-Spender's sense of wonder, which marks the true scientist, was no more. In its place was a sense of deep foreboding that the easy confidence of the three men at his side did not dispel.

'Gamma radiation is at zero.' said Keller politely. 'And we're leaving the rest of the elements in the stand-pipes.'

'You're following the decommissioning programme to shut down the reaction?' asked Cox-Spender.

'Yes, sir. We've continued the staged reduction of boiler pressure so that the coolant absorbs the neutrons and kills the reaction.'

Cox-Spender nodded. 'I understand there's a thermocouple temperature-monitoring computer in the main control room I should like a print-out, please to check the reactor core temperatures.'

'They're cooling nicely,' said Keller respectfully.

'I should still like to see for myself,' said Cox-Spender testily. At least this Keller seemed to know his place.

Keller exchanged a look with Pyne. Pyne nodded.

'And now,' said Cox-Spender, when he had finished examining a fanfold computer print-out, 'I wish to see the hostages.' He tried to make his voice sound insulting.

'I'm afraid that won't be possible,' said Pyne.

'Why not?'

'Because I say so.'

Pyne's grey eyes were hard and cold. Cox-Spender decided not to press the matter. For a moment he could think of nothing to say.

'He's seen the ultimatum,' Pyne said to the others.

'That should make our task easier,' commented Hugh Patterson.

'Terrorism has never achieved long-term objectives,' began Cox-Spender. 'You've only got to look at–'

'I don't think you were sent here to discuss politics,' interrupted Pyne caustically.

'You can't possibly hope to succeed,' Cox-Spender blustered angrily. 'There's only four of you. Eventually, you will tire – your men will turn against you.'

'Perhaps they will,' said Pyne, 'but they've served their purpose, so it doesn't matter. As for tiring, I'll tell you this much, and you can convey this to the Prime Minister when you go back; we will never tire, and we will never give in. I'd sooner commit suicide.'

'It might just come to that,' snapped Cox-Spender.

'And as for long-term objectives,' continued Pyne, ignoring Cox-Spender's outburst, 'they've never been effectively attempted by means of terrorism until now; no one has ever bargained with the lives of fifty million people, with their eventual well-being as the objective. And another thing – you could hardly call the half-lives of some of the isotopes in the silos as 'short-term'. Correct?'

Keller appeared with a sheet of paper which he pushed into Cox-Spender's hand. Cox-Spender gave it a cursory glance before thrusting it in his pocket. It was a list of radioactive materials, beginning with the higher and most dangerous plutonium isotopes.

'The contents of Silo Three,' explained Keller.

Cox-Spender looked at his watch. Determined to sound offensive, he said: 'I've little time to waste talking to you thugs, so if you show me the arrangements you've made with the high explosive, I'll be on my way.'

Pyne gave Cox-Spender a video cassette. 'That's for the Prime Minister,' he said. 'Before we go down, Mr Cox-Spender, there's something you should know if you don't already: the radioactive waste that's in storage here isn't just the power station's spent fuel rods, but waste that's been moved here from all over the country.'

'I know that,' said Cox-Spender frostily.

'Including some high-grade plutonium waste from Japan . . . Remember the cargo ship that the press dubbed the 'Flying Dutchman' last month because no port would accept it?'

'Of course I remember!' At that moment Cox-Spender defiance suddenly melted. He stared at Pyne. 'Are you trying to tell me that that cargo's here?'

Pyne nodded and smiled bleakly at the scientist's thunderstruck expression.

18

The Prime Minister looked up from the large-scale map spread out on his desk.

'What about an attack from the river?' he demanded.

'It would be most dangerous, sir,' replied Cox-Spender. 'Even if the attacking group managed to get on to the apron, they'd be detected by the IRIS system.'

The Prime Minister picked up the Racal infra-red sensor that Cox-Spender had placed on his desk. 'How sensitive are these things?'

'The body heat from a mouse can set one off at fifty metres, sir,' Cox-Spender replied. 'They even have automatic daylight compensators so they don't react to the ambient temperature fluctuations between day and night.'

The Prime Minister wondered what Cox-Spender was talking about, but remained silent. He replaced the detector and toyed with his amber paperweight. 'How about launching CS gas grenades through the control-room windows?'

'That too would be most dangerous sir, CS gas or CR gas grenades don't work instantly. There would still be a few seconds for two of the terrorists to operate the main detonator control.'

'Nerve gas?'

Cox-Spender considered. 'It's quicker, but still not quick enough.'

'What about stun grenades? They were effective enough during the Princes Gate siege.'

'You're thinking of an SAS-style assault, sir?'

'Isn't everyone?'

'That would entail a helicopter assault, sir. They've got radar, and besides – the noise of helicopter engines–'

'Yes. Yes,' said the Prime Minister interrupted testily. 'I had realised that.'

For a while neither spoke. The politician exhaled a thin stream of cigar smoke. It spilled across the map and pooled under the table lamp.

Cox-Spender broke the silence. 'With respect, sir, don't you think it would be a good idea to call a meeting of the Policy Review Committee so that the maximum number of brains could be brought to bear on the problem?'

'No,' said the Prime Minister shortly.

'What about the chiefs of staff?'

'The army would want to storm the place, the navy sink it and the RAF bomb it.'

Cox-Spender smarted at the brusque dismissal of his suggestion. It was an unfair generalization, but he was uncomfortably aware of the coolness, bordering on open hostility, that existed between the Cabinet Office and the chiefs of staff over the recent and most sweeping defence cuts. Cox-Spender had even heard rumours that a number of army officers were seriously considering taking direct action to assume power if the threatened talk of a cen-tralised European defence force became a reality. Neverthe-less, he decided to press the matter – the events of the day had given him a new-found confidence.

'Even so, sir, there are a number of extremely capable brains on the staff. I'm sure they would come up with something.'

A nerve in the Prime Minister's neck twitched. Cox-Spender would have recognized the danger signal had he known the politician better.

81

'The important thing at the moment, Cox-Spender, is to restrict knowledge of this business to as few people as possible until we've had a chance to examine all the options open to us. We don't know yet if these people are bluffing. It is possible that the magnitude of their enterprise will dawn on them, and that they will hesitate to press their demands. If that happens, as I suspect it will, then it follows that they will not carry out their threat to blow up the waste silos.'

This was all too much for Cox-Spender. 'Sir, with all due respect, I've seen these people. They won't weaken – I'm absolutely convinced of it. They've committed themselves too far.'

The Prime Minister banged his amber paperweight down on the desk in fury. 'I selected you for this task, Cox-Spender, because I thought you were the sort of man who wouldn't lose his head in a crisis. Obviously, I was wrong. I'm well aware of the situation, but I refuse to be stampeded into taking ill-considered action on the say-so of advisers who've lost their heads!'

Cox-Spender quailed. The sudden tirade was wholly unjustified, but he lacked the courage to say so. All he could manage was a rather shamefaced, 'Yes, sir.'

The Prime Minister relaxed. 'So you agree with me?'

There was no alternative, but to repeat the, 'Yes, sir.'

The Prime Minister smiled. Cox-Spender's acquiescence was safely recorded on tape. 'Did you give them the phone number?' he asked in a more moderate tone.

'Yes, sir.' Cox-Spender resented having to keep uttering the two words. There had been moments during what had been the longest Sunday of his life when he had thought he had finally broken the habit.

'In that case,' said the Prime Minister, 'we'll wait for them to make the first move.'

He glanced up at the eighteenth-century French clock. 23:05.

The Prime Minister tapped the video cassette from General Pyne. 'I hope you haven't played this.'

'No, sir. I brought it straight to you.'

The Prime Minister yawned. 'Very well, Cox-Spender. You've done as well as can be expected so far. I have a feeling that tomorrow is going to be worse than the usual Monday. It's time you and I were in bed – I'm sure you must be exhausted.'

Again Cox-Spender had to say, 'Yes, sir.'

The Prime Minister reached for a telephone. 'I'll have your car sent round to the Downing Street entrance. Save you that long walk, eh?'

The Prime Minister went to bed at 23:25 and slept soundly from 23:40.

Monday

1

Pyne slept badly during his first night at the power station.

He awoke after one hour's sleep and tried to orientate himself in the strange surroundings. His room had been the station superintendent's office. He could hear the throb of a passing ship. He tried to go back to sleep but gave up. He threw back the sheet, swung his feet on to the coarse horsehair carpet tiles and switched on the light.

03:00 hours. Louise Campion would be on duty in the control room.

The corridor was silent apart from Hugh Patterson's snores from the next office. The pan and tilt servo of a heat-guided closed-circuit television camera whirred briefly as its lens swung towards him.

Louise Campion was sitting at the central console with an open vacuum flask before her. She turned from the television monitors and smiled at Pyne's approach.

'Couldn't you sleep, Conrad?'

Pyne sat near her. 'We should sleep in here, Louise – it's cooler.'

Louise pointed to the computer cabinets. 'The air-conditioning is for that lot. Computers are fussy about their comfort.' She held up a technical handbook. 'I've been reading all about them.'

'Didn't you bring some books?'

'About a thousand on CD-ROMs. I'm saving them. Heaven forbid that we should be stuck in here for–'

'Louise,' interrupted Pyne, 'what happened last night?'

'Hugh gave you a report?'

'I want to hear your version.'

The radiation biologist looked puzzled. 'Well. Ralph and I arrived at about 15:30. He drove the first tanker, and I drove the second – just as we planned.'

'Where was Hugh?'

'Holding the staff in here. About thirty of them.' She paused, 'Look, Conrad, if you've any questions about Hugh and Ralph, you should ask them. We agreed that mutual trust between the four of us was essential. Right?'

'Really, Louise? What about the revised ultimatum? Or have you told Keller?'

Louise flushed. 'That's your job, Conrad.'

'It's also my job to find out what happened to the hostages.'

'Ralph sent them across the river by boat when they'd finished helping to position the explosive.'

Pyne watched her carefully. She avoided looking at him.

'Did you see this boat?'

'Of course not. It was dark.'

'Or hear it?'

'I was too busy checking the supplies.' She poured a cup of coffee without offering one to Pyne.

'Did you hear submachine-gun fire?

'There was some noise. Ralph said he'd been testing some detonators.'

'Louise, among the power station staff, do you remember a girl of about twenty? A pretty little thing with fair hair?'

Louise continued to avoid Pyne's gaze. 'I may have seen her. I can't remember.'

'Keller shot her.'

Louise looked up angrily. 'You're being absurd. Ralph could never–'

'I've seen the body. I didn't do it. I'm certain that you and Hugh didn't, so that only leaves Keller, The girl's body is in the inspection tunnels, and only Keller had business down there at the time.'

Louise pushed the coffee to Pyne. 'You think Ralph killed all the staff?'

Pyne accepted the cup and drank. 'I think so. There're plenty of hiding places down there.'

There was silence. Louise shuddered inwardly, then looked steadily at Pyne and nodded slowly. 'I suspected something. But why would he do such a thing, Conrad? Why?'

Pyne shook his head. 'Christ knows. I was going to tell him about the revised ultimatum at the meeting, but decided to hold back for the moment.'

'You're going to have to tell him sooner or later,' Louise pointed out.

Pyne stared at the detonator controls on a nearby console. There were two simple combination switches three metres apart screwed to the plastic work surface. To activate them required two people to set the combinations and throw the switches simultaneously.

'There's plenty of time,' Pyne said slowly. He ran his hand through his hair. 'If only I could understand him – if only he wasn't so damned polite all the time.'

'You should tell him about the changes we made to the ultimatum, Conrad.'

'No, Louise. Let him find out when the Prime Minister announces the new laws. By then it will be too late for him to object.'

Louise frowned. 'I wonder what the Prime Minister is doing now?'

Pyne stood. 'What I should be doing – sleeping.'

'Even with the problem of us?'

'He'll sleep.' Pyne turned to leave.

'You used to know him, didn't you?' Louise said, looking up at Pyne.

Pyne did not like the question. 'A long time ago when he was at the MOD.' Pyne quickly changed the subject. 'Louise, destroy your copy of the ultimatum. I'll tell Hugh to do the same in the morning.'

He was gone before Louise could reply.

2

From 10:00 that morning Howard Mitchell spent an hour on the phone trying to discover the truth concerning the cause of the Thames Haven explosion. He desperately needed to know whether or not his drill-string had been destroyed or moved. No one could, or would, help him. The oil company's head office in London said the disaster was to be the subject of a Department of Trade and Industry investigation and would say no more. The Department of Trade and Industry said they could do nothing for the time being because there was a danger of more explosions. The Home Office said the area had been sealed off by the police and would remain so until the site had been declared safe. The Ministry of Civil Aviation said the prohibited zone above the Thames Estuary would remain in force until the Department of Trade and Industry said the prohibition could be removed.

Despairing, Mitchell made one last call to his old contact, Paul Weiner, at the American Embassy. He left his office five minutes later, telling his secretary he would be gone for three hours.

Ten minutes later he was driving towards London with Simpson following at a distance in a ten-hundredweight Bedford van. It was an ideal vehicle for the job – the high steering position enabled the driver to follow his quarry at a safe distance without losing sight of it.

Mitchell slid his Mustang tail first into a parking-meter bay near Grosvenor Square. Simpson cruised past in his van and was beaten to a bay by a woman driving a Golf who dived in nose first. By the time Simpson had satisfied his male ego with horn and invective, Mitchell had disappeared.

Simpson found another parking space and went into a McDonald's. He had lost Mitchell but at least he could keep the Mustang under observation from a high stool near the window.

Mitchell found the 'American Dream' without difficulty.

'Mr Weiner says he'll be along as soon as possible,' said a waitress, showing him to a reserved corner table.

Weiner entered ten minutes later as Mitchell was starting his second cup of cup of coffee. The two men exchanged warm greetings. Weiner ordered steak for both of them.

'Long time no see,' said Weiner. 'I was wondering what had happened to you.'

'The political and physical storms in the North Sea have been keeping me busy.'

Weiner grinned impishly. 'And furnishing a new house on St Georges Hill.'

'How the hell do you know that?'

Weiner looked round with a gesture of mock secretiveness. 'We know all there is to know about our boys far from home. Not many make it to St Georges Hill. The oil business must be doing fine.'

'It won't be,' said Mitchell shortly. 'That's why I've come to see you.' He briefly outlined his account of the previous day's flight and his concern about the missing drill-string.

'Wasn't it insured?' asked Weiner.

'Not until today, and, in any event, not if the loss is the result of terrorist activities. British underwriters here have got the jitters at the moment over oil platforms. They're expecting some sort of terrorist action in the North Sea any day now. I've got to pay out a hundred thousand dollars next week for some pumps. I don't want to if I'm going to need the money to cover the loss of the string.'

The waitress brought their steaks.

'I saw on the news last night,' said Weiner when she was gone, 'that there's a danger of more explosions.'

Mitchell opened his briefcase and produced the yellow Kodak envelope. He passed a photograph across to Weiner. 'You don't have to be much of an expert to see there's nothing left to explode. Just look at the place. It's a ruin.'

Weiner examined the print curiously. It was an oblique shot of the devastated refinery taken at a distance of two kilometres. Mitchell was right – there was nothing left.

'There's something else,' said Mitchell. 'You said you saw the television news coverage last night about the explosion?'

Weiner nodded. 'I saw the commercial networks news when I got back after a show. Why?'

'I watched that and the coverage on both BBC networks and on Sky,' said Mitchell. 'None of them had cameras at or even near the site. All they had was a presenter sitting in front of an old blow-up showing the refinery as it was before the explosion. Now I know British television news coverage is crummy, but they're usually pretty good when it comes to a major event just a few kilometres outside London.'

'Sure, but the area has been sealed off,' Weiner pointed out.

'No,' said Mitchell. 'They could've easily staked out cameras with long lenses on the opposite river bank, even though it's four kilometres wide just there.'

Weiner said nothing. Mitchell gave him another photograph.

'If you look at that one, it's possible to tell roughly where the explosion took place. One explosion – right in the middle of the employees' carpark – the last place you'd expect an explosion to happen.'

'Strange,' said Weiner looking up from the picture.

'You're goddamn right it's strange. I'll show you something that's even stranger.' Mitchell gave Weiner a third photograph. 'It's not such a good picture of the refinery – it was taken too far off. That complex looks like a power station, and those two choppers parked in the front belong to neighbours of mine on St Georges Hill: Hugh Patterson and General Conrad Pyne.'

Weiner looked at the prints for some seconds and said: 'Why should that be strange? I've heard of Patterson. His firm manufactures radioactive-waste storage tanks. Maybe he's working extra time on some project.'

'Maybe,' replied Mitchell. 'You once asked me to report interesting developments in the oil business. I thought the information would be fair exchange if you could find out what's happened to my string.'

Weiner gathered up the photographs. 'Can I keep these?'

'Sure. You can have them all.' Mitchell handed him the yellow envelope. 'There's a few more in there that aren't so good.'

Weiner pushed the prints into the envelope. 'I'll see what I can do.' he said. 'I'll check these pictures out, but I can't promise anything.'

Simpson followed Mitchell's Mustang to the roundabout under the Hammersmith flyover and decided he must be returning to Surrey. Simpson had no intention of being out of London that day – not with the events that were looming up. Mitchell continued westward. Simpson went right round the traffic island and headed back to London.

When Weiner reached his office he tipped the photographs on to his desk and examined each one carefully for some minutes. Mitchell's theory about the location of the explosion appeared to be substantiated by the pattern of twisted wreckage, but it was not possible to say with certainty that it had taken place in the middle of the carpark – not without checking the pictures against library covers taken of the refinery on the last UK aerial survey. The pictures were interesting, but Weiner was not certain they were of interest to the CIA – apart from providing another set of covers for the print library.

He decided to make a few inquiries to satisfy Mitchell and then to forget the whole affair. He yawned and pushed the prints back into the envelope. Something was stopping them. He peered into the envelope and shook out a postcard size photograph that obviously didn't belong to the batch taken by Mitchell. It showed a group holding drinks gathered round a Bell JetRanger helicopter. He was about to return it to the envelope, when something in the picture triggered a memory chord.

He placed the photograph on his blotter and stared down at the vaguely familiar face of the man sitting in the helicopter's open door.

Keller . . . Ralph Keller! Jesus Christ!

Weiner picked up his telephone and dialled two digits. He waited, telephone pressed to his ear and the photograph between his elbows.

'Harry . . .Paul. Cast your mind back a few years to Libya. Remember the guy who teamed up with Eric Hoffman and offered to build the Libyans an atomic bomb? . . . Yeah . . . Well, you won't believe this, but I think I've found him.'

3

Two hours after Howard Mitchell had left Paul Weiner following their lunch in the 'American Dream'. James Raven, the duty officer at the Madrid Space Track Center, received a signal from the USAF base at Mildenhall in England. When deciphered, the instructions in the message were simple enough: CYCLOPS was required to take a photographic 'stripe' of southern England.

Raven decoded the positions and wondered why anyone should want to waste the limited amount of film in the satellite's magazines on a series of photographs of the Thames Estuary. Once the magazines were empty CYCLOPS would be useless. Unlike the French SPOT series of satellites which used computer-enhanced high resolution digital TV pictures for remote sensing of the earth, CYCLOPS used film. The problems with film justified the expense: film could resolve down to the granular level whereas the quality of television pictures, even with enhancing, was limited to the line scan rate.

He requested verification in case a cipher clerk had made a mistake. Five minutes later an affirmative clattered out on the center's teleprinter. Raven did not bother to decipher the second message – the code groups were a repeat. He filed both messages in the day book, and decided that whatever happened he wouldn't be held responsible for the expensive operation he was about to undertake.

Raven sat at the CYCLOPS control console and pressed the button which projected the low earth orbit satellite's path on to a fluorescent screen. The illuminated LEO trail was climbing towards the North Pole across Siberia. The computer forecast that in twenty minutes the satellite would be sweeping down the western coast of Greenland – too far west of the required target.

Raven tapped out the course-correction codes. Thirty seconds later a stream of telemetry signals from the Reykjavik relay station triggered CYCLOPS's course-correction vernier rockets.

Raven checked the new orbit.

A few more squirts to orientate the satellite and it was set to pass over southern England only a few kilometres east of the Greenwich Meridian, and exactly over the remains of the Thames Haven oil refinery.

The screen at Raven's elbow showed the required course and the projected course – both lines overlapped exactly. A winking light on the glowing line indicated the satellite's position.

At 15:30 it was over Scotland.

Raven pressed the button that would start feeding the strips of film through the camera-shutter gates and wind the protective visors away from the lenses.

At 15:35 he sent a signal to Mildenhall giving them the position for the recovery of the film capsule. The information was radioed to Colonel Donald Kaufmann, who was flying a Hustler bomber that had left Mildenhall when the instructions to the Madrid Space Track Center were 'first issued.

At 15:45 CYCLOPS was above its objective.

There was no sound in the still vacuum of space as the shutters on the stereoscopic and infra-red cameras opened and closed.

At 15:48 the satellite passed out of the 'area of interest' determined by the Madrid computer. A final signal stopped the shutters. The rest was automatic: the capsule pulled away from its parent satellite and began its long, five hundred kilometre fall to earth – its tiny rocket motor burning brightly to cancel the orbital velocity imparted to it by CYCLOPS.

The capsule's parachute opened at 16:03. Colonel Kaufmann's navigator detected the faint radar echo at 16:15 and extended the Hustler's scoop net.

A few minutes later the capsule was snatched out of the sky.

The Hustler touched down on the hot runway at Mildenhall exactly five hours after Mitchell had handed his photographs to Paul Weiner in London.

4

At 12:30 Simpson made six anonymous phone calls: five to the editors of the national newspapers and one to the chief commissioner of the Metropolitan Police. Each time he identified himself with the codeword 'Moonflower' used only by the Provisional IRA to distinguish genuine bomb-warning calls from hoaxes. He spoke in a thick Irish accent and announced that the Palace of Westminster was to be the target for a bomb attack during the afternoon while it was being used for the special meeting called by the Prime Minister with the 360 members of his parliamentary party.

The police responded swiftly: the chief commissioner telephoned Simpson urging that the meeting should be called off. Simpson said that the meeting would have to go ahead – 360 telegrams had been sent out to members of Parliament demanding that they should break their holidays and return to London. The best thing, Simpson suggested, would be for the police to clear the Palace of Westminster of everyone – even maintenance staff – and ensure that only MPs were allowed to enter.

The meeting was due to start at 15:00 hours. The police took no chances. They stepped-up their usual security measures to an unprecedented level. Arriving Members of Parliament were subjected to even more stringent searches than usual and their identities were double-checked before they were allowed through the cordon.

Not even ministerial cars, which were checked each day as a matter of routine were allowed into the underground car park; drivers were required to remove themselves and their cars once they had dropped their passengers.

The MP's milled round the corridors trying to find out from one another why the meeting had been called. The chief whip's office checked every new arrival, and telephoned Simpson when the number of MPs present reached 345.

Simpson drove. For once the Prime Minister sat in the front, obliging his bodyguard to travel in the back.

'What have you found out about the American?' The Prime Minister demanded.

Simpson slowed in response to the upheld arm of a shirt-sleeved, armed policeman who wanted to see their passes. He examined it carefully, and the two other occupants of the car, before waving it on to the police equipped with ion charge instruments who carefully checked the underside of the car.

'Well?'

'Nothing, sir. I followed him from Walton to London this morning, but was unable to discover whom he visited.'

A knot of MPs gathered on the steps pressed forward as Simpson brought the car to a standstill. The Prime Minister had his hand on the door lock.

'Don't forget what I said, Simpson. Although I'd prefer to have you with me, it's essential we find out what he knows.'

The MPs, crowded into the largest committee room and spilling into the corridor, fell silent when the Prime Minister rose. He had deliberately avoided speaking to his Cabinet colleagues; today they were all equal. Each man and woman present represented one vote – and that was all that mattered.

'I'm sorry to call you all back from your holidays,' he began. 'I wouldn't have done so, but at this moment our country faces the gravest crises in its history.

'Yesterday a group of terrorists under the command of General Pyne seized control of Vulcan Hall nuclear power station on Canvey Island. They are threatening to blow up the radioactive-waste silos unless the government adopt certain stringent measures which they believe will solve the country's economic and social problems.' The Prime Minister paused. Every face in the room was turned towards him.

'My secretary will distribute copies of their demands, which I received yesterday. I want you to read the measures most carefully during the next five minutes. Each copy is numbered and will be collected afterwards, so don't lose them please. No one is to talk and no one will be allowed to leave this room until all the copies have been collected.'

Simpson handed out copies of the ultimatum, including a copy for Cox-Spender, who had been told to attend the meeting. The gathering read in stunned silence, apart from the occasional rustle of paper. As the minutes passed more and more of the ashen faces fixed their horrified gaze on the Prime Minister. He waited until the last man had finished reading.

'Thank you,' he said. 'Now in case any of you think these terrorists are bluffing, they caused yesterday's explosion at the Thames Haven refinery to show they mean business.'

The silence in the room was total. One MP lifted his feet off a table and lowered them to the floor without making a sound.

'Vulcan Hall is not contributing to the national grid – decommissioning was started when it was seized – but I understand that its waste silos hold an unusually large amount of material at the moment as a result of the Cheshire repository problems. The so-called 'Flying Dutchman' plutonium cargo is also stored there. Indeed Vulcan Hall now holds the largest concentration of waste in the country.

'Yesterday, Mr Cox-Spender visited Vulcan Hall. The terrorists showed him the arrangements they have made to carry out their threat unless the government adopt their proposed measures. I'm no scientist, so I've asked Mr Cox-Spender to tell you about his visit . . . Mr Cox-Spender.' The Prime Minister sat down.

Cox-Spender felt Simpson jab him from behind. He climbed reluctantly to his feet. He always felt hopelessly self-conscious when addressing a crowd – even more so when the crowd was completely silent. He spoke hesitantly at first, gradually gaining confidence with the realization that this wasn't a committee meeting and no one was likely to contradict him. The 345 faces watched him intently. Cox-Spender resolutely kept his eyes on his notes. He spoke for fifteen minutes, gradually lowering himself to his chair on his closing sentences.

'A question, please!' The voice cracked out from the back of the room. Cox-Spender looked at the Prime Minister for guidance, but the politician's eyes were fixed pensively on the floor. Cox-Spender's hesitation was a signal for everyone to start firing questions. The Prime Minister rose to his feet and held up his hand. The babble died away.

'Mr Cox-Spender will answer your questions one at a time. I believe Mr Quentin Brieley spoke first.'

Quentin Brieley, the member for Breckon Park, was a small, pugnacious man. Before becoming an MP he had been a physics master in his home town of Cardiff.

He pushed forward until he was nearly face to face with Cox-Spender.

'What I want to know,' he said, in his thin, reedy Welsh accent, 'is what is the exact nature of the radionuclides stored at Vulcan Hall, and what will happen if they are released.'

The use of the word 'radionuclides' did not put Cox-Spender on his guard. Had it done so, he would not have said, 'They are the radioactive byproducts of the nuclear-fission process.'

Brieley snorted. 'I know that. What exactly are they and what can they do?'

'Well, basically, the flasks in the central silo contain up to two hundred isotopes which have been produced from uranium–'

'Such as?' demanded Brieley.

The MPs remained silent. The small Welshman, with his implacable opposition to the nuclear-energy programme, could be relied on to ask all the pertinent questions.

Cox-Spender frantically tried to recall all the isotopes with short half-lives. 'Er . . . Xenon one-three-three . . . Iodine one-three-three–'

Brieley snapped out: 'Wasn't that the stuff that escaped from Windscale a few years back?'

'Yes.' Cox-Spender inwardly cursed the knowledgeable Welshman and wondered why the Prime Minister wasn't coming to his rescue. 'But it didn't kill anyone,' he added.

'Because it has a short half-life – right?'

Cox-Spender nodded.

'And there's the 'Flying Dutchman' cargo. Anything else brewing in there you've forgotten to tell us about?'

Cox-Spender opened his mouth to protest at the man's offensive attitude, but Brieley was too quick.

'What about strontium ninety, Mr Cox-Spender? There'd be a lot of that wouldn't there? It's got a long half-life.'

'There is a quantity of strontium ninety at Vulcan Hall.' Cox-Spender admitted.

Brieley turned to face his colleagues. 'You've probably heard of the stuff,' he said angrily. 'It has a similar atom to calcium so it is readily absorbed by the body to build bones. It doesn't affect adults much.' He turned to Cox-Spender.

'Tell them what it does to children. Tell them what happens to kids who've got bones made of strontium ninety.'

The Prime Minister stood up. 'Mr Cox-Spender didn't invent the stuff,' he said mildly. Cox-Spender thought he was taking over the question-and-answer session, but the Prime Minister avoided his adviser's eye and sat down again.

Brieley remained staring fixedly at Cox-Spender with a mixture of loathing and contempt. 'Iodine and caesium are nothing compared with plutonium. How much of that have you got at Vulcan Hall?'

Cox-Spender looked in vain to the Prime Minister for support. 'I'm not sure. Not much.'

'Christ!' shouted the Welshman. 'It doesn't have to be much!' He held up his fist. 'A lump that size could kill everyone in the country!'

In the world, thought Cox-Spender, but he did not enlighten his opponent.

'Inhale one particle of plutonium, and you get lung cancer. After that, you get dead. Right Mr Cox-Spender?'

'What's its half-life?' asked a voice.

'Twenty thousand years,' said Cox-Spender quickly, frightened that Brieley would use a dramatic simile to express the period of time.

'What does that mean?' asked another voice.

'It means,' said Brieley, 'that after twenty thousand years a few pounds of the stuff can kill only half the world's population, and so on. And they're sitting on tonnes of it.'

No one spoke.

'Shall I tell what will happen if those terrorists blow up the silos?' said the Welshman, turning to the gathering. 'Three Mile Island and Cheynobel will be a kids' chemistry experiments going wrong by comparison. Everyone in the country – perhaps even in Europe, Asia and America – will be dead within a few years, and the land uninhabitable for the best part of a million years. Isn't that right Mr bloody Cox-Spender?'

Cox-Spender nodded. He could argue survival factors, but basically, the Welsh MP was right.

Brieley was no longer angry. 'If the gates of hell do exist,' he said sadly, 'we will find they are made of plutonium.' He looked slowly round at the sea of silent faces. 'It's even named after the Lord of Darkness . . . Pluto . . .'

He sat down.

The silence continued for a few moments, then everyone was firing questions.

The Prime Minister was on his feet again. 'If you will all be patient for a little longer, please, I have something you're all to see. After that, you can ask Mr Cox-Spender as many questions as you wish.'

Cox-Spender sat down. There was a suspicion at the back of his mind that he had been a useful whipping-boy.

Simpson had been busy during the precious few minutes setting up a video recorder and a portable television receiver. He nodded to the Prime Minister that he was ready.

'You are about to see a video recording that the terrorists gave Mr Cox-Spender during his visit,' said the Prime Minister. 'All right Simpson.'

The opening shot showed Pyne sitting at a desk in front of a bookcase. The caption 'MAJOR GENERAL CONRAD PYNE OBE' appeared briefly on the screen.

Pyne interlocked his fingers on the desk blotter and leaned forward, looking fixedly at the camera.

'By now,' he said, in a flat, unhurried voice. 'You will know the truth. You are probably thinking that you face a terrible dilemma. But there is no dilemma, ladies and gentlemen, if you follow the conditions we have laid down in our ultimatum. Indeed you must follow them, because you have no choice.

'Through a mixture of greed and self-interest and a failure to implement straightforward remdial measures, this country is rapidly becoming bankrupt. This is many people's

99

fault – but it is especially yours.' Pyne pointed at the camera to emphasize his words.

'The public broadcasting of Parliament has proved to the British people that the majority of you are an undisciplined collection of self-interested egotists totally unfit to govern a nation of sixty million people. I ask myself – what has this country done to deserve you?' Pyne paused. The MPs sat in shocked silence.

'Perhaps it is not your fault as individuals – it is the fault of your constituency parties who weed out candidates of vision and return to Parliament narrow-minded Union Jack-wrapped Britishers who seem incapable of clear, logical thinking. The sad result that we have a hung parliament of weakness and mediocrity that lacks the drive, initiative, and *courage* to tackle the country's problems with zeal and determination. As a consequence we have rampant infla-tion, unemployment, virtual isolation from our partners in Europe, and a tap-washer and Luncheon Voucher currency that's a standing joke in Europe.

'You've constantly underestimated the British people with your insipid, half-baked measures which merely irri-tate rather than inspire. Just one example but a vital one: look at the mess we are in over house prices. There's no shortage of land or building materials in this country! Making people take out crippling mortgages amounts to a massive self-inflicted wound. We've built on only ten percent of our land! Land is for people! We should use it to allow them to build and extend their own homes over a period as and when they can afford it – not sell them cramped little ready-made hutches on vast, impersonal estates at vast, inflated prices. The amount of land we want released and sold at realistic prices will serve our housing needs well into the next century.

'The housing situation is a symptom of your failure to recognise real needs. Had you had the guts to introduce really tough controls, instead of forever looking over your shoulder at the myth of empty ballot boxes at the next

100

election, you might have won broad support. Instead you've wrung your hands and blamed everyone for our troubles except yourselves.

'While the rest of the European Community has flourished – even former East Germany is now doing better than us – we've had to listen to successive governments prattling on about sovereignty. Substitute the word 'power' for 'sovereignty' in all the political speeches we've endured over the past few years and they begin to make sordid sense. To you political power is more important than jobs, housing, public health – everything. And yet sovereignty does not provide homes or jobs; sovereignty does nothing for our balance of payments; sovereignty doesn't pay mortgages or provide hospital beds or decent schools and motivated teachers. Sovereignty is a negative force – it props up nationalism and greed and inefficiency. To sustain it requires high taxes to pay for independent armies, navies and air forces. It perpetuates the hideous costs of duplication and even jeopardises air safety because sovereignty stands in the way of a Pan-European air traffic control system. For example: sovereignty provided us with the staggering cost of two cellular telephone systems neither of which is compatible with the rest of Europe. The result is that we now have to scrap both systems and write-off *five billion pounds* of capital investment. Sovereignty gave us the absurd MAC television system which no one else wanted and which contributed to the destruction of our television manufacturing industry. Small wonder the Japanese are walking all over us if we tie-up our best engineering brains in electronics to design systems that are useless. Sometimes I think you all forget that Britain is a tiny country that you can drive across in a morning. We can't afford to waste brains and money and resources on senseless duplication in the name of this corrosive enemy of our future prosperity . . . *this sovereignty . . .*'

The last word was almost spat out. Pyne paused and sipped from a glass of water. 'From now on, ladies and gentlemen,' he continued, 'this country is on a war footing. It has worked before against a visible enemy – now we must strive together to ensure that it works against the invisible enemies of greed and inflation which will destroy this country just as surely as Hitler intended to, and just as surely as Vulcan Hall's nuclear fallout will if we are forced to blow-up the silos.'

Pyne paused again and looked straight at the camera. 'I was wrong just now. You do have a choice. You either accept our measures for five years, or destroy our country for eternity.'

The screen went blank. There was a few seconds of stunned silence broken by the video recorder switching itself off with a loud double click. The Prime Minister stood and surveyed the silent faces. 'You now have an idea of the people we are dealing with – utterly ruthless but efficient. But terrorists none the less – no matter what their motives. That is one thing that we must not lose sight of. Questions?'

'What have the armed forces got to say about this?' demanded a voice from the back. 'When are they planning to break in and get these people out?'

I don't think you quite understand,' said the Prime Minister. 'No move has been planned against them. You are the only people in the country who know anything about this. Not even my Cabinet colleagues were aware of the take-over until now. I considered the situation so serious that it must be revealed to all of you, so that we can all discuss what is to be done, rather than recall Parliament and ask you to approve Cabinet action.'

'Easier to get us to agree to something than the Cabinet,' a backbencher remarked.

There were a few guffaws despite the seriousness of the situation. The Prime Minister smiled frostily. 'The diversions within the Party are reflected at all levels,' he remarked. 'Including the backbenches. Right now we need unity.'

'What *are* the chances of launching a successful attack against them?' asked the Home Secretary.

The Prime Minister nodded to Cox-Spender.

'A preliminary examination has ruled out the possibility that any attack is likely to succeed,' said Cox-Spender.

The Home Secretary was unimpressed. It was clear that he resented not being briefed or consulted before the meeting. 'Oh, really? And who decided that?'

Brieley jumped up. 'What the hell are we arguing about?' he demanded. 'We're carrying on as if we've got a choice.' He jerked his thumb at the television. 'You saw that maniac. We've *got* to go along with him otherwise he destroys the country. It's as plain and as simple and as stark as that. We've no choice. We're in what the Americans call a zero options situation.'

His words aroused everyone from their stunned stupor. MPs were on their feet, some shouting that Brieley was right, others yelling that no government should yield to terrorism. The scene was threatening to degenerate into a familiar parliamentary uproar. The Prime Minister had to shout several times to command attention. Gradually the tumult died away and the sea of faces turned to their leader.

'Well now,' said the Prime Minister. 'As Mr Brieley seems to have such a lot to say on the subject, perhaps he would like to suggest a course of action? Mr Brieley?'

The Welsh MP was not inhibited by the Prime Minister's patronizing tone. His entire parliamentary career had been a tirade against nuclear power. Now every embarrassing question and every empassioned speech was vindicated. 'I propose, Prime Minister, that parliament should be recalled immediately to pass an enabling bill before the week is out so that the measures demanded by those thugs can be implemented.'

'Brieley was in good form,' the Prime Minister remarked, as Simpson drove back to Downing Street.

'Well, it was rather expected,' said Simpson.

'He more or less carried the show for us,' said the Prime Minister, relaxing into his seat.

Simpson kept his eyes on the road. A series of shirt-sleeved policemen held up traffic for the car.

'When do you start your intensive surveillance of the American?'

'Don't you think we should get someone else to do it, sir? It's not the sort of work I'm used to.'

'An excellent chance for you to learn, Simpson. Such a talent might come in useful in the future.'

Simpson pressed his lips tightly together and said nothing.

5

Walter Innam's eyesight was such that he could not see the target on a fifty-yard range, let alone hit it. Without thick pebbleglass spectacles everything more than a metre from the end of his nose disappeared into a vague blur of light and shadow.

But for close work, such as staring through the twin lenses of stereoscopic viewers at aerial-reconnaissance photographs, their performance was phenomenal. Innam could pick out fragments of information from the poorest photograph – frequently discovering details that eluded everyone else. It was as if nature had compensated him by giving him the ability to see in reproduction what he could never hope to see in real life.

In the air-conditioned darkness of the CIA's photo-surveillance laboratory he pressed his face to the eyepiece hood of a huge stereoscopic viewer that resembled a submarine's periscope. His left hand grasped a small lever. With this he could move the three-dimensional scene before his eyes in any direction. Pressing down on the lever brought the ground racing towards him with the sensation of plunging earthward in a vertically diving aircraft.

He had been asked to prepare a report on the probable cause of the explosion which had destroyed the Thames

Haven oil refinery the day before. It was the sort of exercise he adored – the opportunity to exercise his talent without having to wonder why anyone should want such a report.

He spent several minutes ranging back and forth over the refinery, merely getting the feel of the place. As far as Innam was concerned, he was not looking at photographs – he was actually there; revelling in the heady sensations of his own private world in which he was flying an aircraft that could dive to within ten metres of the ground or soar to five hundred kilometres at the touch of a lever.

Here, alone in the darkened room, he was the supreme being –far from the painful memories of childhood filled with the cruel, taunting refrains of schoolchildren determined to make the life of a short-sighted eight-year-old abject misery. Here he was God: an omnipotent entity whose penetrating eyes stared down on the puny works of men and sneered in contempt at their feeble efforts to conceal their miserable secrets. He, Walter Innam, had seen all there was to see – couples copulating in cornfields; Libyan engineers building rocket bases in craggy foothills; a European queen and her husband walking in the grounds of their palace – nothing could be hidden from his eyes.

Innam carefully centred himself over the refinery at three thousand feet. The area of devastation filled his field of vision exactly. He twisted a knob and the view was replaced by a shot of the refinery taken before the explosion – it was one of the many thousands of photographs in the CIA library which had been taken on a survey of British industrial installations two years previously. By flicking the knob back and forth Innam was able alternately to destroy and restore the refinery. It gave him the feeling of being a true god, but the purpose of the 'before' and 'after' exercise, with what are known as 'comparative covers' in aerial-reconnaissance jargon was to determine the approximate centre of the explosion.

Refinery – devastation – refinery – devastation–
His hand flicked the knob with increasing rapidity.

An impression began to form on his retinas; he began to see the explosion.

Refinery – devastation–

The coalescing images merged, like the consecutive frames of a film.

Innam could see the explosion. He could see the expanding shockwave racine outwards from the northern end of the refinery –from the carpark. He could see the tall distillation columns splitting open before the massive concussion and slamming themselves to the ground, only to have their remains scooped up and flung hundreds of metres through the air.

The whole fleeting five seconds of appalling destruction was recreated before Innam's eyes in total silence.

He had discovered the position of the explosion in five minutes. Now for the cause.

It would take an expert interpreter as much as two hours. Innam settled more comfortably in his seat and began a painstaking search.

He divided the refinery into a series of squares by superimposing a grid on his field of vision. He centred himself exactly above the square at the centre of the explosion and lowered himself until his view was completely filled by the square. The blur of twisted ironmongery resolved itself into separate but still unrecognizable shards of technology.

Lower. A hundred metres. The unblinking eyes bored down.

Fifty metres. Glittering highlights – undistinguishable from their surroundings at a greater height – suddenly became fractured beams of sunlight captured on the freshly torn edges of sheet steel. The remains of cars.

Innam made some fine adjustments to contrast and lighting levels. He started with the examination of welding seams. The manner in which they had been forced apart would tell him whether the explosion had been inside a particular vehicle or outside.

He meticulously reversed every square centimetre of the grid square, sometimes dictating notes into the microphone of a tape recorder whose reels turned only when he spoke, sometimes pausing to study more closely something that caught his eye – but never blinking.

The irregular piece of aluminium was about thirty centimetres square. It was curved slightly and appeared to have been subjected to an anodizing process during manufacture. It was inscribed with white stencilled stores reference digits that Innam recognized immediately. During the next five minutes he discovered several more fragments from the same piece of aluminium.

Innam stared down in astonishment for some minutes, then relaxed with a feeling of satisfaction, tinged with regret now the operation was over.

He looked at his watch.

Discovering the cause of the explosion had taken him fifteen minutes.

6

Ralph Keller sat alone with his thoughts in Vulcan Hall control room.

For the hundredth time he went over the options open to the British Government, and for the hundredth time he decided there were none: they had to accept the conditions in the ultimatum. There was nothing else they could do – the power station was an impenetrable fortress, sealed on three sides by the army camp and by the river on the fourth side. On the flat roof above his head the radar scanner probed an inviolate bowl that nothing could enter without sounding the alarms. Even high-altitude bombers would have to rise above the horizon. The worst they could do was launch a rocket attack – that would give him thirty seconds warning.

After several weeks' practice he required only five seconds to pull the modified pocket cellphone from his pocket and tap out the five-digit code on the keypad.

He smiled to himself and caressed the little folding phone. The others didn't know about its secondary function. The others were sentimental fools. When it came to action – doing what had to be done – they couldn't be trusted. Their attitude to those men killed in the oil refinery had shown that. It was as well he had taken precautions.

He stroked the keys on the pocket cellphone. They were hard and smooth, yet yielding – like a woman's nipples . . .

His mind drifted back to the Saturday night.

There had been the blonde girl. By the dim lighting in the tunnel he had watched her breasts sway every time she reached down to pick up one of the Cyclonite cartons. He had absolute power over her. This time it would be right.

He pressed the Sterling into her side and gestured down the passage. She didn't understand at first – her eyes were blank when he wanted her to look frightened. Perhaps he should choose another one? No! If he did that, it would mean *they* were controlling *him*.

He prodded her before him and pushed her into a recess in the side of the tunnel and positioned himself facing her so he could also see the power station staff at work stacking the cartons.

She had long silky hair. He liked long hair. He held the gun in one hand and stroked her hair with the other. Perhaps she flinched when he touched her. He didn't know. He was aware only of his own emotions – the blood starting to roar in his ears like an express train. He lowered his hand to her breasts. They had looked so promising when she had been bending down. But now, with her shoulder blades pressed against the concrete, they were unsatisfactory; her nipples were merely a change of skin texture beneath his fingertips. The recurring rage seized him. He grasped her breast, twisted savagely and flung the girl into the passage. Her scream ended with the roar of the Sterling. The impact from the ten shells that poured into her back in one second lifted her bodily and threw her against the sides of the tunnel. She slid to the floor and rolled over.

108

She had no breasts left.

Which was how it should be.

The late-evening sun streaming into the control room was hot despite the air-conditioning. His eyes closed. Memories of the Saturday night had stirred him

He touched himself.

Then a shadow fell across his face. He cringed.

'You disgusting boy!' screamed his mother. 'Wait till your father gets home!'

But the expected blow never came.

He opened his eyes.

Louise Campion was staring down at him.

'I've brought you some coffee,' she said. 'I'm on watch in five minutes.'

Keller took the mug and thanked her. She was wearing tight fitting jeans and an expensive blouse that had been gathered at the front and tied into a knot.

Keller sipped the coffee. There was a stain on the mug but he said nothing; the anger and tension were slipping away as they always did, but he still felt uneasy in the woman's presence. Why hadn't she sat down? Perhaps she was trying to demonstrate some form of superiority by standing while he sat – taunting him, just as all women did. Taunting him with the pale band of flesh below her blouse. Now she was watching his whitening knuckles as the involuntary tension tightened his fingers round the mug. He forced them to relax. Showing outward signs of stress was a mistake he rarely made, but the recollection of the girl in the tunnel had triggered the roller-coaster rhythms that pulsed through his brain and occasionally threatened to smash the delicate psychological mechanism that managed to keep him teetering on the edge of sanity.

'You look as if you could do with some sleep,' said Louise.

'Did you manage to sleep this afternoon in this heat?' asked Keller.

'Oh yes,' she answered lightly. 'Try counting sheep.'

Keller nodded and stood.

109

Maybe her bed was still warm.

Her room had formerly been the office belonging to the power station's chief maintenance engineer.

It was locked.

Keller slipped his Access card between the door and the surround. There was a light resistance as the stiff piece of plastic encountered the convex brass tongue of the Yale lock. He wriggled the cord up and down while easing it forwards. The resistance suddenly ceased and the card slid forward. He pushed the door open and returned the Access card to his wallet; the irony of its name escaped him. For a moment he stood on the threshold, savouring the eager sensations of anticipation at what he would find, before stepping into his childhood and closing the door behind him. He would have to be quick – his mother's shopping trips never lasted more than an hour.

But this wasn't his mother's room. She always made the bed before going out and she didn't sleep on a camp bed.

He kept very still for a moment, picking at the clinging barbs of fantasy in his confused mind.

She was using a typist's desk as a dressing-table. It had her things on it; a hairbrush; a silver-framed head and shoulders of a man in RAF uniform – he was leaning into the picture in the style favoured by professional photographers of a past era. So how old was she? Thirty-five? Forty?

He opened the bottom drawer first. It contained an assortment of empty typewriter-ribbon boxes, pencils and bottles of dried correcting fluid. The middle drawer was the same. He opened the top drawer without closing the lower two. It contained a wallet, some letters, an inventory of medical supplies and a plan showing the power station's radiation detectors. The letters contained nothing of interest.

Keller slammed the drawers shut in frustration.

There were two large crates standing in one corner. One contained cartons of tampons and boxes of new shoes. The other was filled with unworn clothes still in the manufacturer's wrappings. He pulled a small suitcase from under the camp bed; it contained brassieres and panties – all clean and unworn. His calm suddenly ruptured under the pressure. In fury he threw the underclothes across the room and flung himself down on the camp bed. For some minutes he wept bitter frustration into her pillow.

Reason eventually asserted itself. He picked up the garments and folded them before returning them to the suitcase. Then he sat on the edge of the bed, gradually calming down.

The carpet tiles with the sun streaming across them caught his attention. They were all of a uniform colour, but a contrasting shade effect had been created by laying them with the pile at alternative angles to the light. One tile was different – its pile lay in the same direction as two adjoining tiles.

He reached down and picked it up by the horsehair tufts with the intention of repositioning it.

Underneath the tile was a single sheet of typewritten paper. It was a carbon copy – possibly a fifth or sixth copy because the words were blurred and the surface was smudged with carbon. Nevertheless the words sprang clearly off the page as he read them:

Government to commit UK to the setting up of a single defence force for the European Community by the end of the century . . .

Public transport to be free . . .

500,000 hectares of land to be made available immediately and sold in quarter hectare plots to enable people to build their own homes . . .

Disbelievingly Keller read the paper right through. And then a second time with consuming fury.

Conrad Pyne and Hugh Patterson were sitting in the common room when the door burst open. Keller advanced into the room, his face white with anger. Before Patterson could stop him he had yanked Pyne to his feet by his lapels and was screaming: 'Bastard! Filthy, double-dealing bastard!'

Patterson tried to grab Keller but Pyne waved him away.

'What the hell's the matter?' demanded Pyne, trying to pull himself out of Keller's enraged grip. But Keller seemed to have lost control and continued shouting 'bastard' over and over again.

'Look, if you'll just tell me what's wrong!'

Patterson lunged forward but was doubled up by a vicious blow in the stomach from Keller who continued to scream his rage. He released Pyne by thrusting him backwards into his chair. He waved the sheet of paper under Pyne's nose.

'We agreed the conditions. We all agreed!' Keller was shaking with fury.

'Don't be stupid,' gasped Patterson. 'What the hell are you talking about?'

Keller held up the sheet for both men to see.

'Communists!' His voice was a hysterical shriek.

'All right,' said Pyne soothingly. 'Now just calm down and let me see that piece of paper.'

Keller quietened but his face was still deathly white.

'We all agreed on the conditions at the planning meetings. Now I discover you've–'

'Now wait a minute,' said Patterson. 'We couldn't get you to agree to half the terms.'

'Because they were communist-inspired!'

'Look', said Pyne in a reasoning tone. 'Some of the right-wing proposals you wanted – which we all wanted – had to be balanced by socialist measures if we were to win broad support from the people. We want to unite the country – not spark off a civil war. The proposals to set-up self-governing Muslim enclaves within the United Kingdom–'

'Which the Asians want!' Keller shouted.

'Which *some* Muslims want,' Pyne corrected. 'The proposals were mischievous and you know it. You only insisted on them because you knew it would drive a wedge between Muslims and non-Muslims.'

'We don't want to usher in a system of apartheid,' said Patterson. 'None of us want that.'

'Look, Keller,' said Pyne. 'We're extremely sorry for having deceived you, but it's too late to change the proposals now – even if we wanted to – which we don't.'

'No, general. That's where you're wrong.' Keller's voice was now smooth and drained of anger. He reached into his pocket and produced the cellular phone. 'I suspected there was something I was being excluded from, so I took a simple precaution to make sure I should always have a direct say in what was going on.'

Keller held up the handset. The two men stared at it in bewilderment.

'Who are you going to phone?' asked Patterson.

Keller smiled icily at his former employer. He pushed the slide switch with his thumb and held the handset up so that the two men could see the keypad.

'It's no longer a cellphone, Mr Patterson, but it can still transmit. All I have to do is switch it on – as it is now – press five of the keys in a certain sequence, and it transmits a coded pulse which, when picked up by a receiver I've hidden in one of the Cyclonite cartons, will detonate the carton.' Keller smiled. 'And all the others, of course. Your idea upstairs of two switches three metres apart which have to be activated at the same time by two people is ingenious – but not as ingenious as this.'

Keller turned the keypad towards himself and pressed four of the keys. The tactile feedback bleeps were clearly audible in the quiet room.

Pyne held out his hand. 'Give it to me, Keller.' It was as if he was talking to a small boy.

But Keller did not respond: not now he was in full control of the situation. It was only when he felt that outside forces

113

were dictating to him that the aggressive, repressed half of his personality assumed control. Now he was cold and unruffled – master of the situation. He merely shook his head and held his finger poised above the keypad.

'Take one step near me, general, and I press the key. Possibly not all the cartons will explode, but I've made certain there won't be any doubt about those under Silo Three – the one containing the plutonium.'

Pyne stared at Keller for some moments. It was hard to reconcile the coldly infuriated man standing before him with the usually quiet, always polite Keller. The only time he had ever displayed temperament was during the planning meeting to draft the ultimatum, when he had expressed his dislike of some measures Pyne had proposed.

Pyne decided that Keller was not bluffing – he had the knowledge to modify the cellular phone and build a receiver. Pyne inwardly cursed himself for including Keller in the group. He had never trusted him, but Keller had designed the silos – he knew their weaknesses, and where to place the explosive.

'So what do you intend doing?' asked Pyne tiredly. Suddenly he wanted to put an end to the whole wretched business. He was not even aware that it was his sorrow at what was happening to his country, and how he hoped to halt its decline, that prevented him lunging at Keller: his supreme self-control had taken over.

Keller looked at the sheet of paper. 'I presume the deadline for the government to agree to implement the ultimatum is still midday tomorrow?'

'Yes,' said Pyne dully. 'With another seventy-two hours to draft the legislation.'

'What else is there I should know about ?'

'Nothing.'

'You're sure?'

'Yes.'

Keller nodded. 'Very well, general. But you'd better be telling the truth, for all our sakes.'

He spread the sheet of paper on the table and drew a series of bold lines through some of the conditions. He pushed the sheet across to Pyne.

'I want you to call the Prime Minister now, and tell him about those deletions.'

There was a telephone on the table. Keller picked it up and listened before holding the receiver out to Pyne.

'There's a line on this extension. I presume you've stuck to the arrangement of using a secret number?'

Pyne took the receiver and slowly dialled Simpson's direct-line number. He waited, staring down at the floor.

'Don't say anything else.' said Keller. 'Just say what conditions have been deleted, and make sure he understands.'

Pyne wondered if Keller could hear the ringing tone. He pressed the telephone harder to his ear.

'Simpson? This is General Pyne at Vulcan Hall . . . There have been some alterations to the ultimatum we issued on Sunday . . . Yes . . . Certain conditions have been deleted.' Pyne picked up the sheet of paper and read out the numbers of the contentious demands. The conversation took four minutes. Pyne paused occasionally as if the deletions were being read back to him. Finally he said, 'Yes. That's the complete list as it now stands. I want you to see the Prime Minister is informed immediately . . . I'm sorry but I have nothing to add.'

Pyne was about to replace the receiver when Keller spoke:

'Tell him all future communications are to be on the Government's digitally encoded cell phone TAC frequencies, so we won't be overheard.'

Pyne repeated the instructions into the mouthpiece. Keller took the receiver from Pyne's hand and dropped it on to the cradle.

'I suppose you now wish to assume command?' said Pyne.

'No, general. You're the administrative type – you carry on running the power station.' He tapped the handset. 'Just remember that I'll have this little gadget with me at all times,

115

and that I need less than a second to press the keys. Even if you were to shoot me, you can't be certain that I'd die quickly enough to prevent me from destroying the country. And if you were to destroy this gadget with a well-aimed shot . . .' Keller grinned. 'Well – the way I've programmed it, that would be the same as if I'd operated it.'

'Do you expect me to believe that?'

Keller held the handset up. 'Go ahead and shoot it,' he invited.

'What about our guns?' inquired Patterson, bewildered by the transformation in an employee he had known and trusted for a number of years.

For a moment Keller seemed uncertain. Then he came to a decision. 'You'll have to keep them.' He looked at Pyne. 'I want you to issue strict orders to the soldiers that they're not to enter the power station complex under any circumstances. We'll maintain boundary integrity ourselves by increasing the number of IRIS detectors. You and Patterson will have to carry out the morning and evening patrols to check their batteries and reset them, so you'll need your weapons.'

Keller picked up the typed sheet and returned it to his pocket. 'I'm going to move my things into the control room. No one is to go near the floor without my permission.'

He moved towards the door.

'One last warning. Neither you two or Miss Campion is to try escaping. If anyone does, then it's up to the others to stop him. I wouldn't be able to manage things by myself – or even with just three of us, and as you now know – I don't like being a loser . . .'

He left the last sentence in mid-air and was gone.

Two hours later Keller released the safety-catch on his Sterling. He relished the sensation of power that coursed through his fingers whenever they closed round the crude but effective weapon. There was no need to aim at such close range; the soldiers would hear nothing – Pyne had ordered them back to camp and sealed the entrance to the power station with detectors.

He fired from the hip.

The Ericcson switchboard exploded into shards of grey plastic that skittered across the polished floor of the power station's reception area. The thunderous noise was like champagne. He kept firing until the unit was an unrecognizable mass of tangled wire and smashed key-switches. The pine panelling behind the switchboard splintered under the impact of high-velocity ammunition. A few minutes earlier he had sabotaged the communication equipment in Pyne's and Patterson's helicopters.

The noise attracted Pyne and Patterson who had been inspecting the wrecked transceivers in their helicopters. They waited until Keller had gone and stood surveying the wrecked switchboard.

'That's put paid to our first idea,' said Patterson. 'If Keller's going to stay holed up in the control room we won't be able to get near the radiotelephone. So what do we do now?'

'Some how,' said Pyne, 'I've got to escape.'

'What would be the point, Conrad? The Prime Minister will be acting on those changes.'

Pyne shook his head. 'I didn't get through. I was talking to myself.'

The big man looked at Pyne in surprise, and whistled.

'I didn't think Keller would fall for it,' said Pyne. 'Christ – it's such an old hat ruse and yet it worked.'

'Why do it?'

'The opportunity presented itself. I needed time to think.' Pyne gazed across at the far bank, four kilometres away. 'Hugh, you remember we showed Cox-Spender how the detonator control worked, and how it could only be worked by two people? Supposing we're now being watched through high-powered optical equipment on that bank and they notice that from now on there's only one person in the control room – never two?'

Patterson stared at Pyne as the implication of his words sunk in.

'They'd . . . They'd plan a lightning strike, not knowing . . . not knowing . . .'

'Not knowing that the silos can now be blown up by one man in less than a second,' Pyne finished.

Patterson looked thunderstruck. He stared across the river, at the haze hanging over the far bank.

'Put yourself in their position,' Pyne continued. 'Wouldn't you be watching us?'

Patterson nodded.

'That's why I've got to escape.'

Patterson nodded.

'That's why I've got to get word to the Prime Minister,' said Pyne. 'Somehow, I've got to escape.'

Patterson roused himself. 'But Conrad, we're in a hell of a cleft stick. If you were to try escaping. I'd have to shoot you to prevent Keller doing anything crazy.'

Pyne nodded. 'Exactly, Hugh. You'd have to shoot me.'

7

The ten eminent members of the Cromwell Two Committee listened in shocked silence as their chairman related what had happened that day at the Palace of Westminster.

'And so,' concluded the chairman. 'Pyne has stolen a march on us.'

For a few moments there was silence.

'It's what I would've expected from him,' said General Sir Richard Markham. 'Pyne often confided in me that he thought this committee would still be unable to deal with the racial problems unless we revised our ideas about the sort of measures we were in favour of.'

'You were the one who proposed his membership,' the chairman pointed out.

We needed that new force he's been given,' replied Markham. 'I wasn't allowed to have any say in its formation and administration.'

The chairman sighed. 'What do we do now?'

'We'll have to cancel the takeover,' said Sir Oswald Fox.

'Impossible,' said the head of the Special Branch. 'We're ready to move.'

'Sir Oswald is right,' the chairman interrupted. 'What point is there in us taking over if we have to bow and scrape to Pyne and his thugs? No, gentlemen. I suggest we play the Prime Minister's favourite game no matter how much we despise him for it – we wait and see. We let him sort out the problem of Pyne, and then we move. In the meantime I'll keep you all informed of Cabinet meeting developments.'

8

There is no organization within the British Civil Service that resorts to killing as a political function; there are no James Bonds or Boysie Oakes subordinate to retired senior officers in the government's machine. Consequently, Simpson was at a loss when he decided that the best way of dealing with Howard Mitchell would be to kill him.

Then he remembered a list of names and addresses the Special Branch had once supplied to his office in the days when they could be trusted.

At 16:00 hours, he was studying that list intently.

He left his office at 16:05 and drove over Westminster Bridge in search of a suitable telephone box. There was one in an inconspicuous position in the Waterloo Bridge Road.

Patrick Reagan was in his garden, spraying the blackfly on his french beans and reflecting that at least the vegetable crop this year was saving a fortune in housekeeping during the hard times that were upon him and his wife.

Reagan was an instrument-maker. His employers, a small engineering firm, had been forced out of business by spiralling costs. During better days Reagan had supplemented his pay packet by using his skill with the watchmaker's lathe to manufacture bomb and timing mechanisms in his small but well-equipped workshop.

119

Now the cells who had used his services had been mopped-up and the new ones operating on the mainlain consisted of smart, well-educated lads who could build their own mechanisms by buying components over the counter from model engineering shops and electronics shops.

Although things were bad for Patrick Reagan they could be worse. He could be in prison. Fortunately the evidence linking him to the bombing of an Aldershot public house had been too flimsy for the Director of Public Prosecutions to proceed.

Reagan was refilling his garden spray when the telephone rang.

'Mr Reagan?' said a voice he didn't recognize.

'Who's that?'

'Are you interested in earning a couple of thousand pounds, Mr Reagan?'

'Doing what?' said Reagan suspiciously. The caller's accent was right but it sounded slightly contrived.

'I want you to provide a special party for a friend of mine. Using your special talents—'

Fucking law, thought Reagan, and hung up.

The telephone rang again.

'If you go to the telephone box outside Raynes Park Station.' said the voice, 'I will ring you there and give you your instructions . . . Two thousand pounds Mr Reagan. Think about it.'

Simpson saw Reagan's Nissan drive past the café. He paid for his undrinkable coffee and crossed to the telephone box. From inside he watched Reagan park his car and enter the telephone box outside the station.

The telephone surprised Reagan by starting to ring just as he pulled the door open.

'Mr Reagan,' said the voice. 'Look up.'

'What?'

'Look up above your head.'

Reagan looked up and saw an envelope secured to the inside of the telephone directory glass by its gummed flap. It contained a number of £20 banknotes.

'Fifty of them,' said the voice, as if its owner was reading his thoughts. 'And another fifty when you've carried out the task.'

'What do you want me to do?' said Reagan.

Simpson told him.

Five minutes later Reagan sat in his car and considered his problem – namely that he had only ten grammes of plastic explosive. It was hidden in his garden under the compost heap to fool the trained labradors. Ten grammes wouldn't kill a man unless it exploded hard against his body. It was the right amount for a letter-bomb, but they only maimed, and the man on the telephone had been quite clear about the results he wanted.

Reagan turned the problem over in his mind.

Ten grammes exploding hard against a man's body . . .

A traffic warden had spotted his car and was approaching.

Hard against a man's body . . . ten grammes . . .?

Yes. The answer was obvious. Reagan grinned disarmingly at the traffic warden and drove off just as she was preparing to swoop.

The large electronics hobby shop was about to close when Reagan entered. The assistant sulkily found the heat-operated switch he wanted – one set for its contacts to close when the body of the switch was heated to 30 degrees Centigrade – just a few degrees higher than the temperature reached during the hottest part of the afternoon.

And a few degrees below the temperature of the human body.

Reagan was pleased with his purchase. The £2000 was going to be the easiest money he had ever earned in his life.

9

Corporal Garnet stumbled off the Waterloo train at Walton-on-Thames and was carried along the narrow and incredibly filthy pedestrian tunnel by a wave of desperate homeward-bound commuters all determined to get away from one another and into the metallic lava stream of wife-driven cars flooding out of the station forecourt. The train had been the only one out of London on the line for an hour. The journey had been a nightmare with coaches holding four times their designed capacity.

Garnet stood blinking in the bright sun considering his next move. The suit he had purchased in a menswear shop off Piccadilly had been expensive, but now it felt and fitted like a fetid scrotum. He had been lucky in managing to find a seat on the train. A clerk sitting opposite had suspiciously eyed his scar and the general's crested briefcase. Garnet had divided his attention between him and the girl sitting beside him with her skirt hitched round her thighs to ensnare the cooling draught blowing through the open window.

All but £5 of the money in the general's briefcase was gone.

A taxi took him into Walton town and dropped him outside the Midland Bank.

The cash-dispensing machine spat out £100 in new notes after he had fed it with the general's card and punched out the PIN number he had found pencilled on a piece of paper in the wallet.

The corporal tried for another £100 but the machine refused to oblige. It also kept the card.

He now had £105. Enough for several drinks and one woman.

He badly needed both.

10

Late on Monday evening Pyne kept watch while Patterson worked at a lathe in the power station's workshop.

The sweat running down the big man's face was due partly to the suffocating heat and partly to fear of the consequences if Keller discovered what he was doing. His discomfort did not prevent his working quickly. Fortunately his long-neglected skill with a lathe hadn't atrophied over the years.

He gently tightened a nine-millimetre bullet into the jaws of the lathe's bell-collet so that it was gripped evenly round the rim of the case. Next he opened the chuck jaws on the tail-stock and closed them down on the nickel-jacketed slug. The bullet was now firmly gripped at each end.

He carefully rotated the lathe. The entire bullet turned. He cursed and wiped the sweat from his eyes before tightening the tail-stock jaws a fraction. He gingerly turned the lathe again.

This time the jaws held: the slug rotated in its case as the grip between case and slug was broken. Patterson continued turning the lathe by hand, gently winding the tail-stock back at the same time.

The slug was drawn from its case like a tooth pulled from a socket. He removed the empty case and peered inside to ensure the propellent charge was still in place, then used the lathe jaws to crimp the open end shut, taking great care not to distort the case which could jam.

The case could be fired; it would make the normal amount of noise and smoke and that was all.

Pyne studied Patterson's handiwork.

'Okay. Fine. You'd better do enough for a whole magazine.'

Patterson's normally good-humoured face was creased with anxiety. He took the round from Pyne and examined it critically. 'What are the chance's of the magazine jamming, Conrad?'

'It's a chance we'll just have to take,' Pyne replied unemotionally.

123

A committee of twenty Members of Parliament and the two government law officers worked for five hours drafting the enabling bill that would become law within twenty-four hours.

They left Downing Street at five minutes to midnight. All the MPs were also practicing lawyers. Each one had been responsible for the wording of a section, which in turn had been passed to two colleagues for careful checking to ensure that the wording was one hundred per cent watertight.

It had been an exhausting five hours.

The Prime Minister bade them goodnight and returned to the Cabinet Office. Simpson was poring over the sheets of paper written in a wide assortment of handwriting. Each sheet was a mass of amendments and deletions. Simpson held one up.

'The last clause. Written by Beresford. It requires the bill to lapse automatically when pressure on the government has been removed.'

The Prime Minister nodded. 'Provocative, wouldn't you say?' Simpson fed the sheet of paper into a shredding machine.

'Do you know what the Attorney-General said when he left?' inquired the Prime Minister. 'He said, 'It's a good job we haven't got a constitution and that the governments have always opposed a Bill of Rights for the people.'

Simpson looked surprised. 'That's exactly what you said when—'

'I shouldn't attach any importance to it, Simpson.'

The Prime Minister yawned and looked at his watch.

Midnight.

He went to bed at fifteen minutes past midnight and was soundly asleep ten minutes later.

12

At 23:00 hours Reagan reversed his Nissan behind a large rhododendron within fifty metres of Mitchell's house. The baked ground was too hard to leave tyre marks.

He closed the driver's window against the swarms of disturbed mosquitoes before checking his set of watch-maker's tools and transferring them to various pockets: tweezers into the handkerchief pocket where the spikes would not dig into him; a multipurpose screwdriver with a selection of blades in its handle transferred to a trouser pocket; a diamond file into his wallet with the tungsten-wheel glass-cutters wrapped in a piece of self-adhesive decorative plastic film. The small vacuum flask containing the components to make the bomb made a conspicuous bulge in his jacket. He wound a short length of transistor radio earphone wire round the matchbox containing his precious ten grammes of plastic explosive. The wire was fine enough to be cut with his folding nail scissors.

He removed the car ignition key from his key ring and placed it on the floor. If he had to make a quick getaway he would be able to pick the key up without having to fumble with the other keys on the ring. Leaving the key in the ignition was inviting trouble. One of Reagan's recurring nightmares was being forced to flee from a house he had broken into, only to find that his car had been stolen.

He left the car in gear with handbrake off and the driver's door ajar.

He approached the house by skirting the edge of the lawn, keeping close to the shadows and checking the lawn with quick stabs of light from his torch for signs that meant dog. There were none.

There was a light on in an upstairs room but that did not worry him: his immediate concern was to get into the house as quickly as possible. Once inside he could rely on his skill to avoid detection; outside he was at the mercy of curious eyes.

The area round the kitchen door was screened from the garden and road by rustic woven fence panels. There were no feeding bowls on the enclosed rectangle of concrete, no scraps of meat and no scratch marks on the door.

Reagan relaxed a little. The door was locked. He pressed it at the bottom with his foot. It gave slightly. That meant it had not been secured on the inside with a bolt. It was the same at the top of the door – all he had to contend with was the mortise lock. He shone his torch through the keyhole and noted with satisfaction the gleaming end of the key's barrel pointing at him.

It took him two minutes to inscribe a circle on the door's glass pane with the glass-cutters, peel the backing paper off the self-adhesive plastic film and secure it over the circle. The third blow with the inside of his fist caused the disc to fracture from the surrounding pane. He quickly removed the plastic film with glass attached and reached through the hole to unlock the door.

The first thing he did inside the house was to search for an emergency hiding-place. The instinct of a professional housebreaker when he hears noises that suggest his presence is known is not to flee, but to hide. Most people fondly believe that making a noise is sufficient to cause a burglar to leave – it works with amateurs, but not with professionals. And Reagan was a professional.

He found a broom cupboard leading off the hall. He pushed a child's rubber sucker onto the inside of the door so that he could pull it closed behind him if the need arose.

The telephone was in the living-room on a low coffee-table. Reagan positioned his torch and laid out his tools on a handkerchief so that he could pick them up and put them down without making a noise. He could also gather them up quickly if he heard a sound from the floor above. He unscrewed the vacuum flask and shook the bomb components and crushed ice into a clean ashtray. Next he unscrewed the telephone's earpiece cover and placed it on the handkerchief. Using the tweezers to avoid heating the component, he picked the thermal switch out of the crushed ice in the ashtray and positioned it inside the earpiece cover. He rolled the piece of plastic explosive, the size of a thimble, into a slender sausage shape between his palms and then placed it on the bed of ice for a few seconds to cool before carefully tamping it around the inside of the earpiece so that it held the tiny thermal switch in position, but with its two fine wires protruding. Buried in the ice was the pin detonator, which he fished out with tweezers and dried with cottonwool before pressing it firmly into the explosive. The last component was a Mallory cell battery the size of an aspirin. Like the thermal switch, it had two fine lengths of wire attached to its terminals. There was a plastic cap at the end of the wire which prevented the ends touching one another and draining the current. Reagan left it in place until he had pressed the battery into the explosive. Finally he connected the components together with short lengths of the earphone wire. He held the plastic earpiece cover between thumb and forefinger and screwed it back on to the telephone's handset. He tested the weight of the instrument. He doubted if Mitchell would notice the additional weight when answering the phone.

Reagan replaced the handset on the cradle and surveyed his handiwork. The two contacts inside the thermal switch would now be moving towards one another. But they wouldn't touch until they were exposed to thirty degrees Centigrade – another six degrees – such as the human body was capable of providing. When Mitchell answered the phone the heat from his body would cause the thermal switch contacts to close after ten seconds, thus completing the circuit.

The resulting explosion, though small, smaller than even a letter-bomb explosion, would be enough to blow Mitchell's brains out.

Reagan gathered his tools together and tipped the melting ice back into the flask. He dried the ashtray with his handkerchief.

The next phase of the operation was for him to earn the other £1000 he had been promised.

And that required only a phone call.

13

Reagan was heading back towards the main road when he spotted the orange-striped police car with its cherry-festooned roof lurking in the trees.

He drove past, neither slowing nor accelerating. In the rear mirror he saw the police car's headlights suddenly stab across the road then sweep towards him as it pulled out from the trees. The distance between the two blazing lights widened in his mirror. Reagan tried to remain calm and drive normally despite the dazzling lights reflected into his eyes.

The police car made no attempt to pass and wave him down – it seemed content to sit on his tail.

Reagan began to sweat. If they were after him it wouldn't take them long to find the house with the broken window. It would take them even less time to learn some interesting facts about his spare-time career. They'd go over Mitchell's house with a microscope. They wouldn't find prints, but the bloody junky labradors would soon sniff out the plastic explosive.

Unconsciously, Reagan accelerated. Why didn't the sadistic bastards stop him?

The searing lights were now right behind him and blinding him. If he moved his head more lights mocked him from the door mirrors.

Bastards.

All he could see ahead was a narrow band of glittering flint road surface funnelling briefly into his field of vision before disappearing under the Datsun's hood. He did not see the approaching yellow flares of the main-road street lighting until it was too late.

British Aerospace driver Peter Floyd was ferrying a spare Airbus tailplane to London Airport. The police required that such a load should be moved only at night. The road from the aircraft works was slightly downhill. He was doing forty-five miles an hour when his articulated truck struck the car which suddenly shot across his path from a side road.

There was no time for Floyd to transfer his foot to the brake pedal before the front of his cab smashed into the car's rear. The shattering impact spun the car round in the road, with petrol flailing from its ruptured fuel tank.

Reagan might have lived had he driven straight into the side of the truck instead of suddenly spinning the wheel in panic as the yellow street lighting and the side of the truck burst upon his consciousness.

In the time it took for his hand to drop to his seatbelt buckle the car was engulfed by an incandescent fireball. Reagan was still alive three seconds after impact – clawing at an unyielding door welded firmly shut by the rapidly melting rubber draught excluder. He managed to wind down the heat-warped window a few centimetres; flames syphoned into the car, setting fire to the headlining. Then he was screaming as globules of falling molten plastic set fire to his hair and clothing, and he knew he was going to die.

Tuesday

1

Corporal Garnet was at Reagan's death scene, but took no interest.

He pushed indifferently through the small crowd, making his way to General Pyne's house on St Georges Hill.

He had been thrown out of a Walton pub at closing time. The girl had been pretty; she had said nothing about his scar, which pleased him, and had worn a short skirt, which pleased him even more. Short skirts were rare in England, but the birds in Northern Ireland wore nothing else as part of their cock-teasing campaign against British soldiers.

He had bought the girl in the pub three rum-and-cokes. Then she had leaned forward, kissed the scar and said she had to go to the toilet. That was the last he had seen of her.

He had gone to pay for another drink, and discovered the wallet had gone.

So had the last bus, and he hadn't enough for a taxi.

He had walked the six kilometres to Weybridge, going first to the road where the general's snooty bitch of a daughter had bought herself a house with her mother' money.

She wasn't in.

He waited an hour, planning to slip into the house behind her when she opened the front door. The longer he waited, the more he brooded on the treatment he had received at her hands. Well, he was a civvy now – the Redcaps couldn't touch him. The courts would probably give him six months – civvy style.

It would be well worth it.

He had sweated all Friday cleaning out the swimming-pool at her dad's place. When it was nearly refilled he'd asked her if he could cool off indoors. The bitch had turned round and said, 'Not until you've mowed the lawn.'

Her father was decent enough. The sort of man you could admire and respect. How'd he come to have a daughter like that? Her dad had helped him over the business of the teenage joyrider outside Corry's timber yard in Belfast. The stupid kid had driven straight through an army roadblock. The bloody car had backfired and Garnet, his nerves keyed-up because he hadn't been in the province long, pumped five rounds into the back of the receding Toyota. It skidded, overturned and burst into flames.

It was the third case of joyriders crashing roadblocks and the drivers being wasted that year; they were going to hang everything on him. Make an example of him to appease a bloodyminded populace. Then they decided to hush things up and ship him home. He'd still be rotting in a military prison waiting for a court martial if the general hadn't stepped in and said he needed a driver and Scout pilot.

He had enjoyed the new job until the general's daughter had heard about his past. He had been clipping the grass along the edge of the drive when she had slowed down in her MG and said jokingly, 'Just making sure it doesn't backfire.'

A police car cruised by.

Garnet decided to move. Perhaps she was at her dad's home at St Georges Hill.

Her car was outside the house.

Garnet let himself in through the front door with the keys in the general's briefcase, pulled off his shoes and checked the house downstairs. There was no sign of her, although she'd left the kitchen in a mess and there were photographs scattered all over the dining-room. There was one of her in a bikini. A chinless twit had his arm round her and was trying to get his fingertips round her left tit. Looking at it, and the thought that she was just upstairs, made him tremble with anticipation.

But first a drink.

He found a half-bottle of whisky in the sideboard.

Thirty minutes later it was nearly empty.

Now for the girl.

He took off all his clothes in the hallway and mounted the stairs. The night air felt pleasantly cool against his body after the oppressive stickiness of the suit.

Her bedroom door was ajar. He pushed it slowly open. For a moment he thought she had a bedside light on, so bright was the moonlight streaming into the room.

She was lying on top of the bed, curled into a foetal position, wearing a short nightdress. Her legs gleamed with erotic paleness.

Garnet stood trembling in the doorway – encouraging his erection before following it across the room to the girl's bed.

His hand closed over her mouth. She made a choking noise as he forced her on to her back. Her eyes were twin pools of terror that stared wildly up at him from above his fingers – he could feel her teeth trying to bite at the inside of his palm. Her legs thrashed madly, making it difficult to pin her down. Then she was trying to tear his hair out.

He hit her hard on the side of the face. Her hand tried to slide under his elbow and he immediately pinned it against the bed. He grasped her other hand and forced it back against the headboard.

Christ the bitch was strong.

He ground his knees viciously into her shins. A cry of pain gurgled from deep within her throat, and spent itself against the hand clamped across her mouth. The sound encouraged him to increased effort. He pounded his torso up and down – using his body as a pummelling wedge to force her legs apart. She tried to crush him with her hips, but the feel of the inside of her thighs only increased his excitement.

The girl's hand groped on the bedside table. Her fingers closed round the alabaster table lamp.

She brought it down on his head with a wild blow that glanced off his temple. The body on her relaxed. She smashed the lamp down again with all her strength.

The body rolled on to the floor and lay still.

Only when Maggie had staggered across the bedroom and turned on the light did she realize her assailant was Corporal Garnet. A bloodstain was soaking into her clothes under his head.

Her first thought was that her father had arrived home. She ran downstairs calling for him, but there was only silence and hot summer air in the big, still house.

She managed to reach the kitchen sink before being violently sick. The cold edge of the stainless-sink helped revive her. She drank a cup of water, then went into the dining-room for her father's gun.

There was a bottle of whisky standing on the scattered photographs, and something else. She stared at it – not understanding. It was her father's briefcase.

She found the Webley revolver in the sideboard. The museum piece's heavy coldness gave her confidence. She went upstairs – stepping over Corporal Garnet's clothes as if the untidy heap was a dead cat.

He was lying in the same position – completely naked. The bloodstain was spreading to the carpet. Fearful that he might suddenly arise to renew his attack, she crept nearer. His chest appeared to be motionless. There was something she remembered from a television play. She held a hand mirror in front of the corporal's face, above the leering scar.

The glass remained clear.

Suddenly her body was racked with pain. Still clutching the revolver, she went downstairs. She sat in the living-room staring at the telephone, nerving herself to call the police. She had heard about the way police dealt with rape cases, or attempted rape. There was the heap of clothes in the hallway; she'd have to say that Corporal Garnet was not a stranger; Christ – they'd want her to be examined.

Her father's solicitor was someone called Meredith. She opened the address book and punched his number. A bloody answering machine replied. She slammed down the handset and tried to think calmly. She saw Howard Mitchell's name and address on the open page. He would help. He would know what to do.

She called his number, praying he would be at home.

The ringing tone chirruped in her ear. She almost wept with relief when it stopped with the click of a receiver lifted off its cradle.

'Mitchell,' said an American accent, heavy with sleep.

'Mitch! Thank God!' Her voice nearly broke into hysteria as the tension of waiting for the telephone to be answered suddenly snapped. 'This is Maggie Pyne. I—'

She got no further as Garnet grabbed her from behind. She dropped the telephone and clawed desperately at the hand that threatened to choke her.

'Bitch!' screamed Garnet. 'Stinking, cock-teasing bitch!'

The receiver was swinging by its cord. She could dimly hear the puzzled, reedy, distorted voice:

'Maggie . . .? Maggie . . .?'

Garnet let go of Maggie's throat and hit her.

She fell to the floor, twisted round and snatched up the revolver.

Garnet was about to lunge at her. He froze.

Maggie looked up in terror at the livid scar, and aimed the revolver with both hands. She pulled the trigger as Garnet dived sideways.

The hammer fell on an empty chamber.

Bloody hell – an army daughter and she hadn't the sense to check if the damn thing was loaded!

Garnet threw himself at her, but she rolled sideways. He grabbed hold of her hair, screaming obscenities as he tried to tear her nightdress and climb on top of her. She tried to hit him with the gun. He knocked it from her grasp so that it skated across the floor. She doubled her legs under and pushed him away. The nightdress come away in his hands

134

with a loud, tearing noise. Garnet grinned at her. Blood was steaming down his chest from his matted hair. He wiped himself with the nightdress – his eyes never leaving the naked girl cowering on the floor.

She started to crawl away. He jammed her ankle painfully to the floor with his foot so that she cried out.

'Come on, you bitch,' snarled Garnet. 'Let's see you fight.'

She answered by doubling forward and sinking her teeth into his calf. The corporal drew back his other foot and kicked her hard in the crutch – a lethal kick had he been wearing shoes.

Maggie's teeth did not relax their grip. She could taste Garnet's blood.

He swore and dragged her head back by the hair. He slapped her hard across the face. She moaned in pain.

Garnet laughed. He dropped beside her and put his hands on her thighs. Maggie tensed, and drew her legs tightly together. The corporal lifted his fist menacingly. She winced as Garnet dug his fingers into her legs and forced them apart.

He moved over her, the hideous scar now above her face. She stared up at him, unable to feel him because he had kicked her so hard.

He began moving rhythmically, his elbows splayed out on the carpet and his hands crushing feverishly into her breasts.

Garnet's pace quickened. His whisky-laden breath rasped against his teeth and the blood flowed faster from his torn scalp.

Maggie forced her hand down slowly between Garnet's body and her own.

Garnet felt uneasy as the gently questing fingers closed softly, first round the base of his penis before moving delicately down to encircle his testicles.

Maggie crushed, twisted and pulled with all her strength in one smooth, totally devastating movement. Garnet released a shrill, almost feminine scream, arched backwards off the girl as if his spine was a crossbow and Maggie had pulled the trigger. He continued screaming hideously and rolled himself into a tight, protective ball of personal agony.

Maggie pulled herself to her feet. She looked quickly round, grabbed the revolver by the barrel and raised it above her head to hit the corporal.

He looked up at her – his eyes glazed with pain – and pushed himself on to one knee. Maggie dropped the revolver in panic and raced into the hall. For a moment she was uncertain what to do. Garnet was crawling towards her. She flew up the stairs and locked herself in the bathroom. She could hear Garnet crashing about in the kitchen before he came staggering up the stairs after her, bellowing like an enraged bullock.

Then he was outside on the landing.

The lock on the bathroom door was designed to inform rather than to withstand a determined assault. The door splintered away from the surround on Garnet's first charge.

The last thing Maggie saw before losing consciousness was the flash of light on the raised breadknife Garnet was clutching in his hand.

2

The Prime Minister tossed Cox-Spender's phoney report on the cause of the Thames Haven disaster on to the desk and lit a cigar. He watched Simpson covertly through a cloud of blue cigar smoke.

'What are you working on now, Simpson?'

Simpson looked up from his desk and wished the Prime Minister would return to his own office. 'I'm dealing with the discontented families of Vulcan Hall staff who are complaining that their relatives haven't returned home since Saturday night.'

'What are you going to say?'

'I don't know,' said Simpson sourly.

'Unusual for you to be at a loss, Simpson.'

Simpson said nothing.

The Prime Minister stretched luxuriously and watched his cigar smoke define the beams of early-morning sun shining into the room.

'You know, Simpson, were this not such a deadly serious business, I might be tempted to enjoy it. Does that sound callous?'

Simpson met the politician's gaze. 'How much longer do you think we can keep the Civil Service at bay, sir?'

The Prime Minister grinned wolfishly. 'Just as long as I can keep up the pretence that I'm dealing with party business.' He paused, watching Simpson struggle with the report. Simpson's trouble was that he had little imagination.

'Supposing you tell the families that there was an accident with one of the reactors and that the staff have been quarantined?'

'That would bring the press swarming around our ears.'

'A row is inevitable, Simpson. Rows we can deal with once the full story is out. What worries me at the moment are the imponderables.'

'Such as?'

'Such as that American – Howard Mitchell. What's happening on that front?'

Simpson braced himself. 'I've organized a private investigator to watch him'

The nerve in the Prime Minister's neck twitched. 'Dangerous, Simpson.'

'I've arranged everything by phone,' said Simpson evenly.

'Not only dangerous, Simpson, but contrary to my orders.'

'I wanted to be near at hand to assist you, sir. I thought the Nelson touch seemed appropriate.'

The Prime Minister watched Simpson through a cloud of cigar smoke. Simpson knew too much. It would be wiser not to push him too far.

Simpson smiled thinly at the politician. 'I'll be calling him each morning and evening for a progress report.'

Simpson found it easy to lie. His whole life was one huge, complex web of deception.

3

It had been a dream.

Maggie hovered for some minutes in the half-world between sleep and consciousness while one partially open eye and her drugged brain sluggishly co-ordinated their respective images and sensations in an effort to assemble the familiar surroundings into one continuous tapestry, so normal that her reason, struggling up from the depths of sleep, told her that the recent, hideous events uncoiling in her memory had been a dream.

She pushed her feet into the cool corners of the bed and immediately sensed that two things were wrong: the dull ache in her pelvis and the smoothness of the sheets. They were smooth only on Sunday mornings because Saturday was the one day in the week when she made her bed properly.

Then there was something else – she was wearing one of her mother's nightdresses. She sat up and screwed her face up as a lance of pain probed behind her temple. Her fingers traced the outline of a sticking plaster taped to the side of her forehead.

The bedside lamp was missing. It hadn't been a dream. Or had it?

Then she saw the bloodstain on the bedroom carpet and the flood of vicious memories dropped into their slots.

Garnet was still in the passageway outside her door. She pulled the sheet protectively up to her chin.

The door opened.

Mitchell entered the room carrying a tray. He looked at her in concern and said: 'I've been looking in every fifteen minutes to see if you were awake.'

He set the tray down on the bedside table and poured her a hot sweet drink.

'It's tea. Don't try to say anything – just drink it.'

The drink scalded the back of her throat, burning away the taste that lined her mouth. Her hands began to shake. Mitchell sat on the edge of the bed and leaned forward to steady the cup and saucer.

'I'm sorry,' she began, but Mitchell raised a finger to his lips. 'You don't have to say anything. The doctor said you were to get as much sleep as possible.'

'What time is it?'

'Nearly 8:30,' said Mitchell, and added as an after-thought, 'In the morning.' He took the cup and saucer from her and placed them on the tray. 'You need some more sleep, Maggie.' Mitchell gave her an encouraging chuck under the chin and left the room, closing the door softly behind him.

An hour later, with unanswered questions crowding out sleep, Maggie went downstairs. Mitchell was eating a sandwich in the kitchen. He smiled warmly at her.

'How are you feeling now?'

'Awful.' She sat at the table opposite him.

Bruises had appeared on her face that Mitchell hadn't noticed before.

'Maggie, you don't look well. You ought to go back to bed.'

His tone irritated the girl.

'I always look like this in the morning,' she snapped, and immediately regretted it. 'I'm sorry, Mitch. Is that coffee?'

He poured her a cup. 'That was some party you were having last night. The doctor said you were suffering from shock. He's going to look by this afternoon.'

Maggie avoided Mitchell's eye. 'You know what happened?' she asked.

'The doctor told me. You were in a helluva state when I found you.'

'You found me?'

'You called me, remember? I don't know how long you'd been ringing when I answered the phone. I can sleep through

139

anything – even with the extension ringing by my ear. I could hear you yelling so I dropped the phone and got here as quickly as I could.'

'Thank you.' said Maggie.

'He was standing over you with a breadknife, shouting about his crown jewels. I hit him from behind and dumped him in here. I guess I should've tied him up, but I was more concerned about you. By the time I'd cleaned you up, he'd gone.'

God, thought Maggie bitterly. You're attacked by one man, and end up being pawed by two more. It was an ungrateful thought, but she couldn't help it.

Mitchell sensed her embarrassment. He went to the sink and pretended to wash his plate.

Maggie watched him. She remembered the flashing breadknife. She went across to him. 'Mitch, I'm sorry. I didn't mean to sound rude. It was good of you to come so quickly.'

He put his arm round her and steered her back to the chair. 'Don't worry about me, honey. You just sit down and drink your coffee. Then you should go back to bed. I'll stay if you like.'

Maggie allowed herself to be pushed gently on to the chair.

'Do you want to have him charged?' asked Mitchell hesitantly. 'There would have to be an examination by a police doctor'

Maggie shook her head. 'I don't know.' Then she remembered her father's briefcase.

Despite Mitchell's protests, she rushed out of the kitchen. She returned, reading the various papers.

Mitchell read the letter Pyne had written to his bank about Corporal Garnet. 'Why would he want to do a thing like that?' he asked.

Maggie shook her head in bewilderment and held out another paper. 'He's given him the boat, and told him to sell it for whatever he can get . . . And these . . .' She held up an envelope, ' . . .are Corporal Garnet's discharge papers . . . And look – a cheque. Made out to the corporal – for *five hundred pounds*!'

Mitchell took the papers and studied them. 'Why would your father do a crazy thing like that?'

Maggie stared at the cheque. She looked up at Mitchell. 'He's blackmailing him,' she said, her voice low. Then she was screaming, 'That filthy little trigger-happy runt's blackmailing my father!'

Mitchell calmed her down. 'Now, honey. You don't know that.'

The telephone rang. Maggie pulled away from Mitchell and went to answer it.

She returned a few minutes later looking thoughtful. 'That was Weybridge Marina. They said Garnet had just taken the boat out and were checking to see it was okay . . . Mitch, you've got a boat, haven't you?'

Mitchell looked at her. The doctor was right – she was tough. There was a hard light in her eyes.

'Now look, Maggie. Don't you think you should wait for the doctor?'

'I want to find out about my father.'

'We should call the police.'

'No! Not until we know what hold that bastard's got over my father!'

Mitchell decided not to argue. He sighed. 'Okay. I'll go home and get the boat keys. Give me thirty minutes.'

There were a police car and a dog handler's van outside Mitchell's house.

His first thought was that Maggie had changed her mind and had telephoned them.

'Mr Mitchell?' said the senior officer.

'Yes? What's the matter?'

'We've been waiting for you, sir. Were you aware your house had been broken into last night? Your paperboy reported it.' The policeman sounded suspicious, as if people

141

who allowed their houses to be robbed were instrumental in the crime.

The police spent fifteen minutes checking the house. They even let the labrador loose. It sniffed round every room, returning to the living-room several times, but found nothing.

Mitchell finally persuaded the policemen to leave, promising to call them if he later discovered anything missing. They drifted reluctantly back to their vehicles and sat watching the house for some minutes before driving off.

Mitchell ruefully examined the broken kitchen window. He couldn't leave the house empty without carrying out some sort of temporary repair. As he finished hammering the last piece of wood into place he realized that the living-room telephone was ringing.

4

The meeting in a cool, north-facing room above the reservation offices of Mid-European Airlines in Oxford Street was due to start at 10:00 hours.

Walter Innam arrived at 10:05 carrying a briefcase and wearing a ten-year-old suit. The receptionist pointed to the lifts and told him he was expected in Room 101. Innam spent an unhappy five minutes peering at room numbers until he was rescued by a typist.

Paul Weiner arrived by taxi at 10:10.

A man in his early forties, wearing a check suit, arrived on foot. He nodded to the receptionist and went straight to Room 101. Weiner and Innam were already seated at the long conference table. One wall of the room, was occupied by a beaded glass screen with loudspeaker enclosures mounted on each side. A selection of film and slide projectors stood on a long shelf at the opposite end of the room.

'I presume you've converted the pictures to slides?' was the first thing the man in the check suit said to Weiner.

'Yes.' Weiner nodded to Innam. 'Mr Innam has them.'

The man in the check suit seemed to notice Innam for the first time. Then he smiled, and shook Innam warmly by the hand.

'Good to see you again,' he said. 'How are you keeping?'

'Very well,' said Innam, trying to peer closely at the vague face without appearing to be rude.

'We met in Washington a couple of years back. You did some verification work on some suspicious construction work in Iraq.'

'Oh yes,' said Innam politely.

'And now you've found some more surprises for us right here in England?' The man in the check suit looked at Weiner expectantly. 'Right. Shall we start?'

'I think we should wait until Hendricks arrives,' replied Weiner. 'He should be here any moment.'

The man in the check suit looked surprised. 'He's in the country?'

Weiner nodded. 'He flew in from Langley two hours ago.'

'What made him decide to come?' The man in the check suit regarded Weiner accusingly.

Weiner shrugged. 'Hendricks is entitled to do as he pleases.'

'Something must've touched a nerve to drag him across the Atlantic.'

'I sent him Mr Innam's report as a matter of routine,' said Weiner.

'Which I haven't seen yet,' the man in the check suit said pointedly.

'I thought Hendricks should see it first.'

The man in the check suit looked at Innam speculatively. 'It must be something pretty spectacular you've got in that briefcase.'

'Pretty spectacular,' said Weiner, answering for Innam.

The door opened and Hendricks entered. He was a tall, gaunt man with a long craggy face completely devoid of humour that inspired profound gloom and a deep sense of foreboding in everyone with whom he came in contact. There was a rumour circulating in the 'firm', the headquarters of the CIA at Langley in Virginia, that he had once smiled. But it was one of those events, like the falling of Jericho's walls, for which the evidence was slight and largely circumstantial.

Weiner's attempts to introduce him to the other men were waived brusquely aside. He sat at the head of the table facing the screen, positioned his gold pen carefully parallel to the sheets of paper already provided and looked up at the three men.

'Good morning, gentlemen. Shall we begin?' The question was expressed as a command.

Weiner and the man in the check suit looked uncertainly at one another.

Weiner cleared his throat.

'Well, sir, as you know, last Sunday the big oil refinery here at a place called Thames—'

Hendricks held up his hand. 'Quite right, Weiner. I do know. Therefore there seems little point in going over it. I've come all this way to see your covers because I couldn't make much sense of the faxes. I want to hear your interpretation and decide what should be done. So I suggest we get on with the task in hand without preamble.' The sentences were delivered in short, grating bursts in a Harvard accent.

Weiner looked uncomfortable. He muttered a 'yes, sir' and crossed to the windows to close the venetian blinds so that Innam had to grope in near-darkness as he struggled to load his slides into the projector.

The first picture showed the remains of the refinery from an apparent height of a thousand feet. It had hardly been on the screen for five seconds when Hendricks clipped accent rapped out: 'Next.'

It was the same with the following three slides. Each one was allowed barely five seconds on the screen, and the long face would say, 'Next!'

The fifth slide was a close-up of the piece of aluminium which had first captured Innam's attention the previous day. The stencilled white characters were indistinct.

'Do you have a closer picture?' Hendricks asked the darkness.

'There's a zoom attachment on this projector, sir,' said Innam.

'Then use it, please.'

The picture sprang at the audience – the edges spilled on to the ceiling and over the loudspeakers. The white letters and numbers were now much clearer and could be read without difficulty.

'That, gentlemen,' said Hendricks waving his bony hand at the screen, 'is a Federal Stock Number issued from a block of numbers assigned to the Marine Corps by the Defense Logistics Center at Battle Creek, Michigan. The first two digits – one-four – are, as you correctly pointed out in your report, the Federal Supply Classification group for guided weapons. Before leaving, I was able to establish that the rest of the number is the stores identification reference for the after-fairing of an Honest John missile. The number was stencilled on the section in accordance with the Marine Corps normal policy for the identification of spares.'

Hendricks paused, leaned back in his chair and hooked his long fingers behind his head. 'The general consensus of opinion at Langley is that it was most astute of you gentlemen to detect this peculiarity, for which I am asked to thank you.'

A nice back-handed compliment, thought Weiner.

'My own opinion,' continued Hendricks, 'is that fulsome praise should be reserved for when you find out who has been firing American-made missiles. Among other things, you are paid to solve mysteries – not merely find them.'

There was a silence in the room, then Weiner spoke:

'According to the statement issued by the British government, the explosion was an accident.'

145

'All part of the same mystery,' said Hendricks slowly. 'There's no doubt that the destruction of the refinery was the result of terrorist activities, and that the British government know that. Terrorists do not keep their acts a secret.' Hendricks smiled thinly. 'Otherwise there wouldn't be much point committing them. The questions we must ask ourselves, gentlemen, are – firstly, who and what are these people who have fired an American-built missile; and secondly, what are the demands they are making on a friendly government? Demands that the government is apparently keeping secret.'

'Do we know how the missile came to be in the country in the first place?' asked the man in the check suit, wondering what all this had to do with power stations.

'Yes,' said Hendricks unhelpfully. He paused, and continued:

'We believe it must have been one of ten that were sold to the British government some years ago. Very old stock. A truck taking two of the missiles to a Royal Ordnance Factory for decommissioning was hijacked three months age.' Hendricks looked at Weiner. 'You may remember the incident.'

Weiner nodded. He remembered submitting a report to Langley that had resulted in a sharply worded note being sent by the United States Secretary of State to the British government. It criticised the lack of security arrangements for the transport of missiles by road.

'Normally,' said Hendricks, 'I am reluctant to draw conclusions, but it's reasonably safe bet that the missile used to blow up Thames Haven was one of those that disappeared.' Hendricks looked round the room, as if inviting a challenge. None came. 'It would be interesting,' he continued, 'to know where the missile was fired from. We can draw a radius of thirty kilometres around the site of the explosion, which gives us an area of about four thousand square kilometres as a hunting-ground. We need suggestions on probable sites we can work on first.'

This was the opening Weiner had been waiting for.

'Mr Innam has discovered more information from his study of the covers since he filed his report,' he said quickly.

Hendricks turned to Innam.

'Is that so?'

Innam saw a patch of light above Hendrick's shoulders facing in his direction. 'I think I can tell you exactly where it was launched from,' he said nervously.

'Please do,' said Hendricks.

'If I could change the slide . . .' Innam clicked rapidly through the slides. A succession of images flashed on the screen until he reached one that showed the Thames Estuary in strange contrasts. The river was bright green, and the surrounding countryside was a mottled patchwork on various shades of red ranging from pale pink to vivid scarlet.

'An infra-red picture converted to false colours,' Innam explained. 'The shades of red are caused by foliage. If we zoom in closer . . .'

The strange scene moved nearer the four men. Weiner experienced the god-like sensation that Innam enjoyed whenever he plunged towards his reproduction earth.

Weiner looked at the screen with professional interest, but could make no sense of the riotous hues spread across the landscape.

'That's Vulcan Hall nuclear power station in the middle of the picture,' pointed out Innam. 'It's only ten kilometres from the refinery. Those squares are two tanker trucks.'

Weiner studied the picture closely. He could distinguish a stain round one of the vehicles.

'What's that mark?' asked Hendricks.

'A heat blister,' said Innam. 'The sort of thing you get following an explosion. There's a much bigger one around the refinery.'

'And this . . . heat blister was caused around the tanker when the Honest John was launched?' asked Hendricks sceptically.

147

Innam sensed the disbelief in Hendricks' voice, and bristled – his professional ability was being challenged. 'Yes, sir. I'm absolutely certain of it because there's an unfired Honest John in the tanker on the right. There's a gap along the top of the tanker if you look closely. Inside it's just possible to see the nose of an Honest John. It must be an Honest John because the measurements fit exactly!'

There was a silence following Innam's outburst.

Innam's hand was shaking. He wondered what would happen to him.

Hendrick's craggy face turned away from the screen. 'Okay. Let's have some light in here.'

Weiner rose and flicked the blinds open.

'Tell me about this power station,' said Hendricks.

The man in the check suit opened a manilla file and pushed it towards the long talons drumming impatiently on the table. They stopped drumming and picked up the plans and photographs in the file.

'It's a thirteen-twenty megawatt unit powered by two gas-cooled fast-breeder reactors,' said the man in the check suit. 'It's only just been pulled from production and was scheduled for de-commissioning. Yet according to the infra-red pics, two of the cooling towers are still chucking out heat – more than the residual heat you'd expect from even recently closed-down reactors. There's a heat cloud spreading right across the North Sea. My guess is that the British have shipped a helluva lot of nuclear waste to Vulcan Hall for temporary storage. They've run into political problems with their repositories in Cheshire.'

Hendricks tapped the plans. 'In that case, how much waste do you reckon there is at Vulcan Hall?'

The man in the check suit hesitated. 'I've only been able to make a rough calculation based on the size of the heat cloud, but I'd say in the region of two-point-five billion curies, plus.'

'What does that mean in terms of quantity?' Hendricks demanded. 'I'm not a nuclear physicist.'

148

'It means the largest concentration of nuclear waste in the world,' said the man in the check suit.

No one spoke. The walls of Jericho suddenly cracked: Hendricks smiled.

'I have formed a theory, gentlemen,' he said, 'one which ties all these seemingly disjointed facts neatly together.' He turned to the man in the check suit. 'What would be the effect of releasing all that waste into the environment?'

The man in the check suit scribbled on his paper and looked up. In a tightly controlled voice he said, 'It would be another Cheynobel only worse . . . Much worse . . .'

5

An hour later Hendricks was sitting in Paul Weiner's chair studying the photograph of Ralph Keller taken at a St Georges Hill garden party.

He dropped the picture on to the desk and looked up at Weiner. 'Odd that he should turn up.'

'We don't know that he's involved,' Weiner replied.

'We do if my uncanny sixth sense says he is,' said Hendricks, picking up the St Georges Hill electoral register and idly turning the sheets. His shrunken eyes flicked down the printed columns of names and addresses. Several entries were underlined. He pointed a gnarled finger to one and raised a questioning eyebrow.

'People with strong right-wing views,' explained Weiner. 'Strong right-wing views – not extreme. We've eliminated the crackpots and only classified those possessing a degree of sobriety – those who have the ability to form the nucleus of a resistance movement.' Weiner paused. 'Should the need for such a movement ever arise.'

Hendricks studied the list is silence. 'Where's Pyne's name?' he inquired at length.

'Sheet seven. Patterson's name is on sheet five. Louise Campion's name is on the same page. She's the woman in the photograph.'

Hendricks turned the pages. 'What does Pyne do?'

'He's the British government's Logistics Liaison Officer – their hatchet man for supervising the run-down of the armed services. All the defence-cut recommendations carry his signature. He's a leading advocate of a central European defence force.'

'A carpet warrior?'

'A pretty efficient carpet warrior. The Treasury Department like him – that's why he's made the rank of major-general at forty-five.'

Hendricks nodded. 'And it's definitely his helicopter at Vulcan Hall?'

'Yes.'

'How well does your contact – this Howard Mitchell – know him?'

'He plays golf with Pyne on Sundays. Nothing more than that. Howard never used to make friends easily.'

Hendricks stood up. 'I want to see this Howard Mitchell. Call him up and have him come here . . . Like now, please.'

6

It was a woman's voice who answered the phone.

'May I speak to Mr Reagan, please?' said Simpson.

There was a pause, then the woman said: 'Who's that?'

'A friend ,' replied Simpson.

Another pause. 'I'm taking messages for Mrs Reagan,' said the woman. 'If you could tell me who you are . . .'

Her tone worried Simpson. 'I want to speak to Mr Reagan,' he interrupted, keeping his voice calm.

'Mr Reagan . . . He was killed last night in a road accident.' The last sentence came out with a rush.

Simpson placed his hand on the coin box. 'Really? How?' The shock in his voice was genuine.

'It's terrible,' said the woman. 'Mr Reagan was such a careful driver. Always so careful with everything he did. The truck driver said he came straight out of a side road . . .'

'Where did this happen?'

'Weybridge. None of us can think what he was doing there. His wife's in a dreadful state, poor soul . . .'

Simpson let the woman continue for some moments – his mind racing, as one improbable theory after another clamoured for attention.

'Can I say who it was?'

'No. It doesn't matter.' He replaced the handset and stared at the telephone for some seconds, considering his next move.

He called Directory Inquiries and asked for the telephone number of Weybridge police station. Two minutes later he was talking to the desk sergeant.

'I can give you no more information than we've released to the press,' the police officer told him. 'A Patrick Reagan was killed last night at the junction of Brooklands Road with St Georges Hill Road. I can give you the exact time if you hold on a minute . . .'

'Can you tell me which way he was heading at the time?' asked Simpson.

'He was turning out on to the Brooklands Road from St Georges Hill. His car was struck by a British Aerospace truck.'

'Thank you, officer,' said Simpson, and hung up.

He left the public telephone box looking uncharacteristically worried.

7

Keller was woken by the hot morning sun streaming into the control room. He had slept badly during his first night in charge at the power station. Several times he had woken suddenly and reached for the cellular phone in the belief that someone was approaching his camp bed but each time there had been no one.

He crossed to a control console and bent the gooseneck microphone stalk to his mouth. 'I would be most grateful if someone would kindly provide me with breakfast,' he announced with impeccable manners. He could hear his voice booming through distant corridors as a variety of loudspeakers reproduced his nasal accent with varying degrees of accuracy.

'Perhaps Miss Campion would oblige, please?' said the speakers in the staff rest-room where Pyne and Louise were eating a cold breakfast.

Louise looked up at a speaker and grimaced.

'He can get it himself,' she said.

Pyne carefully replaced his cup on the saucer and placed his hand over Louise's wrist. 'It might be a good idea, Louise. Especially if you could get him to eat it near one of the front windows.'

She looked down at the hand covering her hand, and up at the grey eyes. Pyne pulled his hand away.

'How would I do that, Conrad?'

Pyne looked faintly embarrassed. 'Well . . . feminine guile.'

Louise smiled. 'Have I got any, Conrad?'

Pyne avoided her gaze. 'Well, of course.'

'Perhaps I should practise on you first?'

Pyne began to wish he hadn't made the suggestion.

Louise said nothing. She crossed to a small counter and began cutting some corned-beef sandwiches.

'Perhaps we could poison him?' she said.

'We could.' agreed Pyne. 'But you'd have to cook something that could kill a man in one second flat.'

She looked up at Pyne, but the remark was made without humour. His hands were clasped together on the table. He was staring at the far wall with an expression of utter dejection. Several times during the night, when the three had discussed possible ways of overpowering Keller before he had a chance to use the cellular phone, she had wanted to comfort him – to tell him that he was not to blame for the unexpected turn of events. But his unresponsive facade and complete acceptance of responsibility deterred her from

152

making such an approach, Even Hugh Patterson had tried to persuade Pyne against an escape attempt by volunteering to shoot Keller, but Pyne had rejected the suggestion.

'All we've got is these Sterlings.' Pyne had said.

'I thought they were lethal.' said Louise Campion.

'Not lethal enough. The first round has got to kill him outright and you can't be a hundred per cent certain of that with a Sterling. They slay rounds all over the place. Okay in close combat but not much use for picking a man off with a hundred per cent certainty of killing him.' Pyne had paused. 'And we have to be a hundred per cent certain.'

The debate had dragged on all night. By 8:30 when Patterson left to check the IRIS detectors on the western perimeter, it was decided that Pyne's original plan, using a Sterling filled with blank cartridges, was the one that offered the only chance of success. Pyne had stressed the importance of someone escaping to warn the government of the changed situation in the power station in case they were planning a break-in.

Hugh Patterson entered the rest-room as Pyne was finishing his second cup of coffee. He perched his massive frame on a chair and looked in alarm at the sandwiches Louise Campion was preparing.

'They're not for me . . .?'

'They're for Keller,' said Pyne. 'He wants Louise to take him some breakfast. Have you checked the detectors along the river front?'

'No. I've come back for some batteries. I thought I smelt coffee.'

Pyne stood. 'It's time to put the plan into operation.' He picked up a Sterling and held it by the open frame towards Patterson. 'Come on. You can have your coffee later.'

Patterson looked first at the offered submarine-gun and then at Pyne. He shook his head slowly. 'Now?' he queried.

'We all agreed to move when the first opportunity presented itself. Louise will take his breakfast up and get him to eat it near the windows so he can watch you and me checking the detectors.'

Patterson took the weapon and examined it in concern. 'It's too dangerous, Conrad. Supposing it jams?'

Louise Campion finished preparing Keller's breakfast. She watched the two men, making no attempt to intervene.

Pyne shrugged. 'I've never pretended the idea was without risks. I'd rather take a chance that sit about doing nothing.'

'You must let me do it.'

'It was my idea,' Pyne replied firmly.

'And my fault Keller was included in our group.'

Pyne looked at his watch. 'We'd better synchronize. I make it 9:17.' He looked at Louise. 'Do you think you could get him to the windows by 9:30?'

Louise checked her watch.

'Yes.'

'That's settled then. Come on, Hugh.'

Patterson sighed and followed Pyne out of the room.

Louise Campion stopped outside the door leading to the control room and set Keller's breakfast tray down on the floor. In the stillness of the corridors she had heard the faint whirring of the heat-guided closed-circuit television cameras following her progress from the restroom. Now she was standing directly underneath a camera and, she hoped, out of its field of vision. Its lens was tilted towards the floor at the maximum angle the tilt head would permit. It was not the thought that Keller had been watching her that made her tremble, but what she had to do next.

Her fingers fumbled at her blouse until the top five buttons were unfastened.

She looked at her watch.

9:21.

She knocked loudly on the double doors leading to the control room, picked up the tray and pushed the doors open with her hip.

Keller was standing a few metres away holding his Sterling at a casual angle with the cellular phone hanging

154

from his wrist by a short strap. He smiled and came forward.

'Miss Campion. This is extremely kind of you. Let me take that for you.'

Louise moved towards the windows.

'Here?' she asked, watching Keller's eyes to see if they dropped to the unfastened blouse. They didn't.

He took the tray from her and sat at one of the consoles. 'It's much too hot to sit in the sun, don't you think?' he answered with his customary politeness as he sipped his coffee appreciatively. 'This is excellent, Miss Campion. I am most grateful.'

Louise pushed a strand of hair away from her face so she could look at her watch.

9:22.

She had eight minutes to get Keller over to the window.

8

At 9:22 Howard Mitchell dropped the hammer he had been using to nail pieces of timber across his broken window and raced into the living-room to answer the telephone. It stopped ringing just as he picked up the receiver. It started again as he was halfway up the stairs.

He answered it in his bedroom. 'Hello?'

He could hear breathing over the line.

'Mr Mitchell?' said a man's voice.

'Yes. Who is this?'

The line went dead.

Mitchell frowned to himself and replaced the handset. He went into the bathroom for a quick shower and shave before returning to Maggie with the keys to his boat.

The telephone rang for the third time as he was returning his electric razor to its case. As before, he took the call on his bedroom extension. It was his secretary, wondering why he had not put in an appearance at the office.

155

'It's nearly half past nine, Mr Mitchell,' she said reproachfully. 'You said yesterday you wanted to make an early start . . .'

Mitchell cut her short. He said he had changed his plans and wanted to spend the morning on his boat. Urgent calls could be referred to him via the boat's cellphone.

He drove away from the house a few minutes later with the boat keys digging into his hip.

Simpson walked thoughtfully away from the public telephone box. Obviously Reagan had failed in his mission. The Howard Mitchell problem would have to be shelved. If the CIA did find out about the power station . . . Well, it was a problem the Prime Minister could sort out.

9

'I suppose,' said Keller, finishing the first sandwich, 'that we'll have to eat the corned beef first because it has the shortest storage life?'

'I suppose so,' said Louise.

Six minutes.

Keller saw her look at her wrist. He smiled. 'I wonder what being cooped up in here will do to us?'

She realized that his eyes were fixed on her. It took a supreme effort of will-power to resist the automatic impulse to close the partly open blouse and so reveal her embarrassment. 'I don't know,' she replied.

Keller continued eating in silence.

'May I sit down?' she asked.

He looked surprised. 'I'm sorry. I should have said.' He waved his hand round the control room. 'I didn't think you would want to stay. Be my guest.'

Always perfect manners, she thought. It was hard to believe the man was unbalanced. But then, he had fooled everyone – even the shrewd Hugh Patterson. She wandered to the windows overlooking the river and sat down.

Five minutes.

Keller seemed to have lost interest now that she was some distance away. General Pyne and Patterson emerged at the far end of the apron to check the first of the IRIS detectors that guarded the power station's waterfront. Each one was mounted on an aluminium pedestal about two-metres high. The pedestal bases were weighted with a lead plate.

Louise pursed her lips and blew a stream of air up her face so that it ruffled her hair. 'Ye gods, it's hot.'

Keller started on the second sandwich.

'It certainly is,' he said noncommittally.

Four minutes.

She fanned herself with her hand, and pumped her blouse. She stretched her legs and repeated the gesture – enjoying the brief surges of air against her hot skin. She was careful to pull the material out far enough so that Keller would have a glimpse of her body. The behaviour was alien to her nature. It reminded her of her girlhood when she had discovered the sexual powers that girls could exercise over boys. She closed her eyes. Those days were now far away. There had been Clive when she was in her late teens. The halcyon days with him had ended and the memories had begun when he had misjudged an approach, and his Tornado jet fighter had become an incandescent ball of fire in some thick trees at Biggen Hill RAF base.

'Yes, indeed, Miss Campion. Very hot.' The refined, polite voice was immediately behind her.

She opened her eyes and turned slightly. Keller was standing over her staring down. His Sterling was drooping towards her pelvis. A feeling of nausea rose like a poisonous vine in her throat and blossomed into a smile. She glanced casually out of the window. Pyne and Patterson were checking the third detector. Patterson disguised a glance up at the window in a general survey of the power station.

'What are they doing?' asked Keller lightly.

'Checking the IRIS detectors, I suppose.'

'They checked them last night.'

157

'I think they have to be reset each day because of the heat.'

Three minutes.

Patterson paused to tie a shoelace while Pyne moved on ahead.

'Odd.' said Keller casually.

'General Pyne likes to be careful,' Louise replied, hoping her voice was calm.

'I wasn't thinking of that.'

Two minutes.

'You look frightened, Miss Campion.' The voice was flat with a disinterested tone. He rested his hand gently on her shoulders so that his fingers were resting near the top of her arm.

She tried not to shiver, and dared not look up to see if he was looking at her or at the two men below. The sun was glinting on her watch face making it impossible to read the time. She tilted her head slightly towards Keller's hand.

One minute.

The movement was a mistake; Keller thought it was one of affection. His fingers tensed and moved down to the start of the soft skin below her collarbone.

Patterson straightened from tying his shoelace. Pyne was thirty metres from him, walking along the top of the concrete-capped pilings and the water five metres below.

Thirty seconds.

She was certain Keller must be aware of her increased pulse rate beneath his fingertips.

'Can you remember the type of shoes Patterson wears?' said Keller. His voice was soft and gentle, but his nails were now sinking into her flesh like the claws of a mechanical grab.

Twenty seconds.

Pyne was looking down at the water, waiting for Patterson to catch up with him.

'I've worked for him for five years now,' said Keller. 'He wears nothing but expensive elastic-sided shoes.'

She risked a quick glance up at Keller. He was no longer interested in her but watching the two men intently. He suddenly released his grip on her shoulder, swung his Sterling up by the webbing strap and grasped the magazine. For a wild moment, as his attention was fixed on the scene below, she considered trying to snatch the weapon from him. There was a metallic click as his finger released the crude safety-catch.

Then Pyne was running as Keller stepped nearer the window.

'Stop!' screamed Patterson, his alarmed yell carrying plainly into the control room. 'For Christ's sake, Pyne! Stop, you bloody idiot!'

But Pyne didn't stop. He raced along the pilings with Patterson running after him. Patterson stopped chasing Pyne and raised his submachine-gun. His next shout was drowned by the sound of breaking glass as Keller slammed the open frame of his Sterling against the control room window.

'Stop him!' Keller screamed at Patterson through the jagged hole. 'I can't do it at this range!'

Patterson looked quickly up at the broken window and took careful aim at Pyne. He fired a long burst which used two-thirds of the ammunition in the magazine. The impact seemed to spin Pyne round; he teetered on the edge of the pilings before falling out of sight to the water. Patterson ran to the edge and poured a stream of fire into the river.

Two minutes later Keller stood panting beside him at the water's edge.

'Where is he?' demanded Keller, squinting at the dazzling sunlight reflected off the water.

Patterson shaded his eyes and pointed downstream towards the low sun. Keller could just distinguish a shapeless form drifting past the edge of the pilings.

He raised his submachine-gun.

'That's not necessary,' said Patterson sharply. 'He's dead.'

Keller ignored him. He fired a single shot. The water spat near Pyne's body. The recoil jerked the suspended cellular phone strapped to his wrist, but he was unable to see clearly the miniature plumes that spluttered round the floating shape.

Keller lowered the smoking Sterling and turned to Patterson at his side, who seemed too paralysed to move or speak.

'You've employed me long enough, Mr Patterson, to know that I always like to be certain. Just as you like to be sure you're not walking about with loose shoelaces.'

Patterson said nothing. He turned on his heel and walked towards the main entrance, where Louise Campion was staring at the two men in horror. As he walked towards her he half-expected Keller to shoot him in the back. He stopped and looked back at Keller. The nuclear physicist was shading his eyes and staring across the bright water at the lifeless form drifting towards the sea.

It was then that Patterson decide that somehow he would kill Keller before nightfall.

10

'What does your father's boat look like?' asked Mitchell as he inserted the key to start his Chris Craft's diesels.

Maggie surveyed the rows of boats at their moorings.

'Like that one over there. A Freeman.' She pointed to a smart blue and white fibreglass cruiser. 'Except ours has a white hull and a pale-green cabin.'

Mitchell nodded and pressed the starter buttons in turn. He grinned at a boat owner sitting in a nearby cramped cockpit and called out to Maggie:

'Okay. Untie up front.'

He liked to use non-nautical expressions just to irritate the pretentious yachtsmen, some of whom even wore peaked caps to sail pram dinghies.

The two engine temperature gauges were nearing the normal mark as the big cruiser slipped through the marina gates and out on to the Thames.

Mitchell settled into the comfortable helmsman's seat on the flying bridge, while below in the wheelhouse, the stainless-steel wheel and Morse engine-control levers appeared to move of their own accord – as if a ghost were at the helm.

Maggie joined Mitchell and perched on the navigator's seat beside him.

'Do you like boating?' he asked, to make conversation.

'Yes.' Her answer was flat.

Mitchell looked sideways at her. Her face was still lined with the tension of the previous night's ordeal. There was an ugly red mark across her cheek where Garnet had hit her. She had made no reference to the attack during the short drive to the marina.

'How are you feeling now?' It was a stupid thing to say. Why was he always so nervous with women? Why wasn't he able to bubble over with witty remarks that would make her laugh and help her forget?

'Better,' Maggie answered.

'Would it help if you talked about it?'

'No.' Then: 'Can I navigate for a bit?'

The question provided an opening which he seized. 'Do you really think we can get lost on this river?'

Maggie's laugh was immediate and gratifying. 'Idiot. I mean steer it.'

'Sure.' He relinquished his seat and stood behind her. He noticed that she didn't over-correct the steering, as most people do when handling a boat for the first time.

'You've done this before?' he remarked.

Maggie nodded. 'When mother was alive we'd all go on weekend fishing trips to Windsor.'

'With your father?'

'Yes. Always. We were a close-knit family. He always found the time.'

'But not any more?'

'He's been too busy lately.'

They passed a Thames Division motor launch riding at its moorings outside the river police station. An overweight policeman was sunning himself on the bank.

The Thames widened and bisected itself against a tongue of land. The left fork led to Shepperton Manor, the right fork was the Desborough Cut.

'Which way?' asked Mitchell.

Maggie considered for a moment. 'We'll go downriver first, and then come back up the cut. That way we won't waste too much fuel.'

'I'm not worried about that. But supposing he's gone further downriver?'

Maggie swung the helm gently to port before replying. 'He wouldn't get through Molesey Lock. The registration plate is out of date. We hadn't bothered to renew it.'

'Maggie, look. There's a police station back there. Don't you think it would be better to let them deal with him?'

'No, Mitch. Not until I find out if he's blackmailing my father.'

She looked determined. Mitchell decided not to argue.

The muted splutter of the water-cooled exhausts and the subdued mutter of the twin diesels steadily easing the long white hull through the water were not enough to disturb the wildlife thronging the wooded banks and small inlets choked with reeds.

Mitchell had journeyed along this stretch frequently – the first time was shortly after his arrival in England. It was that trip, and the discovery of the tranquil magic of the river, that had prompted him to import the Chris Craft when his business prospered. His great regret was that the increased demands of the business did not allow him to make more use of the boat. The business had also prevented him from making friends. The large house on St Georges Hill had been a mistake: with the exception of General Pyne, the neighbours had not been particularly friendly. And as Mitchell now realized, even Pyne's friendship, slight though it was, had been cultivated only because Pyne was keen to learn about the North Sea oil business. Mitchell suddenly realized as he stood beside Maggie that apart from his secretary, who was wrapped up with her own husband and family, Maggie was the first woman he had become involved with since leaving New York. Perhaps if he had worked and lived in London he would have met more people socially. But after a childhood spent on the Lower East Side he had resolved never to live in a city again.

'Would you like something to drink?' asked Mitchell.

'At this time?'

He smiled. 'Okay. How about a Coke?'

'Something stronger might wake me up. Mitch, I'm sorry I'm being so untalkative.'

'It's a virtue,' said Mitchell, and went down the companionway into the well-equipped galley. He was poking at the ice-cube tray welded into the refrigerator when the engines slowed. At first he thought something had fouled the screws. Then the refrigerator door swung shut as the boat gently heeled.

'Look,' said Maggie when he returned to the bridge. She pointed to the reed-encrusted bank where the roof of a cabin cruiser was visible above the tall fronds.

Mitchell placed his palm over Maggie's hand holding the spoked helm. She withdrew it as though she had been stung.

'I'm sorry,' said Mitchell. 'I was steadying her.'

'It's not your fault,' said Maggie shakily.

'Can you manage?'

'Yes.'

The transom of the smaller boat came into view as Maggie nosed the Chris Craft towards the reeds. Corporal Garnet was dozing in the cockpit. A fishing rod had slipped from his fingers. He did not stir at the sound of approaching diesels – it was the shadow falling across his face that woke him. He opened his eyes and looked up at the towering flying bridge, blinking in surprise, and then in alarm when

163

he saw Maggie at the controls. He stood up just as she sent the big cruiser surging forward with a sudden burst of power that jammed its bows into the reeds, cutting off the smaller boat's escape route.

Garnet considered jumping overboard. He had one leg over the coaming when Mitchell appeared in the Chris Craft's lower cockpit.

'I shouldn't,' said Mitchell, menacingly. 'It's about three metres deep here.'

Garnet hesitated. He felt the general's daughter's eyes on him.

'What do you want?'

'A word with you.'

'Fuck off. You're blocking my view.' Garnet tried to cover his fear with belligerence.

Mitchell stepped on to the Freeman's transom. The sudden motion caused Garnet to lose his balance. Mitchell hit him as he jumped into the cockpit.

The exhaust pipes were the first thing Garnet became aware of when he regained consciousness. His legs were splayed wide apart and crooked over the pipes with his ankles drawn painfully together by a length of rope passed under the exhausts.

The Chris Craft's fully soundproofed engine-room was a readymade torture chamber.

He cautiously opened his eyes. The engine-room was illuminated by a single lamp enclosed in a wire cage. Mitchell was standing over him. Garnet closed his eyes and braced himself for a kick in the testicles.

'You'd better answer a few questions,' snarled the American.

Garnet mouthed a profanity, but the outward display of bravado was diminished by the beads of sweat that appeared on his forehead. He tried to pull himself into a sitting position, and grimaced as the pipes dug into the back of his knees.

'Why did you do it?' demanded Mitchell.

'Do what?'

Mitchell gritted his teeth and hit Garnet. The corporal's insolent expression eased the surprisingly difficult task of hitting a bound man.

'She encouraged me.' Garnet spat.

Mitchell hit him again. It was easier the second time.

'That's not what she says.'

'Then it's my word against hers. For fuck's sake, why am I tied up like this?'

'You'll find out soon enough if you don't answer my questions.'

'Look,' said Garnet. 'Do you know her? She's nothing but a cock-teasing little bitch.' He paused and glanced round the engine-room crammed with expensive machinery. 'I don't suppose she treats you like she used to treat me.'

'How did she treat you?' asked Mitchell, this time resisting the impulse to hit Garnet.

'Like dirt.'

'Maybe there's a good reason for that.'

The sweat trickled down Garnet's face. 'At first I thought it was because I was only a bloody corporal – not her class, but it wasn't that.'

'What was it then?'

Garnet told Mitchell about the Tuesday afternoon in Belfast – about the joyrider's car that had backfired and how General Pyne had stepped in when he heard Garnet had been trained on Scout helicopters.

'You're fond of General Pyne?' asked Mitchell when Garnet had finished.

'He helped me when I needed help. If you can call having to wait on his daughter hand and foot being helped.'

'If you're fond of General Pyne, why are you blackmailing him?'

Garnet stared at Mitchell. 'Don't talk crap. What the fuck are you talking about?'

The third blow jerked Garnet's head back and tore the skin on Mitchell's knuckles.

'For Christ's sake!' Garnet pleaded. 'I don't know what you're talking about!'

The two men glared at one another in the dim light.

'Where's the general now?'

'I don't know,' said Garnet. Blood was trickling from the corner of his mouth.

Mitchell looked at his own bleeding hand. He straightened and lifted an intercom microphone off its hook.

'Okay, Maggie. Start them up. In neutral. Nice and slow.'

As he returned the microphone to its hook there was a loud hiss of compressed air followed by a harsh, metallic grating noise that resonated painfully against the eardrums in the confined space.

The port diesel engine rumbled into life and trembled on its mountings. The noise was repeated until the starboard engine was turning fast enough to run under its own power. The diesels settled down to a regular beat.

The pipes pressed against the inside of Garnet's legs began to get warm. His expression changed from arrogant defiance to fear.

Mitchell forced a smile. There was a difference between hitting a man and what he was about to do now.

'The exhausts are water-cooled so they don't get very hot,' said Mitchell, raising his voice against the reverberating rhythm of the two heavy diesels, 'provided this is turned on.' He pointed to a handwheel. 'But if I was to turn the water off, even slightly, like this . . .' He rotated the handwheel a turn.

Garnet felt the pipes getting warmer. He wondered if the American was bluffing. Mitchell's hard expression was not reassuring.

'Why do you care about the general?'

'His daughter wants to know.'

Garnet was about to risk a grin, when the American turned the handwheel slightly. He felt the temperature increase immediately from the hot gases streaming through the two pipes.

'So why are you blackmailing him and where is he?'

'He told me to say nothing,' Garnet choked out.

Mitchell turned the handwheel a few more degrees. He didn't enjoy what he was doing but the bastard deserved it.

'When did you last see him?'

'I promised to say nothing.'

Garnet sucked in his breath as the pain bit into his tendons.

'Why did he make you promise?'

The handwheel was turned a little more; not much but enough to make Garnet feel that his legs were being amputated at the knees by the searing heat.

'I don't know, for fuck's sake!' he screamed. He tried to arch his back off the engine-room floor, but the tension only pressed his calf muscles harder against the burning pipes.

Mitchell looked at the writhing corporal in concern. He had dropped back on the deck and was twisting his body first one way, then the other, in a fruitless effort to relieve the agony tearing at his legs. Low moans of pain mixed with obscenities escaped from his lips.

Mitchell decided to give up. He was about to restore the cold water when Garnet said:

'All right. Fucking well untie me, and I'll tell you what I know.'

Fifteen minutes later Mitchell dumped Garnet back in the Freeman's cockpit.

'Stay away from St Georges Hill and Maggie, otherwise I'll do a helluva lot worse,' he warned.

'The general said I was to look after his house,' said Garnet sulkily.

'Don't argue with me. Just do as I say!'

Garnet glanced up at Maggie Pyne's cold eyes staring down at him from the flying bridge. He nodded.

Mitchell waved to Maggie to go astern as he stepped over the coaming and back into the cockpit. The screws churned white water under the Chris Craft's hull as they hauled the big cruiser out of the reeds. Maggie swung into midstream and pushed the control levers forward.

'What did he say?' she asked when Mitchell rejoined her.

He related Garnet's scant story about Pyne's Sunday-morning drive to Downing Street. 'He said your father handed a letter to the police officer outside Number Ten. Maybe he's resigned or something,' Mitchell concluded.

Maggie looked puzzled. 'Even if he had, he wouldn't hand it in to the Prime Minister.' She frowned. 'Although, he did once know him.'

Mitchell looked at her in surprise. 'Your father knows the Prime Minister?'

'He used to. I don't think he's got much time for politicians now.' She turned to Mitchell. 'Is that little bastard blackmailing my father?'

'No.'

'You believed him?'

'Yes.' Mitchell paused. 'Maggie, what could your father be doing to be blackmailed?'

She turned her attention back to the river. 'Nothing.'

Her tone aroused Mitchell's suspicions. 'Look, Maggie. If you think Garnet hasn't told me everything, then we'll turn back and-'

'No!' said Maggie sharply.

'Then why–'

'Mitch, if I tell you something, will you swear never to repeat it?'

Mitchell stared at the bruised face turned earnestly towards him.

'Well, sure–'

Maggie paused while she marshalled her thoughts. 'I think daddy's involved with some sort of fraud over government equipment with Hugh Patterson.'

Mitchell looked at her with astonishment. 'Your father? But that's not possible.'

168

'That's what I would've thought. But he's being seeing a lot of Hugh Patterson lately, and I once overheard Hugh mention something about military supplies when I took them a cup of tea in the garden. If something is going on, that corporal could've found out easily.'

Mitchell was silent for a few moments. 'And you really think your father is doing something like that?'

'I don't want to think it,' Maggie replied angrily. 'All I know is that Daddy's been acting differently lately.'

Mitchell shook his head. 'Garnet would've told me. And besides, he respects your father.' He hesitated. 'You're the one he hates Maggie. He said you used to treat him badly.'

Maggie's face went pale with anger. 'He killed a woman. If it hadn't been for my father the ungrateful little bastard would still be in prison.'

Mitchell was unable to think of an immediate reply. He wondered what Maggie knew about service life – real service life, not hunt balls and parties in the officers' mess. Mitchell felt a twinge of sympathy for Corporal Garnet; he had reacted to a car backfiring as he had been trained to. The memory would be with him for the rest of his life.

'Did you hurt him?' Maggie asked.

'Did you want me to hurt him?'

'What do you think?'

'He was drunk,' said Mitchell.

'That makes it all right, does it?'

He was about to reply when the telephone in the wheelhouse emitted a shrill buzz.

It was his secretary. Paul Weiner wanted to see him in London as soon as possible.

'Okay,' he said. 'We're just coming into Walton. Come and pick me up at the Eastwood Marina in ten minutes.'

He explained the situation to Maggie.

'I could take the boat back to Weybridge for you,' she offered.

Mitchell hesitated at leaving his precious boat in the girl's hands. She correctly interpreted his doubtful expression.

'Oh come on, Mitch. I brought it here. You know I can handle it.'

He smiled. 'Sure, better than I can.' He gave her the keys to his Mustang. 'You'll need some transport when you get back to Weybridge.'

'What time will you be back?'

'I'm not sure. Paul's an old schoolfriend.'

'Ring me before you leave London, and I'll try to cook you some supper.' Maggie looked down to avoid his surprised look.

'Thank you. I'd appreciate that.'

Maggie smiled – for the first time that day.

She dropped Mitchell on the towpath at Eastwoods and swung the Chris Craft back upstream, enjoying the sensation of sitting in the sun, controlling a magnificent cruiser on the river she loved, where her father had taken her to feed the Queen's swans when she was a child.

Then she thought of Corporal Garnet also enjoying the river – sitting in her father's boat, fishing with her father's rod. She wondered if Mitchell had hurt him. No, she couldn't imagine it. Mitchell was too kind. It hadn't been him having to stare up at that scar . . .

Five minutes later she came to the island that divided the Thames from the river. She didn't take the Chris Craft up the Desborough Cut but followed the original course of the river towards her father's cabin cruiser.

11

Pyne's immediate concern when he hit the surface was to avoid swallowing the heavily polluted water. The second worry was whether he could swim far enough under water to be out of range of submachine-gun fire if Keller decided to rush out on to the apron. Before his fake fall he had breathed deeply for some minutes so that his bloodstream would be saturated with oxygen, to enable him to remain submerged for as long as possible. The plans he had discussed the night before with Hugh Patterson and Louise Campion – the long underwater swim, the face-downwards drift when he surfaced – began to evaporate as he fought to remain conscious against the numbing shock of the cold water. Luckily the impact had not forced the air out of his lungs as he had feared it might. As he went under he managed a few feeble strokes with no certainty that he was moving in the right direction – he could be swimming against the current and so remaining stationary. Then his brain, with its own indifferent survival instinct, drained his blood of oxygen and clamoured for more. After only thirty seconds beneath the surface he was fighting his way upwards.

As he rolled over he was horrified to see how close he still was to the pilings. He thought he saw Patterson emptying his Sterling into the water. Pyne sucked down one deep breath and allowed himself to drift. He kept his feet low in the water and kicked them in an attempt to move faster than the current.

Another deep breath.

He turned slightly. The pilings had disappeared. He was moving faster than he expected – he was as one with the great mass of water surging towards the estuary.

He felt rather than heard the whack of a bullet striking the water. There was no way of judging how far away it was.

There was no doubt about the next one: it raised a spurt of water a yard from his head. Then he was surrounded by shots smacking into the water. Each one sounded like a thin cane being struck on the surface. He blew the precious air out of his lungs and allowed himself to sink.

There were no more shots.

Pyne surfaced, gulped down air and continued to drift. It was ten minutes before he risked looking back at the power station. He was two hundred metres downstream. The apron, from this angle, was deserted.

And so was the four-kilometre wide expanse of the Thames.

There was a bright orange marker buoy at least four hundred metres downstream and near the far bank. The current was drawing him into midstream. If he could reach the buoy, it would be some thing to hang on to until he was spotted by a passing ship.

He swam with a slow breaststroke — a style he found difficult enough in the ideal conditions of his swimming pool. He dared not risk the faster crawl in case Keller was watching through binoculars. The glare off the water had been one factor in favour of this method of escape, but he couldn't take chances.

He stopped swimming and trod water. The power station was dwindling rapidly now that he was being carried along by the swifter midstream current.

He didn't hear or see the tug hauling a line of refuse barges until it was only thirty metres away and bearing down on him. He stared in bewilderment at the massive coir fender wrapped round the tug's snub bow, and then saved his life by panicking. He struck out for the far south bank just as the tug's bow wave shouldered him aside. He managed to push himself away from the hull as it swept past. Fortunately there was sufficient towline between the tug and the first barge to give Pyne a chance to get clear of the rapidly approaching slab-sided hull. The rusting steel plates tore the skin from his hands as he fought to fend his body away sufficiently to avoid the second barge. He was well out of danger by the time the third barge was passing him. The eddying backwash swept him into the wake behind the last barge. Something caught against his arms and then snaked past his body. It was a long length of mooring rope trailing in the water behind the last barge. He felt it coiling round his ankle. The jerk as the rope tightened would have dislocated his leg had he not grasped it in his lacerated hands to absorb the shock. He held on grimly. The torrent raging against his chest threatened to break his hold. He had to hang on at all costs and drag himself along the rope until his body was clear of the water.

It was that or drown.

By a supreme effort he managed to haul himself four metres along the rope. He tried to rest by wrapping the rope round his body, but it kept pulling straight in the wash from the barge.

Pyne's arms were aching from the strain of hanging on in the boiling wake. He remembered the trick PT instructors had taught him when he was a cadet: he gripped the rope between his instep and ankle, and pushed with his leg muscles.

A few minutes later he was under the barge's raked stern with the rope hanging straight down under his weight. He began to lift his body clear of the water. The rope was dry a metre above the surface; red stains showed where his hands had gripped it.

The motion of the barge swung him from side to side — increasing the load his wrists had to bear. He swung his legs over the remains of a rusting iron pintle projecting from the stern and reached up to grab a bollard before thankfully releasing the rope.

He rested for a few minutes, then carefully balanced on the pintle. As he straightened his head cleared the top of the barge coamings. He could see the other three barges obediently following the tug line astern. Almost fainting with fatigue, he pulled himself on to the narrow side deck. The stench of decaying refuse from the open hold was the most beautiful smell he had ever encountered.

He tried to stand when a sudden heavy wave caused him to overbalance.

It was only a two-metre fall to the refuse hold, but he struck his head on the side of a bottle and lay still. A steady avalanche of wrapping paper, plastic egg boxes and vegetable waste slithered down causing a depression caused by his fall and covered his body.

The crew of the tug were unaware that one of their refuse barges was carrying a passenger.

In five hours they would be in Dover, where a Dutch floating plant would deal with their cargo. Huge vacuum pipes would be lowered into the barge holds and would suck them bare in a matter of minutes. The refuse would be conveyed to hydraulic crushers for compressing into neat one-metre cubes which would end up as back-fill for a Dutch dyke.

12

Paul Weiner introduced Hendricks to Mitchell in his office at the American Embassy as 'my boss'. Hendricks was sitting in Weiner's chair. He waved a gnarled hand at an empty seat.

'Sit down, Mr Mitchell. I'm sorry to have kept you waiting.' He studied Mitchell like a vulture contemplating a piece of meat, and – not being a man to waste time on table manners – got straight to the point. 'Tell me about General Pyne.'

The question surprised Mitchell. 'What about my drill-string?'

'What about it?' inquired Hendricks.

Mitchell glanced at Weiner and then back at Hendricks. 'Isn't that what you dragged me up here for?'

'I daresay it will be possible to see that you're fully compensated for the loss of your equipment, Mr Mitchell,' said Hendricks carefully. 'Provided you tell us what you know about this man Pyne.'

Maggie's right, thought Mitchell. Her father is in trouble. He tried steering Hendricks away from the subject. 'Do you have any idea how much a drill-string is worth?'

'No.' said Hendricks, 'but I expect–'

'More than a million dollars.'

Hendricks nodded. 'Tell me about Pyne.'

Mitchell told him what he knew, but said nothing about Maggie's fears and Corporal Garnet's attack. It was his account of Pyne entrusting his property to Garnet that convinced Hendricks that his theory might be correct.

Hendricks listened carefully, making frequent notes, and produced the photograph of the group standing before a JetRanger helicopter. Mitchell looked at the print in surprise.

'How did you get hold of this?'

Weiner opened his mouth, but Hendricks waved him into silence. 'Do you recognize any of those people?' inquired Hendricks, in an icy tone that discouraged Mitchell from pressing his question.

'No,' said Mitchell, 'But, Mag– General Pyne's daughter showed me an identical picture the day before yesterday. She said the chopper belonged to Hugh Patterson.'

'What about the woman?' asked Hendricks, noting that Mitchell had nearly said, 'Maggie' when referring to Pyne's daughter.

'Louise Campion. A neighbour, and a friend of Pyne's family.'

Hendricks nodded, and turned the picture towards himself. 'And the man is called Keller?'

'Yes. I think that was the name.'

'First name?'

'I don't know.'

Hendricks stroked his nose with a bony forefinger.

'What's all this about?' asked Mitchell.

Hendricks watched Mitchell's fingers on the arm of his chair. 'Mr Mitchell, we would like you to maintain your liaison with General Pyne's daughter, and use it to obtain all the information you can from her about him.' The involuntary movement of Mitchell's fingers confirmed Hendricks' suspicions. 'We're prepared to pay for your drill-string, so you can't complain that we're being ungenerous.' He sat back and smiled frostily at the man sitting opposite him. If

175

he was any judge of character, there would be a reaction now. It came immediately.

'What liaison?' snapped Mitchell.

Hendricks sighed. 'Mr Mitchell, it would be the easiest thing in the world for us to ship you back to the United States, if we so wished. A word in the right ears and the British could withdraw your work permit. I believe you would find it most difficult running your business here from the other side of the Atlantic.' He paused. 'Naturally, I'm confident that we won't have to resort to such measures.'

Mitchell looked at the cold, sunken eyes, and decided that Hendricks, whoever he was, was not bluffing. Also, the promise to cover the lost drill-string would lift a major financial burden.

'Okay then.'

Hendricks stood up. He held out his hand. 'Thank you, Mr Mitchell. You will of course contact Mr Weiner if you have any news.'

Mitchell was at the doorway when Hendricks said, 'Just one more thing, Mr Mitchell. Do you know if Pyne was the sort of man to have strong views on the mess this country is in and how to put it right?'

'Yes,' said Mitchell after a pause. 'His daughter said he often discussed economic affairs with Hugh Patterson.'

Hendricks nodded. 'Not a word to anyone about this meeting, please, Mr Mitchell.'

As Mitchell unlocked his office car he remembered his promise to call Maggie before leaving London. He was about to punch the last digit of her number on his car phone when he suddenly wondered what the hell it was all about, and what he was letting himself in for.

Then the sound of her voice made him forget.

Hendricks picked up the photograph.

'So he's changed his name to Keller?'

Weiner nodded. 'It was the name he used at Oak Ridge.'

176

Hendricks pressed the intercom key.

'I want to speak to the Secretary of State. Tell them it's extremely urgent.'

'Should we tell the ambassador?' asked Weiner.

'I expect so,' replied Hendricks.

13

Police Sergeant Harry Snowdon of Thames Division was resting his fourteen and a half stone — two of them surplus — on the grassy river bank outside his headquarters, having exerted himself for thirty minutes trying to clear the patrol boat's blocked fuel injector.

It was peaceful on the river. On the opposite bank, the Weybridge side, a number of anglers were illegally fishing from the public mooring. Thames by-laws were the province of the water authority, so Harry Snowdon was content to let them continue. A few metres from his large feet the disabled patrol boat rocked gently against the slippery jetty. To his left a weeping willow lazily dipped long tendrils into the water.

It was a perfect afternoon; too hot for messing about in boats.

A cruiser gracefully entered his view. Snowdon recognized it as the Chris Craft owned by the American who lived on St Georges Hill. He watched the boat enviously. In his twenty years with the river police he had learned to judge countries by the luxury cruisers they built. The Americans were high in his estimation, with the Dutch a close second.

There was something familiar about the girl at the controls on the flying bridge. Then he recognized her: General Pyne's daughter. Alone.

Harry Snowdon climbed to his feet and ambled into the headquarters building.

'General Pyne's daughter is out with that big American job from Weybridge Marina,' he announced.

'That's right,' said the duty sergeant, not looking up from his newspaper, 'I saw it go off this morning.'

'With the American?'

'Yes.'

'Doesn't look like he's on board now.'

The duty sergeant stood and looked out of the window over Harry Snowdon's shoulder. Then his face went white.

'Christ!' he yelled, throwing the newspaper on the floor. 'Look!'

Both men dashed out into the sun just as the Chris Craft grazed into the side of the moored patrol boat.

'My boat,' moaned Harry Snowdon.

Maggie cut both engines and leaned over the side of the flying bridge. Harry Snowdon clambered into the patrol boat and fended the cruiser away with a boathook.

'I'm sorry,' said Maggie. 'I'm not used to this boat.'

Harry Snowdon mopped his brow in relief while the duty sergeant made the cruiser secure.

'What can we do for you, miss?' asked Harry Snowdon, looking up at the flying bridge and noticing the bruises on the girl's face.

'I want to report an assault,' said Maggie quietly.

In Harry Snowdon's vocabulary, the journey in the Chris Craft to where the girl said Corporal Garnet could be found was 'hairy'.

The girl had said little during the first ten minutes, then she had turned in her seat and said, 'Would you like a drink?'

Harry Snowdon eyed the approaching bank, and wondered why river users didn't have to take a test like road users.

'You'd better straighten up, miss,' he said politely, noticing that the girl's hand resting on the controls was trembling.

She was suffering from delayed shock. Now that Mitchell had gone, she was unable to ward it off any longer. She didn't want the policeman watching her.

'If you'd like a drink, you're welcome to go below and see what there is,' she told Harry Snowdon.

'I think I'd better stay up here, miss,' said Harry Snowdon.

'There're several tins in the fridge,' said Maggie, grasping the helm tightly to stop the shaking. 'I'd like one if you wouldn't mind, please.'

Harry Snowdon looked at her pale, drawn face. He moved to the companionway.

'Thank you very much, miss.'

The roof of the Freeman cabin cruiser came in sight a hundred metres away. Maggie suddenly wanted to be sick.

'Sergeant,' she called out, 'he's over on the left.'

Harry Snowdon shut the refrigerator door. 'All right, miss,' he shouted up to the flying bridge. 'You take her in alongside, and I'll talk to him.' He slid the wheelhouse door open and stood watching the Freeman. He corrected the girl's approach slightly by touching the duplicate helm. The wheel suddenly jerked beneath his fingers and the boat heeled. Harry Snowdon nearly lost his balance.

'Sorry,' Maggie called down. 'Are you all right?'

'Yes, miss,' was the sorrowful reply.

From her position Maggie could see Garnet dozing in the cockpit. She pressed the horn button. The twin-tone blast woke the corporal. He stared up at the Chris Craft in fear.

'You stay just where you are until I come aboard,' commanded Harry Snowdon across the narrowing strip of water between the two boats.

Garnet's terrified eyes went to the uniformed police sergeant and back to Maggie, who was throttling back.

She leaned back and tossed the stern line to Garnet. He was too surprised to react – the rope fell into the water.

'Let me do it,' offered Harry Snowdon, calling up the companionway.

'It's okay,' said Maggie, coiling the line and tossing it again. The rope fell short as the cruiser drifted. Garnet lunged at the flailing end. His hands suddenly lashed out to grab at the coaming to regain his balance, when his foot slipped on the edge of the Freeman's smooth fibre glass transom. He let out a yell as he fell into the deep water.

For the rest of her life, Maggie was to wonder what really happened during the next few minutes.

'Pull her over!' yelled the sergeant's voice from below, as he dashed along the side deck, looking for a line to throw to the man struggling in the water.

Harry Snowdon suddenly remembered seeing the ropes coiled on the flying bridge. As he shouted, the Chris Craft's hundred-horsepower diesels erupted with a roar of unleashed energy. He dived back into the wheelhouse and saw from the positions of the two Morse levers that the girl had thrown one engine into forward gear and the other one astern.

The big cruiser's stern was swinging towards Garnet, who was screaming that he couldn't swim.

'What shall I do?' Harry Snowdon heard the girl cry out.

He grabbed the two levers and tried to reverse their positions.

As the Chris Craft's stern swung towards him Garnet grasped the mahogany rubbing strake protecting the hull where it joined the transom, His feet encountered one of the under-hull brackets that supported the balanced rudders. He braced his weight against it in relief and stretched an arm out to the swimmers' boarding ladder attached to the big cruiser's transom. The enraged water from the madly spinning propellers boiled past his body, threatening to dislodge him. He was only dimly aware of the girl screaming at the top of her voice.

'Let go of the controls!' shouted Harry Snowdon, but his voice was drowned by the girl's hysterical sobbing as she wrestled with her pair of Morse levers.

'There's something wrong with the controls!' he heard her yell.

For a wild moment Harry Snowdon was undecided whether to climb on to the flying bridge and pull the girl away from the helm, or try to gain control in the wheelhouse. He decided to stay in the wheelhouse – he was stronger than the girl. He hauled with all his strength on the port throttle lever and managed to drag it back to the neutral position.

The roar of one diesel died away.

By now the Chris Craft had rammed its bows into the reeds and was unable to move forward. Harry Snowdon released the lever. It suddenly slammed to the full astern position. The Chris Craft heeled violently as the engine twisted the hull savagely out of the reeds.

The unexpected motion caused the policeman to lose his balance. He reached out to grab at something, and snatched the starboard lever back.

The Chris Craft seemed to leap astern out of the water. Garnet nearly lost his grip on the boarding ladder. His feet slipped off the rudder bracket, and the wash from the Chris Craft, surging hard astern, swept his legs under the hull.

The bronze three-bladed port screw sliced into flesh, bone and marrow, severing his right leg cleanly from his body just above the knee, and flung the limb aside. His unbalanced body slipped sideways from the boarding ladder and was sucked under the hull. The starboard propeller reaped through his torso.

Starting at his groin, it smashed his pelvis, hacked through his spine in several places and scythed his kidneys, liver, heart and lungs to shreds of pulverized tissue.

The spinning remains of his body thundered against the underside of the hull before being snatched back by the port propeller. It continued its work by threshing his arms and skull to pulp. For an encore, it wound several metres of intestines round its shaft.

A marauding pike, undeterred by the presence of the Chris Craft's hull, snapped up drifting threads of spinal cord.

Sergeant Harry Snowdon and Maggie were taken to a local hospital suffering from shock. Despite a heavy sedative, Harry Snowdon kept repeating that it was all his fault.

Three hours after being admitted, Maggie refused all offers of further help. She made a brief statement to the police and was allowed to return home.

She sat by the telephone waiting for Mitch to call. She shivered occasionally despite the heat.

14

Pyne knew exactly where he was the moment he regained consciousness; the smell of rotting garbage was immediate and overpowering.

He pushed himself into a sitting position. Cans and bottles cascaded from him. He groaned and cradled his aching head in his hands. There was a strange roaring noise that seemed to be getting louder. He looked up at the puzzling shadow snaking about in the darkening sky. The strange shape was twisting and pulsing. He could see the open struts of a crane jib high above him. The refuse was moving beneath him. Suddenly he was sliding deeper into the garbage. Then he realized what the noise was – the shape hanging from the sky and burying itself in the barge's hold was a giant vacuum pipe; the roaring noise was caused by refuse thundering into the pipe's metre-diameter opening.

One of the crewmen, perched on the edge of the hold with a shotgun at the ready to shoot rats, thought he saw a movement in the refuse at the far end of the barge.

He peered into the gloom and raised his gun.

Pyne desperately embraced the massive flexible pipe near its consuming maw and cried out as a frenzied stream of broken bottles and jagged cans hurled into the pipe and swept his feet from under him.

The crewman heard the cry and ran down the barge's side deck. He saw a man clinging to the rim of the pipe. One leg had been sucked into the opening. The man was on the verge of losing his grip.

The crewman frantically waved his arms three times to the jib operator – the signal to cut power. The distant howl from the gas turbine which powered the vacuum pump died away.

The man jumped down into the garbage, and went to Pyne's aid.

15

Simpson's phone rang at 20:35.

He listened to the Permanent Under-Secretary with an impassive expression which he allowed to change to one of surprise because no one was in the room with him.

'Surely he gave some indication?' he said when the civil servant had finished speaking.

Simpson pressed his lips together as he listened to the reply.

'Very well,' he said. 'I'll see if he's free.'

Simpson knocked on the Prime Minister's door and entered without waiting for an invitation.

'I'm sorry to disturb you sir, but the American ambassador wishes to visit you this evening on an urgent matter.'

For the third successive evening the fall in temperature brought the race-rioting mobs out on to the streets of London. This time their numbers were swelled by the arrival of thousands of marchers from Wales – Asians who were demanding their own schools, housing estates and legal recognition of their Muslim courts. The police tried to halt the human tide as it neared Heathrow Airport at a steady three miles an hour along the main A4 trunk road, but a determined vanguard of veiled wives with children in pushchairs and prams forced the Home Secretary to order the police to allow the marchers to pass.

Never had so many children taken part in a march. A journalist phoning a report to his editor said it was as if the entire under-sixteen population of Wales had taken to the road. 'It's their future we're marching for,' the journalist had been told. 'So it's only right they should come.' The journalist completed his story by comparing the four leaders of the march with the Pied Piper of Hamelin.

The head of the procession was within twenty kilometres of Hyde Park Corner when the leaders revealed their closely-guarded secret that the marchers were to invade the gardens of Buckingham Palace for a silent sit-down protest. They deliberately kept their plans to themselves until the last minute to thwart army and police intelligence. They believed that communication along the twenty-mile column would be straightforward and made no allowance for fatigue, which would distort the word-of-mouth message.

By 19:00 hours half the weary marchers shuffling along on the outskirts of London believed they were to occupy Buckingham Palace.

At 19:15 the distorted story was picked up by army intelligence.

General Sir Richard Markham, commander-in-chief of UK land forces, with twenty thousand men at his disposal, decided to act – implementing his powers to take unilateral action when the life of the monarch is endangered. His orders were received and acted on by the Aldershot garrison commander.

The London-to-Guildford road was cleared of traffic to provide a free passage for the tanks, personnel carriers and armoured cars that swarmed out of Aldershot and thundered northwards to London.

A second wave of Chieftain and Scimitar tanks abandoned their exercises near Stonehenge on Salisbury Plain, and returned eastward at the maximum speed they could muster.

The commander-in-chief planned and executed his campaign against the marchers with speed and efficiency. No one was to be hurt if it could be avoided, but protection of the monarch was his paramount duty.

The second phase of the operation was to contain the protesters in a square kilometre of West End streets in an attempt to separate them from a mass of National Front agitators who were planning an assault on the Asians. That the American Embassy was right in the middle of the proposed compound did not worry the commander-in-chief; his main concern was to get his men and armour in position before the head of the procession reached Hyde Park Corner.

He achieved his objective with ten minutes to spare.

By a combination of speed and superbly disciplined co-ordination the army, reinforced by units already in London, succeeded in diverting the marchers along Park Lane, and away from Buckingham Palace. Then the heavy battle tanks, belching clouds of blue smoke and pirouetting gracefully on their tracks with incredible speed for their seemingly ponderous bulks, split the angered column into manageable groups for the anti-riot-dressed soldiers to herd into side streets.

In the ensuing confusion, with parents separated from their children, banners forcibly taken from the marchers, the fighting broke out

The Asians, with their wives, families and supporters found the soldiers to be a different proposition from the police. The troops, professionally trained to deal with street riots, did not hesitate to use tactics entirely alien to those employed by the police. A particularly violent battle in Upper Grosvenor Street ended when the soldiers formed themselves into a 'turtle' – a tight group surrounded by riot shields, which waded into the midst of the rioters, seized the ringleaders by their waistbands and retreated, dragging the leaders backwards.

In Berkeley Square Corporal John Stevens flipped up the rearsight leaf on his anti-riot gun, pointed the weapon at the road in front of a chanting mob of National Front supporters and became the first soldier to fire and kill a protester with a plastic bullet under riot conditions in England. The unstable missile, nearly the size of a Coke bottle, rebounded from the kerb and smashed against the chest of a schoolgirl he had not intended to hit.

The crowd erupted with renewed fury and stormed the line of soldiers that retreated behind a line of army trucks. The ambulance summoned to attend to the girl was set on and overturned.

By 21:00 hours the new CR gas canisters had arrived from a factory at Newdigate and were being issued to the soldiers. The main advantage of the experimental gas was that it could be dissolved in the tanks of water cannons, so that the 'riot barriers' could be created across the path of advancing street fighters, although little was known of its long-term effects.

At 21:45, with the battles raging round Grosvenor Square, a Detroit limousine, with eight men crammed inside, pulled away from the American Embassy.

The ambassador dismissed pleas that he should call off his visit to the Prime Minister, but agreed to wear a bullet-proof waistcoat and have extra bodyguards in the car.

Five men sat pressed together in the back – the ambassador, with two men on each side of him. Hendricks sat in the front between Paul Weiner and the marine driver, his bony frame digging painfully into the two men.

The car had just left Grosvenor Square when the driver was forced to brake suddenly as an armoured personnel carrier roared across his path. Missiles struck the side of the car. The ambassador leaned forward to see who was throwing them.

'Keep back, sir,' said a bodyguard politely.

The car was prevented from turning into Oxford Street by a line of steel-helmeted troops, their batons drawn and riot visors down. There were no markings on their mottled combat uniforms to distinguish officers from other ranks. A soldier approached the stationary car with his rifle resting on his hip. He looked curiously at the USA 1 number plate and the eight men crowded into one car.

'I'm very sorry, gentlemen,' said the soldier in a refined accent, 'but you'll have to turn left here.'

'We want to get to Whitehall,' said Hendricks.

'In that case I think your best plan is to head north, and try and work your way down from there. We're containing the trouble between Green Park and Hyde Park, but it's okay to the north.'

The embassy car was driving northwards when rioters broke through the army and police cordons and charged across Oxford Street. There was a sudden harsh rattle of gunfire.

The driver did not hesitate. He swung the car to the right and accelerated down a side street. A tide of yelling rioters storming down another street forced the car to stop. The driver was about to reverse when a convoy of army trucks roared past the stationary car.

'Follow them!' urged Weiner.

The covered trucks, laden with riot troops, turned left with the ambassador's car close behind, then came to an abrupt halt. The street ahead was seething with street fighters.

The marine driver stopped in response to the upheld arm of a riot soldier. At that moment more army trucks appeared at the far end of the street, effectively cutting off the horde of fighting Asians and National Front supporters. The troops in the trucks near the ambassador's car jumped down and began preparing their equipment. The crowd charged but were driven back by a volley of CR canisters. The pale grey clouds were sucked straight up by the warm air rising off the streets, which had been baked all day by the sun.

'You'd better turn back,' Hendricks said to the driver.

'Wait,' intervened the ambassador. 'I want to see how the British manage.'

'They'll manage,' said Hendricks drily.

'We're late,' commented Weiner.

'Then a few more minutes won't make that much difference,' said the ambassador.

The troops were uncovering their equipment truck to expose a squat, ugly barrel that was like no gun the ambassador had ever seen.

'What is it?' said Hendricks.

'A tasser,' said Hendricks.

'What does it do?'

'Rioters,' Hendricks replied caustically.

More troops arrived and formed a shield-to-shield line to thrust the rioters back. Soldiers suddenly fell back to their former positions. The crowd surged forward. The concealed soldiers charged from their hiding-places, seized the ring-leaders from behind and continued their headlong gallop through the line of their own men.

'Clever,' commented the ambassador.

The loss of their ringleaders did not quieten the mob. A voice boomed out, warning people hanging out of windows watching the battle to get back. Few people took any notice.

The men tending the tasser rammed a large package down its muzzle.

'It'll be over in a minute,' remarked Hendricks quietly.

There was a dull boom. Smoke swirled across the street. Troops dashed forward and disappeared into the drifting clouds, which quickly dispersed to reveal a transformed scene. The rioters nearest the tasser were writhing on the ground, shrieking in agony. The others standing further down the street had stopped fighting and were staring at their fallen comrades in shocked disbelief. The troops quickly snapped shackles attached to long lengths of webbing on to the wrists and ankles of stricken rioters.

'What happened?' breathed the ambassador, not taking his eyes off the troops.

'That gun fired a charge of two or three thousand metal barbs attached to lengths of fine wire,' said Hendricks. 'The electrified barbs snag in skin and clothing.'

188

A power winch started. The webbing straps tightened and began hauling the ensnared rioters towards the trucks.

'It's just like fishing,' Hendricks concluded.

The remainder of unaffected street fighters started throwing anything they could lay their hands on. The soldiers fell back. A large, flat-topped truck loaded with what appeared to be racks of lights and loudspeakers swept past the ambassador's car and stopped near the army trucks.

Hendricks studied the equipment thoughtfully, and turned around. 'Mr Ambassador, I think we should make a move now.'

'What is that stuff, Hendricks?'

Hendricks' reply was drowned by the loudhailer telling people to close their windows. The soldiers had pulled right back to the trucks and were putting on what looked like headphones.

'Ear defenders,' said Weiner in surprise.

The flat-topped truck reversed down the street, its lights and loudspeakers trained on the crowd. There came a deep, disturbing sound that seemed to pervade the air from all round.

'Shut the windows!' snapped Hendricks.

Weiner realized that the terrible noise must be coming from the loudspeaker horn mounted on the truck. A red flashing light pulsed out, illuminating the rioters. Each flash seemed to jar Weiner's brain. The deep, mind-chilling noise and flashing light were designed to induce epileptic fits. The note was rising to a shriek. Weiner began to feel sick. The rioters were collapsing in the road and vomiting; some were screaming as the advancing flashing light dealt repeated hammer-blows to their brains; some were suffering convulsive attacks and were uncontrollably jerking their limbs and emptying their bowels. All were affected in some way.

'Let's get the hell outta here!' snarled Hendricks.

The driver slammed the limousine into reverse and gunned the throttle.

'I told you the British would manage,' Hendricks commented some minutes later when the car was clear of the riot zone.

'What the hell was that device?' the ambassador wanted to know.

'A photic driver and curdler,' Weiner answered, recovering from the waves of nausea that had assailed him when he was within earshot of the ultimate anti-riot weapon.

'An appalling device,' commented the ambassador.

He remained silent for the rest of the journey.

16

After his third swallow of whisky, which Simpson poured for him, the ambassador began to feel better.

Witnessing a proud city on the verge of civil war had shaken him badly.

'I'm sorry you had such a bad journey,' said the Prime Minister, concealing his anxiety to find out what the ambassador had come about. 'I understand it's now quiet, so your return should be less hectic.'

The ambassador replaced his glass on the coffee table and took stock of his surroundings. The Prime Minister was seated opposite in a deep leather armchair. Simpson was standing near the door.

After the initial pleasantries the ambassador had asked if he might speak to the Prime Minister alone.

'You don't mind if my secretary stays?' the Prime Minister had asked.

Hendricks and Weiner were shown to an outer office.

The ambassador picked up his glass and put it down again. He might as well get the business over and done with.

'Mr Prime Minister,' he began, 'the question of terrorism is one which concerns our respective governments. And, of course, both our countries are signatories to the new agreement aimed at stamping it out.'

The two men watched the ambassador in silence. I'm making a mess of it, he thought to himself, wishing he had stayed in industry rather than allowed himself to be tempted by the offer of his present job.

'Mr Prime Minister,' he began again, 'we have information that suggests one of your nuclear power stations has been seized by a group of terrorists.'

There was dead silence in the room.

The Prime Minister smiled warmly, but a nerve in his neck twitched. 'Oh yes. That's right. I heard there was something of the sort, but the police now have the situation under control. Isn't that right, Simpson?'

'Yes, sir,' replied Simpson promptly, although his stomach had turned to water at the American's words.

'Fellows wanted a half million pounds,' said the Prime Minister, drawing on skills acquired during thirty years in politics. 'They'll be in Brixton prison by this time tomorrow.'

Either you're a goddamn fine actor, or Hendricks is getting excited over nothing, thought the ambassador.

He checked himself; what he thought didn't matter. He had a job to do, and Hendricks wouldn't hit the panic button without a good reason.

'The purpose of my visit is to deliver a verbal message from the President,' said the ambassador.

The silence in the room was disturbing. He pressed on:

'The President has told me to say he is most concerned about the possible effects of another power station disaster such as Cheynobel. He has instructed me to say that if Her Majesty's Government is ever subjected to extreme threats or pressures imposed by a fanatical group seizing a nuclear power station, he pledges that the United States, with all its resources, is at the disposal of HM government to help end such threats or pressures.'

'However,' he continued, 'the President has asked me to stress that such whole-hearted, unconditional support can be successfully implemented only if there is the fullest co-operation and frankness between us. Such frankness is essential to enable the President to reject any direct course of action he may be advised to take to safeguard the security and well-being of the United States and her people.'

The Americans left Downing Street at 23:10.

The Prime Minister and Simpson listened to a recording of the conversation. They played the closing words of the message three times.

The Prime Minister sat silently for some minutes after the last playback was over. Then he looked up at Simpson, and said softly, 'Christ Almighty. What the hell have we let ourselves in for?'

It was the first time since he had known him that Simpson had heard the Prime Minister swear.

The Prime Minister went to bed at midnight. For once in his long career he was unable to sleep.

17

The supper Maggie cooked for Mitchell tasted of bomb shelters and abandoned basements, but he ate it cheerfully with a straight face.

The forlorn, elfin face watched him across the kitchen table.

Maggie looked exhausted.

Mitchell pushed the empty plate away and smiled at her. 'That was fine, honey, but you shouldn't have bothered.'

'It took my mind off things.'

'Did you see the doctor this afternoon?'

'Yes.' said Maggie truthfully. She tried to summon up the courage to tell Mitchell about Garnet.

'Mitch . . .'

'Yes?'

'Mitch, will you stay the night, please? You could sleep in Daddy's room,' she added hastily.

192

'Wouldn't you rather I ran you back to your place?'

Maggie shook her head. 'I want to be here in case he comes home.'

'Supposing he does, and finds me here?'

Maggie exploded. 'Christ! All I want is someone in the house! Can't you understand that?'

Wednesday

1

It was the large, jagged hole in one of the power station's control-room windows, smashed by Keller during Pyne's escape bid, that suggested to Hugh Patterson a method to kill Keller when darkness fell.

At 1:30 Louise helped him climb through a window in the air-conditioning room, which was on the same level as the control room.

She passed him his Sterling submachine-gun, gave him a light kiss on the cheek and held his hand tightly for a moment. Patterson avoided looking at her pale face.

'Good luck,' she whispered, and closed the window softly.

Patterson padded silently along the narrow roof of the visitors' viewing balcony, which extended along the side of the power station, past the base of the fuelling machine towers perched on top of the main building.

Patterson cautiously approached the corner of the building where the balcony roof stopped. The moon shone from a clear sky, carving a path of flecked light across the oil-black river.

He knelt down and sat on the edge of the roof. Twenty metres below the moonlight gleamed on the dummy petrol tankers and on two helicopters parked on the concrete apron. Patterson had a poor head for heights. His confidence deserted him. The twenty metre drop looked worse in semi-darkness. He shone a pocket torch up at the closed-circuit television camera mounted on a projecting bracket three metres above his head. Its lens was staring across the dark Thames. He directed the torch at the horizontal ledge that traversed the front of the building. It was nothing more than a continuous aluminium box.

Higher up, between each window, was a stout window-cleaner's hook. Patterson reached forward, grasped the first hook and transferred half his weight on to the aluminium ledge. He shuffled his foot along until there was room for the other foot. The ledge seemed strong enough, but he preferred to support most of his weight with his hands. He stretched out an arm, reaching as far as possible until his fingers curled thankfully round the next hook. He worked his toes slowly along the ledge – not daring to move them more than a few centimetres at a time – until his body was in the centre of the window section. There were thirteen such sections between him and the broken pane of glass – he had counted them that afternoon when he had first discussed his plan with Louise. She had been firmly opposed to the idea.

'Supposing he's moved his camp bed?' she had asked.

'Why should he?'

'It's a crazy idea, Hugh. And Conrad said you couldn't be certain of killing him outright with a Sterling.'

Louise had paused. Hugh Patterson, normally good-natured, was proposing the cold-blooded killing of a sleeping man. 'You could do that?'

Patterson thought of Pyne's floating corpse.

'Yes,' he said.

'You'd be aiming into a pitch-black room. You'd be using one hand to hang on. You'd be exhausted.'

'Louise, it's a chance we've got to take. The only chance we'll ever have.'

For a while they remained silent.

'What if you succeed?' Louise had asked.

'We give ourselves up.'

Patterson thought she might argue. She had nodded, and said, 'Okay then. How can I help?'

By the time Patterson reached the third window section sweat was streaming down his face. He hung on with one hand and wiped his sleeve across his forehead.

Thirty minutes later, with only three more sections between him and the jagged hole, he rested. His arms were numb with pain. Sweat was forcibly pumped into the palms of his hands, making it difficult to grip the hooks. He wiped a hand on his trousers. The webbing strap on the Sterling suddenly slipped down his body. He grabbed at it. The weapon's frame clattered against the glass. He waited, counting slowly with his cheek pressed hard on the cool window.

Ten metres away the closed-circuit television camera stirred. Patterson did not hear the faint whir as it swung its lens inward towards the power station's facade.

Patterson resumed his shuffling movement, forcing himself to keep going until the sharp edges of broken glass cut into the inside of his fingers. The sudden jolt of pain nearly caused him to lose his footing.

The smashed hole in the window was before him at last. He closed his eyes tightly for some seconds to adjust his night vision to the control room's dark interior.

He opened them. Stray shafts of moonlight gleamed on IBM machines along the far wall. The horseshoe-shaped main console dominated the scene like a surrealist electronic organ. The shapes in the room were regular, with sharp corners. There was one exception – the shadowy, humped outline of Keller's camp bed.

Patterson carefully supported himself by hooking an elbow over the edge of the broken glass. He slipped the Sterling from his shoulder with his free hand and grasped the magazine awkwardly with the other hand. He released the safety-catch and aimed the submachine-gun at the camp bed.

He fired one long continuous burst. His body shuddered with the hammering recoil. The broken glass gripped between his elbow and stomach began to splinter and pull

196

away from the frame. He felt himself falling backwards and was forced to drop the Sterling and grab at a hook in panic. The gun clattered on to the concrete apron twenty metres below. The smoke stung his eyes and filled the control room, obscuring the dark shapes.

A polite voice not two metres away said, 'I should come in if I were you, Mr Patterson, before you fall and have a nasty accident.'

2

Simpson's bedside telephone rang at 3:00, when he was staring at the ceiling trying to sleep.

He picked up the receiver and didn't say who he was; his number was known to less than a dozen people. There was something familiar about the tired voice which said, 'Simpson, I've just discharged myself from Dover General. You'd better get over here and pick me up.'

'Who's speaking?' asked Simpson, mentally running through the list of those who knew his night number.

'Pyne, you idiot!' snapped the voice.

Simpson's mind reeled. 'Pyne?' Then he recognized the voice.

'Listen,' said Pyne. 'And try to grasp what I'm telling you. There's been a major reshuffle. Keller's taken over as chairman. Do you understand?'

Simpson sat up. 'Did you dial through the nine-three-o-level?'

'Yes.'

'You're not on a cellphone?'

'No!'

Simpson relaxed; there was little danger of the conversation being overheard so he risked firing questions. A lot of questions.

Simpson made his way up to the Prime Minister's flat. He could have used the internal phone, but the walk gave him time to think. He entered the private sitting-room and paused outside the bedroom door, wondering how to break the news.

'There's no need to creep about out there, Simpson,' said the Prime Minister from the other side of the door. 'I'm not asleep.'

Simpson entered. The light was on. The Prime Minister knew immediately from his secretary's face that something was seriously wrong.

Simpson started to repeat the conversation with Pyne. He was on his third sentence when the Prime Minister swore, threw back the covers and started to get dressed – his fingers fumbling at his clothes. Simpson helped him while relating the rest of the conversation. The Prime Minister was thrusting his feet into his shoes by the time Simpson was listing the deleted clauses in the ultimatum.

He stopped getting dressed and stared at his secretary. 'We're going to have to get them out of that power station, Simpson. No matter what the cost.'

Simpson swallowed.

'We agreed that was impossible, sir . . .' he began.

The Prime Minister feverishly fastened his tie. 'You're to call a meeting for nine o'clock this morning. Get on to the best brains in the country. Tell them the security of the country is endangered. Don't tell them more than that. Use the police to drag them here by force if necessary.'

Simpson gaped at the Prime Minister.

'What's the meeting for, sir?'

The stocky figure rounded on Simpson in fury. 'To find a way of getting those bastards out, you idiot! You better have about twenty sets of the power station plans made ready.'

Simpson was rooted. 'Whom shall I ask to attend?'

'Christ, I don't know. Use your imagination.' the Prime Minister stopped dressing and glared at his secretary. 'That's one thing we'll need now Simpson. Imagination. People with plenty of imagination. No more lackies. The head of Defence Studies; someone from the Institute of

Oceanographic Sciences; the retired officer who's written that book on terrorism. Get 'em all here. The whole bloody lot.'

Simpson was halfway across the sitting-room when the Prime Minister called him back. 'You better get on to the Americans and tell them the whole story. They seem to know it anyway. Bloody CIA, pretending to be a bunch of morons while running rings round us.'

Simpson looked aghast. 'The *whole* story, sir?'

The Prime Minister gestured in exasperation. 'You know what I mean. For Christ's sake stop sounding like a bloody butler and get moving!'

'Do we ask the Americans to the meeting, sir?'

The Prime Minister paused. 'Yes. We might need that help they offered. Hendricks struck me as a shrewd bastard. He might be useful.'

'What shall we do about Pyne, sir?'

The Prime Minister sat on the bed. 'Christ, yes Pyne.' He thought for a moment. 'We'll have to keep him under wraps. That house at Inverloch or somewhere. Where is he?'

'Dover.'

The same idea occurred simultaneously to both men: the Prime Minister's holiday bungalow at Broadstairs.

'Ideal,' he said. 'The housekeeper is on holiday for three weeks. There'll be a bobby hanging about, but the place is empty. Get the meeting fixed up first and then go down to pick up Pyne and take him to the bungalow. He's to stay out of sight until we decide what to do with him. Try and be back here before the meeting. I don't think there's anything else.'

The Prime Minister finished dressing when Simpson had gone. there *was* something else – something to do with the CIA. He frowned, trying to remember what it was. Normally, his memory never betrayed him. He wondered about Pyne and reflected wryly on the best-laid plans of mice . . .

What the hell was it he wanted to remember about the CIA? He shrugged at his reflection in the dressing-table mirror. Maybe it wasn't important . . .

Even so, it was worrying.

3

The peasant girl had the most sumptuous breasts Cox-Spender had ever seen. They swayed with their own hypnotic life beneath her thin cotton blouse as she crawled across the bistro floor towards his table. Her long dark hair trailed in the bloodstained sawdust strewn on the floor.

Cox-Spender considered her the best so far — much more beautiful than the three girls he had possessed that night. Brutal men in berets and striped jerseys looked on from the shadows with hate and jealousy smouldering in their eyes as the girl slid her long, sensuous fingers up Cox-Spender's legs.

He smiled down, drew back a foot and kicked her. She fell back scowling, her dark eyes flashing angrily as her fingers curled into the sawdust. A gypsy band gathered round Cox-Spender's table, not missing a note of the savage Slavonic dance as they sawed demoniacally at their shrieking violins.

The girl spat at Cox-Spender and reached up to loosen the laces at her throat which held the front of her blouse together.

She was about to rip the flimsy garment open when the bedside telephone rang and woke Cox-Spender.

It was Simpson. Cox-Spender decided he hated Simpson.

'An important meeting at Downing Street,' said the despicable Simpson. 'In five hours. Nine o'clock. Use the Old Admiralty Building entrance.'

'What about a car?' asked Cox-Spender.

'Your local police station will send a car round to your house at eight o'clock,' replied Simpson, and hung up.

Cox-Spender fiddled with his telephone and eventually managed to program a Star Service 07:00 alarm call. He replaced the handset and lay pondering before drifting back to sleep.

But he was too late: the surly, unshaven musicians had packed their fiddles and gone, taking the beautiful peasant girl and the noisy bistro with them.

4

Mitchell was woken by a noise in the bedroom.

It was Maggie standing in his doorway.

'I couldn't sleep, Mitch.'

Mitchell groped for a light switch, but Maggie came forward and placed her hand over his.

'What's the matter?' Mitchell asked.

Maggie told him about the accident with the boat. She talked haltingly for five-minutes, keeping a tight rein on her emotions.

'Jesus,' Michell breathed when she had finished. 'You poor kid.' He put his arm around her. She shrank away from his touch, then relaxed.

'The police will want to see you tomorrow,' said Maggie. 'I told them they'd find you here.'

'What will they want me for?'

Maggie paused. 'I don't know. I suppose because it's your boat. They'll probably ask you if I could handle it properly.'

Mitchell remembered the way she had steered the boat without over-correcting.

'Maggie . . .' he hesitated, but the question had to be asked. 'Maggie. It *was* an accident?'

There was no reply. He wished the light was on so that he could see her face.

'Maggie?'

'I don't know, Mitch. I keep asking myself. But I swear – I honestly don't know.'

Mitchell pulled her back until her head was resting on the pillow. He stroked her hair away from her forehead.

201

'I'm scared, Mitch,' her voice trembled.

'I'll tell the police the truth – that you had never handled the boat before and that I didn't want to leave you alone with it.'

The girl did not answer. Mitchell moved his arm slightly, and realized she was asleep.

5

'Cox-Spender,' said the Prime Minister, pausing outside the panelled double doors leading to the Cabinet Room and tapping the list. 'Why him? He's incompetent.'

'With respect, sir,' said Simpson evenly. 'I don't agree. He has a capable intellect despite his unfortunate personality. Also, he's the only man who has been into the power station. Exclude him and someone would be bound to ask why. And besides, you'll have someone to steer awkward questions at.'

The Prime Minister grunted and resumed his study of the list of twenty people now waiting on the other side of the door. They included the Ministers of Defence; senior officials from Power Gen; a professor from the Atomic Energy Authority; James Reynolds from the Institute of Oceanographic Sciences; Brigadier Michael Rawlins, who had written the book *Counter-Terrorist*; some well-known engineers, and the two Americans – Weiner and Hendricks.

Simpson noticed the rings under the Prime Minister's eyes. The loss of one night's sleep showed.

'What about the Chief Scientific Adviser?' demanded the Prime Minister testily.

The question surprised Simpson. 'The accident in the Mall,' he said politely.

The Prime Minister folded the list.

You really are losing your grip, aren't you? thought Simpson as he pushed the doors open.

Twenty faces round the long table turned expectantly as the two men entered the room. Only Cox-Spender,

Hendricks, Weiner and the ministers knew what the meeting was to be about.

The Prime Minister greeted the gathering and apologized for the abrupt summons to Downing Street. After introductions had been made he quickly outlined the events since Sunday, omitting Pyne's escape and the revised nature of the ultimatum.

There was no reaction from Hendricks and Weiner when the Prime Minister listed the names of the four holding the power station.

The brigadier was the first to speak, He was about to refer the gathering to his book and say, 'I told you so,' but decided the comment would be inappropriate. Instead he said, 'Why isn't someone from the Special Air Service here? Those boys might have some bright ideas. This sort of thing is right . . .'

'Unfortunately,' interrupted the Prime Minister, 'the Special Air Service has been integrated with the Oil Rig Defence Force under the command of General Pyne. Pyne has been a great advocate of the merging and the rationalization of various armed services units, and has had the drive and personality to push them through.'

'He wouldn't have been able to do so if you hadn't been so keen to rubber-stamp his proposals,' replied the brigadier. 'Damned fellow was a leading advocate of this unified European defence force nonsense.'

The Prime Minister looked frostily across the table. 'I was hoping, brigadier, that you might have constructive suggestions to help with this present problem.'

And then the discussion began in earnest. Simpson distributed sets of the power-station plans. Hendricks and Weiner did not join in. They sat listening as proposals were suggested and dismissed.

'Nerve gas is quick,' said Cox-Spender in reply to one idea, 'but not quick enough for us to be a hundred per cent certain that we could prevent the terrorists from activating the detonators.' He described the system Pyne had shown him during his Sunday visit to the power station. 'A preemptive strike would have to succeed in four seconds,' Cox-Spender concluded.

Less than that now, thought the Prime Minister. Only he and Simpson knew that Keller was now in control. They'd decided that if anyone came up with an idea, that they would insist on certain success in one second as a safety factor before agreeing to the plan.

The arguments and counter arguments dragged on.

'Let's consider the problem on the assumption that they're bluffing,' said Peter Harvey, the Minister of Defence for the Army.

Christ, we're getting nowhere, thought the Prime Minister.

Harvey saw the Prime Minister's expression and said quickly, 'We must look at every angle, Prime Minister. Starting with the improbable . . .'

'I'm not up on these things,' said the Minister of Defence for the RAF. 'My experts would know, but couldn't we use an American laser-guided "Smart" bomb aimed precisely on the quarters occupied by the terrorists?'

Hendricks regarded the speaker with icy contempt. 'Sure. We could drop one from seventy thousand feet with an error of fifty metres. That's pin-point accuracy. But a fifty-metre error is enough to put the bomb plumb through the silos.'

The fruitless discussion went on. After an hour there were ten proposals on Simpson's pad. All had been crossed out.

'Have the Americans got a contingency plan for dealing with similar occurrences in their country?' inquired Peter Harvey.

'Sure,' said Hendricks. 'The main one is making certain all power stations have proper security arrangements. I'm amazed that your nuclear police weren't on duty at the station when it was seized. It's not my place to criticize, but had the British government heeded the warnings of our Atomic Energy Commission, this might not have happened.'

'You're quite right,' said the Prime Minister. 'It's not your place to criticise.'

Hendricks' gaunt face was impassive.

Cox-Spender broke the silence that followed. 'Some sort of unmanned attack through the power station's foundations,' he said to himself.

Everyone stared at him.

The sudden silence caused Cox-Spender to look up from his set of plans. Someone must have said something he had missed. He looked round the table and was horrified to discover twenty-one pairs of eyes on him.

'What was that?' someone said.

'Well,' said Cox-Spender, looking down in terror at his plans. 'I thought some sort of unmanned penetration of the galleries round the radioactive-waste storage silos . . .' His voice trailed away.

'Why unmanned?' asked James Reynolds of the Institute of Oceanographic Sciences.

'It's a silly idea. I was merely thinking aloud. It occurred to me that an unmanned machine might be able to cut the detonator wires without activating the IRIS detectors, but then of course, if there was such a machine, it would probably generate more heat than several humans.'

'It would have to be a pretty fantastic machine,' said the brigadier caustically. Something straight out of science fiction.'

'GOPHER,' said Cox-Spender suddenly.

Everyone looked at him again.

'What's a gopher?' asked someone.

'A North American burrowing animal,' said Weiner.

'An acronym,' contradicted Cox-Spender excitedly.

'A what?'

'I don't know what the letters stand for,' said Cox-Spender, 'but I remember reading about it some years ago.'

'What exactly did this device do, and how can it help us?' demanded the Prime Minister.

'If I remember correctly, sir.' said Cox-Spender, controlling his excitement, 'it was a one-man machine that could bore through rock.' Cox-Spender leaned across the table and pointed to the Prime Minister's plans. 'If we could get hold of such a machine, we could burrow under the riverbed from the opposite bank, and bore right through the power station's foundation. Of course, we'd have to fix up some sort of inertial guidance system for the pilot so he'd be certain of coming up in an inspection tunnel. He could then leave the machine and cut the wires to the explosives.'

There was a silence.

'You've forgotten something,' said the Prime Minister. 'Surely these IRIS detector things they've installed would sound the alarms as soon as they picked up the heat from the man's body?'

Cox-Spender nodded glumly. Then he brightened. 'Not if we were to dress him in a suit that was a perfect insulator so that none of his body heat escaped.'

'Is there such a suit?' inquired the Prime Minister, looking at each man in turn.

'I've heard,' said Hendricks slowly, 'although I'm no expert, that the spacesuits developed by NASA are perfect insulators.'

'No machine is capable of boring such a distance,' said James Reynolds. 'The river is four kilomtres wide at Canvey Island. And there's another problem. This machine, if it exists – which I doubt – wouldn't be able to bore more than a few metres.' He looked at Cox-Spender. 'Presumably it loosens soil or rock and pushes it behind as it moves forward?'

Cox-Spender nodded.

'Then after a few metres,' concluded James Reynolds, 'there wouldn't be any more room behind for the debris it had removed from in front? Yes?'

Hendricks was scribbling as Cox-Spender nodded sadly.

'Shall we move on to the next idea?' asked the Prime Minister.

But the ideas that followed were variations of schemes already suggested. All were rejected after a further hour's discussion.

'So what do we do now?' asked the Prime Minister.

Hendricks looked up from his notes. Without humour he said, 'I suggest we look for gophers.'

6

Mitchell woke up at 9:00 hours.

Maggie had gone. The bedroom was filled with sunlight and the smell of burning breakfast.

He went downstairs.

'Good morning, Mitch,' said Maggie brightly across the smoke-filled kitchen. 'I thought I'd surprise you with breakfast.'

Mitchell was so pleased to see her looking much better that he raised no objection to bacon that looked like fragments of the Dead Sea scrolls and toast like little squares of midnight. The bruise on her face was subsiding. She chatted away during breakfast as if she were making a deliberate attempt to sever herself from the events of the previous day.

Mitchell was nerving himself to taste the coffee when she said, 'I'd like to go to London to find out what's happened to Daddy.'

'I think you should rest, Maggie.'

'It would be best if I did something,' she said with a trace of defiance.

'The police are coming today you said,' said Mitchell, adding quickly, 'I'll do a deal with you. You rest today and I'll call my secretary and tell her I'm taking the rest of the week off, and I'll go with you to London tomorrow. How does that grab you?'

Maggie smiled and nodded. 'You can take me to an expensive restaurant.'

The electric fan the Prime Minister stood on his desk cooled his coffee in two minutes so it was undrinkable. He sipped it, swore and picked up his telephone to order some more.

There was a tap on his door. Simpson entered.

'I've spoken to Keller by radiotelephone,' he said. 'He's agreed to no more than a seventy-two-hour extension to the deadline from midnight tonight.'

The Prime Minister groaned.

'What use is seventy-two hours?'

'I did my best,' said Simpson, 'I explained that a lot of clauses needed rewording to make them watertight. He was extremely polite and accepted that the bill was the most complicated piece of legislation in history, but insisted that it should receive the royal assent and become an Act of Parliament by midnight on Saturday.'

The Prime Minister stared down at his blotter and twiddled nervously with the smooth amber paper weight. His palms were soaked in sweat despite the cooling air from the fan. The paperweight skipped across the desk and fell to the floor. He made no attempt to retrieve it.

'Hendricks wants a week,' he said dully, 'and then he wants us to bluff Keller into agreeing to another week.'

Simpson smiled thinly and noted the proximity of the electric fan. The old rogue was gradually losing his cool. 'Seventy-two hours from midnight might be enough. The CIA have found the magazine article Cox-Spender remembered seeing,' he said.

The Prime Minister frowned. Simpson's mention of the CIA – what was it he was trying to remember that morning? Suddenly it came to him.

'Mitchell!' barked the Prime Minister. 'Howard Mitchell. How is it the CIA haven't mentioned him? What's happened to him?'

The question took Simpson by surprise. 'Nothing, sir.'

Simpson realized he had made a mistake. He was about to amend his answer hastily, but the Prime Minister was too quick. He pounced with all his old parliamentary skill.

'Nothing? What the hell do you mean? How could anything happen to him if you've only had him watched?'

'What I meant was . . .'

'What the hell have you done with him?'

'Nothing, sir.'

'Did you have him watched? Well?' The Prime Minister sighed. 'Look, Simpson. It would take me an hour to get the truth out of you, and time is precious.'

Simpson decided that he might as well tell him about Patrick Reagan.

The Prime Minister listened.

'Why?' he said when Simpson finished.

'We needed time. Just as we need time now. If Mitchell was working for the CIA, as we know he was, then it was important that I should have him dealt with before he learned too much.'

'Christ Almighty! Didn't it occur to you that removing him would only arouse CIA suspicions still further and bring them crashing down on our necks?'

'Mitchell was a plant – a resident, I think they call them. It would take them many months to establish a new one – fix him up with genuine cover. I thought that having Mitchell out of the way would give us the time we needed. Anyway, what does it matter? Reagan was killed in a genuine road accident.'

'Reagan was a bomber?'

'Yes.'

'You gave him Mitchell's address?'

'Yes.'

'Then how the hell do we know there isn't a bomb sitting in Mitchell's house?'

The interrogation irritated Simpson. 'I'll make an anonymous call to Weybridge police and tell them there might be a bomb in Mitchell's house.'

The Prime Minister lost his temper. 'You'll do no such thing, you bloody idiot! We'll keep this to ourselves. You're to go to Weybridge and check Mitchell's house and car yourself! Understand?'

Simpson's face was white. He clenched his fingers together and kept his voice steady. 'I don't know how to look for a bomb, and what if Mitchell is in the house or using his car?'

'That's your problem. You created it. But I'll tell you this much, Simpson, if anything happens to Mitchell at this stage – there'll be one hell of a row with the Americans and I'll see that you carry the can. After that, I'll make damned certain you're finished. Now get out.'

Simpson made no attempt to move. 'With respect, sir. I don't think you could afford to do that.'

He turned on his heel and stalked out of the office.

8

Cox-Spender hated flying.

He knew it was irrational, but he couldn't help it. The most civilized form of transport was the TGV express that carried him four times a year from Paris to Marseilles, to his beloved bistros and the girls lying topless on the beaches.

Knowing he was going to New York didn't help. He had never been to the United States, but he knew all about New York from the television cop series which he watched religiously and found utterly convincing. He would be mugged as he stepped off the aircraft.

Consequently, by the time he was sitting next to Hendricks in a British Airways Concorde at Heathrow waiting to take off he was a nervous wreck.

Hidden loudspeakers welcomed Cox-Spender aboard and advised him that he would be landing in New York in three and a half hours.

'Great airplane,' said Hendricks.

'Yes,' said Cox-Spender weakly.

A few minutes later he prepared himself to meet his maker as the spindly-legged monster hurled down the hot runway and lifted its drooping nose to the darkening sky.

9

By the time Simpson had purchased new shoes and socks, his inner rage at the way he had been treated was beginning to die down.

He paid the shop assistant out of the £1000 he had drawn for Patrick Reagan and added the purchases to the new suit, shirt, gloves and underwear crammed into the second hand travelling bag.

He went by bus to Waterloo Station and changed into his new outfit in the men's toilets. His original clothes went into the travelling bag. He went to the British Rail Red Star counter and arranged for the bag to be sent to his flat. There was nothing on him that would link him to the Prime Minister's secretary should he be caught breaking into Mitchell's house at Weybridge: no keys, no credit cards or letters – nothing. Even the wallet holding £620 in old notes was new.

The only available train was packed. Every time it stopped passengers had to disembark so that those who wanted that station could struggle off.

He found a second hand car dealer within a hundred metres of Surbiton Station. One of the offerings outside the seedy parade of shops was an elderly Sierra. He examined it with a calculated lack of enthusiasm. He argued the price with he salesman and secured a reduction of £200.

He told the salesman that he would have to draw the money from the bank and would be back in an hour. The salesman promised to have the car ready but insisted on Simpson leaving a 10 per cent deposit.

Simpson went away and sat in a cheap café drinking coffee. He decided that he would wreck the Prime Minister as soon as the three terrorists – if they could be called that – were out of the power station.

He had known the Prime Minister for twenty years; he could tell stories to the press – especially the latest story – that would bring the whole rotten structure crashing down about the Prime Minister's ears.

And why not? Why not pay back the old bastard for not even giving him a lousy OBE?

But he would need General Pyne's help.

He would drive down to Broadstairs that evening as soon as he had finished at Weybridge.

Simpson finished his coffee. He found a public telephone and called Mitchell's home. There was no answer. He rang Mitchell's Walton office. His secretary did not know where her boss was – only that he wouldn't be in the office for the rest of the week.

Simpson gave the car salesman a false name and address and paid the balance owing on the Sierra. The car had seen better days, but it handled well and seemed to be in reasonable mechanical condition. He drove cautiously to Weybridge, observing the speed limits.

By the time he was driving into the outskirts of Weybridge he had worked out a detailed plan of action against the Prime Minister with which he felt certain Pyne would agree.

Simpson was pleased with himself.

It was, he thought, an extremely clever plan.

Mitchell's house was deserted.

Breaking in was not the problem Simpson expected: there were several pieces of rough timber nailed across a broken window in the kitchen door – probably where Reagan had broken in. Simpson pulled on his new gloves and prised the lengths of wood away with a garden fork. He levered the remaining pieces of glass out of the frame and climbed into the kitchen.

Simpson set about looking for the bomb. It was a terrifying business: he pulled doors open with pieces of string; he threw books into rooms before venturing in just in case there was some sort of detonator under the carpets; he even turned the electricity off at the mains switch and went round turning on every electrical gadget, pausing occasionally – listening for the sound of a returning car. He restored electric power at the mains switch. The house filled with the sound of radios, televisions, a food mixer, tape recorder and several fans.

Nothing happened.

After two hours' painstaking search Simpson was convinced that there was no bomb in the house. Reagan must have planted it in Mitchell's car – if indeed he had planted a bomb at all.

Simpson left the house by the kitchen door. He was about to walk down the drive, when he saw two men unloading a new television from a van parked outside the house opposite. He quickly returned to the house and watched them from Mitchell's living room – standing well back from the window. The men disappeared into the house. Simpson decided to wait until they drove away. The bitterness he felt at being put in such an absurd situation was offset by the thought of his plan to pay the Prime Minister out. The nagging doubt was, would Pyne agree?

There was a telephone on a low coffee table. He sat in one of Mitchell's armchairs and picked up the handset.

Supposing Mitchell had itemized phone bills? If so it would be certain to show the number he had called and the time. It could be very embarrassing.

Simpson replaced the handset.

What the hell – the chances were that Mitchell wouldn't be receiving his phone bill for several weeks. He lifted the handset and sat with it pressed to his ear while fumbling awkwardly through the dialling code booklet with gloved fingers, looking for the number of the exchange near Broadstairs.

Thirty seconds later, he discovered Reagan's bomb.

He also discovered that death could be a mind-blowing experience.

A kilometre away, Mitchell lifted his head off the aluminium and plastic bed beside General Pyne's swimming pool. He reached out a foot and prodded Maggie.

'Did you hear that?'

She didn't move.

'Did you?' prompted Mitchell.

She yawned.

'What?'

'A bang,' said Mitchell.

'Later,' said Maggie, and went back to sleep.

Thursday

1

Summer was upon New York like a ravening beast that devoured the slight breeze that barely stirred the fringed sunshade above Cox-Spender's head.

He was sitting at the nearest table to the Prometheus Fountain in the Rockefeller Center. Even at 10:00 the appalling heat seemed to be rising out of the ground. The orderly lines of United Nations flags surrounding the humid sunken basin seemed to be too exhausted by the physical effort of hanging from their poles to make any unnecessary move.

Cox-Spender looked at his watch. Hendricks had been gone fifteen minutes. He squinted up at the dazzling golden statue of Prometheus beneath the soaring RCA Building and reflected that had the god known about New York summers, he might have reconsidered his plan to steal fire from the heavens.

A waitress served him with his morning coffee.

Cox-Spender watched the people milling round the Plaza's perimeter. Not one of them was being robbed, except those buying pretzels and ice-cold Cokes from a stand.

He was beginning to like New York: his room a few streets away at the Hilton, was comfortable, and the television seemed to have an inexhaustible number of channels filled with his favourite cops. What little he had seen of the city suggested that it had everything he could wish for, maybe even a bistro. After London, Midtown

Manhattan was surprisingly clean, littered with fountains, crammed with plenty of buses and taxis. And there were no piles of dog shit on the sidewalks. It was very different from London.

Hendricks returned and sat down.

'Delmar Hydraulics is now run by one of Jack Delmar's sons – Henry. He knows nothing about the GOPHER so I've fixed up for us to fly up to see old Jack Delmar at his lodge in the mountains.'

Cox-Spender hung grimly on to his seat as the helicopter threatened to shake itself to pieces in what appeared to be a desperate battle to remain airborne.

He was forced to jam his tongue against his false teeth to prevent the terrifying vibration from dislodging them. Hendricks sat next to the pilot. He turned his craggy face round to Cox-Spender.

'Are you okay?'

Cox-Spender nodded and mumbled something past his mouthful of tongue and oscillating dentures.

'The flight will take a couple of hours. We'll be there by two.'

Cox-Spender looked down and wished he hadn't. The helicopter was flying due north, gaining height as it followed the valley of the Hudson River. He looked longingly back at the Manhattan skyline, dominated by the bland twin towers of the World Trade Center.

Straight ahead was the distant smudge of the Adirondack Mountains.

2

In a land of rich men, Jack Delmar considered himself to be one of the richest.

He had six sons – one to run each of his corporations; several homes across Europe; an apartment on Park Avenue; a photographic memory and a powerful sex drive. Both the latter were still in good shape despite his seventy years. He also had an engaging personality, which he used on the two visitors sitting on his veranda overlooking the lake.

Normally he never entertained strangers, and he wouldn't have been seeing these two had it not been for a call from the White House asking him to meet them. The White House rarely asked favours these days. Maybe they were too scared, or didn't trust so many as they used to. An hour before his guests had arrived Delmar had called up some friends in the Pentagon and given them the names the White House had given him and asked who the hell they were; it was a simple request from an old buddy. He was surprised when they refused to oblige. It also aroused his curiosity.

'Sure I remember GOPHER,' he said to Cox-Spender. 'Must be all of twenty years ago – maybe more. When I was fifty. Crazy things we do when we're young.' He grinned disarmingly at his visitors.

Hendricks showed him the magazine article. Jack Delmar laughed at the pictures.

'Isn't that the weirdest machine you ever saw? This magazine promised to send me some complimentary copies. They never did. A few words to some friends and the editor suddenly found his advertising space hard to sell.' Jack Delmar paused. 'Why are you interested in my GOPHER, Mr Spender?'

Cox-Spender had a story ready. 'A sonar check has revealed what may be an unexploded wartime bomb under Greenwich Observatory. We're hoping it will enable us to recover the bomb without having to disturb the observatory's instruments.'

Jack Delmar threw back his head and laughed. 'GOPHER wouldn't be any good to you. That thing couldn't even cut through warm butter.'

Cox-Spender looked at the industrialist in alarm.

'But these photographs show . . .'

'They show GOPHER drilling down and coming up a few metres away,' said Jack Delmar, grinning broadly. 'That

217

demo was staged on a rented construction site. I had a few hundred tonnes of debris spread around and levelled so GOPHER wouldn't find the going too difficult.'

'What happened to it?' asked Cox-Spender despairingly.

'It was blown up.'

'Do you still have the drawings?'

'Drawings?' Jack Delmar's blue eyes twinkled in amusement. 'In those days we built a prototype first and only drew it up if it worked so we could make another one.'

Hendricks looked at this watch. 'I guess we'd better get back to New York.'

'Do you still have any of the major components?' asked Cox-Spender, frantically casting about for even a slender straw.

'Some went into GOPHER 11.'

Cox-Spender gaped at the old man. 'GOPHER 11.'

Jack Delmar's grin broadened. 'Worked like a dream. Could bore its way through twenty metres of Manhattan rock. No problem.'

Hendricks had half-risen. He sat down again, letting Cox-Spender ask all the questions.

'Have you still got it?'

'Sure thing. And I'm still sitting on the patents. I figured they might come in handy some day.'

Cox-Spender sat on the edge of his chair. 'Mr Delmar, could GOPHER 11 Bore under a four-kilometre-wide river, and then through, say . . . two metres of rock?' Cox-Spender nearly said 'concrete'.

Jack Delmar shook his head. 'Four kilometres? That would be asking a lot of any machine.'

'But the article in that magazine said that a later version would be able to bore under the Hudson or East River to rescue trapped subway passengers.'

Without looking at the magazine Jack Delmar said, 'If I remember rightly, it said, bore *through* the riverbed.'

'Then how . . .?'

'When we got GOPHER 11 working properly, we presented the Port Authority with a complete scheme, and laid on a demonstration. We made several dozen thirty-metre lengths of two-metre diameter plastic pipe – once we had the mould we could punch out as many lengths as we wanted. They were made to be easily joined together to form a watertight seal. A team of scuba divers fitted them together on the bed of the Hudson. They started on the West Side and pushed out until they were over on the New Jersey side. They sealed a prefabricated dome to the submerged end of the pipeline with the open base of the dome held against the riverbed by water pressure. Takes some doing. Once everything was ready the City Fire Department pumped the pipeline and dome dry.'

'So after that, you were able to take your GOPHER along the pipeline to the dome, and bore down from there?' said Cox-Spender excitedly.

Jack Delmar grinned. 'You've got it. The GOPHER operator went straight down, levelled out and broke through into the side of the Lincoln Tunnel within a few metres of the spot marked by the railroad engineers.'

'When was this?'

'Fifteen years back.'

'I never heard about it,' said Hendricks.

'Washington asked me to put the lid on the story as a favour. They were worried in case someone thought of using the idea to break into bank vaults – or even missile silos. I was angling for a big government contract at the time, so I agreed.' Jack Delmar grinned at his visitors.

'Have you still got GOPHER 11 and the pipe sections, Mr Delmar?' asked Cox-Spender, trying to control his eagerness.

'Sure. And the prefabricated dome. They're in our West Fiftieth warehouse, unless Henry's had them shifted. I don't run things now.'

Cox-Spender mentally crossed his fingers before asking the next question. 'Can you remember how many lengths of pipe there were, Mr Delmar?'

Jack Delmar looked curiously at the British civil servant. He wondered why everyone was getting so excited over an unexploded German bomb. It had to be one helluva bomb. He noticed that the Englishman's hands were clenched tightly together. Hendricks was gazing boredly across the lake.

'A hundred and sixty lengths,' said Jack Delmar. 'Enough to construct a five kilometre line. The sections split into halves so they can be stacked and not use too much room. They snap together under water with special latches on the inside.'

Cox-Spender edged forwards until he was nearly falling off his chair. 'Mr Delmar, the British government would like to purchase your GOPHER and its ancillary machinery together with the pipe sections and the prefabricated dome. I'm empowered to negotiate on their behalf.'

Jack Delmar shook his head. 'I wouldn't sell it.'

Cox-Spender goggled at him. 'But you must!' he blurted. Annoyance flicked across the industrialist's wrinkled face.

'Now see here . . .' he began.

Hendricks intervened. 'I think the British government would be willing to pay substantially for the equipment.'

Jack Delmar gestured round him. His hand encompassed the air-conditioned lodge, the lake and a twin Mercruiser boat.

'When you get to my age, you discover that friends, and maybe a little excitement to relieve the boredom, are more important than money. I was about to say you can have the stuff in return for two small favours.' He studied Cox-Spender. 'Have you the authority to grant favours, Mr Spender?'

Cox-Spender nodded.

Jack Delmar sat back and gazed up at the trees. 'One of my boys – Carl – runs Delmar Instruments in the UK. Carl's been having a struggle lately to keep the business going. It's not his fault – he's a good kid, works hard – but he can't raise cash for investment, and he won't come to me. But he would accept a two million dollar grant from the British government – without strings, and without my name being mentioned. Okay?'

'Okay,' said Cox-Spender, using the affirmative for the first time since he was a boy. 'And the second condition?'

'That you ship me to the UK with the equipment and two of my engineers to help run the operation.'

Cox-Spender agreed with alacrity; Jack Delmar's condition was to have been a Cox-Spender proposal. He felt he had scored a point over the shrewd industrialist.

'One thing, Mr Delmar. How long did it take to break into the Lincoln Tunnel?'

'Twenty-six hours from starting to put the pipeline together to when GOPHER showed her nose to the Penn railroad engineers. Do you know what GOPHER stands for? Geophysical Orbital Power Head Earth Explorer.' He grinned and stood up – eager for action. 'When do we get to ship the stuff?'

'Within the next twenty-four hours,' said Hendricks, uncoiling his frame. 'Sooner, if I can get the transport fixed in time.'

The featureless concrete prongs of the World Trade Center were in sight when Jack Delmar yelled to Cox-Spender above the noise of the helicopter's motor, 'That story about a German bomb is a load of crap?'

'Yes,' Cox-Spender agreed solemnly. 'A load of crap.'

Jack Delmar grinned delightedly at the British civil servant.

The police were very considerate to Maggie and even allowed Mitchell to be present when they questioned her about the accident with Mitchell's boat.

The detective-sergeant closed his notebook and stood up. 'Thank you, Miss Pyne. We'll have this typed out then we'll be asking you to sign it.'

'What will happen next?' Maggie asked.

'There'll be an inquest early next week. The coroner will no doubt have something to say about the responsibilities of river users, then record a verdict of accidental death. It won't take more than fifteen minutes.'

'What happened to the river policeman?'

The detective-sergeant looked levelly at Maggie. 'Sergeant Snowdon? He's still suffering from shock.'

When he had gone, Maggie said to Mitchell. 'I'd like to go to London now, Mitch.'

'Why not call his office and ask them where your father is?'

'You promised, Mitch.'

Mitchell looked at his watch. 15:00 hours. 'Yes, but look, honey. We didn't know the police would be so late coming. It's going to take at least an hour to get into London – there are probably road blocks after yesterday's rioting.'

But Maggie was determined. 'In that case, we'd better leave now.'

She marched out of the room.

Mitchell sighed, and followed her out to the car. He wanted to go back to his place and change, but decided against upsetting her.

It took two hours of driving along nerve-racking police and army diversions before Maggie and Mitchell reached the Ministry of Defence overlooking the Thames in London. The rioting was over but obviously there was still a major alert on.

'Sorry,' said the security officer. 'But everyone's gone home now.'

'But you can at least call his office!' said Maggie angrily. 'Room 1702.'

'It's gone half past, miss. They've all cleared off.'

'Look,' said Maggie calmly, 'my father often works late. You could at least ring his extension.'

The security officer glowered at the angry girl, and decided it would be best not to have a row with a general's daughter. He called the extension. No one answered.

'Do you know where this new camp is that my father's in command of?' demanded Maggie.

'I wouldn't know things like that, miss. Your best bet would be to come back first thing tomorrow morning.'

Mitchell and the girl walked out into the early-evening sun. They crossed the Victoria Embankment and stood leaning against the parapet, looking down at the Thames, swollen with drifting islands of rat-infested refuse.

'God. Just look at it,' said Maggie bitterly.

'What?'

'Everything. When my father came back from a visit to Singapore, he said how clean it was because they had such tough penalties for dropping litter. He said that that was half the trouble with this country – that we don't crack down hard enough to solve problems.'

Mitchell slipped his arm round her and steered her back to the car. 'Come on, honey. We'll find a hotel, and give those bureaucrats hell in the morning.'

4

New Yorkers are more accustomed to helicopters than most inhabitants of large cities. At most times of the day the air space above and round their city is thick with twenty to thirty helicopters either pleasure-tripping tourists round Manhattan, ferrying mail and passengers to La Guardia and

Kennedy airports, or just hanging about making a noise. But the spectacle of fifteen in-line Sikorsky S61s, painted in the mottled green and brown camouflage of the US Air Force Recovery and Rescue Service, thundering across Manhattan from the direction of Queens caused many of the late home-going crowds thronging the sidewalks to look up. The immense machines ignored city ordinances controlling the movement of helicopters; they swept across Central Park, turned sharply above the Parks Department Boat Basin on the Hudson and formed an orderly line of disciplined, hovering thunder between the basin and the Dwight Eisenhower Passenger Terminal.

The Circle Line Ferry nosing towards its berth after the last trip of the day listed dangerously to port as excited passengers swarmed to one side.

Ex-Sergeant Dean Forester from Colorado Springs, pointed out the machines to his son.

'Know what they are, Ben?'

'A lot of noise and lot of pollution,' said Ben distastefully.

'Jolly Green Giants, we used to call them. One of those whirly-birds picked up your Pa when he was shot up bad. If it wasn't for them, you wouldn't be here. What do you think of that, hey?'

It was one of those statements that parents are wont to make for which their unsuspecting offspring have no ready answer.

The first Sikorsky swung towards the West Side water-front, lowering its cargo hoist to the men clambering over the stacks of thirty-metre pipe sections. It hovered for thirty seconds. The whine from its turbines deepened. The heavy machine lifted, swinging away from the waterfront with a cluster of pipe sections suspended from its hoist. The helicopter thrashed down river and the second machine in the line moved in to take its place.

Don Marchant of Oklahoma was on second honeymoon with his second wife and his three cameras. Even on the balcony of the observatory on the eighty-sixth floor of the

Empire State Building there was no wind to upset his shutter finger. The second honeymoon had been a disappointment, but he was amply compensated by his magnificent Polaroid shot of fifteen big helicopters flying in line towards Kennedy with the setting sun flashing on their twisting, suspended cargoes.

Operation GOPHER was underway.

5

Paul Weiner was shown into the emergency operations room at five minutes to midnight. His heart sank when he saw the number of people present. Senior army officers were gathered round a large plotting-table bearing a huge large-scale map of the Thames Estuary. Engineers were aiming spluttering soldering irons into the maze of coloured wires sprouting from the end of a massive cable that entered the room through a ragged hole in the wall. A man was mounting a public address speaker on a wall bracket. Girls were hovering near the officers with shorthand pads at the ready. The Prime Minister was at the centre of a huddle grouped round a television monitor showing a surprisingly clear picture of the Vulcan Hall nuclear power station. Another engineer had the back off a second monitor and was probing its innards with a test meter. Two senior police officers were playing StarGlider III on a microcomputer.

No one took much notice of Weiner. He had passed through five security checks to get near the room. He stood looking round. The windows were shut and the blinds pulled down. There was no air-conditioning.

Weiner pushed his way across to the Prime Minister.

'May I have a quick word with you, please, sir?'

The Prime Minister looked up from the monitor. Weiner was surprised by the transformation in the man's face since he had last seen him. He had an expression of elation – the look of a soldier eager for battle.

'Ah, Weiner. What do you think of the picture from opposite Vulcan Hall? We've set up hidden cameras fitted with something which lets them see in the dark. Image intensifiers or something.' The politician left the huddle and drew Weiner into a corner. 'How's everything going?'

'All the equipment has left New York. It's on its way.'

The Prime Minister looked surprised. 'Already? I'll introduce you to the Marshal of the Royal Air Force so you can arrange for Biggin Hill . . .'

'It's all arranged,' said Weiner. 'But we're not using Biggin Hill. It can't handle the long-range strategic heavy transports we're flying in.'

'We agreed it was the best place.'

'Our aircrews were against the idea. They've suggested Dunsfold.'

The Prime Minister had never heard of the place.

'It's owned by British Aerospace and has one of the longest air strips in the South of England,' explained Weiner. 'So we'll need all the helicopters diverted to Dunsfold.'

The American's attitude had annoyed the Prime Minister all through the day during their frequent telephone conversations. The Americans were trying to take over the entire operation.

'We've decided against helicopters,' said the Prime Minister firmly.

The statement astounded Weiner.

'But we decided . . .'

'*You* decided.'

'But Prime Minister, helicopters are the most logical way of transporting the pipe sections to Chatham Dockyard.'

The Prime Minister grasped Weiner gently by the elbow and steered him into the corridor. 'Listen, Weiner, dozens of helicopters buzzing across the country with thirty-metre lengths of pipe hanging from their hoists will start a whole spate of rumours which it will be impossible to suppress. If the story about the power station gets out, it could easily start a panic. Naturally, we're extremely grateful for all the help your country is giving us, but we're the ones who have to govern here when this business is over. Not your President, and certainly not the CIA.'

The Prime Minister gave Weiner no time to reply.

'You give Sir Dudley McBryan full information on when and where your transport is expected, and he'll arrange for them to be met by the fleet of trucks and low-loaders he's laid on. How far is Dunsfold from Chatham?'

'About a hundred miles.'

'What time will your transport be arriving?'

'Ten hundred hours.'

'Then there's no problem. The navy say the ship won't be ready until sixteen hundred hours so there'll be plenty of time to shift the stuff from Dunsfold. There's no point in a lot of unnecessary panic, Weiner. We British are used to keeping cool in adverse circumstances.'

And being offensive, Weiner wanted to say, but he managed to remain silent.

'What about this GOPHER contraption and the space-suit? When's that arriving?'

'They'll be on the transports arriving at Dunsfold in the morning.' said Weiner. 'The team of technicians will be arriving with them; two men to look after GOPHER; the NASA spacesuit experts and, of course, the GOPHER operator. He's our only astronaut who's also a first-class marksman.'

'I've changed my mind about that, too. The operator who breaks into the power station will have to be British.'

Weiner was appalled. 'We can't change the plans this late in the day, sir. besides, he's on his way.'

'Maybe you can't change the plans, Weiner, but we can,' said the Prime Minister smoothly. He was gratified by Weiner's expression. The CIA man was badly shaken.

'We can't substitute the operator,' Weiner nearly shouted. 'Jesus, he's a trained astronaut. He's accustomed to working in a spacesuit. He's been shown how to operate the machine–'

'According to Cox-Spender's last instruction,' the Prime Minister interrupted, 'operating the machine is relatively simple.'

'You don't understand. We have to use an old pattern spacesuit because they've got a hundred per cent heat-insulating properties. Those spacesuits were individually made. You can't just get anybody to wear one!'

'I'm sorry, Weiner. But my colleagues and I have made up our minds. The man who breaks into the power station must be British. On that we are firmly decided.'

The American shook his head in disbelief.

'Christ. What does the man's nationality matter?'

'It matters to us.' The politician paused and patted Weiner patronizingly on the shoulder. 'As a matter of interest, I've already made a personal choice of the officer who is to break in. He's a capable man and, I understand, an excellent marksman.'

Weiner saw no sense in arguing further. He merely said, 'The agreement was that we supply the equipment and the specialized personnel. In view of this change, we will have to revise downward our estimates of the probable success of Operation GOPHER.'

The Prime Minister grinned. 'So you've taken it upon yourselves to allocate a code name?'

'It's necessary for communication purposes.'

'Have you read Churchill's memoirs on the Second World War?'

Weiner moved towards the operations room.

'No.'

'I think it was Volume Two,' said the Prime Minister, now enjoying himself. 'In it, he published the directives he issued to be applied when deciding the code names to be used for wartime operation. He stressed that the name selected should not be trivial – it would not do, he said, for the relatives of those killed in a particular action to have to recall an operation with an absurd name. He also said the name should in no way reflect the nature of the operation.'

'I'm surprised that you should concern yourself with such minor points, sir.'

'Churchill also said that the greatness of an organization manifested itself in its attention to detail.'

Weiner choked back an impulse to tell the Prime Minister what he thought of a country that allowed its nuclear power stations to be seized by a handful of terrorists. Instead he said coldly, 'If it's detail you're concerned about, you'd better let me have the measurements of your operator so we can have another spacesuit flown in from Houston.'

With that, Weiner turned and walked away.

The Prime Minister spent another hour in the operations room. He left at 2:30 and went to bed at 3:00 hours. As he undressed he reflected that here were only forty-five hours left before Keller would carry out his threat.

He lay awake for some minutes wondering what had happened to Simpson, and then fell soundly asleep.

Friday

1

The Lockheed Galaxy's wings drooped as it lost speed, lowering its twenty-eight landing wheels to Dunsfold's runway. By the time it had rolled to a standstill the tips appeared to be touching the ground. Then the massive transport kneeled by partly retracting its undercarriages into their vast pods.

The load master wasted no time.

The Galaxy's nose swung upwards like the visor on a suit of armour, and the two Queen Mary vehicles reversed smartly up to the yawning cavern.

Beads of sweat rolled down the soldiers' faces as they laboured to load the curious lengths of half-section plastic pipe on to their long trucks. The vehicles were quickly loaded to safe height and moved away to allow two more to take their place. After thirty minutes under the dawn sky eight low-loaders were loaded to capacity. The last two pulled clear as the great visor swung down. The ponderous bulk of giant freight aircraft heaved itself up from its kneeling position and taxied away to the far end of the long runway. A few minutes later the great shadow swept over a farmhouse, its engines bellowing at the sustained effort required to keep the improbable mass in the air.

The next arrival at Dunsfold was a flying nightmare: a hideous bloated Super Guppy Owned by Aero Spacelines Inc. of Santa Barbara, California.

The Super Guppy had started out to be a graceful Boeing Stratocruiser, and then things had gone badly wrong for it.

The wings and the underside of the fuselage were Stratocruiser, but its upper half was a grotesque swollen balloon that swept up from the nose until its height matched the tailplane. The sides bulged sickeningly over the wings and continued bulging until they reached the tail, where sanity was restored. The weird aircraft had been designed to transport the top stage of the Saturn/Apollo moon rocket, and was now available to anyone with a bulky load that required urgent transportation.

The monstrous creation sat pregnantly on the runway while its crew performed a Caesarean section on its fuselage. The opening disgorged more of the pipe halves, a large crate, several giant reels of flexible hose, a number of smaller crates and ten passengers. All were spirited away in the remaining trucks.

The Guppy waddled to the end of the runway and waited while the airfield-control officer nerved herself to give it permission to take off.

2

Hendricks arrived in London at 8.00 hours. He went straight to Paul Weiner's office. Weiner was asleep on a folding bed. Hendricks shook him roughly.

'What's this bull about the British wanting to use one of their own men?'

Weiner sat up yawning and rubbing his eyes. Hendricks repeated the question.

'National pride,' said Weiner. He looked at his watch. 'Jesus, I need more sleep than this.'

The long bony fingers hooked the covers on to the floor 'You've had some, which is more than I've had. Come on. We're going to make them change their minds.'

Weiner shook his head. 'We'd be wasting our time. I've tried. The Prime Minister won't budge.'

Hendricks sat in Weiner's chair. 'You told him we had someone lined up?'

'Sure.'

'An astronaut who's a marksman?'

'Yes,' said Weiner wearily. 'He said he too had picked an ideal man.'

'The British don't have astronauts.'

'You tell him.'

Hendricks drummed his talons on the desk.

'Does it matter?' asked Weiner. 'The machine isn't difficult to operate. All we need is for NASA to get off their asses and fly out a spacesuit that matches the measurements I've faxed them.'

'That's the whole goddamn trouble,' growled Hendricks.

'Haven't they got one?'

Hendricks gazed at Weiner sadly. 'Sure they got one. But nothing less than a personal directive from the President will persuade them to part with it, even for a week. I got their message an hour before I landed. I thought, in a moment of rashness, that I could leave you to look after things at this end.'

'What's so special about one lousy spacesuit?' demanded Weiner, stung by Hendricks' comment.

Hendricks picked up the phone and fished in his pocket for a piece of paper, which he tossed to Weiner.

'*That* is what is special about it.'

Weiner read the slip. He looked at Hendricks with a mixture of surprise and dismay. All he could think of to say was, 'Oh shit.'

'My reaction precisely,' said Hendricks, and gave the switchboard the day code that would put him through to the White House.

3

By noon, the seven-thousand-tonne ore-carrier *Barrow* lying at the navy dockyard at Chatham was beginning to look like a ship again. Most of the two hundred skilled dockyard workers who had been swarming over her since she had been commandeered the previous night had completed their frenzied operations and were clearing up the mess. They had laboured first under floodlights and then under the hot morning sun to cut a three-metre diameter hole in her side into the midships hold. The position of the hole had been carefully calculated so that it would be well below the waterline when the forward and aft holds were laden with gravel and equipment.

When everything was ready the signal was given to the cranes that were holding the *Barrow* at a thirty-degree list. The ship slowly righted herself. Water roared through the gaping hole. A steel hawser parted with a sudden twang, The *Barrow* heaved herself over on to an even keel and settled lower and lower as water continued to flood into the midships hold. The engineers looked on anxiously. Their main concern was whether the reinforced bulkheads separating the hold from the rest of the ship would withstand the water pressure normally directed on the hull.

The *Barrow* stopped sinking and rode serenely at her mooring. No one went near her for thirty minutes – there was a chance that a bulkhead might collapse without warning.

Two dockyard engineers ventured cautiously aboard. They looked down at the flooded hold.

'Just like a bleedin' swimming-pool.'

'I reckon there's enough freeboard for the gravel.'

'I wouldn't go out on it. Bloody dangerous with this lot sloshing about in any sort of chop.'

'I've heard they're taking it up river – not out to sea.'

'Why do they want them extra anchors then?'

'Nice ship until we buggered her up.'

'Wonder what it's for? I've not heard there's a market of ships with bleedin' great three metre holes in their side.'

'Maybe it's a new method of fishing. They sit up here waiting for a fish to swim through the hole them chuck gavel at it.'

The first engineer spat into the brimming hold.

'Why should we worry? Just so long as they pay us that bleedin' treble time they promised. Come on. Let's get the gravel loaded before that stuff turns up.'

'Do you know what's it's all for?'

'Dunno. Who cares?'

The first engineer nodded to one of the many closed-circuit television cameras recently installed on the *Barrow*'s bridge. 'Not me. But someone does.'

4

'I'm sorry, Miss Pyne,' said the principal officer at the Ministry of Defence. 'But I'm afraid I cannot disclose where your father is.' He smiled sympathetically at Maggie, finding it hard to believe that she could have been responsible for all the scenes throughout the building which resulted in him agreeing to see her personally.

The American with her seemed to be embarrassed by the whole business.

'General Pyne is in command of the new oil and gas platform defence force?' said Mitchell.

The principal officer nodded. 'Quite right. There's no secret about that. But I'm afraid I'm not at liberty to disclose where the camp is. Not until the minister decides to release the press statement.' He nodded to Maggie. 'As the daughter of a senior army officer, Miss Pyne, you must be accustomed to your father being called away on business.'

Maggie stood. 'He's always told me when he would be away, and when he would be returning. If you won't help me, then I'll find him by myself.'

She turned and marched out of the office.

Mitchell looked at the principal officer in embarrassment. 'I'm sorry.'

The civil servant smiled good naturedly. 'Don't worry, Mr Mitchell. You'd better go after her. A few more like her and we wouldn't need an army.'

'Take me home Mitch,' said Maggie when they were outside the building.

'Hey. I thought you were a fighter?'

'I'm sick of London. I never thought I would be – but I am.'

'It's possible,' said Mitchell slowly, 'that Paul Weiner might know where your father is.'

'Your friend at the American Embassy? How could he?'

Mitchell considered telling her about his interview with Hendricks and Weiner and their interest in Maggie's father. He recalled Hendricks' threat and decided against it. Still – it wouldn't hurt to take Maggie to see Weiner.

'Maybe not,' he said in answer to Maggie's question. 'But it might be worth looking him up.'

Mitchell steered Maggie back to the Mustang.

5

The officer the Prime Minister had selected to break into Vulcan Hall nuclear power station was one of the few in the country who knew about the terrorist takeover.

He was watching a television programme when two plain-clothes men called for him. They were polite, but firm. They allowed him to change out of his shorts, then pushed him into the back of a two-door sports car.

'Where are you taking me and why?'

'We only know where, sir.'

And that was all they said during the entire journey.

They took him to a drab, inhospitable mansion in a tree-lined road off the Bayswater Road and left him to contemplate the view across Kensington Palace Gardens from a comfortable flat on the top floor.

He sat on a window seat wondering what was going to happen next.

He was a lean, muscular man with grey eyes and dark wiry hair that was beginning to go grey at the temples. After five minutes in the flat he crossed to the door. It was unlocked. two soldiers were standing on either side of the door.

'Can we help you, sir?' one of them asked.

The officer returned to the window seat. He was still sitting there when the Prime Minister walked into the room, sat in an armchair and proceeded to unwrap a cigar. The officer gaped at him in surprise.

'You know about the power station takeover, of course,' said the Prime Minister, as if unaware of the impact his appearance had had on the officer. 'What you don't know is that with a little American help, I've devised a scheme to get them out.' The Prime Minister paused to light his cigar before explaining about the *Barrow*, the prefabricated riverbed tunnel and the GOPHER boring machine. The Prime Minister concluded by saying that the officer would have to go to the Royal Aircraft Establishment at Farnborough to be shown how to use the spacesuit and to check that it was effective against the IRIS detectors. He was about to enlarge sightly, when the officer interrupted him:

'You said "me", sir.' The officer was puzzled.

The Prime Minister examined the glowing end of his cigar.

'That's right. As one of the most loyal officers in the country, you're going to be the one to break in.'

The officer stiffened. 'Whose idea was this?'

'Mine,' said the Prime Minister, grinning. 'Rather ingenious, don't you think?'

The officer's face relaxed. He nodded slowly and allowed himself a faint smile.

'There is one thing,' said the Prime Minister. 'If you were unable to cut all the detonator wires, you'd have to find this Keller and be absolutely certain of killing him with your first shot before he saw you. There'd be no second chance. Could you do it?'

'Yes. I'm a good shot.'

236

The officer had misunderstood the question, but the Prime Minister let it pass. There was a silence, then the politician said, 'I've told my Cabinet colleagues that the identity of the officer carrying out this task must remain a secret known only to me. If you succeed – well and good. But if you don't . . . Well, I don't think it fair that your name should be remembered in history, if there is any history should you fail, as the man partly to blame for the death of millions of people.'

The officer nodded. The explanation made sense. 'And that view has been accepted?'

'Yes,' said the Prime Minister. 'For that reason, I've decided you should have a code name – Phoenix.' He paused. 'Your identity will never be known. You're prepared to accept that?'

'Yes.'

The Prime Minister nodded. Loyalty was a commodity to be exploited first, and respected second.

The two men discussed details for an hour. At the end the Prime Minister crossed to a cocktail cabinet and poured drinks. They drank a silent toast to their plan's ultimate success.

'I must go now,' said the Prime Minister, 'and you must get down to Farnborough to see about that spacesuit.' He paused at the door. 'One thing, for God's sake be careful with it. The Americans are rather attached to it. It was the suit worn by Neil Armstrong when he took his giant leap for mankind.

6

Cox-Spender dragged his suitcase off the circulating conveyer and tottered towards the customs hall.

He was not feeling his best. He had persuaded Hendricks to allow him to return on a slower aircraft than Concorde. The flight from New York had taken nine hours instead of the usual seven. There had been storms all across the Atlantic. Belts of severe clear air turbulance from all over the ocean had gathered in the path of his Boeing and lain in ambush — arranging themselves so that each succeeding air pocket was worse than the previous one.

On top of that a baby had been sick all over his suit.

Two men approached him. One was wearing a sailcloth suit which Cox-Spender thought he must have purchased in a dark boutique during a power cut.

'Mr Cox-Spender?' Sailcloth suit smiled disarmingly.

'Yes?'

'Will you come with us please.'

It was an order, not a question.

They were very kind to Cox-Spender. They told him that they had been told to say what a magnificent job he had done, and that he was to be rewarded with some well-earned leave at Inverloch in Scotland.

'Inverloch?' echoed Cox-Spender. 'You mean the safe house?'

'I expect so, sir,'

'But it's been closed since the war!'

'Deliberate rumours, Mr Cox-Spender. You'll find it cooler that London.'

'What would I do there?'

'Well, there's golf.'

'I don't play golf.'

'We'll teach you.'

'And Commander Crabbe will teach you fly fishing,' said the second man. 'He's an expert now.'

'A trout stream prima donna,' said sailcloth suit, taking Cox-Spender's case.

Ten minutes later Cox-Spender was sitting between the two men on a flight bound for Edinburgh.

7

The navy dockyard at Chatham had not seen so much activity since the war.

At 14:00 hours a convoy of low-loaders, with tarpaulins covering their loads, rumbled along the naval town's sun-blistered streets and into the dockyard, where cranes transferred their loads on to the thousand tonnes of gravel spread evenly in the *Barrow*'s forward and aft holds.

The level of the gravel was three metres below deck, so there was plenty of room for the pipe sections, the pumps, the prefabricated dome and the GOPHER boring machine.

A team of shallow-water divers arrived from the navy's HMS *Vernon* underwater training school, followed by trucks loaded with oxygen rebreathing sets and additional equipment delivered from Westlands in Yeovil.

The Prime Minister watched the final preparations with ill-concealed satisfaction on the monitor screens in the operations room.

Hendricks was standing beside him.

The politician waved a hand at the tiered television screens fed from cameras mounted on the *Barrow*.

'Supposing all this hadn't been possible, would you have carried out that veiled threat?'

'I can't speak for my government,' replied Hendricks.

'Your ambassador had no inhibitions on Tuesday night.'

Hendricks watched a crane lowering a cluster of plastic pipe sections.

'That was Tuesday night,' he replied.

8

'Would you wait in the outer office please, Miss Pyne,' said Weiner.

Maggie made no attempt to move. 'So you won't help?'

Weiner glanced at Mitchell. 'We don't know where he is. I'd like to speak to Mr Mitchell alone. It won't take a minute.'

Maggie regarded Weiner coldly. She left the room without speaking.

'Now see here Mitch,' said Weiner when the door closed behind her. 'Do you want us to cover your drill-string or not?'

'Sure.'

'Then why bring her here? You heard what Hendricks said.'

'I've told her nothing. We were in town, and I thought you might be able to help. Why *are* you interested in Pyne?'

'I can't tell you that.'

'This fraud or whatever it is he's mixed up in, does it involve American equipment?'

Weiner came around from his desk. 'Listen Mitch. Take the girl home. Take her away on vacation somewhere – anything to stop her worrying about her father. She'll find out soon enough, but I can't tell you anything at this point.'

'Can I tell her that?'

Weiner shrugged. 'Why not. Just take her away somewhere where the press and the crackpots won't be able to give her a hard time.'

'So he is involved in a serious crime?'

Weiner nodded. 'In a way – yes. But don't for Chrissake tell her.'

Saturday:
The final hours

1

'Phoenix' arrived at the Royal Aircraft Establishment at 00:15 hours.

The untidy test laboratory was busy with technicians milling round a spacesuit suspended from a frame. A long bench against a wall was strewn with the component parts of the suit's backpack. A loud Texan accent was yelling for a six-mill wrench. A white-coated man was chipping at a block of ice.

Earl Kramer's name was embroidered on his coveralls. Phoenix introduced himself. Kramer stared at Phoenix, then yelled, 'He's here!'

Everyone stopped work and gathered around.

'How's it going?' asked Phoenix.

'Lousy,' said Kramer. 'Come back next week.'

'What's the trouble?'

'Heat absorption.' Kramer looked at Phoenix curiously. 'This thing you've got to do. Could you do it in an hour?'

Phoenix was surprised by the direct, no-nonsense approach. 'I don't know. Why?'

'We have a problem with your body heat. Come over here, and I'll show you what I mean.'

Kramer stepped across to the bench and picked up a garment that resembled long underwear to cover arms, legs and torso.

'Feel,' he said, as if he were a tailor trying to convince a customer about the quality of some material.

Phoenix could feel minute tubes sandwiched into the material. The entire garment was a mass of them.

'Water-cooling tubes,' explained Kramer. 'You wear this next to your skin over the absorbent underpants, and these tubes carry your body heat to the PLSS on your back, where it's pushed through an exchanger out into the environment. Now as I understand it, we can't do that.'

'That's right,' said Phoenix. 'No heat must escape.'

'So what the hell do we do with it?' demanded Kramer.

Phoenix shrugged. 'I'm sorry. I'm not an engineer. What do you do with it?'

'Instead of getting rid of it, we absorb it – into crushed ice. We've modified the PLSS–'

'PLSS?'

'Personal Life Support System,' explained Kramer patiently. 'The backpack. We've modified it so you'll have a an insulated flask containing thirty pounds of ice. Ice can absorb a helluva lot of heat, but as soon as it's all melted, its temperature starts to creep up. That's why you only have a hour to do whatever it is you're going to do. Maybe two hours if you take it easy, but we can't be sure, so we've fixed you up with an ice-weight indicator. That way you'll know when you're heading for trouble.'

Phoenix frowned. No one had mentioned this problem during his long telephone conversations with various experts.

'Couldn't you provide more than thirty pounds of ice?' he asked.

Kramer shook his head. 'We've tried, and run up against a law of diminishing returns. The more ice you carry, the more heat you generate having to hike it around, and the faster the ice melts. Besides, thirty pounds is half the weight of the suit. You'll have ninety pounds over your body weight to shift around. It's enough.'

'One hour?'

'Two if you don't rush around. Okay, let's get you suited up. The guys in the next lab want to run some tests.'

242

Phoenix found the spacesuit, or 'extra vehicular mobility unit', as the NASA technicians called it, was surprisingly comfortable and permitted an unexpected freedom of movement – the one thing that had worried him since he had learned he was to wear one. The only uncomfortable feeling was caused by the urine tube fitted to his penis and leading to a bag on the right leg of the suit above the knee.

'The absorbent underpants will cope with anything else,' Kramer said.

Phoenix commented on the crude arrangement.

'If you can come up with an improvement on diapers,' said Kramer, grinning, 'then we'd be glad to hear about it.'

The first garment had been the one-piece cooling suit. This was followed by he eighteen-layer 'integrated meteoroid suit' with an outer covering of non-flammable Beta cloth, finally the abrasion-resistant Teflon fabric covering designed to protect the suit against mishaps on the rugged lunar terrain.

Tinted pull-down visors were provided on the helmet to protect the astronaut against ultra-violet and infra-red radiation, and micro-meteoroids. It was impossible to see the wearer's face when they were lowered.

Kramer secured the backpack and connected the water cooling, oxygen purge and communication umbilicals. He guided Phoenix's gauntleted hands to the control box on the suit's chest.

'I'm going to switch you on now,' he said into a two-way radio.

Phoenix suddenly felt water flowing through the tubes next to his skin. It was like being plunged into a cool bath. The sensation was a welcome relief from the heat building up in the suit.

'How does it feel?'

'Great.'

Kramer grinned. 'For the first time in your life, you're completely independent of Mother Earth in your own little

243

self-contained space-ship. If this planet was to blow apart suddenly, you'd outlive everyone. But only for a few hours.'

Kramer checked the suit's controls. 'Okay. Try moving about a little, but lean forward – remember, you've got a high centre of gravity.'

The backpack was a deadweight on Phoenix's back. The straps dragged at this shoulders. He took a few unsteady steps. Sweat streamed down his face despite the cooling system.

'Well?'

'God, it's heavy.'

Kramer nodded sympathetically. 'Yeah. They're not designed for EVA in one gee. And you've got an extra thirty pounds of ice.'

'Why are you using pounds instead of kilos?'

'Because all this kit was designed before NASA adopted the metric system. What's the gauge reading?'

Phoenix looked at his right wrist – holding it high in front of the visor.

'Twenty-nine pounds.'

'You see? You've melted a pound of ice already, and you've hardly started moving about.'

Kramer's easy-going manner annoyed Phoenix. 'Why the hell couldn't you arrange something better than this ludicrous system? Christ, even a sixth-former would've thought of refrigeration.'

'Easy on,' said Kramer's voice inside the helmet. 'All refrigeration does is move heat from one place to another: it doesn't get rid of it. Ever put your hand down the back of an icebox?'

'I'm sorry.'

Kramer brushed the apology aside. 'Don't let it bother you. You'd better get next door.'

'Just as I am?'

'Sure. It's meant for moving about in. Through the door. First door on the right.'

244

As Phoenix swayed unsteadily towards the door, he heard a click in his helmet as Kramer cut communications. He did not hear him say loudly into a telephone for the benefit of everyone:

'One astronaut on the rocks coming up, fellers.'

Phoenix turned in the corridor and saw the technicians mouthing silent laughter.

The spacesuited figure shuffled towards an IRIS detector. His external microphone was switched on so he could hear the sounds in the laboratory. Four men and a woman doctor were watching his progress from behind a glass panel set into the wall. A loud speaker relayed their talk.

The detector was mounted on a pedestal. The dome on top of the unit discarded ambient heat radiation, and concentrated on any dense sources of heat that moved.

'Hold it a minute,' said the loudspeaker.

Phoenix paused.

'Okay. Carry on. We thought we were getting a reading.'

Phoenix moved nearer the detector until he could reach out and touch it.

'What do you want me to do now?'

'Move a hand in front of it.'

Phoenix waved a gauntlet up and down a few centimetres from the detector.

'Fine,' said the loudspeaker. 'Now turn around slowly, and put your face near it.'

Feeling slightly ridiculous, Phoenix did so.

'Now push one of the visors up.'

Phoenix complied.

'Now the other one.'

He had only just pushed the visor halfway when the loudspeaker shrilled with a continuous, discordant note.

'Just thought you'd like to hear the result,' said the loudspeaker.

'How much ice is left?'

'Nineteen pounds.'

'Right. There's just one more test, then you can get some sleep.'

The four men and the woman entered the laboratory. They guided Phoenix to a cycling machine and helped him on to the saddle. He had to hang grimly on to the handlebars to prevent the backpack's weight from toppling him off. He was unable to see his boots, so they secured them to the pedals with straps.

'Just pedal slowly,' said the doctor. 'As if you were cycling along a flat country lane and enjoying the view.'

While Phoenix busily pedalled nowhere, the laboratory staff surrounded him with a fence of detectors before returning to their booth.

'How much ice now?' said the loudspeaker ten minutes later.

'Thirteen pounds.'

'Slow down a little.'

The needle on the wrist gauge crept downward. After twenty minutes it was hovering over the figure five.

'Ease up little,' said the loudspeaker after Phoenix had relayed the information.

Phoenix slowed the pumping action. The movement of his legs was causing the urine attachment to chaff painfully on his penis.

Fifteen minutes later the needle was on zero.

'It'll take a while for the water to warm up and trigger the detectors,' said the loudspeaker.

Phoenix continued pedalling. The heat in the suit began to rise.

'Speed it up a little,' said the loudspeaker.

He pedalled faster, tightening his abdomen muscles against the desire to urinate.

Another five minutes passed. There was no sound in the laboratory apart from the creak and whir of the cycling machine and the rustle of Teflon fabric.

Then the room suddenly filled with a violent shrieking tone from the loudspeaker. The mind-numbing noise caused

Phoenix to relax his stomach muscles. Hot urine coursed through the tube and gurgled into the bag on his thigh. The shrieking rose to a deafening crescendo.

'Christ,' breathed one of the men in the control booth. 'He's set them all off. Every fucking one.'

2

At 2:00 hours, Jack Delmar was hardly able to contain his excitement. He leaned on the bridge rail beneath a bright moon and breathed deeply, savouring the feeling of anticipation now that the operation was about to begin. God, how he hated retirement.

There was a flooding tide, the *Barrow*'s navigation lights were switched on and her mooring lines singled up. A tug eased across the still water and between the dark shapes of mothballed warships.

The shallow-water divers sat in orderly rows on polythene sheeting spread over the gravel in the aft hold. They were dressed in neoprene wetsuits and wearing oxygen rebreathing sets. Their masks hung down on their chests. Some passed the time threading weights on to their quick-release belts, a few smoked. None talked. A chief petty officer checked the spare lithium hydroxide canisters the divers would be using to purify the oxygen in their rebreathing sets. He was unhappy having so many men on oxygen. He preferred aqualungs, which used compressed air and were much safer. Oxygen under pressure could kill a man in a few minutes, especially if he had to be dragged out of a four-kilometre long underwater pipeline.

'Scubas are out,' Jack Delmar had told the chief petty officer. 'We don't want exhaust bubbles pooling in the pipeline and forcing it to the surface before we've pumped the gravel in.'

The chief petty officer moved across to his men. 'You okay, Jones?'

The diver he addressed nodded nervously. 'Fine, thanks, chief.'

The chief petty officer grunted and moved on. Jones was recovering from a perforated eardrum after diving with a head cold he had not reported. Normally he wouldn't be allowed near a pair of flippers for another month, but those in charge, whoever they were, sitting God knows where, and watching every move with the television cameras, wanted every diver they could lay their hands on.

The tug left the *Barrow* when the two ships reached the widest part of the River Medway. The bridge rang down 'slow ahead both' to the engine-room. White water boiled under the ore-carrier's stern. Black water heaved in the flooded hold as she moved downriver alone.

In one hour she would be entering the Thames Estuary; and another hour's steaming up river towards London would bring her to Canvey Island.

Keeping well over to the south bank, away from the power station, she would gradually lose way, pay out her anchors and use her engines to drag their flukes deep onto the mud until the *Barrow* was held firmly fore and aft. Then, below the high sides of the holds and screened from the distant power station, everyone on board would start work. Even the *Barrow*'s original crew had a task to perform: they were to laze in the sun in full view and show no interest in the power station whatsoever.

While *Barrow* was lifting her bows to the gentle waves, Phoenix was in a sedative-induced sleep at the Royal Aircraft Establishment.

A pilot boat would take him to the *Barrow* when everything was ready. That would be at 14:00 hours if everything went according to plan.

Ten hours before Ralph Keller's Doomsday Ultimatum deadline.

3

Phoenix raised the M1 automatic rifle and fired three times.

The first round tore a piece off the top of his target's skull, the second smashed through the back of the neck and the third shattered the remains of the head.

'Not bad,' said the major grudgingly. 'You're getting the hang of it now. The first one would've been enough.'

'I like to be certain,' said Phoenix, pulling off the space helmet and gauntlets. They were the only part of the spacesuit he had been wearing. He examined the rifle. 'Sawing off the trigger guard was a good idea.'

The major looked curiously at the strange gauntlets.

'Damned difficult shooting with those things on. Is it absolutely essential?'

'Yes.'

The major walked down the indoor firing range and collected the fragments of wax. He assembled the skull in his hands and showed it to Phoenix. There was a neat hole where the second shot had penetrated the back of the neck, but at the front was a crater the size of a man's fist. The major put the skull down and examined one of the unjacketed bullets disapprovingly.

'Nasty things,' he said. 'Don't know why MOD buy them. A bullet goes in and an express train comes out.'

A nice way of putting it, thought Phoenix.

'I suppose you'll be shooting the real target from behind?'

The telephone rang.

'For you,' said the major, holding out the receiver.

Phoenix took the telephone and waited for the major to move away.

'How's it going?' asked the Prime Minister.

'Very well indeed, sir.'

'You're now going to have to deal with Keller no matter what happens. The Americans know something about him. It's his presence which has caused all the trouble.'

Phoenix was intrigued. 'What do they know that we don't know?'

'A hell of a lot. It seems he was involved in some mischief concerning nuclear fuel when he was working in the United

249

States. It's something we should've known about. Anyway, the important thing now is for you to deal with him so that we can make them a present of his body. That way, they'll lose interest and go home. Do you understand?'

'Yes, sir.'

'I'll wish you the best of luck,' said the Prime Minister. 'See you on television.'

The line went dead.

The major lifted the space helmet off his head.

'Will you be wearing the rest of it? A full spacesuit?'

'Yes.'

'Where exactly is the target? On the moon?'

'Somewhere just as difficult to get to,' said Phoenix, and changed the subject.

4

With six anchors dragged deep into the riverbed, the *Barrow*'s captain was satisfied it would be impossible for the ship to move, apart from up and down with the tide.

He glanced at the bridge chronometer: 4:45 hours. Fifteen minutes ahead of the operations schedule on the chart table.

He gave the order for work to begin.

On the word from Jack Delmar, the chief petty officer herded the first team of twenty divers into the flooded hold.

The black-clad figures guided the lower half of the first pipe section into the hold and through the hole in the *Barrow*'s side without difficulty. Three divers swam out into the Thames and supported the end of the pipe while their fellow-divers pushed out the upper half and allowed it to settle on the lower half. A diver swam along the inside of the pipe fastening the latches that pulled the two halves tightly together against their seals.

An inflatable collar was pushed round the pipe so that it was trapped evenly between the pipe opening and the side of the hole in the hold. The collar was inflated slowly, with divers pulling out the creases until a tight seal was formed.

The *Barrow* now had a flooded thirty-metre length of plastic pipe protruding from her side into the Thames three metres below the surface.

'Current's dragging it a bit,' said Jack Delmar. 'Get another five sections in position right away so we can anchor them to the riverbed.'

The first team worked well. By 5:20 ten sections were in place and the pipeline was three hundred metres long.

'I'm going to have to rest them,' said the chief petty officer.

'Okay, chief. Put your next team down,' said Jack Delmar.

'I'm sorry, sir. But I've put my most experienced divers into the first team so they'll know all the snags that are likely to crop up. Each one of them is to be a divemaster for the other teams, so I can't put any more men down until they've rested.'

Jack Delmar nodded. 'How long do you need?'

'Thirty minutes, sir.'

'Thirty minutes then chief. But no more.'

The second, less experienced team tired in forty-five minutes and managed to increase the pipeline by only five sections. It was exhausting work: each new length added sixty metres to the distance the divers had to swim from the *Barrow*'s hold to the end of the pipeline, and back again.

The third team tired in thirty minutes and succeeded in adding only four sections.

'It's this business of having to shove the sections along the tunnel,' said the chief petty officer despondently. 'Each section makes it more and more difficult. It's a six hundred metre swim as it is, without having to handle the pipes.'

'The pipeline is going to be four thousand metres long, chief,' Jack Delmar pointed out.

The chief petty officer nodded glumly. 'We'll have to think of another way of getting the sections out to the end, sir. At this rate, all the men will be exhausted with only half the sections in position.'

The American considered the problem. 'Okay, chief,' he said. 'You carry on, I'll see if I can up with something.'

5

As each new section disappeared into the hold a girl in the operations room stretched a rod across the plot-table and pushed another length of plastic on to the end of the line that was creeping from the model of the *Barrow* towards a replica of the power station. The Prime Minister, Hendricks and senior officers watched the agonizingly slow process in concern.

Weiner had disappeared in response to an urgent telephone call from his office.

'Ten past nine, Prime Minister,' said Hendricks. 'There should be fifty sections out.'

The Prime Minister picked up a telephone and pressed the button that would sound the buzzer on Jack Delmar's two-way radio. They talked urgently for five minutes.

'They need another two hundred divers,' announced the Prime Minister when he had replaced the receiver.

6

There was very little of Simpson's face left, but enough for Paul Weiner to recognize him as he gingerly turned the body on to its back in Howard Mitchell's sitting-room.

'Do you know who it is?' asked Mitchell.

Weiner stood up and stared down at the body, baffled. Mitchell repeated his question.

'No,' lied Weiner.

'I thought you might,' said Mitchell coldly. 'That's why I called you.'

'Why should I know who it is?' demanded Weiner.

'Come on, Paul. I wasn't born yesterday. You call me up to London. You tell me I'm to spy on General Pyne in return for covering my drill-string which would cost you a helluva lot of money.' Then Mitchell was shouting, his face a few centimetres from Weiner's. 'And now I find this on my carpet, and my telephone blown to bits by what looks like a bomb!'

Weiner groped for words. The bedroom telephone rang. He followed Mitchell upstairs and stood in the doorway. The telephone call had given him time to think.

Mitchell picked up the receiver. 'Yes?'

It was Maggie. Excited. 'Mitch! I've found Daddy! I was an idiot not to have realized before. Those photographs you took last Sunday. I've just made another print from one of the negatives. You remember all those huts and things at the back of that power station that I thought was a holiday camp? Well, it's an army camp! Daddy's new camp! It must be!'

Weiner could hear an excited voice from where he was standing but was unable to make out what was being said. He was grappling with the mystery of Simpson's body, and suddenly realized that Mitchell was speaking to him – his hand cupped over the mouthpiece.

'You know London, Paul. That power station near Thames Haven: is it called Vulcan Hall?'

Weiner was too shaken by the question to speak. He could only nod dumbly.

'Yes,' said Mitchell into the mouthpiece. 'And you couldn't? Sure you dialled the right number?'

Weiner tried frantically to attract Mitchell's attention. Mitchell turned his back on him.

'Sure. I'll take you there, honey.'

Weiner thought he was going to have a heart attack. 'You can't!' he shouted.

Mitchell finished talking and replaced the receiver. He looked up at Weiner. His friend's face was ashen.

'You can't go to Vulcan Hall, Mitch.'

'Sure I can. Who's going to stop me?'

Weiner grabbed his arm.

'Mitch! You can't! You've got to keep away. Both of you!'

Weiner was scared. Mitchell knew him well enough to know that he didn't scare easily.

'Supposing you tell me what all this is about, Paul? Right from the beginning.'

Weiner hesitated, then nodded. 'Okay,' he said reluctantly, and sat down.

Half an hour later Weiner was driving fast back to London, wondering if he had done the right thing. The car clock said noon. Weiner shrugged inwardly. In twelve hours it wouldn't matter what Mitchell knew. It would all be over.

One way or the other.

7

Charlie Davidson was the secretary of the West London branch of the British Sub-Aqua Club. The police called for him at his Ealing office and drove him home through the streets of Acton with sirens howling and lights flashing.

He searched through his club papers and gave the police a list containing the names and addresses of every first-class and second-class diver who was a member of the branch.

'Are any of these people experienced in the use of oxygen rebreathing sets?' asked the police officer, reciting a question he had been told to ask.

Charlie stared at the policeman.

'Hell, no. We only use compressed-air aqualungs. Oxygen sets are too bloody dangerous.'

Charlie followed the policeman out to the car.

'Look,' he said, as the officer called his headquarters. 'None of these people will be any good to you. They know nothing about diving with rebreathing sets.'

'Looks like they're going to get the chance to learn,' said the policeman, and started reading out the names and addresses.

8

The spacious modern bar on the lower deck of the Thames pleasure boat *Chay Blyth* was crowded with over a hundred bewildered members of the British Sub-Aqua Club who had been ruthlessly press ganged into leaving their homes or places of work and driven to Westminster Pier.

The *Chay Blyth*'s master cut his engines and allowed the vessel to drift so that it would pass between the anchored *Barrow* and the south bank. As the *Barrow*'s bulk obscured the distant power station, the divers, on a signal from the plain-clothes policeman, filed quickly out of the bar and jumped into the water. Although they were all good swimmers and covered the thirty metres to the *Barrow*'s side without difficulty, some of them were not so good at climbing scrambling nets and had to be helped aboard.

The chief petty officer divided them into teams and appointed a navy shallow-water diver to put each group through a crash training course in the use of oxygen rebreathing sets.

The *Chay Blyth* continued down river for a little way before turning in a wide circle and pushing her way back towards London to collect another party of reluctant, shanghaied day-trippers.

9

Phoenix helped Kramer and two of his NASA technicians to manhandle the crate containing the spacesuit on to the pilot's boat at Greenwich Pier, under the eyes of indifferent tourists who had grown bored with the *Cutty Sark* and were waiting for the return boat to London.

The pilot's boat pulled away from the pier at 14:10. The crate was carried below. Kramer helped Phoenix into the suit and connected it to a portable air-conditioning unit.

The afternoon was heavy with heat and humidity. Hot diesel fumes soaked through the boat's lower decks.

'You're better off than us,' said Kramer to Phoenix. 'At least you're in the cool.'

Phoenix said nothing. A fan in the air-conditioning whirred quietly as it removed the heat from his spacesuit.

10

By 13:30 the pipeline was over three thousand metres long and was within a kilometre of the power station.

'Okay,' said Jack Delmar. 'Let's get some more ballast pumped in.'

Gravel hurtled along the flexible pipes that snaked through the flooded pipeline.

Barrow was shedding her cargo at a rate of thirty tonnes a minute. The marks painted on the sides of her hull climbed slowly out of the water.

A member of her original crew finished his cigarette and flipped it over the side. He watched the butt curving down. Something caught his eye. He leaned over the rail.

'Christ,' he whispered to himself.

Jack Delmar and the *Barrow*'s captain leaned over the rail and tried to look casual.

'So what do we do now?' asked the captain bitterly.

Jack Delmar looked at the power station crouching beneath its four ghostly cooling towers and then down at the first two pipeline sections extending from the *Barrow*'s side. They were awash on the surface like an elongated drugged whale.

'Once all the gravel is in the pipeline, we can flood the fore and aft holds so we ride lower in the water.'

256

'Can't we do it now?' asked the captain. 'Will it matter if the gravel gets wet?'

'We can't pump wet gravel,' said Jack Delmar. 'We'll just have to take a chance that they can't see anything.'

'A hell of a chance,' said the captain grimly, and gave the order for work to resume. He looked up at one of the television cameras. 'I'd better tell them the good news.'

Weiner slipped unnoticed back into the operations room and looked at the plot table in concern: 18:00 hours was the latest time for the pipeline to be completed and pumped dry. He was about to whisper to Hendricks about his trip to Weybridge, when the Prime Minister spoke:

'This business of sending divers along the inside of the pipeline with the sections seems slow and cumbersome.'

'It prevents divers getting lost,' said a naval officer. 'And it prevents them being swept away by the current, sir. The tide's just turned, so it's going to get worse.'

The Prime Minister pursed his lips. 'Surely they won't get lost if they follow the pipeline? We could have one team pushing the pipe halves through the pipeline and two teams on the outside at the same time. Treble the speed at which we're getting the damned thing assembled.'

'Visibility is under a metre, sir,' said the naval officer, trying to keep his voice polite. 'I'm sure the men on the site would suggest the idea if it were feasible. And besides, if divers were to be swept away, it wouldn't be possible to rescue them.'

'Divers are expendable,' said the Prime Minister. 'Time is not.'

He reached for his telephone.

Between 14:30 and 15:20 the *Barrow* lost two naval divers and five members of the British Sub-Aqua Club team. The water was too turbid for anyone to have seen them disappear. The divers, struggling with the long plastic pipes in open water, soon learned to recognize the sudden increase in their burden as a sign that another of their comrades had lost his hold. They tried lifelines, but there was nothing to fasten them to – only thirty-metre lengths of plastic pipe endowed by the current with a malignant life force of their own. Three lengths were lost – swept away by the strengthening black tide with divers secured to them.

At 15:50 the *Barrow*'s captain counted the remaining halves of pipe, and calculated that the pipeline was now only three sections short of its required length. A quarter of an hour later a divemaster surfaced in the hold, spat out his mouthpiece and yelled that the last section ferried out couldn't be fitted because it fouled against the power station's steel and concrete pilings. There was a half-hearted cheer from the exhausted divers huddled in the holds.

A diver manning an electric underwater scooter was sent along the pipeline to count the reinforcing buttresses between the pipeline opening and the western extremity of the pilings. He returned with the figure fifty-one.

The pipeline opening was in the correct position.

The final task of swimming out with the twelve curved petals that comprised the dome was assigned to a team who had not dived for five hours. They had spent most of the time practising assembling the dome in the aft hold.

The heavy steel petals were lifted over the side of the *Barrow* away from the power station, and passed under her hull. Plastic floats neutralized 95 per cent of each petal's weight. One of them had a hole cut in it to accommodate the pipeline opening. This petal would be positioned first and the others bolted to it to form a dome, with the open base sealed to the riverbed by an inflatable skirt. When the water was eventually pumped out, the pressure of the Thames bearing down on the dome would be greater than the dome's buoyancy.

By the time the under water convoy had set off from the *Barrow*, with each petal assisted by four manned scooters, operation GOPHER was thirty minutes behind schedule.

Jack Delmar was helping to break open the crates that contained the electric golf carts for use in the pipeline after it had been pumped dry, when the pilot's boat was sighted.

11

Phoenix and the NASA technicians were welcomed aboard the *Barrow* at 17:25 by Jack Delmar. He looked curiously at the impenetrable visors and wondered why they were down.

'You might as well take your helmet off,' he told Phoenix, gesturing to the throbbing diesel pumps. 'We won't have the pipeline pumped dry for another half hour. Maybe more.'

'I prefer to keep it on,' said Phoenix. 'It's air-conditioned in here. Why the delay?'

'I couldn't even begin to tell you,' replied the American. 'As soon as we'd shifted some gravel into the pipeline, the ship began to lift. That's why we're pumping the pipeline water into the holds. Do you want to meet the captain?'

'I'd sooner see your boring machine.'

'It would be better if you'd come earlier to get the feel of the thing.'

'I was told it was simple to operate,' replied Phoenix.

The GOPHER was resting on the ramp with most of its weight supported by the outstretched arm of a derrick. It was an odd-looking machine about four metres long and just over a metre in diameter. One third of its length consisted of the spiral cutting-head.

Phoenix leaned into the open hatch. Jack Delmar joined him and pointed out the controls.

'That lever at the side controls the cutting speed and the column in the middle is for going up or down or turning.' He spoke for five minutes, with Phoenix listening attentively.

'How do I control the forward speed?' asked Phoenix, when Jack Delmar had finished.

'You don't. The cutting action of the head pulls you forward. The faster you turn the head the faster you move forward.' He pointed to a group of digital displays. 'That's your INS navigation computer. All you've got to do is keep the displays reading zero, otherwise you're off course. It's been programmed so you'll come up in the power station's Number Three inspection tunnel.'

Phoenix nodded. He had been over the maps of the galleries until he knew them by heart.

'Do you want to see the cutting-head working?' asked Jack Delmar.

'Yes, please.'

Jack Delmar had to yell above the noise from the pumps to attract his engineers. He gave them orders. They connected hydraulic hoses to the couplings at the rear of the GOPHER. A hydraulic pump started up, adding its noise to the existing racket.

'GOPHER's like a road-drill,' Jack Delmar explained. 'It has to be connected to a separate power plant by those hydrualic hoses.' He reached into the cockpit. The massive cutting-helix started turning with a loud clanking.

'Don't worry about the row.' he yelled. 'It quietens down when it's biting into something.'

He shut the machine off and waved to the men manning the hydraulic pump to do the same.

Phoenix noticed that the water level in the midships hold had dropped two metres since he had come aboard. The top of the pipeline entrance was visible above the surface.

The chief petty officer bullied a reluctant team back into their rubber wetsuits.

A third of the opening was visible by the time the first diver edged past the GOPHER, gave Phoenix a curious look and dropped into the hold. He swam into the gaping hole; the last diver was able to wade in carrying a powerful lamp.

'This is the dangerous part,' said Jack Delmar. 'There's plenty of gravel in the pipeline, but if it's not properly distributed a section could be buoyant and suddenly break loose. If that happens, we cash our life insurance and go out on the town.'

The chief petty officer allowed three more divers into the tunnel when the first diver reported that the first ten sections were holding. By the time the entire four-kilometre length of pipeline had been inspected, the bottom of the hold was covered with only a few centimetres of water. The two-metre diameter tunnel entrance in the *Barrow*'s side yawned dark and forbidding.

Alan Roberts of the British Sub-Aqua Club was fixing a portable lamp to the smooth inner surface of the pipeline when he thought he heard a faint creaking noise. He lifted the lamp off its hook and shone it on the nearest seal between two sections. It was weeping discoloured Thames water, but then so were many of the seals. The American had said some seepage was inevitable. He heard the noise again and experienced a twinge of alarm. He tried calculating the water pressure bearing against the outside of the pipeline while straining his ears. There was no more noise. Perhaps his ears were playing up after all the diving he had been doing that day.

He finished connecting the lamp and climbed onto the electric golf cart. Its tyres crunched on the gravel floor as he drove back to the *Barrow*. The strange noise was forgotten by the time the pipeline floor was sloping upwards to the daylight.

12

Maggie fell silent.

No matter how much she screamed at Mitchell, swore at him and heaped abuse on him, he remained steadfast in his determination to keep her a prisoner.

She decided on a different approach.

'Mitch? I'm sorry if I was rude.'

He smiled faintly, but still looked extremely worried. 'Forget it.'

She sat on his knee and lifted his forearm on to her shoulder. 'It's hot. How about a swim?'

'Okay. But only if you promise not to try anything.'

'I promise.'

Maggie's timing in the swimming-pool was superb. She grasped the waistband of Mitchell's trunks and heaved just as he was pushing off from the side. He turned over in the water spluttering in fury.

'Hey! Gimme my shorts!' he bellowed.

Maggie hopped out of the pool and ran towards her car, clutching Mitchell's trunks like a trophy.

Mitchell dived naked into his Mustang just as Maggie's MG disappeared out of the drive.

The Mustang was the more powerful of the two cars. He overtook Maggie on the golf club road. He gave her a safe stopping distance, then swung his car sideways, blocking the road. Maggie responded by swinging on to the golf course and accelerating down the fairway, scattering a foursome teeing up for the fourth hole. Mitchell swore and shot after her. In the four-minute chase round the golf course Maggie tried several times to turn back to the road only to be headed off by the Mustang. Mitchell eventually forced her into a bunker. He yanked the MG's door open as its back wheels spun uselessly in the soft sand.

'I'll take you after midnight, you silly bitch!' He yelled at Maggie.

'Now!'

'Midnight!'

They both stopped arguing, aware of four pairs of eyes watching them.

'You'll be hearing from the club secretary about this, Mr Mitchell,' said one of them, whose game had been interrupted. He turned to his three guests who were regarding Mitchell solemnly.

'An American,' he explained.

The three guests nodded sympathetically.

13

The dank interior of the dome, pressed against the riverbed like a giant rubber sucker, was lit by a string of battery lamps. Perforated steel plates had been placed over the mud to distribute the GOPHER's weight.

The machine was now upended – its cutting-head buried in the mud at a carefully calculated angle.

Jack Delmar was sitting in its inclined cockpit carrying out a last-minute check when the one diver who had remained with him said he could see lights approaching along the tunnel. The golf carts stopped near the dome. Kramer and a NASA technician entered, supporting Phoenix between them. Jack Delmar scrambled out of the cockpit and pulled the GOPHER's power hoses that snaked down the tunnel to one side. The two NASA men helped Phoenix into the GOPHER's cockpit. He kneeled awkwardly on the sloping floor while Kramer attached his backpack and connected the spacesuit to the spare pack Phoenix was to use during the journey under the power station's foundations. A loaded M1 rifle was placed in the cockpit. A pair of wire-cutters and a cold-light discharge tube were stowed in the spacesuit's utility packets.

'We thought we heard a noise back there,' Kramer said to Jack Delmar without stopping work. 'A sort of creaking noise.'

'You'd better take a look,' Jack Delmar said to the diver. 'Use one of the carts.'

The diver drove along the tunnel. After five minutes he too could hear the noise. He slowed down and steered the golf cart with his knees while directing a portable lamp on the sides of the pipeline. He found the broken seal immediately. It was halfway up. Water was running down the tubing and being absorbed into the gravel. The creaking was caused by fractured plastic surfaces being slowly forced inward. Even as the diver watched with mounting concern, a new fissure crept hypnotically across the concave surface. Beads of water appeared along the crack and began to swell.

Phoenix stretched out on his stomach. The GOPHER's steep angle caused him to slide forward over the controls.

'Grip the restraint-bar with your feet,' Jack Delmar advised.

Phoenix eased himself back and hooked his boots over the bar.

Jack Delmar picked a field telephone to call an engineer standing by on the *Barrow*. 'Okay. Give us power.'

The hydraulic hoses connected to the GOPHER stiffened.

'Test the rams,' said the industrialist. 'One at a time.'

Phoenix operated the burrowing machine's controls. Rectangular sections set into the GOPHER's body extended slowly.

'Okay. That's fine.'

The steering pads were withdrawn until they were once again flush with the GOPHER's skin.

Kramer made some final adjustments to the backpack and rapped affectionately on the space helmet before stepping back.

'Good luck,' said Jack Delmar, shutting the hatch. Darkness closed in on Phoenix. He twisted round, fastened the latches and looked at the luminous watch Kramer had given him.

Operation GOPHER was forty-five minutes behind schedule.

The diver picked the golf cart up by the rear and swung it round. He was about to climb back on to the seat to warn the men in the dome, when the pipe suddenly caved in with a tremendous roar and inrush of water that swept the golf cart over and threw the diver against the opposite side of the tunnel.

The men working in the dome looked anxiously down the pipeline as the sound of the imploding water echoed out of the black opening.

'What the hell was that?' asked Kramer.

264

Jack Delmar plugged a communication-jack into a recep-
tacle on the GOPHER's side.

'Okay! Get going!' he barked.

The machine's cutting-head began churning down into
the mud before he finished speaking. The sound of the
GOPHER's hydraulic motor mixed with the thunderous
noise booming out of the tunnel. It was getting louder.
Kramer was about to speak when the tidal wave boiled into
the dome and swept him off his feet. The wave scoured the
perimeter of the dome as if seeking a way of escape.

'Full speed!' Jack Delmar screamed into the communica-
tor. 'We've had a cave-in!'

Kramer and the technician struggled to their feet. The
water was swirling round their waists. They tried to push
their way to the opening against the black torrent surging
into the dome. Kramer's assistant became ensnared in the
thick coils of hydraulic hose and started screaming. Kramer
fought his way to the opening. Jack Delmar grabbed him.

'You've got to stay and help me pay out the hoses!'

GOPHER was driving down into the riverbed.

'Christ no! We'll drown!'

'We can't drown, you fool! There'll be a pocket of air
trapped at the top of the dome!' Jack Delmar gripped
Kramer by the shoulder. 'You must stay and help me!
Please!'

Kramer looked wildly round. Water was creeping up the
tunnel opening. There was no sign of his assistant. 'You can
stay!' he shouted. 'I'm getting out!'

Jack Delmar hung on to Kramer with both hands.
'Please,' he implored. 'You must stay!'

Kramer tried to pull away from the old man's clutching
hands which were gripping like claws. 'For Chrissake
leggo!' the water was up to his chest. He swung his fist back
and hit the elderly industrialist in the face with all his
strength.

Jack Delmar released his grip and sank slowly beneath the
black, swirling water.

14

Louise Campion stared across the water. She reached out and touched Patterson. He was awake immediately.

'What's the matter?'

Louise glanced round the canteen and pointed across the river.

'There's a whirlpool out there. Right in the middle. About halfway between us and that ship.'

Patterson shaded his eyes against the burnished glare of the evening sun shining on the river. 'A whirlpool? Are you sure?' Then he saw it: a whirling vortex spiralling around a hole in the water.

'What do you suppose would cause that ?' asked Louise.

Patterson shook his head.

'I've never heard of them on the Thames.' He turned his attention to the *Barrow* anchored on the far side of the river. 'That ship's been there all day. Do you suppose something's being hatched?'

Louise stared at the strange pattern of circling water.

'If there is, it looks as if it's just gone wrong.'

15

Hendricks was quietly telling the Prime Minister about the discovery of Simpson's body when the sudden silence in the operations room made him break off.

Everyone was staring at the television monitor that showed *Barrow*'s midships hold filling with water. The Prime Minister was about to pick up his telephone when it rang. He listened, his eyes fixed on the plot table with its miniature pipeline extending across the river from the model of the *Barrow*. He replaced the receiver and looked at the anxious faces waiting for him to speak.

'There's been a collapse in the pipeline. It's now flooding very quickly. There was a message from Jack Delmar a few minutes before the collapse, to start the pumps that power the GOPHER. The captain said the pumps are still operating, so it's possible they're still connected to the GOPHER. Whether or not it started on its journey before the collapse, we can't tell. The captain will send a diver along the pipeline when it's fully flooded to inspect the dome. We won't be certain until then.'

16

Phoenix wondered what had happened in the dome as he drove the GOPHER downward through the mud. He heard Jack Delmar's voice in his helmet yell: 'Full speed,' and then the communication link was cut.

He concentrated on keeping the inertial-navigation displays showing a zero reading.

The machine continued to burrow downward smoothly with all deviation displays showing hypnotic rows of glowing zeros. Sometimes the cutting-head slowed with a deafening noise as it chewed its way through a layer of gravel.

Suddenly the forward display flashed a positive reading. Phoenix pulled the control column yoke. The reading still glowed mockingly at him. He hauled the column back even further. He felt the machine level out and the strain on his feet relax. The digits on the forward display winked back to zero.

The GOPHER had bored successfully down until, if the miniature on-board navigation computer was correct, it was now at a greater depth than the lowest part of the power station's foundations.

The machine levelled out forged steadily through the million-year-old deposits.

The illuminated rows of zeros continued to glow out of the darkness.

Phoenix became troubled by his imagination. He found himself contemplating the tonnes of concrete above him and wondering what would happen if something went wrong with the machine. 'The only real problem is making sure your power hoses don't get tangled.' Jack Delmar had said. 'But we'll be in the dome paying them out to make certain that doesn't happen.'

Supposing something went wrong with the inertial-navigation computer? Supposing he bored right up into one of the radio-active-waste silos?

The rear display was showing a reading. Phoenix stared at it. How long had it been like that? In his confusion, he pushed the control yoke forward. More digits flashed up on the display. He slowed the cutting-head until it was barely turning so that he could unravel the sudden whirl of confused thoughts.

When the rear display showed a reading, you pulled the column back!

The rams set into the GOPHER's side pressed out, nudging the machine upward.

The digits started sliding back to zero.

He hauled the column right back against his visor until the display was once again showing a neutral reading. His weight slipped back until his lunar overshoes rested on the restraint bar.

GOPHER was now driving upwards – aiming for the metre thick concrete floor of Number Three inspection tunnel.

Phoenix looked at his watch. 21:25. Two hours thirty-five minutes before Keller's deadline, and he still had to break into the power station.

Suddenly the GOPHER gave a shuddering jerk and came to an abrupt standstill.

17

The underwater scooter purred smoothly along the flooded pipeline, towing the outstretched body of a diver. He steered the machine by gentle twists of his body. The powerful headlight on the front of the scooter was virtually useless in the opaque, polluted water. A faint trace of daylight marked the rupture where the section had collapsed. He slowed to pass the sharp edges of torn plastic, and sped on towards the dome. A white hand reached out. The fingers hooked on to the scooter's propeller guard, upsetting the steering. The corpse of the NASA technician was dragged fifty metres before the diver managed to release it. The diver pressed on – gathering together the shattered remains of his nerves.

Jack Delmar was waiting for him in the dome. The diver kept the headlight away from the dead, watching face. The body performed a slow somersault as he pushed it to one side. The diver explored the mud floor. There was no sign of the GOPHER. He found a shallow depression where the hoses disappeared into the yielding ooze. Grimacing with distaste he pushed an arm into the mud until his probing fingers encountered one of the golf carts. A hydraulic hose was wound tightly round it and had pulled the vehicle down into the riverbed. He thrust his arm deeper feeling with his fingers until they closed round the hydraulic hose below the golf cart. It felt like an iron bar so tightly had it been stretched, He pulled his arm out of the mud and returned along the pipeline with scooter's motor set at maximum speed.

'It seems,' said the Prime Minister, replacing his telephone, 'that the GOPHER managed to get away before the collapse, but one of its hoses is tangled round an electric golf cart. A team of divers is now on its way to the dome with cutting equipment.'

Hendricks looked up from his copy of the Operation GOPHER schedule. The wall clock said 22:30. 'It would also seem that we're now too late, Mr Prime Minister.'

The politician sat silently for a few minutes. The room was now crowded with cabinet minsters and service officers. The American ambassador had arrived at 22:00 hours.

'I'm going to ask Keller for a three-hour extension,' said the Prime Minister.

18

Phoenix gave up wondering what had happened and resigned himself quietly to fate.

The whole scheme had been absolutely crazy, he thought. Doomed to failure from the start. He should've told the Prime Minister what he thought of the idea when it was first put to him.

Breathing was getting difficult. He fumbled in the cramped darkness to switch his cooling and oxygen systems over to the backpack. The wave of coolness travelling down his body as the ice absorbed his body heat, and the fresh oxygen flooding in to the space helmet, cleared his head.

He had kept the cutting-head turning slowly: first in the hope that the GOPHER might free itself and suddenly and lurch forward; and then, as that hope faded, because the GOPHER would be as quiet as a tomb without the gentle vibration.

He wondered what future archaeologists would make of his body mummified in eternal Teflon. At least they would know his name: Neil A. Armstrong.

It said so on his shroud.

Phoenix started laughing.

19

'No,' said Keller's polite voice in the Prime Minister's ear. 'I'm extremely sorry, sir, but I cannot permit another extension. I take it the bill has now received the royal assent?'

'No yet,' said the Prime Minister testily. 'The palace have raised a number of queries. All I'm asking for is three hours to resolve them.'

Keller sounded concerned. 'I appreciate the difficulties, sir, but I earnestly implore you to sort them out within the next hour. Fifty-five minutes to be exact. I've got a portable television set and I'm looking forward to your appearance at midnight when you announce to the nation the terms of the new Act of Parliament based on my ultimatum. If you do not appear, then I will not hesitate to blow up the silos.'

The line went dead.

Keller replaced the radiotelephone microphone on its hook. He turned and looked thoughtfully at Louise Campion and Hugh Patterson.

'I'm afraid I'm going to have to lock you two up – just in case you have any more ideas. I'll let you out after midnight.' He paused. 'If there is an after midnight.'

He waved his Sterling towards a door at the back of the control room.

20

Phoenix had dozed off to sleep because there was nothing else to do and it conserved oxygen. He was woken by a sudden lurch – the one thing he had ceased praying for an hour earlier. He touched the sides of the cockpit. He wasn't dreaming – they were vibrating with renewed vigour. Another lurch, and the note from the cutting-head deepened.

The GOPHER had resumed boring and was now being dragged upwards by the action of the cutting-head. The displays winked. He automatically corrected course, too dazed to realize what he was doing.

The machine continued driving smoothly upwards through the compressed mud and gravel beneath the power station. Phoenix steered to one side and pulled back on to the correct course. Everything was working perfectly.

His feeling of exaltation ended when the cutting-head rammed into concrete with a terrible scream. The noise frightened and confused him. He thought the gods were striving to make him mad before they destroyed him. He shut the power off and the noise stopped.

Concrete! He had reached concrete! All he had to do now was run the head very slowly until he broke through.

'It's no good driving vertically up through concrete,' Jack Delmar had told him, 'otherwise the cutting-head goes through, and you're trapped, unable to open the hatch. You've got to go through at a shallow angle – like a jet taking off.'

For fifteen minutes the massive helix bored relentlessly. Rubble and debris rattled along the side of the cutting-head and was ground to powder.

He looked at the watch 23:23. He was too late. Even if he got into the inspection tunnel within the next few minutes, there wouldn't be enough time to cut all the detonator wires.

Suddenly the GOPHER was turning about its axis. He was rolling sideways off the mattress and on to the side of the cockpit. He fought back waves of panic and tried to reason out what was happening. Another spasm shook the GOPHER. It twisted again with a sickening noise as its unprotected flanks grated against the side of the hole it was cutting. He suddenly realized that the entire machine was trying to rotate about its axis while the jammed cutting-head remained stationary.

He pressed the control yoke down as Jack Delmar had told him to do. All four steering rams extended simultaneously and arrested the turning motion. He waited until the cutting-head was turning freely again before easing the pressure off the yoke.

There was something he had to do. He slowed the cutting-head and wrestled with his memory. Cooling water! He thankfully turned the control that would pass water to the cutting-head to prevent it activating the IRIS detectors when it broke through.

He eased the GOPHER forward very slowly, centimetre by centimetre.

272

The GOPHER was through.

Phoenix cut the power, For the first time since he had climbed into the machine there was silence. Complete and utterly overwhelming silence. He twisted around, released the cockpit latches and pushed. The hatch remained firmly closed. He pushed harder. It yielded slightly, but snapped shut when he lowered his arms. He turned carefully and pressed his foot against the hatch. He tensed his thigh muscles and heaved. He placed both feet on the hatch and heaved again. The hatch opened slightly and snapped shut. Another hard push that caused something to break in the backpack and he succeeded in forcing the hatch open a few centimetres. He grasped it and jerked it from side to side, easing it forward at the same time. It suddenly fell away into the darkness with a loud clatter. He lay quietly for a few moments while the spacesuit's cooling system drained the excess heat generated by his exertions.

He climbed stiffly out of the cockpit, feeling in a utility pocket for the cold light discharge tube. He broke the seal. The clinical light from the reacting chemicals filled the inspection tunnel. Grey cartons of Cyclonite were stacked four high along one side for as far as the light could reach. An IRIS detector gleamed menacingly less than a metre away. He was about to unfold a small sketch-map to check his position, when he suddenly remembered that he was existing on the backpack. He raised his wrist to his visor and gazed at the reading in numbed disbelief.

There was less than five pounds of ice left.

The watch said 23:40. There was no time even to think about cutting the detonator wires. He snatched up the automatic rile and stumbled along the tunnel as quickly as the unwieldy suit would permit.

At 23:42 the Prime Minister sat calmly before the hastily installed television cameras. Engineers buzzed round making final adjustments to microphones and lights. The closed folder before him contained two speeches: one based on the ultimatum General Pyne had delivered, and the other based of the ultimatum imposed by Ralph Keller. The Act of Parliament which had just become law was modelled on Pyne's ultimatum. Now that Simpson was dead, only he knew that Pyne had escaped.

The red telephone was connected direct to Keller. The chances that its red light would flash with a message from Phoenix to say he had gained control now seemed extremely remote.

At 23;43 Phoenix discovered the riddled bodies of the power station staff piled on top of one another. He leaned against the side of the tunnel and tried not to be sick. It could be fatal in a spacesuit – he could drown in his own vomit. He had no choice but to climb the terrible heap to reach the lower rungs of the shaft. His lunar overshoes slipped several times on the rigid corpses. The bodies sighed as his weight forced air from their lungs.

He fastened the rifle to a clip and started to climb the fifty steel rungs set into the side of the shaft. He wondered which would run out before he reached the top – his strength, the ice or time.

At 23:51 Phoenix pushed the steel cover open at the top of the shaft and looked quickly around. There was no ice left, and no point in waiting.

He heaved himself on to the concrete and staggered to his feet. He had no way of knowing whether the IRIS system had detected his presence. The alarms would sound in the control room – not down here.

He shuffled quickly across the apron towards the main entrance.

It was unlocked.

Heat was beginning to build up in the spacesuit now that the ice was gone. He mounted the stairs. The lunar overshoes slipped on the smooth marble. He fell backwards, crashing the backpack against the railings. He picked himself up and continued up the stairs. Sweat ran down his face. Something was wrong with his breathing system. He twisted and pulled the oxygen-purge controls. A small quantity of oxygen trickled into the helmet, but not enough to sustain him as he climbed the stairs. The heat was getting worse. A film of mist began to form on the inner fixed visor. Keller wouldn't have moved IRIS detectors into the power station – they would've caused too much nuisance. He paused on the second floor to unfasten the space helmet. The restricted field of vision through the visors and a spreading film of mist prevented his seeing the detector of the wall beside him.

Ralph Keller picked up his modified cellphone cum detonator and switched it on. A portable television standing on the console was showing a late-night film. He looked at his watch.

23:55.

He stood watching the television – his fingers caressing the cellphone.

Phoenix gave up fumbling at the space helmet – the clumsy gauntlets made the task impossible, and removing them would waste valuable seconds. His aching lungs sucked painfully at the meagre oxygen supply as he raced up the stairs. The mist spreading across the inner visor was now much worse. He paused outside the control room, fighting for breath and pressing his hands together to stop them shaking.

Christ! What the hell was he to do about the helmet misting up? How long would it take to get it off?

There was a circular window in the control room. Through the fogged visors he could just make out Keller at the far end near the main console.

By now Phoenix was in despair. His hands were shaking uncontrollably – he aimed the M1 experimentally down the stairs. The foresight waved all over the place.

23:59.

His breath rasped out of his lungs – fogging the helmet until Keller was a blur.

Too bloody bad.

He kicked the door open, launched himself into the control room and fired.

Keller turned, his finger reaching automatically for the cellphone.

Phoenix emptied most of the M1's magazine at Keller before collapsing on to one knee, his blood pounding in his ears from lack of oxygen. He was vaguely aware of noise all round him as bullets from Keller's Sterling smashed into the steel filing cabinets near the door. A ricochet shattered the space helmet and three bullets tore into his stomach just as his lungs clawed down acrid, cordite-impregnated air. He slipped to the floor and lay face down.

At five minutes past midnight the red telephone flashed. The Prime Minister snatched it up and, remembering eyes were upon him, placed it casually to his ear.

'Yes?'

He listened.

The television director in the outside broadcast van noticed a nerve in the Prime Minister's neck that twitched.

'I see,' said the Prime Minister. He listened for a few seconds, then: 'How badly?' Another pause. 'Very well.'

He replaced the receiver slowly and looked at the faces round him.

'Phoenix has failed,' he said in a flat, unemotional voice. 'He's been shot. Keller wants me to go down to the power station alone.'

There was a deathly silence in the room.

'You can't, sir,' said the Home Secretary.

The Prime Minister stood, and gave the Home Secretary the speech based on the original ultimatum. 'I've got no choice,' he said. 'You're to do the broadcast for me.'

The Home Secretary took the document with trembling hands. 'Let me go, sir,' he begged.

The American ambassador spoke. 'You shouldn't go, Mr Prime Minister. You'd be—'

'It must be me.' said the Prime Minister, moving to the door. He called one of the armed marines into the room and told him to allow no one near the red telephone.

'I'll give you that, he's got guts,' the ambassador said quietly to Hendricks when the Prime Minister had left.

Hendricks nodded.

The lungfuls of air revived Phoenix. It was quiet in the control room. There was a terrible pain in his stomach. He picked at the smashed fragments of visor and tried to pull himself up. His legs wouldn't work. There was no sign of Keller.

He looked at the watch. Three minutes past midnight. He hauled himself across the control room floor by his elbows. There was a good deal of blood splattered over the main console and the remains of Keller's cellphone detonator on the floor. Phoenix grimaced when he saw it. Keller had been wrong that destroying it would detonate the explosives. He crawled to the radiotelephone and dragged the microphone off its hook.

'Yes?' crackled the Prime Minister's voice.

'Phoenix, sir. I've shot Keller . . .' He broke off as the pain in his stomach racked his body. 'The cellphone detonator didn't work.' There was blood rising in his throat, choking his exultation. 'But the danger's over.'

'I see,' said the Prime Minister's voice.

'Keller's gone – he's wounded, but—'

'How badly?'

The Prime Minister's voice seemed to fade as the control room spun round. 'There's a lot of blood . . . Must be badly hurt . . .' Phoenix's voice was a whisper.

'Very well,' said the Prime Minister.

Phoenix was about to speak again, but realized the line was dead. He became dimly aware of hammering on a door at the back of the control room. Patterson and Louise

Campion. Keller must have locked them up. It would be best if they remained out of the way until he had dealt with Keller.

He turned away from the radiotelephone and saw the thick trail of his own blood across the control room floor.

The Prime Minister sat silently in the darkness in the back of his chauffeur-driven car. He unwrapped a cigar and reflected that everything seemed to be turning out well.

It was the whine of the fuelling machine that attracted Phoenix. The sound of the giant machine that lowered the nuclear-fuel elements into the two reactors could be heard all over the power station.

Doomsday

1

Captain Stacy clutched his clipboard protectively.

'Miss Pyne, your friend's car is blocking the road. If you aren't gone within thirty seconds I shall have both of you arrested.'

Stacy nodded to the soldiers. They gathered closer round the Mustang that was parked in the road outside the main gate leading to the new Oil and Gas Rig Defence Force camp.

'Come on, honey,' said Mitchell, 'He's not going to let us in.'

'I'm not leaving until I've seen my father,' said Maggie firmly.

Stacy peered into the darkness and thought he could see headlights approaching. He turned angrily to the Mustang. 'For the last time, Miss Pyne, he's not here. I'm expecting an important visitor and I want this car out of the way!'

'You're lying!' snapped Maggie. 'I know he's here, and I'm staying here until you agree to let me see him!'

The headlights were now within four hundred metres. 'Take them away,' said Stacy urgently. 'And shift this car.'

Mitchell did not argue with the submachine-gun pointing at him. He opened the door and stepped out. Maggie refused to budge. A soldier opened her door and gestured with his gun.

'You'll have to drag me out,' said Maggie defiantly.

The soldier reached into the car. Maggie bit his hand when he tried to grab her.

Stacy groaned. The car was fifty metres away and slowing down.

Three soldiers dragged Maggie from the Mustang. Mitchell took a step towards her as she fought and yelled, but was pushed back by the soldiers.

'Get the car shifted!' barked Stacy. The headlights stopped a few metres behind the Mustang. Goddamit – a ministerial car. Its rear door opened and slammed before the chauffeur could move. Footsteps approached.

Maggie nearly broke away.

'What's the trouble?' asked a voice that Stacy recognized immediately from the radio and television. It was the Prime Minister.

'I just want to see my father!' Maggie yelled.

'Let her go,' said the Prime Minister.

'She's creating a disturbance, sir,' said Stacy, cursing inwardly.

'Let her go, Captain Stacy.' The voice car was quiet and authoritative.

Stacy ordered the soldiers to release Maggie.

The short, stocky figure moved forward. 'Miss Pyne, isn't it? I'm the Prime Minister. How do you do?'

'I don't care who you are,' retorted Maggie. 'All I want is–'

'To see your father. And so you shall. I'll take you to him. But first, I have some urgent business to attend to.'

The Prime Minister turned to Stacy and issued a series of orders.

Ralph Keller's right shoulder was a mass of blood and the arm hung uselessly at his side. He was standing on the catwalk watching the fuelling machine lower the deadly uranium rods into the reactor. He stared across the great vault of the power station with mad fascination as the machine completed the loading operation. The cluster of mechanical claws released the rods and began lifting themselves clear. An electric motor started. The machine, suspended from overhead rails whirred towards Keller to collect the last of the rods hanging in the circular water-tank ten metres below the catwalk. The heavenly blue glow of Cerenkov radiation from the immersed rods bathed his face.

The great machine clanked nearer, its empty claws hanging down between the overhead rails like obscene ruptures.

Just these ten more rods, thought Keller. Just these ten more rods lifted out of the tank and lowered into the reactor with its cooling system switched off, and there would be an uncontrolled chain-reaction. The concrete and steel round the reactor core would hold for a few seconds, but nothing could withstand the terrible unleashed energies. The catastrophic explosion would blast radioactive particles across the face of Europe. It was a pity his clever methods of overriding the safely devices wouldn't survive; but it didn't matter – the memorial to his genius, the poisons that would fill the air and seep into the ground, would last for generations.

The machine was nearly over the tank – the cluster of claws level with Keller's eager eyes. He moved to a control board and pressed a button. The machine stopped within a few metres of the catwalk. The hum from the motors changed. The claws opened, and the whole machine began sliding gently down the four gleaming shafts that suspended it from the overhead gantry rails.

There was something wrong with the shafts. Thick red fluid was running down them and turning blue as it neared the glowing water. Keller looked up at the top of the descending machine. Phoenix was aiming a rifle at him.

'Switch it off, Keller.'

Then, for the first time. Keller saw Phoenix's eyes – staring at him past the shattered visor fragments, moving nearer, growing larger. Keller's surprised expression changed to terror. It was as if all the screaming monsters of his savage nightmares had risen as one to torment him. He backed across the catwalk, away from the terrible, approaching apparition and turned to run.

Phoenix fired. It was a difficult shot from a moving platform at a moving target.

The bullet tore into Keller's thigh. It flattened and became an anvil, smashing and tearing its way through bone and tissue. The impact spun Keller round and threw him against the safety rail. His fingers clutched at the side of the fuelling machine as he over-balanced and fell ten metres into the shining water.

Phoenix pulled himself to the edge of the machine and looked down. Keller was struggling in the flowing water, trying to climb the smooth sides of the tank.

Phoenix felt the machine stop. The twenty claws, each with three open steel fingers extended downward to the water on the ends of long shafts. Keller saw them coming and screamed. Although the tops of uranium rods were twenty feet below the surface of the water, the fingers were designed to shut when they encountered an obstruction.

They closed on Keller. They closed on his arms, his legs and his neck. The shining water seemed to burn with increasing intensity as it rose round his body. His screaming stopped abruptly as he was pushed under. The terrified face staring up at Phoenix receded into the iridescent depths until his entire body was obscured by the swirling clouds of blue smoke rising from his thigh.

The top of the fuelling machine had stopped level with the catwalk. Phoenix grasped the safety rail and hauled himself on to the narrow walkway. It took ten minutes of superhuman effort to drag himself to the control panel and push the button that stopped the fuelling machine from completing the loading cycle.

The whine from the electric motors died away.

Phoenix leaned against the railings, too weak from the loss of blood to make another move. He was cold. Numbing fingers of death were probing his body, exploring his bowels, moving through his organs.

He became aware of footsteps echoing across the open vault of the power station's central gallery.

A short stocky figure was mounting the steel steps to the catwalk. Phoenix watched the Prime Minister approaching. The polished shoes stopped near his outstretched legs. The Prime Minister knelt down.

'Well, Pyne, you seem to have managed better than I thought you would.'

The man who was Phoenix nodded weakly. 'Be able to–' His face twisted with pain. He moved a gauntleted hand over his stomach. 'Be able to pick up from where I left off.'

'No, Pyne. I don't think that's necessary now.'

Pyne tried to struggle up. 'But the bill, sir,' he whispered. 'You need me to carry on here.'

'The bill became law at midnight, Pyne.'

Pyne shook his head inside the helmet. His lustreless grey eyes stared up at the politician. 'I thought you'd scrapped it after Keller's takeover?'

The Prime Minister smiled at the dying man. 'After all that planning, Pyne? You misjudge me. Just as you misjudged Keller. That was the one mistake Simpson and I made when we planned all this – letting you choose your team. By the way, where are the other two?'

'Locked in a room off the control room. They know nothing about this. I never told them.' Pyne's words were a whisper.

'I didn't think you would,' said the Prime Minister easily. 'You're much too loyal to disobey orders.' He felt in his pocket and produced a sheaf of papers which he held out to Pyne. 'There it is, Pyne. A copy of the Special Powers Act which makes me the most powerful man in Europe. Just think, Pyne; no more forced divisions in the House; no more worrying about legislation being watered down in committee; no more worrying about which way rebel backbenchers are going to vote. There it is, Pyne. Doesn't it seem worthwhile after the worrying time we went through when you told me about the existence of the Cromwell Two Committee, and our arguments over which power station should be seized?' The Prime Minister laughed easily. 'I'm more powerful now than Cromwell ever dreamed possible.'

Pyne fell back, his body drained of strength and blood. The cold was reaching into his chest.

'What's going to happen to me, sir?'

The Prime Minister glanced at the blood on the top of the silent fuelling machine. 'Well, it looks as if you're going to die, Pyne. I'll keep you company until you do.'

Pyne looked up into the calculating eyes and began to understand. 'You're forgetting something, sir.' The 'sir' was automatic – the product of Pyne's loyalty, which even the approach of death could not entirely eradicate. 'Simpson hates your guts. He'll tell everyone.'

'Simpson is dead, Pyne. Just as you will be in a few minutes.'

Pyne shook his head disbelievingly. 'You need the threat from the power station to stay in office. You said that when you wrote the ultimatum. I remember your words . . .'

The Prime Minister smiled. 'Read the bill, Pyne. It's been drafted by the best legal brains in the country. It's one hundred per cent watertight. It sailed through the House and now it's received the royal assent. There was a clause that required the act to lapse once the threat from the power station was removed, but it was deleted. That's why I don't need you any more.'

Pyne said nothing. His eyes were closing. Air rattled noisily past his lips as his lungs laboured against the blood flooding into his throat. The Prime Minister made himself comfortable while waiting for Pyne to die.

'Oh yes, I nearly forgot. Your daughter's outside.'

Pyne's eyes opened and flickered with eagerness. 'Maggie? She's here?' He tried to pull himself up. 'May I see her, please?'

The Prime Minister shook his head. Pyne summoned his strength and leaned forward. The politician pushed him back. He looked at the blood on his hand with distaste and wiped it off on his handkerchief.

'You're a true bastard,' said Pyne softly, barely able to move his lips.

'At last you're beginning to understand me, Pyne. But when I walk out of here, I'll be the biggest hero in the country.'

The Prime Minister's voice was fading.

'But you, Pyne, will be remembered as a traitor. A traitor who was given the chance to redeem himself, and failed. You won't even get the credit for shooting Keller.'

Pyne only heard the words 'a traitor' before he died.

The Prime Minister leaned forward. 'Are you dead yet, Pyne?' he asked softly.

He placed his ear near the smashed visors. Pyne's lungs were silent.

The Prime Minister waited ten minutes to be certain, then stood up.

Maggie was waiting by the main entrance with Mitchell when the Prime Minister emerged. Stacy's men were holding her back.

A pretty little thing, thought the Prime Minister. Had her father's looks. If she had half his loyalty, she'd make the American a good wife.

'Is he in there?' she asked.

The Prime Minister smiled warmly at her. 'Yes, my child. you can go in and see him now. Straight down the corridor and into the main reactor room. He's at the top of an iron catwalk waiting for you.'

'May I go with her, sir?' asked Mitchell.

The Prime Minister gestured expansively. 'If you wish.'

He waited until the couple had entered the building and turned to Stacy.

'Captain Stacy, do you know what's been going on here?'

Stacy fingered his clipboard and nodded. 'I saw the Home Secretary's broadcast, sir.'

The Prime Minister unfolded a piece of paper and gave it to the officer. 'You and your men are in for a busy night, Stacy. That's a warrant for the names on the attached list. They're all members of a group calling themselves the Cromwell Two Committee. You're to round them up.'

Stacy looked at the list aghast. 'These people?' he croaked. 'But they're all—'

'Politicians, top civil servants, service officers. Pillars of society. I don't care what they are,' interrupted the Prime Minister. 'All I know is that they're traitors.'

'But one of them is the Home Secretary,' Stacy protested.

'The ringleader. You'll also find two of the terrorists in there.' The Prime Minister jerked his head at the power station. 'I've locked them in a room off the control room. A man and a woman. Arrest them too. When you've done that, send a bomb disposal team into the silos to remove the high explosive. Have you got all that?'

Stacy repeated his instructions in a trembling voice.

'Excellent, Stacy. One more thing. I've a sense of the theatrical in me tonight so haul them all off to the Tower of London.'

The Prime Minister did not wait for a reply, but turned and walked to his car. The driver jumped out and opened the rear door.

'Downing Street,' said the politician.

He paused before getting into the car and looked up at the stars. The clear sky was tinged with the first flush of dawn.

He inhaled deeply.

There was the smell of a new day in the air.

A CAGE OF
EAGLES

FOREWORD

In 1979 I wrote a novel, *U-700* (US title: *The Wotan Warhead*), which was based on the circumstances surrounding the surrender to the RAF in 1941 of a German U-boat and the subsequent 'trial' of the U-boat's first officer by his fellow prisoner of war officers at Grizedale Hall in the Lake District. Research for the book produced an astonishing flood of accounts from former POWs, guards, and even London 'Cage' interrogators. The useful material was very useful indeed, but it was outweighed by a mass of fascinating material that had no bearing on the incident I was concerned with.

Stumbling on such a motherlode of exciting material and not being able to use it rankled considerably. I had prospected for emeralds – and found them, but I had also stumbled upon gold. For example: try as hard as I could, there was no logical way that I could work into *U-700* the amazing story of the two escaping *Luftwaffe* officers who stole an RAF aircraft. It simply refused to fit. Nor could I use any of the material relating to the remarkable lengths that the senior German officer at Grizedale Hall went to in his attempts to warn the German High Command of the existence of 'Huff Duff' – seaborne high-frequency radio direction finding.

The obvious solution was to write another book.

This novel is not a sequel to *U-700*, although there are

unavoidable parallels with that earlier novel simply because the settings and some characters are the same. In *U-700* I described the 'trial' of a U-boat officer by his fellow POWs for cowardice. A similar kangaroo court-martial is covered in this book. Both events took place; both ended in a tragedy that still haunts those involved to this day.

I am indebted to the many individuals who provided such a wealth of material but particular thanks are due to Alan Graydon for supplying me with a detailed account of the time when, to use his own words, he 'gave' two *Luftwaffe* escapees an RAF trainer.

Having lived with the story of Grizedale Hall for so many years, I was also most grateful for being allowed to pick over the sad ruins of the hall (it was demolished by the Forestry Commission in 1957) so that I could build some of its slate blocks into the walls of my house. Strange to think that part of the original fabric of the 'Cage of Eagles' is now standing in a Surrey village.

James Follett
November 1987

Part One

ARRIVAL

The *Luftwaffe* had been busy over London.

In contrast with the devastation wrought by the bombers, Commander Ian Lancaster Fleming looked immaculate in his expertly cut Royal Navy Volunteer Reserve uniform. He was well aware of the admiring glances of office girls on their way to work as he motored his Bentley tourer into Seacole Lane off Fleet Street.

He was sorry to see that Pallisters had taken a direct hit: no more leisurely evenings whiled away before a roaring log fire under mellow oaken beams. The curious blast patterns from Goering's 1000-pound bombs had left a number of neighbouring buildings unharmed apart from shattered windows – now staring out on London like the eyeless sockets of a blind man. In other cases entire internal walls of four-storey buildings were exposed – each wall on each floor contributing to a clashing mosaic of coloured distemper, patterned wallpapers, and the tiled surfaces of what had once been bathrooms and kitchens. A fireplace, two floors up, even had a clock sitting unconcerned on its mantelpiece. Fleming's keen powers of observation, which would later stand him in good stead as a thriller writer, were such that he noticed the clock was showing the right time.

Fleming drove slowly down Seacole Lane, threading his way past hastily erected barriers around partly demolished buildings that council workers and Air Raid Precautions wardens were shoring up with baulks of timber. He was relieved to see that Louis Bros tailors' shop was still standing, albeit minus a few windows. Max, the surviving partner, was re-rolling a bolt of cloth that had been blown into the street. He was a distinguished-looking man in his early fifties, a man who took great care with whatever he was doing. So intent was he on re-rolling the cloth that he did not hear the Bentley sidle up to the kerb like a docking ship.

'Morning, Max,' said Fleming cheerily, stepping down from the Bentley's running board. 'Looks like I'm going to end up having to pay your bill after all if the Jerries keep missing you every night.'

Max looked up and gave a broad beam of genuine pleasure while at the same time running a critical eye over the cut of Fleming's uniform. 'Commander Fleming! Delighted to see you. Josie will put the kettle on while I see to that right shoulder pad.'

Fleming chuckled and held up his hand. 'Sorry, Max, old boy, but it'll have to wait. Can't stop.'

'But it needs trimming, commander,' Max protested. 'A simple alteration. It will only take five minutes.'

Fleming knew all about Max's idea of simple alterations that would take only five minutes. He shook his head regretfully. 'Later, Max. Meanwhile I've got a little job for you. Go and fetch your tape measure and tell Josie to cancel your appointments.'

Max looked puzzled, 'Now, commander?'

Fleming climbed behind the steering wheel of the giant car and reached across to open the passenger door. 'Right now, please, Max, old son. I've got a very important new client for you.'

After a twenty-minute drive in which Fleming talked animatedly about his schooldays in Switzerland, Max followed the naval officer into the hallway of a large, nondescript, Edwardian mansion standing in its own grounds in a cul de

10

sac off the Bayswater Road. A man in civilian dress was sitting at a desk. He examined Fleming's blue Admiralty pass, gave Max a cursory glance, and nodded to the broad staircase.

'He's just had breakfast, sir.'

'Excellent,' said Fleming. 'Let's hope he's in a good mood this time.'

Max accompanied Fleming to the first floor, where an armed corporal was lounging against the wall outside a door. He snapped to attention when he saw Fleming and gave a crisp salute. Max caught a whiff of pungent cigar smoke. Fleming smelt it too; his aristocratic nostrils twitched. He frowned and said to the corporal, 'It would seem that our friend has got hold of some more of those infernal cigars.'

'Smells like it, sir,' said the corporal. 'Gawd only knows how he can stand them at this time of the morning.'

'Or indeed at any time,' Fleming murmured, rapping on the door.

There was a silence. Fleming rapped again.

A man's voice answered, 'Come!'

The single word was correctly pronounced but there was a curious clipped quality about it. Max was certain that the speaker wasn't English. He followed Fleming into a sparsely furnished sitting-room. The acrid smell of cigar fumes stung his eyes. He wiped them and saw a man sitting in an armchair, partially hidden by a copy of the *Daily Telegraph*.

'Morning, old boy,' said Fleming breezily. 'I've brought you the promised visitor.'

The man slowly lowered the newspaper without speaking and rose to his feet. He was in his mid-thirties and was tall – at least six foot three inches. He was wearing a badly stained shirt and ill-fitting trousers that did nothing to ease the sudden feeling of dread that Max experienced. It was the man's eyes – the hard, unwavering, hypnotic stare – that

11

held the Jewish tailor's entire consciousness in a compelling, irresistible grip which seemed to bore straight into his soul, probing its innermost recesses for concealed guilt and hidden secrets.

'Good morning, Commander Fleming,' said the man stiffly, not taking his eyes off Max for an instant.

Max's stomach performed a double somersault and tried to crawl into his bowels. He had heard a whisper that Fleming was involved in 'hush-hush work'. If so, was this Fleming's method of arresting suspects? Was he about to be interrogated about the gossip he had overheard from his influential clients?

'Meet your first U-boat "ace", Max,' said Fleming affably. 'This is Korvetten Kommander Otto Kruger – commanding officer of *U-112*. Or, rather, he was until two days ago. Your job is to run him up a new uniform. We can't have him meeting the press in his present state, can we?'

Admiral Godfrey, the Director of Navy Intelligence, and his assistant, Ian Fleming, watched the newsreel in silence. The wailing air-raid alert sirens howling across London could be heard faintly by the two men sitting in the private cinema because the sound track of the *Movietone* newsreel rush they were watching was not ready.

The darkened room, with its deep, comfortable chairs for an audience of ten, was the same as that used by Winston Churchill when he wished to unwind by watching a favourite film such as *Gone with the Wind* or Chaplin's *The Great Dictator*.

The five-minute monochrome clip that the two men were watching with close interest showed Commander Otto Kruger disembarking down a ship's gangway in the company of two armed marines. His haughty, aristocratic features were fixed in an expression of sardonic inscrutability. Beside Kruger, the well-scrubbed marines guarding him looked decidedly scruffy; the captured U-boat commander was wearing a beautifully cut *Kriegsmarine* greatcoat, unbuttoned at the front to reveal his double-breasted uniform jacket and knife-edge-creased trousers. His Knight's Cross and Oakleaves, awarded by a grateful Hitler to his top-scoring U-boat 'ace', gleamed dully at his throat. Every detail of Kruger's uniform was correct – right down to the white cap-cover that U-boat commanders wore so that they could be distinguished by other members of the U-boat's crew at night.

Kruger disdainfully ignored the camera and the reception committee of two NCOs by pausing at the foot of the gangway to light a cheroot. The camera moved in for a close-up of the hawk-like, impassive features. The German officer's brooding eyes regarded the camera in contempt for a few seconds and then, as if to underline his disdain, he exhaled a cloud of cigar smoke straight at the lens.

The brief newsreel insert ended with Kruger exchanging crisp, very correct salutes with an army officer and entering the back seat of a Humber staff car.

The lights came on. Fleming languidly stubbed out his cigarette and consulted his notes. He chuckled and said to Admiral Godfrey: 'The commentary will run something along the lines, "Well may you strut and preen, Herr Kruger; well may you sneer and try to look proud, but you're not so proud now, are you, you Nazi rat? Not with your U-boat two and a half miles down on the floor of the Atlantic. But don't worry, Herr Kommander – it isn't alone because our brave boys on the high seas are sending it plenty of your Fuehrer's submarines to keep it company and there'll be plenty of company for you with all your U-boat cronies at your prisoner of war camp somewhere in England."'

'Good grief,' Admiral Godfrey muttered.

Fleming grinned. 'I think I could do better, sir.'

'I don't doubt it for one moment,' the admiral murmured drily.

'Actually, sir, Kruger isn't a Nazi. He has no interest in politics and appears to hold all politicians in contempt.'

'And the British, of course.'

'I don't think so, sir. He did admit to me that his loyalties are to the Fatherland, his flag officer – Admiral Doenitz, and his crew.'

'How about his family?'

Fleming shook his head. 'He refused to discuss it.'

'A wife or girlfriend?'

'He gave us two names and addresses for his Red Cross notifications. A secretary, Alice Kramer – a girl in his home town of Bremen, and Doenitz himself.'

Admiral Godfrey gave Fleming a shrewd glance. 'Why was he kitted out with a new uniform?'

'Major Charleston at the Ministry of Propaganda agreed with me that it would look more effective that way.'

'I see. And whose budget has the cost dropped on? Ours or theirs?'

'Ours, sir. I thought it might be useful if they owed us a few favours.'

Admiral Godfrey sighed. 'How much?'

Fleming looked uncomfortable. 'The clothing depot at Didcot provided the material. It's not a perfect match but it's near enough.'

'I didn't ask where the material came from.'

'Three hundred guineas, sir.'

Admiral Godfrey's eyes opened wide. 'For a uniform?' His voice was deceptively mild.

Fleming fiddled sheepishly with his briefcase. 'Kruger refused to be filmed unless he was provided with a complete wardrobe, sir. Shoes, socks, shirts, greatcoat, gloves, ties – everything.'

'We could have filmed with or without his permission,' Admiral Godfrey pointed out.

'Yes, sir. But I thought it would be a good idea if audiences saw a top German at his best so that they'd realize that appearances alone don't make them invulnerable.'

Admiral Godfrey grunted. 'And all we've got out of it is a scowl at the camera. Fleming, has it occurred to you that Kruger may be using you rather than the other way round?'

'I'll get more than a scowl out of him before I'm through, sir,' said Fleming smoothly.

Admiral Godfrey looked unconvinced. 'Well, we don't appear to have got anything out of him yet,' he remarked testily. 'I've not seen a report from you.'

'I haven't really interrogated him, sir, if that's what you mean.'

The admiral looked sharply at his subordinate. 'After two weeks? Why not? I put you on to him because you speak fluent German – not so you could take your time.'

'Kruger's a unique prisoner, sir. My guess is that he's one of the few U-boat commanders to be issued with the new magnetic torpedo. He's sunk more shipping than any naval commander in history. He's shrewd and he's cunning. Orthodox interrogation methods won't work.'

'The magnetic torpedo isn't the only thing we're interested in right now,' Admiral Godfrey interrupted caustically.

Fleming looked surprised. 'But I thought –'

'The G7e torpedo will be issued to an increasing number of U-boats as it goes into full production,' said Admiral Godfrey. 'It's only a matter of time before we get our hands on a talkative torpedo officer or, better still, we manage to get a boarding party on to a U-boat before it's scuttled. The information we need from Kruger is much more vital than that.'

'What information, sir?'

The admiral regarded Fleming thoughtfully. 'Is it true that you met Kruger before the balloon went up?'

'Yes, sir. During the Coronation Spithead Review in

1937. The *Admiral Graf Spee* was lying alongside the *Hood*. Kruger was a lieutenant then. He was amongst a party of German officers who were invited on to the *Victory* for a drink by the C-in-C of the Home Fleet.' Fleming smiled diffidently. 'Actually Kruger and I got on somewhat famously together. He spent his weekend in London at my flat.'

Admiral Godfrey nodded. He unbuckled his briefcase and handed Fleming a folder marked 'Most Secret'. 'Two reports for you to read,' Fleming. The first one is from our naval attaché in Montevideo. One of his staff managed to get aboard the *Graf Spee*'s hulk in the River Plate and climb its wireless mast. The sketches he supplied of what was left of its radio aerials have convinced the PM's scientific advisors that the Germans have developed a method of radio ranging for gunnery control. Do you know what radio ranging and location is?'

Fleming had heard the expression mentioned in the Admiralty but he prudently shook his head.

'Well, I'm no boffin,' said the admiral. 'Everything you need to know is in the reports. Basically, radio ranging is a method of using the echoes from beamed wireless transmissions to plot the position of an enemy ship over a distance of twenty miles – maybe more.'

Fleming was silent for a few seconds as the full import of what the admiral had said sunk in.

'I hope we're working on something similar, sir.'

'I expect we are,' said the admiral noncommittally. 'The second report details some of the extremely sketchy information we have on radio ranging research that the Germans carried out during the thirties. There was a committee set up in Berlin in 1934 to co-ordinate research. Around 1937, when the German U-boat arm was re-established, a special *Kriegsmarine* subcommittee was set up to develop radio ranging and location equipment that was small enough to be installed in U-boats.' Admiral

Godfrey paused. 'It's one thing to build several tons of cumbersome gear for installation in a battleship – quite another to make it small enough to fit in a U-boat. And if it can be built to go in U-boats, then it can be installed in aircraft. I don't have to spell out what that would mean.'

Fleming nodded. 'Did they succeed?' he asked.

'In 1938 the U-boat subcommittee authorized the production of an equipment called *Drehturm Gerat*,' Godfrey replied.

'Revolving turret apparatus,' Fleming translated.

'Something like that. Anyway, it was fitted into several U-boats. How many – we don't know. How effective it was – we don't know. Nor do we know which company made it – probably Siemens in Berlin – or what frequency it operated on.'

'What has all this got to do with Kruger, sir?'

Admiral Godfrey stood. While Fleming was helping him into his overcoat he said, 'What we do know is that a certain Otto Kruger was on both *Kriegsmarine* committees.' He gave Fleming a hard look. 'It's my guess that Kruger's presence on the *Graf Spee* before this lot started had something to do with his knowledge of radio ranging and location. He must know a hell of a lot about this *Drehturm Gerat* equipment. There's also the possibility that it was fitted to his U-boat, which would account for his uncanny ability to track down convoys – either that or it was sheer good luck.' The admiral moved to the door and gave Fleming another hard stare. 'As far as the War Cabinet is concerned, Kruger is the most important prisoner to fall into our hands so far. The *Graf Spee* equipment was installed over two years ago and therefore must be out of date by now. Therefore it's imperative that we discover just how advanced the Germans are now with their radio ranging and location equipment. You've got to know Kruger, Fleming. That's why, as from now, you're being

17

given a free hand to find out all you can from him and other prisoners about *Drehturm Gerat*.'

Fleming looked alarmed. 'Kruger's no fool, sir. It won't be a simple matter of asking a few quest –'

'You're the one who's always advocating subtle and unorthodox interrogation methods,' Admiral Godfrey interrupted testily. 'Well, now's your chance to practise what you've been preaching. I'm having you posted to Kruger's POW camp as a special intelligence officer.'

Fleming looked aghast. 'You mean that I'm being posted away from London?'

'The experience of the Shap Well Hotel camp is that the prisoners are not on their guard once they're no longer being interrogated. The intelligence officer there has picked up a great deal of information. You must do the same. And, as I said, you have a free hand. Thank you for the film show. It was most interesting, although I'm not sure treating Kruger like that has served any useful purpose. The Prime Minister is taking a personal interest in this matter. I've told him that my best operator is dealing with the problem and that he will have some concrete information by the end of the month, and regular monthly reports thereafter. Straight, factual reports, please. And try to keep the melodramatic cloak and dagger content to within reason. You will be writing reports, not thriller novels. Good day to you, Fleming.'

The senior intelligence officer strode out of the private cinema leaving an appalled Ian Fleming gaping after him.

The wind howling round the windscreen and the shrill scream of the Amerhurst-Villiers supercharger, sounding as though it was about to blow itself into a thousand pieces, made ordinary human speech in Fleming's Bentley tourer an impossibility, especially when the throttle pedal seemed to spend most of the journey in Fleming's favourite position: hard on the floor. The only variation in his driving technique was when the brake pedal was hard on the floor.

Even if talk had been possible, Fleming guessed that Kruger would have spent most of the eight-hour drive north in a stoic, brooding silence. Over lunch in a Preston restaurant that specialized in drab food and shining prices, Kruger had unbent slightly to recount his days as a cadet on the *Kriegsmarine*'s sail training ship, *Gorch Fock*. He had made no mention of when or how he had joined the U-boat arm, and Fleming, biding his time, had not pressed him on the matter. Fleming, in turn, was a little surprised that the U-boat ace had shown no interest in where he was being taken.

It had been a magnificent day with a blazing May sun traversing a clear blue sky and promising that the summer of 1941 was going to match the glorious summer of 1940.

By 4 pm the car was skirting the panoramic sweep of Morecambe Bay at a modest forty miles per hour. Fleming waved a languid arm at the vast expanse of sand where the sea was a band of molten light, barely visible on the horizon. He remarked in German, 'In the spring and autumn the tidal bore comes in at thirty miles an hour. In the last century the stage-coaches would chop about twenty miles off their journey by risking a short-cut across the sands. A lot of them were never seen again. If the quick-sand didn't get them, the tide did.'

'Interesting, Commander Fleming,' answered Kruger in his clipped but perfect English. He lit a cheroot and looked as bored as a caged eagle on a hot afternoon.

Fleming grinned at his passenger. 'Any idea where we are, Otto?' He had started using Kruger's first name during the journey.

Kruger inhaled on his cigar and glanced across at the dashboard in front of Fleming. 'We've driven three hundred miles due north from London – nearly five hundred kilometres. The sun's on our left, therefore we are on the western coast of northern England, nearly into Scotland. This must be Morecambe Bay near the Lake District. Correct, commander?'

It was the longest sentence that the aloof U-boat ace had uttered so far; Fleming was delighted. 'Spot on, Otto,' he answered in English.

Kruger gave a ghost of a smile at the Englishman's capitulation. 'Why are there no road signs? When I was studying at Exeter University there were many road signs.'

'Ah. That's to confuse the invader.'

'I see. You believe that the German army will have to depend on road signs when they arrive?'

Fleming wasted one of his disarming grins on Kruger whilst making a mental note to check up on the period of time that Kruger had spent at Exeter. That he had studied in England was a new piece of information which might be worth following up. 'Well,' he replied cheerfully, 'I daresay we've been judging the map-reading ability of the German army by the map-reading ability of the British army, Otto.'

Kruger did not respond to Fleming's jibe at his own countrymen. Instead he studied the scenery intently as though he were imprinting it on his mind.

Fleming swung the car inland and followed a winding main road that took them through the craggy splendour of the granite-scarred Cumberland fells. He cut the supercharger and trickled the tourer along at a steady twenty miles per hour, occasionally reducing speed to pass fell walkers togged out in full hiking kit despite the hot afternoon. Sheep browsed on the rolling green slopes; hedge sparrows intent on nesting fought among themselves over wisps of wool that the sheep had left on the ragged drystone walls that snaked over the hills like grey varicose veins, and an invisible skylark, high up in the cloudless sky, presided over the spring awakening with a sweet, continuous song.

'Makes you wonder why we're bothering to fight a war, eh, Otto?' said Fleming, wondering what the impassive German officer was thinking.

'I don't need magnificent countryside to make me think that, commander,' was the curt reply.

Despite Fleming's debonair, easy-going nature, his armour against such barbs was exceptionally resilient. He chuckled and made no reply.

As they motored deeper into the mountains and away from the coast, Kruger noticed that the British enthusiasm for removing signposts appeared to have waned: the little town of Newby Bridge, with its neat houses and shops built of blue slate from the nearby quarries at Coniston, was clearly marked, and so was the bridge across the River Leven that the town was named after. It was as they were crossing the river that Kruger caught his first glimpse of an English lake.

'Windermere,' said Fleming in answer to Kruger's question. 'Over ten miles long and the largest lake in the Lake District. The smaller ones are called tarns.'

The scenery changed dramatically fifteen minutes later when the winding country lane Fleming was following plunged into the deep valley of Grizedale Forest. The pleasant views across broad fields gave way to thickly wooded, sombre hills which were completely hidden by countless acres of spruce and Douglas fir. The pines stood tall and silent in their regimented rows, as if well aware that they were out of character with the surrounding countryside. So closely planted were they that there was no natural light to sustain ground cover; the straight trunks grew out of bare soil that had been poisoned by generations of pine needles. There was little insect life and therefore the birdsong was conspicuous by its absence.

Fleming pulled up outside a magnificent pair of wrought-iron gates set into a high slate wall. The gates' piers were crowned with large, decorative, stone balls. A soldier emerged from a wooden guardhouse and carefully examined the documents that Fleming showed him. Satisfied, the soldier nodded to a second guard, who grudgingly unlocked the gates and waved the Bentley through.

The car swept up a curving drive and skirted an unkempt lawn that covered several acres. A whooping mob of about thirty men, all wearing shabby, unrecognizable uniforms, were storming across the grass. They were laughing and cheering themselves hoarse. The object of their adulation was a good-looking young man with blond hair who was being carried in shoulder-high triumph by two of the men. Someone shouted and pointed to the car. The mob fell silent and gazed in astonishment at the sight of an immaculately dressed *Kriegsmarine* officer riding as a passenger in an open-tourer Bentley.

Even the phlegmatic Kruger showed some interest in the large and very elegant Edwardian mansion that suddenly came into view. Fronting the mansion, and facing south to take advantage of the view across the valley, was a broad, paved terrace guarded by a slate block retaining wall whose balustrade was capped with more of the decorative stone balls. There were even stone balls along the parapets of the huge dormer-windowed hall itself; whoever had built the mansion obviously had a strong liking for stone balls.

There were some more men on the terrace. They were wearing shapeless, unrecognizable uniforms, and were gathered around garden tables playing cards. They too stopped to stare at the new arrivals.

Fleming followed the drive round to a cobbled courtyard at the rear of the mansion and stopped the car. He switched off the engine and gave Kruger an amiable smile.

'Welcome to Grizedale Hall, Otto. Number One Prisoner of War Camp for captured officers. This is now your home until the war's over.'

*

Leutnant Willi Hartmann was a plump, balding Bavarian whose taste for bribery, graft and a spot of corruption here and there was a sharp contrast to his strong aversion to any form of physical exercise other than counting money.

Willi had shrewdly joined in the riotous celebration of Dieter von Hassel's release from twenty-eight days' solitary confinement following his latest escape bid, because the revellers' ringleader was Hauptmann Paul Ulbrick, the camp's senior officer. That was the only reason; the perspiring little Bavarian felt that galloping around the grounds on a hot afternoon was an enterprise that was definitely very low on fun and non-existent on profitability. He fervently hoped that von Hassel's inevitable next escape bid – his sixth – would be more successful.

Willi wiped the sweat from his moon-like face with a grimy handkerchief and jogged gamely into the courtyard with his fellow officer POWs. They stopped a respectful distance from the car and stared bug-eyed at the apparition of a resplendent *Kriegsmarine* commander stepping down from the tourer and exchanging salutes with Major James Reynolds, Grizedale Hall's commanding officer.

Willi blinked several times. Maybe the mixture of a prison diet and American chocolate bars was affecting his eyesight. But there was no doubt about it: the German officer was wearing a greatcoat made of best-quality worsted wool, top-quality black leather shoes polished to perfection, kid gloves, and, as a final touch, the Knight's Cross and Oakleaves pinned to his black tie. To round off the image, the new arrival was smoking a cigar.

'My God,' breathed Ulbrick. 'Maybe we've won the war and the *tommies* haven't had the guts to tell us?'

The two prisoners carrying von Hassel on their shoulders allowed him to slide to the ground. The flamboyant young *Luftwaffe* pilot looked slightly aggrieved at no longer being the centre of attention.

'We've not won anything,' said a U-boat officer despairingly. 'That's none other than Otto Kruger of the First U-boat Flotilla.'

The news was greeted with a buzz of comment.

'What's he like?' asked Ulbrick, noticing that he was outranked by the new arrival.

'There was a joke at Lorient that there was a plan to have him pulled down and a human being built instead.'

A *Luftwaffe* officer gave a loud groan. 'He's a commander, Paul – that means he'll be taking over as the senior officer.'

Willi gazed in mounting alarm at Kruger as he accompanied Fleming and Reynolds to the administration block adjoining the kitchens and converted garages on the far side of the courtyard. Kruger's hard, sardonic expression and hawk-like features suggested that the relatively easy days at Grizedale Hall under Hauptmann Paul Ulbrick were over.

Kruger's inscrutability was put to the test. He put down his cup of coffee on Reynolds' desk and stared incredulously at the Canadian officer. 'A holiday camp?' he echoed. 'You mean to tell me that the British are housing us POWs in a *holiday camp*?'

Major James Reynolds, Canadian Army Corps, DSO, adjusted his black eye-patch to cover his embarrassment. He found Kruger's piercing gaze as disconcerting as his perfect English.

Reynolds had lost his left eye at Dunkirk the year before and had been ruled unfit for further active service. He had been offered early retirement, a pension, and a free, army-issue, pink eye-patch. He had declined all three: the early retirement because he was only thirty-three, and the pink eye-patch because he thought that his black one gave him Douglas Fairbanks' swashbuckling air. He glanced irritably at Fleming, who was doing his best not to laugh.

Avoiding the German officer's hard stare, he replied, 'Well, hardly a holiday camp, Commander Kruger. Grizedale Hall was built in 1905 for Harold Brocklebank, a shipping millionaire. He died in 1936. The Holiday Fellowship used it until last year – 1940 – when it was requisitioned by the War Office.'

'Who's the senior German officer at the moment?' inquired Kruger, lighting a cheroot.

'Hauptmann Paul Ulbrick of the *Luftwaffe*,' Reynolds replied. 'You outrank him, of course, therefore you are now the senior officer.'

'Has he maintained good discipline?'

Reynolds scowled. 'Hardly. He's a close friend of Dieter von Hassel – our dedicated escapee who has spent most of his time here in solitary confinement for his hare-brained bids. He's tried five times now with Ulbrick's connivance. As the senior officer, he should know better.'

'Isn't it a POW's duty to escape, old boy?' inquired Fleming.

'It's one thing to escape from Grizedale Hall, Commander Fleming,' Reynolds replied testily, wondering whose side Fleming was on, 'but it's quite another to escape from the fells.' He turned to Kruger. 'I'm sure you must have noticed on your drive here just how remote we are. The pikes may look beautiful but you'd be surprised at the number of walkers who've died on them.'

'Pikes?' Kruger queried. 'I am sorry – it is a new word.'

'The local name for the mountains,' said Reynolds curtly. 'I'm from Montreal and I thought I knew everything there was to know about hard winters, but here they can be really something. Last January a German officer died of exposure on Heron Pike. He'd spent two days in a blizzard wandering in circles. And if the pikes don't get you, the bogs and tarns most certainly will. Another thing – the Home Guard and War Reserve Constables here are all

25

local lads who know the fells like the backs of their hands. It never takes them long to pick prisoners up. Incidentally, tunnelling is out of the question because Grizedale Hall is built on rock – there's only a few inches of topsoil.'

Kruger exhaled boredly on his cheroot and regarded Reynolds steadily through a cloud of curling smoke.

'There're one or two other things we need to get straight,' Reynolds continued. 'Firstly this is a "white" camp for non-Nazi officers. The borderline cases go to the "grey" camps, and the hard-liners go to the "black" camps run by the Free Polish in a manner the War Office turn a blind eye to. Any suggestion of Nazi bullying – indoctrination – anything like that – and the prisoner concerned is sent immediately to a "black" camp.' Reynolds paused and gestured to the window. 'Secondly, as you've seen, Grizedale Hall is a magnificent stately home, one of the finest in the country, and I aim to keep it that way. After the war the War Office will have to hand it back to its owners in its original condition. If it comes to any harm, we'll be only too happy to rehouse you in huts. The prisoners have freedom of movement in the hall and grounds during the day and they're locked in the hall between sunset and sunrise. How they organize their accommodation is up to their senior officer. He's reponsible for internal discipline – we look after security. It's a simple system and it works. There's a Queen Alexander's Royal Army Nursing Corps sister, Brenda Hobson, who has a sickbay next to the downstairs shower rooms. She works here twenty hours a week and looks after the medical records of all eighty-two prisoners. All prisoners are required to help out in the kitchens. Organizing the rota is your job. There's a daily roll-call in the courtyard at 0800. Snap roll-calls can be called at any time. Any questions?'

Kruger shook his head.

'Sergeant Finch!'

The camp adjutant poked his head around the door from

the adjoining office. He was a stocky, belligerent-looking little man who, with his toothbrush moustache, bore a striking resemblance to Hitler. He was a shrewd man, a clear thinker with a capacity for cunning that belied his somewhat absurd appearance. He glowered resentfully at Kruger. It wasn't a case of hate at first sight because Sergeant Finch hated all Germans even before he saw them.

'Saar?'

'Show Commander Kruger around the hall please, sergeant, and see that he is supplied with a list of all the prisoners.'

'Yes, saar!' The NCO glared at Fleming. He wasn't over-fond of the Royal Navy either. 'Excuse me, saar. But how much longer is that car going to be parked outside? Only the Jerries are showing a lot of interest in it so I've had to post two men on it.'

'Commander Fleming will be leaving shortly,' said Reynolds irritably.

When the two men had left, Reynolds said to Fleming, 'It's unusual for a prisoner to be delivered here personally, commander.'

Fleming grinned. 'As I was coming up anyway, I thought it would be a chance to get to know him. I presume you've been told about my posting here?'

'I received a letter last week.'

'Don't worry, I won't be here full-time. Just flitting in and out as the mood takes me.'

'I don't mean to sound rude, commander, but just what the hell is going on?' Fleming's casual tone had irritated the Canadian.

'It's all to do with obtaining intelligence from POWs after they've been placed in their camp. Can you provide me with an office please, old boy? Nothing pretentious.'

Reynolds referred to the letter that Fleming had given him. 'I guess so.'

'I take it you have no objection to me having access to your prisoners?'

'Do I have any choice?'

'Not really, old boy. Just observing a few courtesies.' Fleming grinned broadly. 'Incidentally, our friend Kruger is believed to be a mine of useful information, so please don't lose him.'

'My prisoners don't escape. Well, not for more than forty-eight hours.'

'Oh? What about our missing torpedo officer – Leutnant Herbert Shultz?'

Reynolds looked uncomfortable. Leutnant Herbert Shultz was his least favourite topic of conversation. 'What about him?'

'He's now been missing since last October. Six months.'

'He escaped before I took over.'

'Oh really?' said Fleming innocently. 'I thought it was a week after. A pity he's not around. I looked at his interrogation transcript the other day. It was bungled. If he was questioned properly, he might provide some useful gen on the latest German torpedoes. Everyone seemed to be too obsessed by the fact that he was a vet in civilian life.'

Reynolds groaned inwardly. First it was War Office busybodies poking their noses into the affair of Leutnant zur See Herbert Shultz, now it was the Admiralty. He decided to change the subject. 'Will you be staying around here, commander?'

'You must call me Ian,' said Fleming affably. 'And I'll call you James. Yes, I daresay I'll be staying here on and off. The Eagle's Head at Satterthwaite looks comfortable.'

Reynolds cursed his misfortune. Satterthwaite was the neighbouring village whereas most London visitors opted for the comfortable hotels of Ambleside ten miles to the north.

Fleming looked at his gold wristwatch. 'I don't suppose they'd thank me for turning up at this time of the afternoon,

James. My inner man is screaming for attention so I don't suppose your mess could fix me up with a bite, could they?'

'Yes,' Reynolds muttered, standing up. 'I'll join you.'

As the two men moved to the door, Fleming noticed some fishing tackle standing in a corner. 'Is the trout fishing any good around here?' he inquired.

'It's great,' said Reynolds, warming to his favourite subject. 'Mrs Standish lets me fish in her tarns.'

'Mrs Standish?'

'One of the local landowners. She actually owns most of the Grizedale Estate – that is, the bits that the Forestry Commission didn't want. She's very rich and very widowed.'

'Ah. Think she might let me join you one afternoon?'

'I guess she might,' said Reynolds heavily, thinking what a rotten war it was turning out to be.

In the courtyard a group of prisoners were admiring Fleming's Bentley under the watchful eyes of two guards. The leading admirer was Leutnant Dieter von Hassel.

'A magnificent car, commander,' the young flier remarked to Fleming as he and Reynolds walked past.

Fleming paused and replied in fluent German: 'The finest in the world, leutnant. Perhaps, when the war is over, we'll see some more duels between Bentleys and Auto Unions at Brooklands?'

At first Hassel was nonplussed by Fleming's command of German but he recovered quickly and smiled. 'With the Auto Unions winning as usual, of course,' he replied. He knelt down and pointed to the wide gap between the cobbles and the tourer's running board. 'That's the trouble with the Bentleys, commander, they're too high off the ground. The centre of gravity is wrong. The banking at Brooklands was built especially for Bentleys but our Auto Unions do not need it.'

'I'm sure you're right,' agreed Fleming, not wishing to be drawn into an argument.

*

29

Fleming and Reynolds left the camp by a guarded side gate set into the perimeter wall and crossed the narrow lane to the converted outhouses that served as the guards' quarters.

Dieter von Hassel, deep in thought, continued to study the Bentley. While watching the two guards every bit as carefully as they were watching him, he ran his hand lovingly along the graceful bonnet. Suddenly he had an idea that he considered nothing short of brilliant.

Willi was sitting in the open doorway of the common room's French windows that opened on to the terrace when he spotted Kruger mounting the terrace steps that led from the garden. He started whistling – the signal to the other prisoners on the terrace and in the common room that a guard was approaching.

Willi suddenly felt somewhat foolish: although Kruger wasn't a guard, the U-boat commander's sinister demeanour had triggered Willi's in-built alarm system which had developed as a result of being a prisoner of war for a year.

Kruger paused on the steps and stared contemptuously at Willi and then at the prisoners playing cards. 'Your name, please?'

Willi was pleasantly surprised by the unexpected friendly tone in Kruger's voice. He scrambled to his feet and gave Kruger a hurried salute. 'Leutnant Willi Hartmann, commander,' he blurted out.

Kruger's gaze moved to the Army School of Motoring 'MS' insignia embroidered on Willi's grubby shoulder marks. 'What are you doing in a prisoner of war camp, leutnant?'

'I was shot down, commander.'

'You're a motor transport officer?'

'Yes, commander.'

'What vehicle do you normally drive?'

'A Benz truck, commander.'

'You were shot down in a Benz truck?'

'No, commander.'

'So what were you shot down in?'

'A Heinkel bomber, commander.'

Willi flinched away from the hard stare.

'What were you doing in a Heinkel?'

It was a question that Willi had been dreading. 'My unit had been posted to Chartres in France where there was a Heinkel bomber group,' he replied, trying hard not to look embarrassed. 'I scrounged a flight as an observer on a daylight raid on the Isle of Wight.'

'Why?'

'I wanted to see England, commander.'

Kruger gave a ghost of a smile and glanced at the panoramic view south down the valley. 'Well, you're seeing a lot of England now, aren't you, leutnant?'

'Yes, commander,' said Willi miserably.

'Are you ever bored?'

'Sometimes, commander.'

'You won't be for much longer. The British NCO, Sergeant Finch, told me that the short fat one knows everything that's going on here. His words were that you can scrounge anything and that you've got your thieving, pudgy little fingers into every pie and that one day he's going to break them off one by one. I presume he meant you?'

'Yes, commander.'

'Excellent, Willi,' said Kruger. 'As from now you're my executive officer. I've found two suitable rooms on the top floor for my office and bedroom, which I shall require you to furnish, but first I want you to pass the word that all officers are to assemble in the common room in thirty minutes.' Kruger looked at his watch. 'At 3.30 pm precisely.'

While Willi was wearily trudging around the four acres of Grizedale Hall's grounds, passing on Kruger's message, a group of twelve prisoners entered the courtyard at the rear of the hall and started a lively game of football. They used a goal that had already been chalked on the slate buttressing wall at the northern end of the courtyard. The two guards standing boredly by Fleming's Bentley were only too glad to have something to watch. They didn't notice Dieter von Hassel and Peter Ulbrick emerge from the laundry room and lean casually against a wall.

Play stopped after five minutes over a hotly disputed goal. The claim by the *Luftwaffe* team that they had scored was met with hoots of derision from the defending *Kriegsmarine* side.

Von Hassel and Ulbrick became very tense and braced themselves against the wall.

In the absence of a referee, the argument developed into an all-out row. A U-boatman suddenly swung a vicious punch at a fighter pilot and within seconds all hell broke loose with fists flailing and boots seeking targets that were not the football. The two guards cursed roundly and ran across the courtyard. They waded into the midst of the brawl, blowing their whistles and hauling the combatants clear of the battle zone by their arms and legs.

Ulbrick and von Hassel moved as one despite their lack of rehearsal. They raced forward, threw themselves down on the cobbles and rolled under the Bentley in one neat, well-co-ordinated movement. Ulbrick yanked several leather laundry hamper straps from under his jacket while von Hassel hooked his legs over the car's rear axle and pushed himself off the ground by his hands. Working quickly and silently, Ulbrick passed three straps around von Hassel's body and lashed the ends securely to the vehicle's chassis. He did the same with the young flier's arms and legs, leaving a hand free so that von Hassel could cut the straps with a knife.

'Okay, Dieter,' Ulbrick whispered. 'You can let go.'

Von Hassel relaxed his grip on the underside of the car. The makeshift leather harness held his body six inches clear of the ground. 'How do I look?' he grunted, trying to ease his cheek away from the rough surface of a cross-member.

'Like a trussed chicken.'

The clatter of guards' boots and yelled orders in English announced the arrival of reinforcements.

'See you when you come out of the cooler,' chaffed Ulbrick, grinning.

'This time I'm not coming back, Peter.'

'That's the sixth time I've heard that from you.'

'I mean it, Peter. This time I'm going home.' The *Luftwaffe* officer's voice was deadly serious.

Ulbrick grinned at his friend. 'Don't forget to write,' he said, pushing a sheathed kitchen knife into the front of von Hassel's jacket where it could be reached easily.

Von Hassel grinned. 'Good luck with the new senior officer.'

Ulbrick made no reply. Instead he grasped von Hassel's free hand briefly and peered across the cobbles to where the fight was dying down. Gauging the right moment, he rolled out from under the car, crawled towards the wall and stood. He propped himself against the wall with his hands thrust casually into his pockets.

Sergeant Finch pounded into the courtyard like a demented walrus. He didn't join the tangle of prisoners and guards but braked to a standstill some paces away, his eyes darting everywhere and missing nothing.

'Stop!' he bellowed.

All activity ceased. Prisoners and guards alike gaped apprehensively at the puce-faced apparition confronting them.

'What's going on here?'

'A fight, sarge.'

Sergeant Finch moved his face to within a fraction of an

inch of the hapless guard who had spoken. 'What have I always said about diversions, Corporal White?'

The guard pointed to a *Luftwaffe* officer who was nursing a split lip and a U-boatman in charge of what held the early promise of turning into a Technicolor eye. 'It was too serious to be a diversion, sarge.'

Finch glared suspiciously at the Germans. 'Okay, you lot. The party's over.' He gave a slow, malicious grin. 'In more ways than one, I fancy. Your new commanding officer wants to meet you all in the common room in twenty minutes.'

Of the eighty-one expectant faces filing into the ornate, oak-panelled common room that had been Harold Brocklebank's drawing room, the dozen faces that belonged to the two football teams looked in need of urgent repair.

Kruger stood with his back to the magnificent white marble mantelpiece and consulted the list that Sergeant Finch had given him. Willi took his place at a small writing desk and waited, pen and paper at the ready.

'You may all be seated, gentlemen,' said Kruger, glancing up at the prisoners and returning to a detailed study of the list.

Some of the Germans dropped into the large, easy chairs while others distributed themselves on the floor or on the carved staircase that led to the gallery. Two posted themselves near the French windows and one stood guard near the main doorway. All were silent, waiting for Kruger to speak.

The U-boat ace cleared his throat. 'I take it there's a system for ensuring that we're not overheard?'

'Yes, commander,' said one of the officers by the open French windows.

Kruger nodded. 'Good afternoon, gentlemen,' he said in a clear voice. 'Firstly, I will introduce myself. I'm Otto

Kruger, the former commander of *U-112* and, whether you like it or not, I'm taking over from Hauptmann Ulbrick as senior officer until we're liberated.'

The blunt opening produced an exchange of glances.

'I propose,' Kruger continued, 'to run this camp along the same lines that I ran *U-112* – that is, at maximum efficiency. Therefore there are going to be a number of changes. Within a week I will have Grizedale Hall running like clockwork. To achieve that, every man will have a task to perform and there will be monthly rotas so that no one need ever get bored.'

'Are you suggesting that we do menial work?' queried Ulbrick from the back of the hall.

Kruger turned a cold stare on Ulbrick. 'Your name?'

'Hauptmann Peter Ulbrick.'

The U-boat ace gazed steadily at Ulbrick. 'No, Hauptmann Ulbrick, I'm not *suggesting* that you do menial work. I shall be ordering you to do so – because that's the only work there is. If I could put you on to something useful such as building Heinkels or U-boats, I would do so.'

Kruger's rare approach to what might be termed a joke was rewarded by chuckles; it effectively discouraged Ulbrick from further argument.

'As I call out your names,' said Kruger, tapping his list, 'I want you to stand up so that I can see who you are. But first, can anyone tell me why Leutnant Herbert Shultz's name has a question mark against it on the roll?'

'He escaped, commander,' said Ulbrick.

'When?'

'October 1940.'

Kruger arched his eyebrows. 'It's now May 1941. Has he reached home?'

Ulbrick shrugged. 'We would have heard by now if he had. The British won't admit that he has escaped. Every morning at roll call, Finch yells out his name, and every morning he doesn't answer.'

'Have you tried to find out what has happened to him?'

'From whom?'

Kruger lit a cigar and snapped the spent match in two with his thumbnail. The U-boatmen who knew Kruger from their days at Lorient recognized the danger signal. 'From the Red Cross, Hauptmann Ulbrick,' said Kruger icily. 'As the senior officer at the time, it was your duty to find out.'

'Well, it's now your duty, commander.'

Kruger realized that a face was missing. 'Where is our habitual escapee?'

'Von Hassel is sleeping,' Ulbrick replied promptly, deliberately omitting Kruger's rank.

'I passed the word that all officers were to muster in here,' said Kruger mildly.

'Be reasonable,' said Ulbrick. 'He's just been released from twenty-eight days in the cooler. This is the first time in a month that he's been able to sleep in a decent bed.'

Kruger considered for a moment and appeared to come to a decision. He glanced down at his list. 'Very well. The first name is Aisne, Hubert R. Hauptmann Aisne, will you please stand.'

While von Hassel was waiting patiently, trussed like a potato peeler blade to its handle beneath Fleming's Bentley, the weather set about doing something that it was exceptionally good at doing in the Lake District: it started raining. It was proper Lake District rain that went sideways, lashing itself to a fine spray with the ferocity of a thousand demented bullwhips.

Von Hassel heard some shouted 'goodbyes' followed by running footsteps. He twisted his head slightly and saw Fleming's polished shoes dancing around the car as their owner pulled the Bentley's hood up. The driver's door opened and closed. The finely tuned engine fired on the first crank of the self-starter. A linkage moved near von

Hassel's hand as the handbrake was released. The car swung in a circle, drove out of the courtyard and down the uneven drive to the main gates. The jolting caused the leather straps supporting von Hassel to bite painfully into his body. He managed to twist his leg away from the rapidly heating exhaust pipe. Water thrown up by the huge wheels drenched him; it ran along the underside of the vehicle and trickled down his neck. He realized that he was in for the most uncomfortable car ride of his life.

The car stopped at the main gate in the middle of a large puddle. Hassel twisted his head round and his heart nearly stopped when he saw the reflection in the puddle of his right leg under the Bentley's running board. A guard had merely to glance down at the puddle when checking the car and it would be another twenty-eight days in the cooler for Dieter von Hassel.

'Thank you, gentlemen,' said Kruger when the last prisoner had identified himself. 'It will take me a week to remember all your names. Willi Hartmann will be issuing my work rosters within the next seven days. Who are the members of the escape committee?'

'There isn't one,' said Ulbrick. 'I didn't see the point of one. If a man came up with an idea, then it was up to him to carry it out if he wished.'

Kruger nodded. 'Perhaps that's just as well because from now on, my express orders are that escapes are strictly forbidden unless the would-be escapee can convince me that every detail has been thought out, including plans for getting home.'

The guard's boots splashed through the puddle, breaking up the reflection of Hassel's leg, but splattering the escapee's face with muddy water.

'All okay, sir,' the guard called out.

The wrought-iron gates squealed open. Fleming drove

out of the camp. Von Hassel offered up a silent prayer of thanks when he heard the gates clank shut. The next minute he was grimly trying to lift his body as high as possible as Fleming accelerated along the winding country lane.

In the driving rain, Fleming missed the Satterthwaite fork and only realized his mistake after ten minutes motoring along a lane that had degenerated into little more than a rough track. He turned the car around in the entrance to a field and drove back the way he had come. He wiped the inside of the windscreen clear of condensation while trying to peer through the torrential rain. He passed a farmhouse that he hadn't seen before and realized that he was hopelessly lost. He had no choice but to continue down the hill because the lane, with its high banks, was too narrow to turn the car around.

Fleming swore roundly and braked hard. The Bentley's wheels locked and brought the big car to a standstill at the edge of a ford that crossed a wide stream. From underneath the car, von Hassel couldn't see the stream but he could hear broken water surging past rocks.

Fleming wiped the inside of the windscreen again and tried to assess the depth of the ford. From the way the water danced over small rocks, he guessed that it couldn't be more than a few inches deep and would therefore be no problem for the Bentley with its high ground clearance. Also the road on the far side was in good condition and looked as if it might go somewhere. He revved up the engine, engaged first gear, and released the handbrake.

Contact with the icy mountain water made von Hassel gasp with shock. He put his free hand down and touched the gravel-strewn bed of the stream. Although the water was shallow and therefore he wasn't in danger, he decided that now, with the car moving slowly, was a good time to cut himself free. He pulled the knife from its sheath and was about to cut the first strap when the Bentley's rear wheel slipped off a small boulder and dropped the car six inches.

The sudden jolt caused the knife to slip from his fingers. It dropped into the water. He tried to snatch it from the bed of the stream but the forward movement of the car put it out of reach.

Suddenly the Bentley's rear wheels were spinning impotently and von Hassel could hear Fleming's faint curses above the roar of the engine. The wheels stopped and went into reverse, churning up muddy water that swirled over Hassel's thighs.

After four attempts in forward and reverse which only served to bog the car down even more in the mud, Fleming decided that he would have to walk back to the farmhouse to fetch help. Cursing his misfortune, he removed his shoes and socks, rolled up his neatly pressed trousers, and stepped down in the water.

Von Hassel waited for a minute after the British officer had left and set to work with his fingers to untie the nearest knot in the leather straps.

After tearing his fingernails and lacerating his skin for five minutes, he realized that the water was causing the leather straps to tighten. He started sawing the strap back and forth on the rough edge of a chassis member. A crumb of comfort was that at least the water was supporting his weight to some extent so that the straps weren't cutting into him so much. It was then that he experienced the same sensation of raw fear that he had felt the previous year when the Hurricane's machine-gun shells had raked his Me109 and set fire to his fuel tanks: the reason the water was supporting his weight was because the level of the stream was rising. And it was rising fast.

He frantically renewed his efforts to saw through the strap. If only he could cut one strap, he might be able to wriggle free.

The surging water crept up to his face which he then had to press hard against the underside of the Bentley in order to breath. He could no longer see what he was doing and the rising water deadened the diminishing effort that his aching arms muscles could put into the hopeless task of sawing through the unyielding strap.

Suddenly the water was over his chin. He began desperately tearing at the strap with terror-induced strength but to no avail. He started choking on a mouthful of water. In that moment, Dieter von Hassel did something that he had never done before: he panicked but there was no one to hear his sobbing cries.

'But you can't ban escapes!' Ulbrick protested. 'Not in the spring when the escape season's just started!'

'I didn't say I was banning them,' said Kruger, addressing all the prisoners and not just Ulbrick. 'I said that I would not permit any escape that had not been properly prepared or thought out. If someone comes up with a sound scheme, then it is likely that I will approve it. In due course, I will set up a new escape committee with myself as chairman to vet all plans placed before it. For the time being, anyone with an escape idea can forget it unless it is a first-class idea. That is all, gentlemen. The meeting is closed.'

Cathy Standish was a forty-year-old widow who knew how to wear her sexuality like most women knew how to wear slippers. Her horse knew it and so did Fleming but neither did much about it: the horse was too busy hauling Fleming's Bentley out of the swollen stream, and Fleming was in no mood for dalliance – not even with someone as dalliable with as Cathy Standish.

'Come on, Brutus. Come on,' said Cathy, giving the Suffolk Punch an encouraging slap on the rump when the car got stuck again. 'That's my boy. Heave ho.'

The horse threw its weight on the collar. The rope tightened, squeezing water from its fibres, and the Bentley lurched out of the swollen stream. Water streamed off its running boards which had been partly submerged by the time Fleming had returned with Cathy and Brutus.

'Mrs Standish,' said Fleming gratefully, bending down to untie the rope from his car's front axle. 'I don't know how to thank you.'

Cathy placed her hands on her hips and laughed. The rain enhanced her voluptuousness by causing her denim trousers and blouse to cling to her body like wet wallpaper to a pillow. 'You can start by calling me Cathy, commander. Do you think she'll start?'

'Only one way to find out,' Fleming replied as he climbed behind the wheel.

After ten attempts, Fleming ended up with a flat battery and a flooded, silent engine.

'Water in the petrol I expect,' Cathy diagnosed. 'Hitch the rope up again, commander, and we'll haul you back to Grizedale Hall. Some of the prisoners there are mechanical geniuses.' She gave Fleming a mischievous smile. 'Or we could tow it back to the farmhouse to try out your skills.'

Fleming grinned amiably. With water streaming down his face, he said. 'Perhaps I could take a rain cheque on that kind offer, Mrs Standish?'

Ulbrick was playing table tennis in the billiard room when word reached him that Fleming and the Bentley had returned on the end of a towrope attached to one of Cathy Standish's horses.

It had stopped raining when he strolled casually into the courtyard. His mind raced when he saw the Bentley. Had there been enough time before the breakdown occurred, or whatever had happened, for von Hassel to have cut himself free? Was he still strapped under the car?

Major Reynolds was listening sympathetically to Fleming as the naval officer related his catalogue of misfortunes. Cathy Standish was nearby holding Brutus by his reins.

Ulbrick moved nearer the car and combed his hair. He deliberately dropped the comb and stooped to pick it up, glancing towards the Bentley as he did so. He saw a lifeless hand resting on the cobbles.

Suddenly Ulbrick wanted to be violently sick.

All of the prisoners had seen the guards removing von Hassel's lifeless form from beneath the Bentley, and the supper that evening at long trestle tables in the common room was an unusually subdued affair. The blond, happy-go-lucky flier had been one of the most popular men in the camp. Ulbrick had spent the entire meal staring with unseeing eyes at his untouched plate of sausage and mashed potatoes. There was very little conversation to die away when Kruger stood and rapped his spoon for silence.

His speech was short and to the point. 'In view of today's events, I am imposing a total ban on all escape attempts until further notice. Any prisoner who disobeys me will be court-martialled at the first opportunity after our liberation.'

'What will happen to von Hassel, commander?' asked a fighter pilot.

'His body is to be sent home,' Kruger replied dispassionately. 'I suppose it can be said that at least von Hassel will have finally achieved his objective.'

Part Two

HUFF DUFF

Willi broke the War Office censor's seal on his letter and read the typewritten contents in some dismay. It was the third warning he had received from the Feldgendarmerie at Chartres. The oberst in charge of investigations regarding the disappearance of certain motor spares from Willi's old depot and their reappearance on the black market was not interested in the feeble excuses that Willi kept trotting out. Unless Leutnant Willi Hartmann presented himself to the Feldgendarmerie within twenty-eight days, he would be summarily arrested, no matter where he was, and taken back to Chartres by armed escort.

The War Office censor had scribbled in German at the foot of the letter a somewhat gleeful 'Bad Luck, Leutnant Hartmann'.

Willi sighed and broke the seal on the envelope with the Bremen postmark that was addressed to Kruger. The woman's handwriting and her scented envelopes were familiar; he was groping in his drawer for his magnifying glass even before unfolding the letter.

Alice's letters to Kruger were long, verbose affairs, full of gossip about the goings on in her solicitors' office. Who was sleeping with whom; who had been sacked, and so on. The closing paragraphs were couched in affectionate terms and always ended with a string of 'Xs'.

Willi studied the epistle through the magnifying glass and found the first tiny break between one letter and the next almost immediately. He wrote down the letter preceding the break on a separate piece of scrap paper. His magnifying glass continued tracking along the line and stopped when it came to the second break. That letter too was written down.

After ten minutes Willi had a brief message for Kruger from Admiral Doenitz. The simple letter code, which Kruger had shown Willi how to operate, had been devised by Doenitz in collaboration with all his U-boat commanders so that in the event of capture, they could continue to send intelligence back home.

A distant whistling of the opening bar of Beethoven's Fifth warned Willi that Kruger was approaching.

'Willi,' said Kruger, marching into the room. 'If you insist that I should have a signature tune, please find someone who can whistle in the right key.' He spotted the letter that Willi had decoded. 'What has the admiral got to say this time?'

'He wishes you a happy birthday,' said Willi boredly.

Beatrix Potter, or Mrs Heelis as she preferred to be called, was a formidable seventy-five-year-old Lake District landowner. She was dressed in grimy, ill-fitting tweeds, a moth-eaten bonnet and several layers of old cardigans – the few remaining buttons of which were fastened to the wrong buttonholes.

As she chatted animatedly to Reynolds on their tour of Grizedale Hall's grounds, the Canadian officer couldn't help thinking that she looked exactly like Mrs Tiggy Winkle, the character that she had created many years before. Unlike Mrs Tiggy Winkle, Beatrix Potter was a phenomenally rich woman, thanks to the royalties that her children's books continued to earn, even though she had given up serious writing many years before. The great interests that now dominated her cloistered life were her Lake District estates, her herds of prize-winning Herdwick sheep, and the National Trust of which she was a founding member and one of its principal benefactors.

It was this latter interest that had brought her to Grizedale Hall in a chauffeur-driven car from her farm at the neighbouring village of Near Sawrey.

'Of course, I never knew Harold Brocklebank personally, Major Reynolds,' she said when they paused on the eastern side of the estate, near the overgrown vegetable gardens which a party of prisoners were clearing. The men stopped work to gape at the unlikely couple. 'But I do remember Grizedale Hall being built. My late husband was involved in some of the legal work you know.'

Reynolds didn't know. 'About Commander Kruger's suggestion –' he began for the third time.

'Of course, it was the Ainslie family that owned the original estate.' She gestured to a hill to the west which had always puzzled Reynolds by its symmetrical shape. 'That mound is artificial. Brocklebank had it built because he couldn't stand the sight of the Ainslies' house. He was an eccentric, you know.'

My God, thought Reynolds. That's rich coming from you. 'Miss Potter –' he began.

'What's that monstrosity?' Mrs Heelis interrupted, pointing an accusing finger south at a crude tower made from pine trunks that was rearing above the shrubbery.

'It was a Forestry Commission firewatchers' tower,' Reynolds explained. 'I requisitioned it and had it moved to the corner of the barbed wire fence to serve as a watchtower for my guards.'

Mrs Heelis grunted. 'It's a disgrace the way the Forestry Commission and War Office seem to be able to do exactly as they please without consulting the National Trust. Planting ugly pines everywhere, turning people's homes into concentration camps.' She waved an imperious hand at the working party. 'At least you've got some gardeners in. High time too. The place was going to rack and ruin.'

'They're German POWs, Mrs Heelis,' said Reynolds patiently, wondering if it would ever be possible to bring the conversation around to the subject of her visit. He also wanted to ask her endless questions about Peter Rabbit, Tom Kitten, Ginger and Pickles, and all the other characters he had read about during his Montreal childhood.

'At least they're working,' said Mrs Heelis, running an approving eye over the acre of land that had been cleared.

Reynolds saw an opportunity and seized it. 'They're extremely hard-working, thanks to their new commanding officer, Miss Potter. He believes in keeping them busy. The War Office say that his suggestion is a great idea, so if –'

Mrs Heelis pounced on a chocolate wrapper. 'A Hershey bar,' she cried indignantly. 'You see? Even the Americans leave their litter everywhere.'

'A prisoner must've dropped it.'

'Where would he have got a Hershey bar from?'

'Miss Potter, this camp is flooded with food parcels from pro-German sympathizers in the United States. You wouldn't believe the amount of chocolate they receive.'

'Anyway,' said Mrs Heelis abruptly. 'I think your German's idea is an excellent one, major. Matters are a disgrace around the popular spots. Whenever I complain, people throw up their hands in despair and say that there's a war on. I shall suggest at the next National Trust meeting that the trustees fully support the scheme.'

Reynolds managed to conceal his sigh of relief.

Willi loved a good argument provided he was present but not involved. Very often choice pieces of gossip were let slip when tempers got frayed. Back home in Munich, during his motorcar double-dealing days, he had run a nice little blackmail sideline based on information gleaned from eavesdropping on rows.

The row that finally erupted between Kruger and Ulbrick a month after Kruger's arrival fulfilled both Willi's requirements. The only trouble was that it was a bit one-sided: nothing that Ulbrick said elicited a flicker of response from Kruger. The U-boat commander sat impassively at his desk, inhaling occasionally on a cheroot and staring at Ulbrick while the angry *Luftwaffe* officer took advantage of Kruger's permission to speak freely by delivering a harangue concerning Kruger's changes, which were, in Ulbrick's opinion, making it easy for the British to administer the camp.

'Examples, please,' Kruger requested when Ulbrick paused for breath.

'This business of us all having to work the vegetable gardens.'

'Don't you like fresh vegetables?'

'That's not the point. The more food we provide for ourselves, the more we make available for British mouths.'

Kruger shook his head. 'The agreement I entered into with Major Reynolds was that whatever extra food we grow will not affect our rations. Also, the work is good for the men and it eases the boredom.'

'With the American food parcels, it's not as if we're short of food.'

'We don't get sent fresh vegetables.'

Ulbrick realized that he was losing the argument. 'It's undignified for officers to do labouring work while watched by British conscripts,' he stated.

Kruger shrugged. 'Boredom is even more undignified, Ulbrick.'

'They wouldn't be bored if they were allowed to plan escapes.'

Kruger nodded to Willi. 'Show him the survey, Willi.'

Willi opened his desk drawer and passed a handwritten sheet of paper to Ulbrick.

'A survey I've carried out of every escape since the camp was established,' said Kruger. 'Ninety per cent of them weren't planned. They were a matter of opportunities being seized as they arose: a guard's back turned for an instant on an exercise walk, that sort of thing. The ten per cent that were planned weren't planned properly. The escapees had little or no money, inadequate travel and identification documents, and no proper clothing.'

Ulbrick was unimpressed. 'The object of escaping is to tie down enemy resources,' he said. 'The more soldiers there are guarding us or searching for us, then the less soldiers the British have to fight us.'

Kruger carefully tapped the ash off his cheroot. 'The object of escaping is to get home and rejoin one's comrades in the fight. Also, I doubt if searching for escaping prisoners does tie down British resources. The British use volunteers to a greater extent than we do: Home Guard, War Reserve Constables and so on. Read the British newspapers and you will learn about the thousands of girls who've left service to work in the factories and how former ladies of leisure have mobilized themselves into volunteer organizations – nursing, bandage-making, driving ambulances, fund-raising – a whole host of activities that we would never allow our women to join in.'

There was a low whistle from the corridor. Willi moved with astonishing speed despite his bulk. He crossed to the window and released the sash lock which enabled him to slide back a section of the wooden windowsill from its frame. Beneath the sill was a cavity filled with documents. He snatched the survey from Ulbrick, dropped it into the cavity, slid the sill back into place and locked it with the sash catch. He was back behind his desk by the time the door was thrown open by Sergeant Finch, accompanied by Corporal White and Private Jones.

The sergeant's suspicious glare at the three German officers was completely ruined by the acrid fumes from Kruger's cheroot which made his eyes smart and water. He made a mental note to check the next consignment of food parcels to find out who was sending Kruger the poisonous weeds.

'I have a message from Major Reynolds,' the British NCO announced, wiping his eyes on the sleeve of his battledress.

'And *I* have a message for Major Reynolds,' said Kruger coldly, rising to his feet and fixing Finch with an icy stare. 'Inform him that I am organizing a series of instruction courses in various subjects for the men in my charge. If he would like me to include a course of lessons in manners for his NCOs, then I will be happy to do so. The first lesson will be on the correct way to enter a room.'

Finch was unmoved. 'My apologies, sir,' he said crisply. 'Major Reynolds says that the National Trust are in favour of your suggestion to use POW working parties to clear litter from picnic sites.'

Ulbrick looked dazed. 'Clearing picnic sites?' he echoed.

'Before agreeing,' Finch continued, 'Major Reynolds will require a parol from you – a binding promise – that there will be no escape attempts from the working parties.'

'He shall have my word on it,' Kruger promised.

Ulbrick stared at Kruger in frank disbelief. 'Clearing picnic sites?' he repeated. 'I'm sorry, commander, but have you gone completely insane?'

Leutnant Hans Schnee stared at the questionnaire. The form had been handwritten: all the questions were printed in pencil in Willi's neat block capitals.

'This is lunacy,' he protested. 'Do I have to answer every question?'

'Every one,' Willi affirmed. 'Every new prisoner has to fill in the form. Commander Kruger's orders.'

Schnee turned the sheet of paper over. 'But there's at least thirty questions. Service details, special skills, civilian occupations, special training, hobbies. Everything.'

'Well, how do you think I feel?' Willi complained. 'I've

had to draw up over a hundred of those forms, so don't you go messing it up.'

'But I'll have to give information that I refused to give the British when they interrogated me.'

'Just answer the questions please,' Willi pleaded.

'Supposing this form fell into British hands?'

'It won't.'

Schnee read carefully through every question. He was a well-scrubbed, fresh-faced U-boat 2nd Watch Officer barely out of his teens. He looked up at Willi. 'Supposing Kruger decides from my answers that I'm not eligible to be a POW? Will he send me home?'

Willi groaned.

'Anyway,' said Schnee emphatically. 'I'm not going to write down anything about my capture. If Commander Kruger wants to find out, then he'll have to question me himself.'

Kruger was lost in silence for some seconds, staring with unseeing eyes out of his office window as he brooded on the loss of *U-100*. The U-boat had been from the 1st U-boat Flotilla based at Lorient: the same flotilla as his *U-112*. Its commander, Joachim Schepke, had been one of his few close friends. He turned round to face Schnee and relit his cheroot.

For once Willi was not present. Nettled at being told by Kruger to make himself scarce, he had crept into the next room, a disused boxroom, and was listening to the conversation with the aid of a tumbler purloined from the kitchens. He was holding it sandwiched between the adjoining wall and his ear.

'I'm very sorry to hear about Schepke,' said Kruger, sitting at his desk. 'He was a fine U-boat commander.'

Schnee nodded and remained silent.

'Are you sure that the destroyer came straight at you out of the darkness?'

Schnee nodded again. 'Yes, commander.'

'What was *U-100* doing when the destroyer rammed you?'

'We were shadowing a convoy that was under attack. We had expended all our torpedoes. Commander Schepke hoped that there might be a chance to pick off stragglers with our 88-millimetre.'

'How far astern of the convoy were you?'

'About six miles.'

'And a warship broke away from the battle to attack you?'

'Yes, commander.'

Kruger was baffled. Schnee's story tallied with accounts from other recently captured U-boatmen who told of convoy escorts that had left their station and 'came straight at us from out of the darkness'.

The deadly 'wolf pack' tactics that Admiral Doenitz had insisted on his U-boats adopting after the decimation of Convoy SC7 the previous October depended on a surfaced U-boat, when sighting a convoy, to shadow it while radioing frequent reports on its course and to speed back to headquarters, which would then direct other U-boats to the target for a massed, surface attack. The advantage of the surface attack was that a U-boat could use its diesels, giving it a top speed of 18 knots as opposed to a submerged speed of 5 knots on its electric motors. Also, a surfaced U-boat was difficult to spot, especially in heavy seas and driving rain; and under-water detection equipment such as ASDIC was rendered impotent. Additionally, a surfaced U-boat was highly manoeuvrable, so its commander could use one torpedo per ship instead of the wasteful submerged attack technique of firing a fan of four torpedoes across the bows of a single ship.

But the recent spate of British successes against shadowing U-boats suggested that the enemy had developed an efficient method of detecting a surfaced U-boat at night, at

53

a distance of several miles, regardless of the weather conditions.

From the experiments he had been involved with before the war, Kruger knew that radio location using impulses reflected from a target was useless in mid-ocean against a U-boat's low profile because the top of a U-boat's conning tower was invariably below the level of the swell.

'What was the weather like when you were rammed?' Kruger asked.

'Filthy, commander. Force Seven and we were shipping it green down the bridge hatch.'

'So why did you refuse to enter the circumstances of your capture on my form?'

Schnee hesitated and said guardedly, 'I didn't want to write anything down because I know that the British have got some sort of equipment for plotting the position of surfaced U-boats.'

Kruger stubbed out his cheroot and lit another one. 'Why do you think that, leutnant?'

'I was on the bridge with Commander Schepke and the lookouts when we were rammed. Visibility was less than four hundred metres and yet that destroyer was dead on course for us when she appeared out of the squall. She hit us square on the bridge. I was thrown into the water and was picked up by the destroyer about thirty minutes later with six other members of the crew.

'At daybreak we were transferred to an armed merchantman, the *Farnham Castle*. It was crammed to the bulwarks with survivors of the convoy battle. Dutch, Poles, Lascars – the lot.' Schnee gave a wry smile. 'Conditions were chaotic below decks. We were wearing these overalls – none of us were in uniform – so we thought it best if they didn't discover that they had some U-boatmen among them. We kept quiet and stayed out of the way.

'The next day I found a paint scraper and a wire brush and discovered that I could move about the ship without being challenged. I overheard two officers talking about a "Huff Duff" fix on a U-boat.'

'A what fix?'

'"Huff Duff",' Schnee repeated.

Kruger pushed a pencil and paper across his desk. 'Spell it,' he ordered.

Schnee thought for a moment and wrote 'HUF DUF' in block capitals. 'It sounded like that, commander.'

Kruger frowned at the two meaningless words.

'I decided to find out what "Huff Duff" meant,' Schnee continued, 'so I started cleaning the paint off the companionway ladder that led to the radio shack. The door was open. A radio operator was sitting in front of an ordinary wireless set but there was another apparatus that was like no other set that I'd seen before. The radio operator heard me. He turned round and told me to clear off.'

'Can you describe the apparatus?'

'I can do better than that,' Schnee replied. 'I can draw it. I memorized everything I could. I wasn't close enough to read what the controls were for and my English isn't that good anyway.'

'Could it have been nothing more than a new type of ordinary wireless set?'

'I suppose so, commander. But there was a queer-looking antenna array above the radio shack. I can draw that as well. I've got a rough idea of its size because someone was working on it.'

Kruger considered for a few moments. 'What do you think the apparatus was?'

'A radio direction-finding system?' Schnee ventured.

Kruger looked faintly contemptuous. 'Direction-finding at sea, leutnant? Firstly, accurate direction-finding requires large, steerable aerials operating from at least two land bases. Secondly, the stations have to be over four hundred kilometres apart in order to obtain reliable triangulation fixes on a radio transmitter operating in the mid-Atlantic.

And thirdly, the radio transmitter you're trying to get a fix on has to operate for long periods. As you well know, U-boat transmissions rarely last longer than thirty seconds.'

Schnee looked suitably crushed. Kruger moderated his tone and added, 'I think it's safe to assume that the apparatus you saw was nothing more than a new type of communications wireless set.'

'I suppose so, commander,' Schnee admitted, although he didn't sound convinced.

A week later Fleming arrived at Grizedale Hall in the company of a man in civilian dress. Schnee was in a small working party that was clearing the drive when the Bentley hooted. The prisoners stood to one side to allow the vehicle past. Schnee stared in astonishment at the man dressed in a British Merchant Navy uniform who was sitting beside Fleming. The young U-boat officer made a hurried excuse to his comrades and went looking for Kruger. He found him in the common room leafing through a consignment of National Geographic magazines that had just arrived from America.

'I'm sorry to disturb you, commander, but the radio operator who saw me in the *Farnham Castle*'s radio shack has just arrived here.'

Reynolds frowned and glanced at Fleming and the Merchant Navy officer in turn. 'An identity parade?' he queried. 'May I ask why, gentlemen?'

'Sorry to mess up your routine, old boy,' said Fleming blandly. 'But we're scooting all over the place checking the survivors that were brought into Liverpool on the *Farnham Castle* last month. One of them may have seen something on the wretched boat that he should not have seen.' He opened his briefcase and handed Reynolds a list of four names. 'Those are the four Jerries you're sitting on who were on the *Farnham Castle*. I'd like this gentleman to take a look at them to see if he recognizes one of them.'

Reynolds looked none the wiser.

'I'm sorry about this, Major Reynolds,' said the Merchant Navy officer. 'But the man who looked into my radio shack was doing some maintenance work on the ship at the time. I told him to go away and thought nothing more about it until I mentioned it to the bosun. He told me that he hadn't given orders to any member of the crew to do any work around the radio shack.'

'So whoever it was,' murmured Fleming, 'we aim to find him. Wheel out those four Jerries please, old boy.'

The Merchant Navy officer stood in front of the four prisoners who were lined up in Reynolds office and stared hard at each man in turn. He seemed to hesitate when he studied Schnee's face and then he shook his head.

'Alright, sergeant,' said Reynolds to Finch. 'Wheel them out.'

'The trouble is,' said the Merchant Navy officer as he climbed into the Bentley, 'I only got a glimpse of the blighter's face as I turned round. And he was standing against the light.'

'Next stop is the POW camp at the Shap Fell Hotel,' said Fleming, starting the Bentley's engine. 'They're looking after a couple of U-boat NCOs who were on your ship.'

Kruger examined the two sketches that Schnee had drawn. One was of the apparatus that the U-boat officer had seen in the *Farnham Castle*'s radio shack and the other was of the antenna array. Both drawings were neatly inscribed with estimated dimensions and were captioned 'HUF DUF'.

Kruger lit one of his evil-smelling black cheroots and inhaled on it while gazing across his desk at Schnee. The young naval officer fidgeted uncomfortably.

'Alright,' said Kruger at length. 'It's obvious that you

saw something important in the ship's radio shack and that the British are very jumpy about it. The question is: what is it that you saw?'

Schnee was still convinced it was a radio direction apparatus but Kruger had already demolished that argument so the junior officer was reluctant to bring it up again. Instead he shook his head.

There was a silence while Kruger absentmindedly doodled on the sketches by pencilling-in the letter 'u' in 'HUF' and in 'DUF'.

'Perhaps it was radio ranging and location apparatus?' Schnee ventured.

Kruger made no reply: he was staring at his handiwork. His normally impassive expression was one of surprise. The two words amended by his doodling now spelt 'HF DF'.

The letters 'DF' were familiar to Kruger. In English they stood for 'direction finding'. But 'HF'?

Schnee sensed that something was amiss but was wholly unprepared for what happened next. Kruger suddenly thumped his desk and exclaimed: 'My God! "Huff Duff"! High Frequency Direction Finding!'

Schnee goggled anxiously at his senior officer, wondering what he had done wrong. 'Commander?'

'Schnee,' Kruger declared. 'I owe you an apology. The British *have* developed a seaborne direction-finding system.'

Willi looked at Schnee's sketches of the 'Huff Duff' apparatus and its antenna array and shook his head doubtfully. 'I'm sorry, commander, but it would take weeks of coded letter writing to convey this information to Admiral Doenitz. And they'd probably get it wrong even then.'

'Yes, I agree, Willi,' Kruger conceded. 'And yet it's vital that we get the information home somehow.'

'I suppose it could be done,' said Willi, anxious to please. 'But it would involve such long, rambling letters – full of

58

numbers. The War Office censors would be certain to stop them.'

The same thought had already occurred to Kruger. 'I can't take that risk and we don't have the time,' he murmured.

'Why is it so important, commander?'

Kruger inhaled thoughtfully on his cheroot. 'The U-boat arm was sinking half a million tonnes of allied shipping a month when I was captured. Our only hope of defeating the British by the end of the year is by maintaining that figure.' He tapped the sketches. 'If this equipment is as good as I suspect it is, it may turn the tables against us.'

Willi could think of nothing constructive to say.

Kruger was lost in thought for a moment. And then he appeared to come to a decision. 'A pencil and paper, Willi. I want to dictate a draft letter to "Alice". After that I want you to look through the questionnaires to find out if any of the prisoners were once tailors.'

Willi found a pencil and paper.

'And Willi.'

'Commander?'

'Not a word about this to anyone or I'll have you court-martialled.'

If Hauptmann Dietrich Berg had existed in fiction he would have served an aspiring writer well as a mad scientist, although he was neither mad nor a scientist. He was an extremely clever, eager to please young technician who happened to be accident-prone on a scale best described as monumental.

He first blew himself up at the age of six with the aid of a children's chemistry set that its makers had guaranteed was harmless. At school he decimated a chemical laboratory in addition to losing two fingers during his first attempt at building a perpetual motion machine. His three years at university were punctuated by an assortment of minor explosions and a number of major ones. He became obsessed with geology and took up pothole exploring in the Hartz Mountains because they were rich in minerals. His experiments with underground explosions in order to open up new galleries led to him spending a week underground, trapped in a very new gallery that was the fruit of one of his experiments.

When asked by the army for a reference, his university authorities had recommended that Berg should be posted to a department dealing with some form of research, possibly explosives. The German army, with its remarkable ability to put square pegs in round holes – a talent it shared with the British army – sent Berg to an infantry regiment as a wireless operator because they discovered that he had been an amateur radio enthusiast until Hitler had revoked all 'ham' radio licences in 1936 on the day after Berg had been issued with his.

After that Berg had to content himself with blowing up the odd radio valve here and there, although he did succeed in shooting off his big toe during rifle drill. The injury left him with a slight limp that contributed to his capture at Dunkirk and later being run over by a Post Office van at Euston railway station while in the company of two guards who were quicker on their feet than he was.

Despite the loss of two fingers, he was an accomplished engineer. The alarm system he rigged up in his workshop at Grizedale Hall consisted of a cocoa tin cum electric gong operated by a strategically placed prisoner on lookout duty. It worked perfectly; nothing incriminating was in sight by the time Kruger strode into the workshop. The dozen or so prisoners present were intent on the wooden cuckoo clocks they were making under Berg's guidance.

The two officers exchanged salutes.

'Any luck with the wire-cutters?' inquired Kruger.

Berg went to his cupboard and produced two lengths of flat spring steel from underneath a heap of rock samples.

He showed them to Kruger. 'These are just the job, commander,' he said enthusiastically. 'We'll drill a pivot hole at each end and file a notch in each cutting edge. They're long enough to provide the leverage needed to cut through a ten-millimetre iron bar.'

'Just so long as they can cut through barbed wire,' said Kruger acidly. 'I'll want them by Wednesday evening.'

'Two days? They'll be ready,' Berg promised.

Kruger fingered the two pieces of steel. 'Where did you get these from, hauptmann?'

Berg grinned. 'Sergeant Finch will insist on parking his Austin near the laundry room. We removed a leaf spring from each side of his rear axle.'

'Is his car safe to drive?'

'No, commander.'

Kruger gave a ghost of a smile. 'Unfortunate.'

Berg hesitated. 'Er – may I ask who will be escaping, commander?'

Kruger's smile froze. 'No,' he said curtly. He turned on his heel and went off to look for Willi. He found him in the common room. 'Willi, what sort of pressure can you put on the guards?'

The little Bavarian looked baffled. 'Pressure, commander?'

'Blackmail,' said Kruger bluntly.

'I would never dream of blackmailing anyone,' Willi protested indignantly.

'Of course you don't dream about doing it – you actually do it. I need one of those flashlights that the guards are issued with.'

Willi looked relieved. 'Oh, I won't have to blackmail anyone for one of those, commander. Just a little bribery: two bars of chocolate ought to be enough.'

Sergeant Finch levered his bulk behind the wheel of his baby Austin. His head pressed against the soft canvas roof

61

and he wondered for the hundredth time whether or not he should have bought the larger Wolseley. But the insurance money his mother had left him had just been enough to buy the Austin outright. And besides, he was in love with the tiny car even though it didn't have enough power to pull the skin off a rice pudding.

He drove it down the drive. A bumpy ride because the narrow wheels hopped from one rut to the next regardless of what the steering wheel told them to do.

He simmered with impatience at the main gate while Corporal White made a great show of examining his pass and peering underneath the vehicle.

'Going to get a new flint for it, sarge?' inquired Chalky, opening the gates.

Finch scowled, revved up the engine and shot forward into the lane. The front wheels took the pothole in their stride but disaster struck when it was the turn of the rear wheels. There was a loud crash and a deafening scream of metal on asphalt caused by the Austin's body hitting the ground where it had parted company from the rear axle. The tremendous jolt punched Sergeant Finch's head through the car's canvas roof and trapped it by the neck.

Chalky gaped in amazement at the sight of his NCO's head jammed through the car's roof like a hog's head on a platter and then he doubled-up over his rifle in helpless laughter, tears streaming down his cheeks.

'Corporal White!' snarled Finch, twisting his head round in its new collar. 'You're on a charge!'

Oberleutnant Max Kluge, foot-sore and half dead on his feet, toiled wearily up the gloomy back stairs that led to Kruger's office. He had the sort of backache that could be framed and put on display in an osteopath's waiting room.

Max and a party of nine fellow prisoners had spent the day walking the entire length of Cunsey Beck, picking up litter under the watching eyes of three guards on horseback. They had cleared the southern bank in the morning and the northern bank in the afternoon – working in the opposite direction. Cunsey Beck was a pretty little mountain stream near Grizedale Hall that discharged into the western shore of Lake Windermere. Max couldn't imagine why the beck was so popular with walkers because it seemed to flow uphill in both directions. But popular it was, as was evidenced by the number of sacks that his team had filled with litter.

He tapped on Kruger's door and entered when bidden. The office stank of cigar fumes. Max exchanged polite greetings with Kruger while wondering where the seemingly inexhaustible supply of the lethal cheroots was coming from.

'Anything of interest, oberleutnant?' inquired Kruger.

Max was too tired to answer. He had just about enough strength left to empty his specially deepened trouser pockets on to Kruger's desk. The U-boat officer's eyes widened very slightly at the cascade of miscellaneous items that tumbled out: bus tickets, letters, bills, receipts, nail scissors, combs, a full packet of English cigarettes, a box of used Swan Vestas matches and another box that looked half used. The packet of Durex condoms was definitely unused, and there was even a hiker's compass – all litter that somehow had not ended up in the sacks loaned for the occasion by Windermere Urban District Council.

'Well done, oberleutnant,' said Kruger, examining the compass. 'This is a remarkable find.'

Max sat down without being invited. 'The *pièce de résistance*,' he grunted, producing a wallet from beneath his blouse and handing it to Kruger.

Kruger opened the wallet. Inside were four pounds in banknotes, an identity card, a driving licence, and a 'Ramblers' Association' membership card. All were made out to a Mr Ian Proctor of Liverpool.

'This is fantastic, oberleutnant,' said Kruger in genuine

astonishment. 'Absolutely amazing. I had no idea your first sortie would produce such results. Don't forget to draw the maps while the details are still fresh in your mind.'

Max's answer was a deep snore.

The news was a bombshell. Schnee gaped bug-eyed at Kruger. 'I'm to do what?' he stuttered.

'You're to escape,' Kruger repeated with a flash of irritation. 'You're in possession of valuable information which we can only get to the OKM if you escape. What's the matter? Don't you want to go home?'

Schnee collected his reeling thoughts. 'Well, yes, commander. But how? When?'

'Through the wire. Tonight,' answered Kruger cryptically. 'Escaping from Grizedale Hall is not difficult. Staying escaped is impossible unless proper plans have been made – which they have in your case. Any questions?'

Schnee had a thousand and one questions.

The game that the prisoners played in the courtyard that afternoon was rough, and one that the guards hadn't seen before. Two teams of ten men each, one man carrying a team mate on his shoulders, squared up to each other. Battle commenced on a blast from Kruger's whistle. The teams charged into each other. The object of the game was for the men being held aloft to topple a rival from an opponent's shoulders.

The pitched battle surged unsteadily back and forth across the courtyard. Men went crashing down amid loud cheers from onlooking prisoners and guards, and there was some brisk wagering with cigarettes.

One team got the upper hand and drove the opposition under the high granite archway of Grizedale Hall's rear entrance.

The mêlée of wrestling, yelling prisoners provided a screen for Berg while he unscrewed the fusebox cover. The guards, sensing that the battle of the archway was a diversion, obligingly looked in the opposite direction. It took Berg less than thirty seconds to wind a length of coat-hanger wire across the terminals of the main fuse and to replace the cover.

The game ended when Kruger blew his whistle. He walked over to Berg. 'Everything alright, hauptmann?'

Berg looked very pleased with himself. 'Yes, commander. I've uprated the hall's main fuse from a hundred amperes to about five hundred amperes. The floodlighting fuse is now certain to be the weak link in the hall's entire circuit.'

'Let us hope so,' Kruger murmured.

As usual, the floodlights that illuminated Grizedale Hall like a granite ballerina came on an hour before dusk.

At 9 pm, after the prisoners had been locked in the hall, an expectant group of them gathered around Berg in one of the dormitories to witness his latest piece of insanity.

All had unlit cigarettes in their mouth and all watched in silence as Berg, wearing gloves, picked up a sharpened pencil in each hand. The lead graphite core at the end of each pencil had been exposed and connected to lengths of cable whose ends had been inserted into an electric power socket. The reason why the crude arrangement looked lethal was because it was.

Berg glanced at his watch – one minute to go.

Three floors below, Kruger and Schnee were crouched by a window that opened on to the terrace. The junior U-boat officer was wearing a heavy woollen jersey and denim trousers. On his back was a small hiker's rucksack that had been made from a *Kriegsmarine* haversack. If a guard chose to patrol along the terrace, Schnee was certain that his pounding heart would be heard.

*

'The pencils will work on the same principle as the carbon arc lamps in cinema projectors,' Berg explained enthusiastically to his sceptical audience. 'When the guards come to see what has happened, I will explain that I was merely creating a continuous spark to light our cigarettes because we'd run out of matches.'

Berg gave a boyish grin and brought the pencil points closer together so that there was a twelve-inch gap between them. 'All right. Who wants to light their cigarette?'

Berg was not exactly overwhelmed by eager volunteers.

'Oh, come on, fellows. It's perfectly safe.'

'Okay,' said a prisoner, moving forward and offering his cigarette gingerly in the direction of the makeshift electrodes. He closed his eyes tightly. 'I'll try it.'

'What you must appreciate,' said Berg, bringing the pencil points even closer together, 'is that I've never actually done this before.' He chuckled. 'I'll probably get seven days in the cooler.'

The points were less than half an inch apart when he finished speaking. Nothing happened.

Berg looked disappointed. 'It doesn't look as if it's going to work,' he commented.

Suddenly there was a tremendous bang and a blinding blue flash in the dormitory, followed by the sound of a distant explosion, followed by all the lights going out, including the floodlights, leaving Grizedale Hall plunged into total darkness.

An aroma of charred wood and burnt human hair filled the pitch-black dormitory. There was a silence and then a respectful voice in the darkness said, 'Berg?'

There was a long pause before Berg answered. 'Yes?'

'I think you'll definitely get your seven days.'

The instant the floodlights went out, Kruger opened the window and shook hands hurriedly with Schnee. The young U-boat officer tightened his grip on Berg's homemade wire cutters and jumped out on to the terrace. He leapt over the balustrade and dropped the eight feet to the lawn. It took him less than forty seconds to cover the three hundred yards down the slope of the lawn and across the vegetable plots. He weaved through the shrubbery, threw himself flat on the ground in front of the barbed wire fence and started cutting his way through. The strands weren't difficult to cut but they parted with loud cracks that Schnee was certain could be heard by the two guards perched in the nearby firewatchers' tower. There was a sudden uproar of pounding boots and shouted orders from the direction of the hall as a company of guards turned out to investigate the power failure.

Schnee cut through the final strand and gingerly twisted the severed ends of wire to one side. Before crawling through the hole, he buried the wirecutters in a pre-arranged spot so that they could be recovered for future use. He wriggled through the wire and raced towards the cover offered by the pines. Once safe in the shadows, he rested for a few minutes to allow his thumping heart to return to its normal rhythm. Curiously, there was no feeling of elation at being free; perhaps it was the thought of the daunting twenty-kilometre cross-country walk to Grange-over-Sands on Morecambe Bay that lay ahead of him that night.

He checked his bearings with the aid of the compass and a hand-drawn map, and struck out due south, threading his way through the dark, brooding pines of Grizedale Forest.

The lights had been back on five minutes when Reynolds, wearing pyjamas and dressing gown, examined the charred remains of the two pencils that Sergeant Finch had placed on his desk. He poked at the two lengths of cable.

'All right, sergeant. I'll ban all games in the courtyard. But what do you think of Berg's story?'

'Well, it's possible, sir. They don't receive that many

matches in their parcels – plenty of cigarettes, yes – but no one seems to think about matches.'

Reynolds was suddenly reminded of something. 'Who sends Kruger those lousy cigars?'

'No one, sir,' Finch reluctantly admitted. 'I don't know where he's getting them from.'

'Okay. We'll look into it another time. I guess we'd better let Berg have the benefit of the doubt but I'm giving him seven days for damaging government property. That ought to be long enough for him to grow new eyebrows.'

A weak moon broke through the clouds a few minutes after midnight just as Schnee was crossing the lonely little bridge over River Leven at Backbarrow near the southern tip of Lake Windermere. He left the deserted road and crouched beneath a hedgerow to check his position against the map.

He worked out that he had just crossed the Lakeside and Haverthwaite Railway, which meant that the main road nearby had to be the A590 to Grange-over-Sands. Apart from the occasional call of a nightjar and the barking of dogs in distant farmyards, the night-shrouded countryside was still and silent. He decided to stick to the main road; he could always jump over one of the low dry-stone walls into a field if he heard anything suspicious.

He made good time walking on the metalled surface. Twenty minutes later, after skirting the village of High Newton, he saw the moonlight gleaming on the sea in Morecambe Bay. He stared for some seconds, hardly believing his luck and, after picking out his objective – the Humphrey Head peninsula – he started walking again with renewed vigour.

From now on the sketch map was vague, but by swinging south-west across the fields, he was able to keep the Humphrey Head in sight. The route took him west of the tidy little Victorian resort town of Grange-over-Sands. He crossed the Furness railway line and came to a bank of sand dunes. He paused at the top of the dunes and saw with dismay that what he thought was the sea was in fact a vast expanse of wet sand. There was no sign of the sea nor was there any sign of the barbed wire entanglements defending the coast that Kruger had warned him to expect near the town. Obviously the British didn't think it likely that the invasion would take place in Morecambe Bay, a useful snippet of intelligence to take home.

Schnee checked his watch. 3.05 am. In forty minutes he would be among his own countrymen and on his way home. His feet sank alarmingly into the sand. It was far softer than he had anticipated. Also, the beach was absolutely flat – there was no slope to indicate in which direction the sea lay. He assumed that he would eventually reach the water's edge if he walked with his back to the land.

Schnee trudged on for fifteen minutes and paused for a rest. It was hard going through the soft, clinging sand, and his ankles were beginning to ache. No wonder the British weren't expecting an invasion force to land in Morecambe Bay: anything heavier than a lawnmower attempting a landing from the sea would be bogged down. But where the hell was the sea? He battled on for another ten minutes and decided that it was time to send the prearranged recognition signal. He aimed the flashlight due south and sent four dashes and a dot. He waited a minute and signalled again, this time sending a dot and four dashes. To his joy, the U-boat responded immediately with four dots and a dash. The signal was barely discernible which meant that either the U-boat was using a low intensity lamp or it was standing off a long way from the shore.

He took a few steps forward and immediately sank up to his knees in the half-mud, half-sand. From then onwards forward progress became a tedious, ankle-wrenching business of having to haul his feet out of the clinging quicksand with every step. Suddenly he sank up to his waist. He cursed out loud and threw himself forward. By pushing down on outspread hands he was able to lift one leg clear, only to have his arms sink up to the elbows. His struggles to free himself from the glutinous ooze caused his body to sink until he was trapped up to his chest. Every movement of his body produced obscene sucking noises as though the quicksand was a living creature. He stopped struggling because he thought he heard a strange hissing noise like a distant waterfall. Maybe it was his imagination. He was about to curse again but the expletive died on his lips and his eyes widened in horror. Straight ahead, shining clearly in the moonlight, was a line of white water that stretched into the distance on either side for as far as he could see. The hissing noise grew steadily louder as the menacing tidal bore hurtled towards him at what seemed to be the speed of an express train.

Schnee cried out in terror and renewed his futile struggles to escape the grip of the treacherous ooze. The three-foot high wall of charging water was one hundred yards from him when he began to scream out and claw dementedly at the engulfing sand.

'Seawater and sand in the lungs. It'll be death by misadventure on the report,' said the green-overalled pathologist, marching ahead of his two visitors through the gloomy, marble-lined corridor at the Barrow-in-Furness mortuary.

The pathologist showed Fleming and the Merchant Navy officer into a high-ceilinged room where the naked body of Leutnant Hans Schnee lay on a dissecting table. The three men approached the table and regarded the body of the young man in silence.

'We get several drownings every year,' complained the pathologist. 'People simply won't read the warning signs. The sands look innocent enough but they're lethal. And at this time of year, the tidal bore comes in at thirty miles an hour. Not even a horse can out-gallop it.'

'Well?' Fleming asked the Merchant Navy officer.

There was a silence. The officer studied Schnee's face carefully for a few moments before looking up at Fleming. He nodded. 'Yes,' he said. 'It *was* him. I'm certain of it now.'

'If he ever had an identity disc, he'd lost it,' said the pathologist. 'So who was he? A serviceman on holiday?'

'Something like that,' murmured Fleming, moving to the door.

Part Three

RADIO GRIZEDALE

After two months under Kruger's leadership, the prisoners' morale was remarkably high, and the rift between Kruger and Ulbrick had largely healed. Ulbrick's initial hostility to Kruger's many changes had been gradually replaced by the realization that demanding work rotas were eliminating the corrosive effect that boredom had on the men's minds and souls. Where work didn't exist, Kruger created it. He persuaded Reynolds to allow those prisoners with catering skills to take over in the kitchens for one day a week. Following the success of the experiment, this was later increased to two days. Another concession he won – despite opposition from Sergeant Finch – was to assume responsibility for the distribution of the prisoners' mail and food parcels. Even the prisoners' leisure time was occupied with compulsory attendance on any two of the ten or so instruction courses that were now running every day. The most popular, after Kruger's English language classes, was Hauptmann Dietrich Berg's clock and model-making course.

As Berg climbed the stairs to Kruger's office, his most fervent wish was to be left alone in his workshop. He cursed his willingness to try to please as many people as possible, especially Kruger. If only he could learn to say 'no' now and then, he would not have these problems.

His face was lined with anxiety as he knocked apprehensively on Kruger's door. He was so preoccupied rehearsing a string of excuses regarding his failure to produce a satisfactory pocket compass that he forgot to wait outside the door until summoned. He was sent scurrying out of the office by a blast of invective from Willi and a blistering scowl from Kruger.

Berg re-entered correctly. His apologies were silenced by a gesture from Kruger, who indicated the chair in front of his desk. Willi sat with pencil poised ready to take notes while Berg perched nervously on the edge of the chair. Kruger took his time reading carefully through a form which Berg recognized as the questionnaire he had completed upon his arrival at Grizedale Hall. Kruger opened his box of cheroots and hesitated before selecting one. Willi noticed the uncertainty. He had already noticed that Kruger was smoking less than usual. Obviously the mysterious supply was not inexhaustible after all. Willi decided to carry out a thorough search of Kruger's quarters when the senior officer was on one of his inspection tours. Willi hated mysteries.

'Good afternoon, hauptmann,' said Kruger, lighting a cheroot and regarding Berg through a cloud of smoke.

'Good afternoon, commander. Commander, I'm extremely sorry about the delay in producing a pocket compass. I'm doing my best but –'

'I'm not interested in compasses at the moment,' Kruger interrupted. He tapped Berg's questionnaire. 'You say here that you were once a licensed amateur radio operator?'

'Only for one day, commander. I got my licence on a Wednesday and they were all revoked on the Thursday.'

'But you passed the examinations?'

'Yes, commander,' said Berg, wondering what all this was leading up to.

'And you were a radio operator in the army?'

'Yes, commander. But only for six months before my capture.'

Kruger steepled his fingers and stared at Berg. 'Hauptmann Berg. Could you build a radio transmitter?'

Berg goggled in alarm. 'What – here, commander?'

'Where else do you think I mean?'

The young army officer was lost for words. He was always eager to help and he had a measure of self-confidence that frequently led him to attempt anything. But building a radio transmitter? He resolved to say 'no' and risked a sideways glance at Willi as a possible source of support. The chubby little Bavarian was pretending to be busy writing.

Berg caught Kruger's eye and his resolve began to collapse. 'Well,' he said cautiously. 'I'm not sure, commander. It all depends.'

'On what?'

'Er – well, the frequency you want it to operate on for one thing.'

'15,460 kilocycles,' said Kruger succinctly. 'It's one of the standard U-boat frequencies.'

Berg swallowed. A thousand problems crowded into his fertile brain. 'And the power output, commander?'

'Enough for me to communicate with the headquarters of the 1st U-boat Flotilla at Lorient in western France.'

The young army officer looked as though he was about to faint. 'Commander, that would be extremely dangerous.'

'Why?'

'Sending directional signals south – down the entire length of England – they would be certain to be heard and bearings taken on their source.'

Kruger considered for a moment and nodded. 'Very well then, hauptmann. How about sending directional signals due west across to southern Ireland – which is neutral anyway – and out into the Atlantic?'

'Commander,' said Berg desperately. 'Even assuming I could build a transmitter and a directional aerial, who would hear such signals?'

'U-boats,' Kruger answered curtly. 'They operate in mid-Atlantic where the convoys have no air cover.'

Berg wanted to close his eyes and open them again to discover that the interview was really a particularly bad nightmare. 'Mid-Atlantic?' he croaked. 'A distance of about three thousand kilometres?'

'About that,' Kruger agreed. 'The transmitter will require a power output of at least fifty watts.'

By now Berg's eyes were permanently glazed with shock. 'Fifty watts? But ten watts would be adequate.'

'I have a considerable amount of text to. send,' said Kruger. 'Repeating the signals three or four times would be dangerous because the British monitor the U-boat frequencies. One powerful transmission will ensure that HQ will be able to piece together the entire signal from the logs of several U-boats. Could you build a fifty-watt transmitter?'

Bracing himself for the worst, Berg said, 'I'm very sorry, commander, but I have to be honest with you. No.'

'Why not?'

'There are so many components I would need – valves, condensers, resistors, potentiometers, wire and solder, *and* a soldering iron. The list is endless. To build just a receiver would be difficult enough, but a transmitter will be impossible.'

Kruger inhaled on his cheroot without saying a word.

'I'm very sorry, commander,' Berg repeated, feeling foolish. 'But it is impossible.'

Kruger broke the silence that followed. 'Hauptmann Berg, have you noticed anything unusual about the thirty or so new prisoners who've joined us this month?'

Berg looked puzzled. 'No, commander.'

'Most of them are U-boat officers,' said Kruger coldly. 'The reason for that is because the British have developed a new equipment that enables them to pinpoint the position of surfaced U-boats. Last week, Leutnant Schnee gave his life attempting to get valuable information home concerning this new equipment. We owe it to our country, our U-boat crews, and to the memory of Leutnant Schnee to get the information home somehow. It's too complicated and too long to be incorporated in coded letters, so I intend transmitting it by radio.' The U-boat ace paused and fixed the unfortunate Berg with a hard, unblinking stare. 'Therefore, Hauptmann Berg, you will build a suitable transmitter-receiver to communicate with U-boats and you will have it working within two weeks from today. All the talents we have in the camp and all its limited resources are at your disposal. Brief me on your progress every morning immediately after roll-call.'

'Yes, commander,' Berg muttered.

'And, hauptmann.'

'Commander?'

'Good luck.'

Standing exactly five feet in his bare feet when they were clean, radio officer Leutnant zur See Fritz Brunel, one of the *Bismarck*'s junior radio officers, was the smallest POW at Grizedale Hall.

He was also the most agile, which was why none of the guards watching over the litter-gathering party of perspiring POWs saw him execute a neat dive into the thick undergrowth at the edge of the picnic area. The other prisoners studiously avoided looking in his direction as he hopped over a dry-stone wall like a marauding dung beetle and catapulted himself into a ditch.

He ran, bent double, along the bottom of the dried-out ditch, vaulted another stone wall and worked his way across two fields. His objective was a row of holiday cottages about half a mile away. He was within a hundred yards of them when he saw that an end cottage had an aerial wire strung up the length of its garden. Had the woman dozing in a deckchair in the back garden opened her eyes, she would have seen Brunel dart through her open kitchen door and emerge a minute later clutching the family radio under his arm. But she didn't open her eyes and Brunel was able to race, unchallenged, in the direction he had come. He reached a spot where the working party was moving towards him through the undergrowth and went to work on the radio receiver with a screwdriver. He removed the component-encrusted chassis from its cabinet, eased the valves from their sockets and laid them carefully in the long grass. He also removed other bulky components such as the tuning condenser and spread them around on the ground. Small, detachable items such as control knobs went into his pockets. He scratched a hole in the thick peat beneath the trees and buried the unwanted wooden cabinet.

A litter-gathering prisoner approached and, without a word to Brunel, started putting the various components and the chassis into his sack. Brunel stood up and helped him.

None of the guards noticed that Brunel had been absent.

Berg carefully and methodically dismantled the fourth domestic wireless receiver that had come into his possession during the week. As always, he had started by unsoldering the resistors and reading their coloured rings to determine their resistive value before placing them in appropriately marked matchboxes. His soldering iron consisted of a brass bit mounted on a steel shank thrust into a file handle. Occasionally he reheated the bit by holding it in the flame of a home-made Bunsen burner. The short lengths of wire that he removed from the set were tied into neat bundles according to their colour.

When all the components had been removed, he turned his attention to the largest one of all: an aluminium-encased electrolytic condenser the size of a hand grenade. The other characteristic that such condensers shared with a hand grenade was a tendency to explode when overloaded.

Berg decided that a protective shield for the condenser would be a good idea. He wrapped a strip of aluminium around the condenser and tried to hold the assembly in place while he bored the holes for the clamping screws. The awl slipped and punched right through the condenser's casing, releasing toxic aluminium borate on to his workbench. It wasn't a disaster because of an identical spare condenser removed from another stolen radio. But it was the only one, so maybe trying to make a shield wasn't such a good idea.

He carefully cleaned the poisonous chemical off his bench and shook it out of the window.

Suddenly the cocoa tin electric alarm rattled as though a stag beetle with St Vitus' Dance was trapped inside. Berg picked up the false top to his workbench, opened the door of a large, unfinished, wall-mounted cuckoo clock, and tipped the incriminating items into the clock's base. The half-dismantled radio set disappeared under a floorboard that had to be slid, not lifted. He failed to notice a resistor that rolled on to the floor.

By the time Sergeant Finch strode into the workshop with two guards in tow, Berg was quietly tempering a piece of the cuckoo clock's escapement mechanism in the Bunsen burner flame.

Finch sat down and lit a cigarette while the two privates carried out a snap search of Berg's workroom. The POW was well-liked by the guards, so they refrained from ransacking the place. They checked his cupboard containing finished and unfinished cuckoo clocks without harming the contents and prodded his collection of rock samples to see if they were hollow.

'Good afternoon, Corporal Finch,' said Berg in the best English he could manage.

Finch scowled ungraciously. 'It's *Sergeant* Finch, jerry.'

Berg shrugged and continued with his work while Finch

called out occasional orders to the two guards, telling them where to search. He picked up the chunk of Coniston granite that Berg used as a paperweight.

'Can't imagine why anyone would want to collect lumps of rock,' Finch observed, juggling several of Berg's prized geological samples.

'Always I wanted to be geologist,' Berg explained.

'Nothing, sarge,' reported one of the guards.

Finch grunted. As he stood and turned to leave, Berg spotted the resistor on the floor where it was about to be trodden on by the sergeant.

'Sergeant Finch!'

Finch gave Berg a suspicious look. 'What?'

Berg's mind raced. 'Sergeant Finch. You would like a cuckoo clock, yes?'

'A cuckoo clock?'

'I have a fine clock. Just made. Wait please.' As Berg brushed past Finch, he managed to kick the offending resistor under his bench. He took a small, neatly carved clock from the cupboard and returned holding it out with a beguiling smile on his face. It was his first and therefore least successful attempt at making cuckoo clocks.

'Look, you will see that it works.'

Berg proudly held the clock up and tripped its mechanism. A tiny door flew open and out popped a creature that resembled a raped, one-eyed sparrow. It managed a strangled 'Uck yoo' and disappeared.

Berg held the strange timepiece out to Finch. 'It is yours. I am sorry that it has one eye only. They are difficult to make.'

Finch accepted the clock with a muttered 'thanks'. To cover his embarrassment at Berg's gesture, he barked an order at the guards and marched out of the workshop with the clock tucked under his arm.

'This was in today's post,' said Willi, handing 'Alice's' latest decoded message to Kruger when the senior officer entered his office.

Kruger took the slip of scrap paper and read it through twice.

BDU TO U112. CONTENTS YOUR 12/41 AGREED. URGENT YOU CONVEY FULLEST DESCRIPTION OF HFDF. IN PARTICULAR OKW REQUIRE DIMENSIONS OF AERIAL ARRAY. U-BOATS IN OPERATIONAL AREA WILL MAINTAIN DAILY 1155 TO 1230 LISTENING WATCH FOR YOUR CALL SIGN.

'Did you also arrange a radio call-sign with Admiral Doenitz?' asked Willi curiously.

'It cost nothing, Willi,' Kruger murmured enigmatically. He lit a cheroot and burned the slip of paper in his tin lid that served as an ashtray. 'So – it would seem that I'm going to write a long signal for Brunel to transmit.'

'Still no sign of Leutnant Herbert Shultz, old boy,' murmured Fleming, inexpertly casting a fly into the centre of the tarn.

Reynolds' cast was equally abysmal. He swore. 'You know something, Ian? Before I lost the sight of one eye, I could drop a fly within a couple of inches of a fish.'

'About Leutnant Herbert Shultz,' Fleming reminded him.

Reynolds scowled. 'After all this time, the guy's dead,' he said, trying to hide his irritation at the question. 'He has to be.'

'But no body, James.'

Reynolds spooled in his slack line. 'The summer visitors are starting to flock into the Lake District. His body will turn up on a pike or somewhere.'

'Good afternoon, gentlemen.'

Both men turned round and called out greetings to Cathy

Standish, who was urging her horse along the track to where they were fishing in her lake. Her riding companion a youngish man dressed in neat tweeds, allowed his horse to graze some two hundred yards away. Reynolds returned his wave.

Cathy reined in and jumped down from her saddle. She was wearing a tight-fitting gingham blouse and even tighter jodhpurs. She gave the two men the special smile that she reserved for men in uniform, even though Fleming and Reynolds were dressed in old clothes. 'Commander Fleming. Major Reynolds,' she said breezily, shaking hands with the two men. 'Had any luck?'

Fleming shook his head. 'We've only been here a few minutes, Mrs Standish.'

Cathy gave Fleming an impish smile. 'Commander, if you wish to drop your rod in my tarn I have a right to insist that you call me Cathy.'

'Hey, ma'am,' joked Reynolds. 'Does that go for me as well?'

'Certainly not,' said Cathy with a severity that was diminished by the laughter in her eyes. 'Not so long as you let your prisoners go roaming all over the Lake District stealing wireless sets. Mine's now disappeared.'

Fleming was immediately intrigued. 'Stealing what?'

'There's been a spate of break-ins round here,' Reynolds intervened. 'Radios and valuables disappearing from houses. The police are satisfied that it's not the prisoners because the break-ins always occur at least a mile away from where they're working.'

'Interesting,' Fleming observed.

Reynolds didn't share Fleming's view. The visits by the police had made the issue a sensitive one as far as he was concerned. 'Windermere CID think that it's a gypsy who operates near a POW working party in the hope that the prisoners will be blamed. Anyway, if the POWs wanted a radio, they'd steal one set, not four.'

'Five,' Cathy corrected, chuckling mischievously. She swung a not unshapely leg over the saddle. 'I daresay they've got a home-made crystal set hidden somewhere in that vast hall.'

'No, they haven't,' said Reynolds defensively.

'Well, if you find it, let me have it. There's not a wireless set to be had in any of the shops in Windermere or Ambleside.'

'Cathy,' said Fleming quickly. 'I'm returning to London tomorrow. If you'd like me to look out for a wireless for you, I shall be happy to do so.'

'Super, Ian,' she replied, matching his smile. 'You bring me one back and I'll lay on a special wireless-warming party just for you.' Her smile became decidedly mischievous. 'And you've yet to cash that rain cheque, Ian . . . Must go now. Bye.'

'Rain cheque?' Reynolds queried as the two men watched Cathy riding away. 'What did she mean by that?'

'Heaven only knows,' Fleming murmured sagely.

'Her parties are really something,' said Reynolds, reeling in his line. He added hastily: 'So I've heard say.'

It was after midnight when Kruger entered the linen storage cupboard in the labyrinth of Grizedale Hall's attics. He rapped on the back of the cupboard. The thin plywood panelling that had been made into an inward opening door was opened by Brunel. The tiny naval leutnant saluted Kruger and ushered him into the cavernous, elongated space under Grizedale's steeply pitched slate roof which ran the entire east-west length of the hall. The gloomy space, lit by a string of naked, low-wattage light bulbs, was broken at ten-foot intervals by fans of timber trusses supporting the weight of the roof.

Brunel indicated a taut, inclined wire that appeared to be stretched the length of the roof space. 'Mind your head on the aerial wire, commander,' he said, leading the way along narrow catwalk planks laid across the ceiling joists to where Berg was working at a bench he had built over the main water tank.

The reluctant radio engineer looked up from the tangle of valves and wiring he had assembled on the chassis of the largest of the stolen radio receivers. His attempt at a salute resulted in him cracking his hand painfully on a roof truss.

'Good evening, commander.'

Kruger nodded and ran his eye over the radio that was lying on its side. It had no enclosing cabinet. Despite all the problems Berg had, the results of his labours looked remarkably professional: the radio's wiring was neatly routed around the various components and the soldered joints were smooth and gleaming. Even the mahogany baseboard on which the home-made morse key was mounted had been french polished with a concoction that Berg had made from pine resin and methylated spirits.

'It all looks very smart,' said Kruger with less ice in his voice than usual.

Berg's anxious expression cleared slightly. He gave a nervous smile. 'I've been lucky, commander. One of my biggest worries at first was finding a suitable solder. I tried some lead from the roof but its melting point was too high. Then I realized that the bulges in the lead pipes in the shower rooms were wiped solder joints. I scraped some of the metal off and found that it worked perfectly. For flux I used some pine resin that a litter clearing party brought back – the stuff oozes out of the trees around here.'

'Does the radio work?' Kruger inquired.

Berg, warming to his subject, turned the radio upright and pointed to an identical pair of valves that were mounted side by side. 'They're the main RF power valves, commander. I was able to match a pair from two receivers. The only way to get their power output up is to have them working together in a push-pull circuit.'

86

Kruger wasn't interested in the technicalities. 'Does the radio work?' he repeated in some irritation.

Berg hesitated. 'Er – well – yes.'

'What's that supposed to mean?'

'I think the output's about half a watt.'

Kruger regarded Berg steadily. 'You only think?'

Berg looked embarrassed. 'I'm sorry, commander – I don't have a power meter. I can only guess at the power output by the temperature the dummy load reaches when the morse key is operated.'

'The chances of a U-boat hearing a half-watt signal are almost nil, Berg. I ordered you to provide fifty watts.'

'Well, I can't,' said the army officer showing uncharacteristic spirit. He had worked virtually day and night for a week to get the transmitter to its present state, and precious little thanks he was getting. He gestured to the radio. 'Maybe those valves could pump out fifty watts for a short period before they blew up, but there's no hope of that without a suitable power supply.'

'So build a power supply,' Kruger ordered dispassionately.

Berg looked despairingly at Brunel who was hovering in the background. He showed Kruger the disembowelled remains of the stolen radios. 'Look, commander. These radios had power supplies designed to provide one watt of audio output – a nice, comfortable volume for listening in a small living room. What we need is the sort of power supply that you find in public address system amplifiers. When we're liberated, you can have me arrested, court-martialled, stood up in front of a firing squad – whatever you like – because there is no way that I make this thing deliver more than one watt.'

Surprising himself with his own courage, Berg met Kruger's piercing gaze without flinching.

'I've got an idea,' said Brunel brightly.

*

As soon as it was dark, Brunel crawled out of an attic window and on to the highest point of Grizedale Hall's roof. Fortunately, the floodlights had been arranged so that their beams were concentrated on the façades of the building. A prisoner passed him a roll of stair carpeting and a coil of rope that was attached to a grapnel made from the business end of a gardening fork.

Brunel ran along the ridge towards the eastern end of the hall and slithered down the tiled slope to the eaves. He braced himself, launched himself into space, and landed lightly astride the ridged roof of the kitchen outhouses which ended under the overhang of the hill.

Brunel whirled the grapnel around and sent it sailing up to hook on to the barbed wire fence. The fence, tucked into the cliffside overhang, was over thirty feet above ground level but it was only five feet high because the British never expected any prisoner to attempt an escape by the cliff route.

Brunel lashed the roll of carpet across his shoulders and shinned up the rope hand over hand. He clung to a fencing post, untied the short roll of carpet and managed to fling it over the barbed wire so that it provided a safe route for him across the vicious entanglement.

Fifteen minutes later, after a difficult climb up the precipitous hillside, he was loping along the lonely road towards Ambleside seven miles to the north. Owing to his fitness, he wasn't out of breath and nor would he be, even if he maintained his present pace all the way.

On occasions, when he neared pedestrians, or when vehicles approached him, he slowed to a casual saunter, but for most of the way he was able to travel at an easy jog.

His luck held. In the blacked-out streets on the outskirts of Ambleside he even asked a woman the way to the cinema. As Kruger had rightly guessed, his accent aroused no suspicions because the little lakeside town was a popular centre where Free French, Poles and Dutch servicemen spent their leave. The woman directed him along Kelsick Road to the market place and even told Brunel that he would just catch the main film if he ran.

He found the cinema near the old Salutation Hotel without trouble, purchased a shilling ticket in the stalls from the five shillings that Kruger had given him, and settled down in the packed, darkened auditorium to watch the pre-war film *Band Wagon* about a gang of comedians running a pirate television station. He found the antics of the comics as incomprehensible as the plot but the audience enjoyed it hugely.

Before the end of the programme, he disappeared into the toilets and folded his tiny frame into a cleaners' cupboard. The national anthem was played and a few men used the urinal. After that there was silence apart from the final check by the cinema manager to make sure that everyone had left.

He waited an hour, surrounded by buckets and mops, slowly getting cramp, before cautiously emerging from his hiding place. The auditorium was pitch black and deserted. He lit a candle and made his way to the back of the cinema. A door marked 'Private' took him to his objective – the projection room. The projector used for the final reel was still warm to the touch as Brunel began his search. His luck continued to hold: the cinema had a standby sound amplifier concealed behind a dusty stack of film cans. He dragged the heavy, steel-cased instrument from its hiding place and examined the maker's label. It was exactly what Berg needed: a 100-watt cinema amplifier manufactured by Western Electric. Brunel swung it on to his shoulder. It weighed at least seventy pounds.

Despite his superb physical condition, getting the unwieldy amplifier back to the camp was a nightmare: the blackout proved a blessing in the back streets of Ambleside because he was able to hide whenever he heard approaching footsteps, but the seven-mile trudge along the country lanes – having to crouch behind dry-stone walls or hedges at the slightest sound – quickly developed into a back-breaking murderous slog.

The eastern sky was tinged with the dawn by the time he was dragging the amplifier over the carpet-covered barbed wire fence. A prisoner helped him lug it across the out-house rooftop, and a third prisoner dropped a rope down so that it could be hoisted on to the roof of the hall.

Ten minutes later it was safely on Berg's bench.

Berg removed the amplifier's outer casing and examined the huge rectifier valves. 'Marvellous,' he breathed to Kruger. 'Marvellous. I'll have the transmitter working by tomorrow, commander. *And* it will be delivering at least sixty watts.'

Kruger turned to Brunel. The diminutive officer was grinning from ear to ear. 'Brunel, as soon as we're liberated I shall recommend that you receive the Knight's Cross.'

Two days later, at 11.40 am, Berg and Brunel finished checking the fencing wire aerial. The single strand of taut steel was stretched the entire length of the roof. It was anchored as high as possible at the western end of the roof and sloped down to the ceiling joists at the eastern end. In places Brunel had sawn niches in the timber roof trusses so that no part of the aerial's forty-metre length was earthed.

'Why isn't the wire horizontal?' asked Kruger.

'So that the eastward signal shoots into the sky,' Berg explained, sitting at the bench to check the connections to the morse key. 'It means that there's less radiation for any monitoring stations to pick up.' He pointed up at the wire. 'Actually, commander, a wire aerial like that – two wavelengths long – is very directional; most of our signal will be going due west in the direction that the aerial's pointing.'

'Will there be emissions to the north and south?'

'There's certain to be some, commander,' Berg replied,

inspecting the wiring that linked the modified cinema amplifier to the transmitter. 'Without proper filtering, this transmitter will be splattering harmonics all over England.' He switched on the power and watched the transmitter's valves as they began glowing. 'But if any British monitoring stations to the south do pick us up, they'll probably think we're a U-boat off the Faroe Islands or somewhere.'

'Especially as we'll be using a weather station U-boat call sign,' Kruger remarked.

Berg made sure that the morse key was switched off. He stepped back to admire his handiwork. 'She's ready, commander.'

Kruger looked at his watch and glanced at Brunel. 'Have you practised on the morse key?'

'Yes, commander,' Brunel replied, sitting at the bench. 'It's a bit mushy but I've got the feel of it.'

Kruger pulled a sheaf of book flyleaves from his pocket and dropped them on the bench. Each sheet of paper was covered in neat, hand-printed text. 'That's the signal, Brunel. Start transmitting *en clair* at 1100 precisely at a speed of no more than ten words per minute. The message must be received in its entirety on the first transmission.'

Berg snatched up the signal. 'But all this is going to take at least ten minutes to send!'

'So?'

'But I thought you'd be transmitting for only a few seconds at a time!'

'Did I say anything about the length of the transmission?' inquired Kruger, his voice deceptively mild.

'Commander,' Berg beseeched, pointing at the transmitter. 'Those valves are going to be about three hundred per cent overloaded as it is. They won't stand a continuous transmission – they'll blow up!'

'I'll be the one that blows up if they do,' Kruger threatened softly, taking the papers from Berg and placing them in front of Brunel. 'They have only to last for the one transmission.' He nodded to Brunel. 'My call sign is "UBW58". Send it five times. The "standing by" acknowledgement from a U-boat will be the usual six "V"'s. Off you go.'

Brunel gave nervous smile and switched on the morse key.

Fifty miles to the south at the Royal Navy's Liverpool monitoring station, Wren Chief Petty Officer Jenny Linegar heard Brunel's 'UBW58' call sign in her headphones. She switched on the pen recorder and carefully adjusted the aerial selector knob on her 'Huff Duff' receiver until the pulsating ellipse of light on the set's cathode ray tube was tuned to hard line. The graticule around the edge of the circular screen showed that the signal bearing was due north. Switching on her recorder had illuminated a warning light above the huge wall map of the western approaches at the far end of the operations room. The duty officer left his rostrum and crossed to Jenny's console.

'A UBW weather station U-boat, sir,' Jenny reported. 'Bearing due north. Signal strength three.'

The lieutenant glanced at the pen recorder that was busily spiking the U-boat's morse on to a moving roll of paper. The pen stopped oscillating and drew a straight line while the transmitting U-boat awaited an acknowledgement. It came with a weaker string of 'V's that the pen faithfully reproduced.

'UBW58,' mused the lieutenant, reading the morse straight off the recorder when the U-boat started transmitting again. 'Have we heard him before?'

Jenny checked her log. 'No, sir.'

'Mm. Well, he looks out of harm's way. Probably up in the Arctic Circle. Chatty too. Who's east of us to give us a decent cross-bearing? Just to be on the safe side.'

'There's 90 Group's Baker Six, sir.'

The lieutenant groaned. 'Blasted army. Their trouble is

that they don't understand anything that's not on dry land. Oh well, let's give them a chance to shine.'

The lieutenant picked up a telephone.

Brunel frowned in concentration as he keyed out the long signal. The dull ache in his wrist brought home to him just how rusty his morse had become since his imprisonment.

The strange light illuminating the roof space prompted him to glance at the transmitter. What he saw almost caused his wrist to falter in the middle of a word: the transmitter's driver valves were glowing with an intense blue light and the energies building up inside the big electrolytic condenser were causing its maker's label to blister and flake. He could even feel the heat from the grossly overloaded components on his face.

Berg was staring at the condenser in alarm. He opened his mouth to protest but Kruger silenced him with an impatient gesture.

'Yes, well that's jolly interesting and all that, old boy,' said the lieutenant patiently, talking into the telephone and winking at Jenny. 'And I'm sure your D/F gear is spot on, but I'm afraid your cross-bearing puts our U-boat smack in the middle of Lake Windermere.'

There were accusing squawks from the receiver's earpiece. The lieutenant looked pained. 'Yes – I know a U-boat got into Scapa Flow, old boy. But Lake Windermere isn't the same as Scapa. . . . Look, I hate to be too dogmatic about this, but the only way that a U-boat could get into Lake Windermere would be to carry it overland on the backs of pink elephants.'

The unfriendly squawks coming from the earpiece became distinctly more hostile – to the navy in general and the lieutenant in particular.

'I daresay. I daresay,' said the lieutenant boredly. 'But I seem to recall that it was a lot of piddling little boats that brought a certain army back from Dunkirk last year.'

The squawks degenerated into expletives and then the line went dead.

'Strange creatures, soldiers,' the lieutenant remarked to Jenny. 'Never able to admit when they're wrong. Anyway, there's not much point in worrying just yet about a U-boat on a weather station billet.' He leaned forward, switched off Jenny's pen recorder and looked speculatively at her. She was definitely the most beautiful Wren in the place. 'Tell me, chief, are you doing anything special tonight?'

Jenny gave the naval officer a sweet smile. 'That all depends on what my husband has in mind, sir.'

Berg jerked his hand away from the burning condenser.

Brunel ignored him by turning to the second page of the signal with one hand and maintaining the staccato rhythm on the morse key with his other hand.

Berg watched the near-molten valves and the bulging condenser knowing full well that the transmitter had no more than a few seconds left to live.

'Commander,' he pleaded. 'You must –'

'Quiet!' Kruger snapped.

'But –'

'I said, quiet!'

'I'm halfway, commander,' muttered Brunel, not breaking his concentration.

Kruger glanced in some concern at the tortured transmitter. 'All right, hauptmann, you'd better put a screen or something over those valves.'

Berg picked up the metal case that had housed the cinema amplifier. He was about to lower it over the transmitter when the condenser suddenly split with a loud crack and blasted fragments of aluminum foil in his face. He cried out, dropped the heavy case on the valves – causing them to implode, and fell back clutching his face and moaning in agony. Blood starting welling between his fingers.

It took Brenda Hobson nearly fifteen minutes to pick as many fragments of aluminum foil as she could out of Berg's face with her tweezers and drop them one by one into a sterile dish. She looked up at Reynolds as he walked into her sickbay and shook her head.

'I'm sorry, sir, but he needs hospitalization. I can't get all these bits of metal out from around his eyes because of the swelling, and I think some have gone in his eyes as well. What I don't understand is why the bits of foil, or whatever they are, are causing such inflammation. It doesn't make sense.'

'Has he said how it happened? Or what he was doing?'

'No, sir. I've asked him several times but he refuses to answer.'

'Goddamn stubborn jerry,' Reynolds muttered. 'Okay. I'll call an ambulance.'

'I've already called one,' said Brenda.

Kruger stood impassively to attention in front of Reynolds' desk, staring straight ahead at the wall as though Reynolds didn't exist. He had refused to answer any of Reynolds' opening questions.

The Canadian rose to his feet, walked round his desk and stood close to Kruger, their faces inches apart.

'Okay,' said Reynolds, staring Kruger straight in the eye. 'If you won't do any talking, I will. Some straight talking that you won't like. Firstly, the hospital Berg has been moved to is St George's Royal Eye Hospital. Secondly, the surgeons there think they may be able to save his eyesight if only they knew what the hell it is that's causing the infection. Thirdly, he won't tell us what he was doing when he had the accident, and fourthly, I've got a goddamn shrewd idea that you do know.'

Kruger's icy gaze went briefly to Reynolds and returned to the wall. 'If Berg refuses to speak, then I have nothing to say either.'

Reynolds stared at Kruger in contempt. 'Have you ever wondered how I got this eye-patch, commander?'

Kruger remained silent.

'No,' said Reynolds. 'I guess you haven't. Maybe I'm wrong but I've got a pretty shrewd idea that you don't give a damn about other people. I lost my eye at Dunkirk when a shell exploded nearby. I went through three weeks' hell in hospital wondering if I was going to go blind. I know exactly what Berg is going through now. My opinion of anyone who would deliberately put a comrade through that sort of torture doesn't bear repeating. Words such as coward and skunk come to mind plus a few others.'

Kruger's silence continued.

'Get out,' said Reynolds wearily. 'I don't want to see you in this office again. In future you will pass all messages through Sergeant Finch – at least he knew you for what you were from the moment he saw you. I'm only sorry that I've turned out to be such a lousy judge of character, but not as sorry as I am for that poor bastard lying in St George's.'

'I have only your word for it that Berg is in danger of going blind,' said Kruger calmly after a pause.

'For Chrissake!' Reynolds exploded. 'You saw his face! You saw the blood!'

Kruger's face remained expressionless.

'Anyway,' said Reynolds, calming down. 'At least I won't have the job of writing the letter home to his parents telling them what has happened to their son. Nor will I be the one who has his blindness on my conscience for the rest of my life.'

Kruger was lost in thought for some seconds. He met Reynolds' gaze for the first time and seemed to come to a decision. He felt in the pocket of his great-coat and placed the remains of the electrolytic condenser on Reynolds' desk.

'This was found by a litter clearing party and was given to Berg. He was doing something to it when it blew up in his face.'

Reynolds examined the remains of the condenser, turning it over in his hands. 'What in hell is it? I can't even read the maker's name on it.'

'It was made by the Telegraph Condenser Company,' informed Kruger. 'It's a radio component but I've no idea what was in it or what Berg was using it for.'

Reynolds picked up his telephone receiver and asked to be put through to St George's Hospital. He looked up at Kruger while he was waiting for the connection to be made and gave the German a wry smile. 'I guess I didn't misjudge you after all, commander.'

'Perhaps,' said Kruger. 'But I definitely misjudged you.'

The deputy director of the Telecommunications Research Establishment at Malvern gingerly pushed the wrecked condenser across his desk with his pencil. 'One electrolytic condenser that's been subjected to about a five hundred per cent overload, I'd say.'

'How?' asked Fleming.

'Too much juice pumped through it. Serves you right if the navy's started using domestic spec components in service equipment.'

Fleming looked depressed. 'So you definitely think it's been used in a transmitter?'

'No doubt about it,' said the scientist emphatically. 'A powerful one, too. That condenser was intended by TCC for use in domestic wireless receivers. There isn't, or rather, wasn't, a receiver on the market that could do that to an electrolytic.'

Fleming carefully folded the burst condenser into a handkerchief and returned it to his briefcase. He stood and shook hands with the scientist. 'Thank you, Mr Nicolson, you've been most helpful.'

'If you're staying overnight in Malvern, I can recommend the Foley Arms. Roast lamb on Tuesdays.'

Fleming's diffident smile concealed his concern at the scientist's opinion about the condenser. 'I have to be getting back to London today.'

The scientist grunted. He had hoped for dinner at the Navy's expense.

'So what did TRE have to say?' Admiral Godfrey wanted to know as soon as Fleming arrived back at the Admiralty.

'Definitely used in a transmitter, sir,' Fleming replied.

Godfrey sighed. 'And I suppose those blighters at Grizedale had time to concoct a story that they've all stuck to?'

'I'm afraid so, sir. I spent about four hours with every POW involved. I couldn't shake them. They're all sticking to their story that they were listening to a home-made receiver when the condenser blew up.'

'What about the one who's in hospital?'

'He's refusing to talk,' Fleming replied glumly.

Admiral Godfrey came to a decision. 'Very well, Fleming. We're damn certain that they transmitted. Probably on a U-boat frequency. So we must work on the assumption that the transmission was heard. I'll arrange for all recently-captured U-boat crews to pass through the London "Cage". Officers *and* ratings. You're to stay in London until you get results. I'm sure I don't have to remind you just how important it is that we find out what those blighters at Grizedale Hall know.'

Fleming thought wistfully about Cathy Standish's rain cheque that he had yet to cash but wisely remained silent.

Part Four

THOSE MAGNIFICENT MEN

Oberleutnant Harry Wappler and Leutnant Heinz Schnabel did things together: both belonged to the same *Luftwaffe* group; both were pilots; both had been shot down over Southern England and both had been interrogated at the London 'Cage'. To round off this achievement in comradeship, marred only by Heinz's inability to speak English as well as Harry, and a failure by Harry to share Heinz's passion for trains, both arrived at Grizedale Hall in the same truck.

The canvas-covered Bedford ground to a standstill in the courtyard. The three soldiers guarding Harry and Heinz vaulted over the tailboard and unlatched it with a loud crash.

'Out!' yelled the lance-corporal.

Harry and Heinz dutifully jumped down and hoisted their Red Cross issue kitbags on to their shoulders. They looked around in bewilderment. Guards were yelling orders, prisoners were piling out of the hall and forming up into neat lines, while other soldiers were running around the grounds, blowing whistles and shouting at prisoners tending the vegetable plots. From within the hall came the sounds of organized ransacking. To add to the confusion, the weekly laundry van, loaded with giant hampers of soiled linen, was pounced on by two privates under the command of Chalky, who overturned all the hampers, tipping their contents on to the courtyard like camels going berserk in an Arab bazaar. Three soldiers even crawled under the vehicle.

The truck that had delivered Harry and Heinz was searched before roaring away, leaving the two new arrivals standing in the midst of all this frenetic activity, puzzled and uncertain what to do next.

Harry was the taller of the two, a calm, methodical man with a droll sense of humour. By contrast, Heinz was a tortured, uncertain soul, torn between two conflicting desires. The first he shared with Harry: a craving to escape and rejoin his group. The second was his burning ambition to maintain his skin in one pristine piece throughout the war, which, like most German servicemen, he expected to be over by the end of 1941.

'What's going on?' Heinz asked a *Kriegsmarine* leutnant.

'Another blitz,' the naval officer replied, hardly glancing at the two men as he hurried by. 'Reynolds thinks we've still got a hidden radio. You'd better get in line.'

Harry and Heinz moved to the rear of the parade and joined the prisoners forming into lines. Harry nudged a major standing beside him. 'Who's the senior officer here?'

The major gave Harry a puzzled look. 'Commander Kruger, of course. Surely you've met him? He personally briefs all new prisoners.'

'We've not met anyone yet,' Harry replied.

The major pointed out Kruger and Reynolds, who were exchanging salutes at the head of the parade. He motioned Harry to silence as two British NCOs moved along the ranks counting the prisoners.

'One hundred and thirty-two, sir,' the first NCO reported to Reynolds.

Reynolds looked pained. 'Goddamn it,' he muttered. 'There should only be a hundred and thirty. Count them again.'

'One hundred and thirty-two prisoners, sir,' the NCO reported a few minutes later.

The news seemed to sadden Reynolds. 'Sergeant Finch!'

Sergeant Finch had heard the news, which he treated as a

personal insult. His face was thunder as he gripped his clipboard under one arm. He took two paces forward and crashed to attention. 'Saar!'

'We have two prisoners too many.'

'Yes, saar! I heard, saar!' He did an about turn and was about to bawl out an NCO when Reynolds quickly intervened.

'We'll have a normal roll-call, sergeant. Each prisoner to fall out when his name has been called.' He turned to Kruger. 'Will you translate please, commander.'

Kruger acknowledged and repeated Reynolds' order in German.

At the end of the roll-call, which included Leutnant Herbert Shultz's name being called out, Harry and Heinz were the only prisoners left in the courtyard, standing rigidly to attention and looking very worried about all the fuss. After much consultation of documents and poring over clipboards, the reason for their presence was discovered. They were marched off by a smouldering Sergeant Finch to Reynolds' office to face the Canadian officer's standard 'welcome to Grizedale and escape is impossible' spiel.

After lunch Willi ushered the airmen into Kruger's office. They stood to attention while the senior officer studied the questionnaires they had completed. He looked up at Harry while slowly lighting a cheroot. Willi watched the ritual with interest. He knew from his surreptitious searches of Kruger's quarters that the senior officer was down to three boxes of a hundred each of the poisonous weeds. The stock was definitely dwindling. Willi wondered gloomily what the senior officer's temper would be like when the supply was exhausted.

'Exactly how good is your English?'

Harry was taken back. The question had been asked in English.

'Please reply in English,' Kruger added.

'I've been told that my English is very good,' Harry answered in English, trying not to be intimidated by Kruger's hard stare and not succeeding.

'Did you tell the English during your interrogation that you spoke their language?'

'No, commander.'

'Why not?'

Harry shrugged. 'Why make it easy for them?'

Kruger gave a faint smile.

'Commander . . .' said Heinz tentatively, not having understood what had been going on.

Kruger raised a questioning eyebrow.

'How easy is it to get out of this camp?'

Kruger exhaled a cloud of cigar smoke. 'Very easy. All you have to do is join the morning cross-country exercise walks. Only thirty prisoners at a time, so you will have to wait some time before I include your names on the weekly rota.'

Heinz was at a loss. '*You* organize the walks, commander?'

'Yes. But the British like to supervise them. Understand-able, of course.'

'Of course,' Heinz agreed.

'I take it you're thinking of escaping?'

Heinz nodded emphatically. 'Those wire fences looked easy enough to get past.'

'I'm sure they are,' said Kruger drily. 'However, I'm extremely difficult to get past. Listen to me, both of you. Despite what Major Reynolds may have told you, escaping from Grizedale Hall is not impossible. What *is* virtually impossible is escaping from these shores. And that's what you have to plan right down to the last detail if you wish to have an escape proposal approved by the escape committee. Bright ideas for getting out of the camp are not enough.'

Heinz looked disappointed. 'How many people on the committee do we have to convince?'

'Only one. The one with the vote. And that's me. It's a very democratic committee.' Kruger paused and nodded to Willi. 'Hauptmann Hartmann will show you to your quarters. Good day, gentlemen.'

'I can see that Kruger is going to be a problem,' Harry declared dolefully when he and Heinz were installed in the tiny bunk-bedded garret that they had been allocated. In Harold Brocklebank's day, the room would have been occupied by the most menial of his household staff. 'His aide – the little fat one – said that Kruger's never sanctioned an escape unless it was his idea.'

'Whose idea? The little fat one's?'

'No, Kruger.'

Heinz nodded and peered out of the grimy, south-facing window. In the distance he could just make out the silvery gleam of Lake Esthwaite Water. 'It's crazy, Harry. We could just walk out of this place. One watchtower that looks as if it's about to fall down, and a fence sheep could stroll through.'

'Sheep don't stroll. They gambol and frolic – but they don't stroll.'

The beginning of their argument was drowned by a formation of four single-engine light aircraft flying low over the hall. The two men pressed their noses against the window.

'Miles Magister trainers,' Heinz declared.

They watched wistfully as the little aircraft dwindled into the distance. As if mocking the captivity of the two men on the ground, the neat little formation broke up to perform a series of exuberant low-level aerobatics over the lake.

'We've *got* to get back,' said Harry resolutely. 'There'll be no more flying if we don't, and who's going to be at the bottom of the list when the decorations are handed out, eh? The ones sitting on their arses in POW camps when there's a peace settlement or an invasion.'

During the weeks that followed, Harry and Heinz slipped into the routine of life at Grizedale Hall. They tended the vegetable plot that they had been allocated, joined in Ulbrick's gruelling physical training sessions, and even did terms of duty as lookouts for Kruger's weekly meetings of the escape committee in the music room. The high spot of each month was the summons to Brenda Hobson's sickbay for the ritual routine with her weighing machine, the search for creatures in their hair, and the check on their fingernails for signs of dietary deficiency.

Although she was the only woman that the prisoners came into contact with, she knew enough about men to know that they rarely made passes if they were forced to stand naked in a chill, acorn-shrivelling draught.

On one occasion a sadistic dentist was present who insisted on filling one of Heinz's many neglected cavities. He used an ancient, foot-operated treadle drill and a bit that was blunt, and announced that he would fill another of Heinz's cavities the following month.

'We've got to escape before that damned dentist comes back,' said Heinz, examining his new filling in a shaving mirror. After two days his jaw was still aching abominably from its rough treatment.

'Your trouble is that you're a coward,' Harry observed unsympathetically, his lanky frame stretched out on his bunk where he was reading a British comic.

Heinz grunted. 'I'm not afraid of Spitfires or Hurricanes, but that dentist terrifies me.'

There was a knock on the door. Willi entered, a beaming smile on his moonlike face. 'Good news, gentlemen.'

'The dentist has been assassinated?'

'Nothing like that,' said Willi, who had also suffered at the hands of the dentist. 'Your names are now on Commander Kruger's list for inclusion in the cross-country exercise walks.'

*

'Right, you lot,' said Sergeant Finch on horseback, addressing the party of prisoners assembled outside the main gate. He glared down at Harry and Heinz. 'This is for the benefit of those of you who've never been on one of our little exercise walks before. Those of you who understand English can translate.' He gestured to the other four guards, who were also on horseback. 'Firstly, although there's thirty of you and only five of us, we're the ones who are armed. My lads are all local and they're all bloody good at shooting rabbits, which means that they won't have no trouble bringing down any of you lot who thinks he'll try making a run for it. You'll keep to the path we indicate, stay four abreast like you are now, and there'll be no singing. Understood?'

'*Jawohl, mein Führer,*' said a voice from the back of the column. The comment prompted sniggers.

Finch's face went puce. 'How many times do I have to tell you bloody Huns to speak to me in English!' He glowered down at the prisoners. 'Okay,' he ordered grudgingly. 'Open the gates.'

The wrought-iron gates swung open and the prisoners trooped out four abreast flanked by guards, with Finch at the head of the column. They turned south towards Satterthwaite, marching at a brisk pace. Finch kept the party in the centre of the road, with the guards evenly dispersed on each side so that there was no possibility of a man trying to dive unseen into a ditch or leap over a dry-stone wall.

After thirty minutes' hard slog up the steep, wooded slopes of Carron Crag, Harry and Heinz decided that walking was their least favourite form of travel. Heinz maintained that the best form of travel, after flying of course, was by rail. Indeed the high spot of his enforced stay in England had been the eight-hour journey from London to Lancaster in a train hauled by the *Coronation Scot*.

'Number 6223,' Heinz panted, toiling up the steep slope

behind Harry. 'A fantastic locomotive. I would have loved to have stayed on it for the climb up Shap Fell. Did I ever tell you that Shap Fell is the steepest –'

'Heinz,' Harry interrupted. 'Did I ever tell you that I'm not in the least bit interested in trains? Since meeting you, my lack of interest in trains has become a pathological hatred of them. Doesn't that make you feel just a little bit guilty – instilling this hatred of trains in a fellow human?'

'All right, you lot!' Sergeant Finch bellowed, reining in his horse. 'We'll take a five-minute rest.'

The party of weary prisoners sank gratefully to the ground. Harry and Heinz propped themselves against a rock and savoured the warmth of the late August sun on their faces. Harry pulled a bar of American chocolate from his pocket. He broke off a piece for Heinz and noticed Chalky and his horse looking enviously at him. He snapped a generous chunk off the bar and held it out.

'Please, you would like some?'

After a brief glance at Sergeant Finch, Chalky gratefully took the chocolate and bit into it with relish. 'Thanks, mate,' he said with his mouth full. 'Oh, bloody marvellous. Haven't had chocolate for months now. Here, boy . . .'

The horse disappeared the piece of chocolate off Chalky's outstretched palm with adroit promptness. It chomped noisily, baring its teeth in appreciation and dribbling threads of brown saliva.

'What's you name, corporal?'

'White. Alan White. Me mates call me Chalky.'

Harry nodded sagely. 'Ah, yes. Chalky White. We can call you Chalky – yes?'

Chalky nodded and took another bite out of his chocolate before his horse got it. 'Funny thing,' he mumbled. 'Here you are, prisoners and that, and yet you get all the sweets and everything you want from the Yanks, and we don't get nothing.'

'You get Lend-Lease tanks and destroyers and airplanes

from the Americans,' Harry pointed out. 'In a war such things are more useful than chocolate, I think.'

Four dots in the distant haze hardened into the droning outlines of Tiger Moth biplanes.

'RAF trainers,' Harry remarked in German to Heinz.

'Really, Harry? And to think I thought they were a squadron of heavy bombers.'

'Sometimes Magisters, sometimes Tiger Moths,' Harry observed, ignoring his comrade's sarcasm. He turned to Chalky. 'In such aircraft we learned to fly. Just like those.'

The guard nodded. 'Funny little things. I went for a flip in one once when Alan Cobham's air circus was up here. Wouldn't do it again, I wouldn't. No bloody fear.'

Sergeant Finch swung into his saddle. 'All right, you lot. On your feet. We'll take the Millwood Forest Trail back to camp. Come on! Fall in! Fall in!'

Kruger rose to his feet when dinner was over. The meal had been Thursday's customary offering of shepherd's pie: grey, watery mashed potato flecked with almost invisible specks of what could be ground meat which looked as if it had been added to the ingredients by means of a spray gun with an extremely fine nozzle.

He tapped his spoon on the table for silence and the buzz of conversation died away immediately.

'Our experts tell me that our vegetable harvest is exceptionally good this season,' Kruger announced without preamble. 'As you have seen, we are now enjoying generous portions of vegetables. Therefore I have decided that we will save at least twenty-five per cent of our produce as seed for next year. Potatoes and beans will be stored, and selected plots of other vegetables will be allowed to go to seed.'

There was a chorus of groans.

'What's the point, commander?' Ulbrick demanded. 'The war will be over before the year's out.'

'I pray that you're right,' Kruger replied. 'If the war is

over by the end of the year, then I promise you all the biggest feast of your life. But I always believe in planning for any eventuality, therefore my ruling stands.'

There was complete silence as Kruger sat down.

'He's crazy,' Harry whispered to Heinz. 'Everyone knows it'll all be over by the end of the year.'

'You know that,' Heinz retorted acidly. 'I know that. We all know that. The trouble is that the British don't know.'

'We've *got* to escape,' Harry whispered vehemently. 'I mean, well, it's not even a proper camp. We'll be a laughing stock when it's all over if we do nothing.'

'The guards have got proper rifles and proper bullets,' Heinz pointed out. 'And the fence is made of proper barbed wire.'

'You're scared?' There was an accusing note in Harry's voice.

'Of rifles and bullets, yes. And barbed wire is bad for my skin.'

'Your skin is all you think of,' Harry retorted.

'It's the only one I've got.'

'We'll have to think of something.'

'I'll tell you what, Harry,' Heinz suggested. 'You do the thinking. You're the one with brains.'

Harry wondered what he could say that would stir his friend out of his lethargy. He had an inspiration: 'That dentist will be back next week. And his drill will be even blunter.'

Autosuggestion at the mention of the German-hating driller-killer was enough to renew the throbbing in Heinz's abused jaw. He brooded for some seconds. 'We escape,' he decided.

On the next exercise walk, Harry nudged Heinz and pointed to a man in a blue uniform who was having a picnic with a girl. The couple were sitting on the grass where they could enjoy the view across Lake Windermere. It was an idyllic day. The girl was in a pretty summer dress, gathered modestly around her ankles; the man's tunic was unbuttoned; the lake was speckled with white triangles of sailing boats.

'What do you think of those two?' Harry asked.

'You can have the fellow, I'll have the girl.'

The man stood up for a closer look at the enemy as the ragged column approached. Some prisoners whistled appreciatively at the brief glimpse of underwear that the girl gave them when she scrambled to her feet. She clung to her escort's arm and stared at the Germans, her eyes wide and a little fearful.

'RAF,' Heinz murmured.

Harry was about to agree but they passed close enough to the couple for him to have a good look at the man's uniform. It was plain, unmarked. Harry switched his attention to the insignia embossed on the man's gilt buttons.

'No, he's not, Heinz. My God! He's Dutch! Royal Dutch Air Force. No wings. He's either ground crew or he's . . .' Harry's step faltered so that the prisoner behind nearly crashed into him. 'Heinz!' he whispered urgently. 'Memorize every detail of that uniform! I've got a brilliant idea!'

Not a flicker of emotion showed on Kruger's face as he regarded the two airmen. He tipped his chair back and exhaled slowly on his cheroot. 'So you propose stealing an aircraft,' he commented. 'Interesting. Tell me more.'

Harry did all the talking. 'Commander, those aircraft that keep appearing over here are trainers – two-seater RAF basic trainers. The biplanes are De Havilland Tiger Moths, and the monoplanes are Miles Magisters. The formations they fly and the sort of stunts they perform are typical of any service flying training school.'

'So?'

Undeterred by the scathing tone that had crept into Kruger's voice, Harry pressed enthusiastically on. 'They won't have a range of much more than five hundred kilometres – half that with the sort of aerobatics they do over the lakes. The formations come from the north and they always return north. That means that there's a flying training school no more than a hundred kilometres from here – about sixty miles.'

Kruger held up his hand for silence. He thought for a few moments, his eyes fixed unblinkingly on Harry, who returned the hard stare without flinching.

'So let us take one step at a time,' said Kruger at length, carefully tapping the ash off his cheroot. 'We assume that you escape from here. We assume that you find the flying school. We assume that you get into the flying school, that you find an aircraft that you've never flown before, and that it has full tanks, and that you manage to take off. Having assumed all that, oberleutnant, you will find yourself flying an aircraft with a range of no more than three hundred and fifty miles – which is not enough to reach France or Holland. So what, may I ask, is the point of your plan?'

'Simple, commander,' Harry replied. 'We never said anything about flying to France or Holland. We'll fly to southern Ireland where we'll be interned. And as for flying an unfamiliar aircraft – there's nothing to trainers: a control column, a rudder-bar, a few instruments – compass, rev counter, oil – and that's all.'

'That's all?'

'That's all,' Harry confirmed.

Kruger looked far from convinced. 'And how about the security at this . . . flying school?'

'If it's anything like the security at training schools, it'll be non-existent. We're not talking about an operational base, commander.'

'We're not talking about an escape yet,' said Kruger icily. 'How do you propose travelling north?'

Harry nodded to Heinz. The younger officer was hesitant at first but he warmed rapidly to his favourite subject. 'We were brought here on the London to Carlisle line, commander,' he said respectfully. 'We were taken off the train at Lancaster where we changed on to the branch line that took us to Windermere.'

Kruger nodded. It was how the majority of prisoners arrived at Grizedale Hall.

'North of Lancaster,' Heinz continued, 'the Carlisle line goes over Shap Fell. It's a very steep climb. In fact there was a lot of argument among railway engineers in the last century when the line was being planned because it was thought that the climb would be too steep for locomotives. The gradient is –'

'You mean the trains have to slow down when they're climbing Shap Fell?' Kruger interrupted impatiently.

'Yes, commander,' Heinz replied.

'All right,' said Kruger, stubbing out his cheroot. 'How do you propose getting out of here?'

'In two laundry hampers,' Harry answered promptly.

Amusement showed fleetingly on Kruger's face. He gave a theatrical sigh. 'Tell me, oberleutnant, have you read any escape stories of the Great War?'

'No, commander.'

'I think you should. In all of them, POWs on both sides were pouring out of their camps in laundry hampers. It's the oldest trick in the book. That's why the guards turn out all the hampers as they're loaded into the van. They've read all the stories even if you haven't.'

'But they don't *measure* the hampers,' said Harry evenly. 'They're nearly a metre high. A false bottom about a third of a metre up from the base will provide just enough space for us. We know, commander, because we've tried it. And they won't know about the extra weight because they always make us load them into the van.'

Kruger lit another cheroot to give himself time to think. He dropped the match in his tin lid that served as an ashtray. 'All right, gentlemen,' he said at length. 'You have my permission to make a start on serious planning.' He immediately killed the look of elation on Harry's and Heinz's faces by adding sternly, 'And that's *all* I'm giving you permission to do. If your plans aren't ready to my satisfaction by the end of October – before the onset of winter – I shall not permit your escape attempt until the following spring. Is that clearly understood?'

'Understood, sir,' said Harry crisply, saluting and breaking into a broad grin of triumph.

'Forty-one, sarge,' Chalky reported to Sergeant Finch.

Sergeant Finch scowled. 'You sure, White?'

'Positive, sarge. I counted every doorstop twice.'

Sergeant Finch's scowl deepened. Devilment was afoot. Jerry devilment. 'That's twenty less than last week. Did you check Hartmann's room?'

Chalky looked apprehensive. 'Well, no, sarge.'

'Why not?'

'Because . . .' Chalky floundered. 'Er – well – because –'

'Because Willi Hartmann bribes you with chocolate bars! Just like he bribes all of you!' Finch thundered. 'I know everything that goes on this camp. Everything! So don't you try pulling the wool over my eyes, corporal!'

Chalky decided that it might be unwise to point out that if Sergeant Finch knew everything that was going on, he would know what was happening to the disappearing doorstops.

Finch pulled on his forage cap and glowered at Chalky. 'This is a very serious matter, White. I shall take personal charge of an investigation. And if I don't get to the bottom of what's going on, it will be reported to Major Reynolds.'

Major Reynolds was not in the best of moods as he and Kruger confronted one another on the terrace. With the exception of Willi, who was eavesdropping behind the french windows, the prisoners had sensed trouble and had made themselves scarce.

'As far as I'm concerned,' Reynolds declared, 'we had an

114

agreement that you would ensure that the hall was not structurally damaged in any way.'

'It was an understanding, major,' said Kruger blandly. 'I don't recall entering into any agreements.'

'It amounts to the same thing, commander.'

Kruger lit one of his poisonous cheroots. For once Reynolds was too preoccupied to wonder where the German officer was obtaining them.

'Personally,' Kruger murmured, 'I would have thought that you had more important things to worry about than twenty missing doorstops.'

'Sergeant Finch takes it seriously,' said Reynolds, inwardly cursing his over-zealous adjutant. 'Therefore I have to back him up. Twenty, round wooden doorstops are missing. He has rightly pointed out to me that they're fixtures, that they're on the inventory of fixtures and fittings agreed between the War Office and the owners of Grizedale Hall, and that they will have to be replaced when the hall is de-requisitioned.'

'I will look into the matter,' Kruger promised.

'They will have to be replaced.'

Kruger nodded. With a deadpan expression, he said, 'I will set up a committee of inquiry.'

'You can't go holding court-martials,' said Reynolds, alarmed. 'That's contrary to the Geneva Convention.'

'It will be a *committee*,' Kruger stressed. 'It will report back to me with recommendations as to the best way to replace the missing doorstops.'

Reynolds looked relieved. The two men exchanged salutes.

'Willi!' Kruger called out when Reynolds had departed.

Willi sheepishly emerged from behind the french windows. 'Commander?'

'Have you got those forms for me?'

Willi looked unhappy. 'I've been promised them tomorrow, commander.'

'How much?'

'Twenty half-pound bars of chocolate,' said Willi miserably.

'Twenty?' Kruger exclaimed. 'Well – I daresay you have at least a hundred bars in your room. How about the money?'

'Ten pounds in ten shilling notes, commander.'

'That's ample, and there'll be plenty left over for the escape fund. Incidentally, I am now a committee of inquiry. Who's been stealing the doorstops?'

Willi contrived to look suitably puzzled.

'Willi,' said Kruger mildly. 'Nothing goes on in this place that you don't know about. If you don't tell me who has been stealing the doorstops, Major Reynolds will receive information about a certain prisoner who bribes the guards to ensure that his room is never searched.'

Willi looked sorrowful. 'It's only a suspicion, commander. I'm not an informer but I think Oberleutnant Wappler and Leutnant Schnabel may know something about them.'

'What the hell do they want with twenty, round, wooden doorstops?'

'I don't know, commander,' Willi replied truthfully.

'Buttons,' said Harry proudly, reaching into his mattress and holding out a collection of domed, wooden buttons for Kruger's inspection. 'We discovered that the doorstops were made from a wood that was easy to carve. Each one took about four hours.'

Watched nervously by Harry and Heinz, Kruger carefully studied one of the home-made buttons. The embossed insignia of the Royal Dutch Air Force had been painstakingly carved on the domed surface, and the finished product had been carefully covered with chocolate foil wrapping paper. He handed the button back to Harry without comment.

116

'And this is Schnabel's finished tunic,' Harry continued, producing the garment. 'Our colour is the same as the Dutch uniform, so it was only the buttons and the shoulder marks that gave us trouble.'

If Kruger was impressed, he gave no sign.

Unnerved by the senior officer's silence, Harry pressed on. 'We've learned from Chalky that the Royal Dutch Air Force men who we sometimes see on the fells are what the British call "Free" Dutch. Most of them are pupil pilots at an elementary flying training school near Carlisle. There's also a lot of Poles there.'

'How near is Carlisle?' Kruger inquired.

'We didn't like to press him, commander. But at least we now know that the school is near Carlisle.'

Kruger nodded. 'Well, so long as you keep clear of the Dutch, your accents will pass unnoticed. When will you be ready?'

'In time for next week's visit by the laundry van,' said Harry hopefully, sensing that Kruger was about to give his consent for the escape to go ahead.

Kruger reached into his pocket and produced two type-written documents which bore the Royal Air Force crest. 'These are British Air Ministry form Twelve-fifties. They're temporary passes that will enable you to enter RAF establishments provided the smudged date stamps aren't looked at too closely.'

While Harry and Heinz were gazing speechlessly at the two documents, Kruger counted out some ten shilling notes on to one of the bunks. 'There's three pounds each in British currency, plus bus tickets, torn cinema tickets, and so on. All the bits and pieces that one would expect to find in a serviceman's pockets.'

'You . . . you mean that we can go?' said Heinz, speaking for the first time and omitting Kruger's rank in his excitement.

'Your plan is the best that has ever been submitted to

me,' said Kruger, turning to the door. He paused and nodded to the forms lying on the bunk. 'Make sure that you know your identities. I shall be testing you. One more thing – why did you have to use doorstops for the buttons? Why didn't you prise knots out of the floorboards? I'm certain Sergeant Finch hasn't counted them.'

Heinz gaped at his senior officer. 'Knots? You know, commander, we never thought of that.'

Kruger grunted. 'I shall inform Major Reynolds that you sliced up the doorstops to make a draughts set.'

Heinz was the first to speak after Kruger had left. 'The best plan ever submitted to me,' he said, reciting Kruger's words. 'Harry, I do believe he *actually* paid us a compliment!'

Harry grinned at his friend. 'There's only one problem from your point of view.'

'What's that?'

'The dentist comes on a Monday and the laundry van comes on Tuesday.'

The cramped space in the laundry hamper's false bottom made Heinz realize that the dull ache of his recently filled tooth was the least of his discomforts. Through the gaps in the wickerwork, he had a depressingly close-up view of khaki as the guards milled around the prisoners who were loading the hampers into the back of the van.

A jolt banged his jaw as the hamper was lifted. Another jolt banged it again when it was bundled roughly into the van. He heard the lid thrown open, a sound of rummaging in the soiled linen, shouted orders, and yet another jaw-jarring jolt as the hamper containing Harry crashed into his hamper. The prisoners were deliberately handling the hampers casually so as not to arouse the suspicions of the guards concerning the extra weight that had to be lifted.

'Okay, Mike!', yelled an English voice. 'Take her away.'

Darkness closed in as the van's rear doors were slammed

shut. The engine started up, gears were crashed, and the van started moving.

After ten minutes Harry decided that it was safe to make a move. He heaved upwards, dislodging the false bottom, and pushed himself upright amid a cascade of sheets and pillowcases. He helped Heinz disentangle himself from his hamper, then the two men busied themselves in the swaying van by fitting the false bottoms back into the hampers and replacing the linen.

Heinz cautiously released the internal locking bar on the vehicle's rear doors and peered out. The van was travelling over Hawkshead Moor, heading towards Windermere. As it slowed to negotiate a junction, Harry and Heinz pushed the door open wide and jumped out. They picked themselves up and leapt over a dry-stone wall where they spent a few minutes cleaning their disguised uniforms and taking stock of their surroundings.

Harry grinned at his friend. 'There's no doubt about it, Heinz, the old methods are the best.'

Heinz gingerly massaged his aching jaw. 'That's what that damned dentist said.'

The two escapees reached Windermere station without being challenged. Harry purchased two tickets for Carlisle. The prisoners' main worry was that most servicemen on leave in the Lake District would be using travel warrants instead of money. Their anxiety was alleviated when they saw a polish major ahead of them in the ticket office queue pay cash. Luckily there were no Dutch servicemen about. Two hours later, after an uneventful journey to Oxenholme, they changed trains and boarded a northbound train to Carlisle. To Heinz's delight, the locomotive turned out to be a class G2, normally used for hauling freight.

The two airmen found an empty third-class compartment and settled down. They decided that the best way to pass the journey was by pretending to be asleep. This would minimize the chances of them being drawn into conversation with gregarious passengers.

After a short stop at Tebay, the train pulled away from the slate and granite station and began the long climb up Shap Fell. It was one stage of the journey during which Heinz found it impossible to feign sleep: he spent it with his nose to the glass, gazing out across the harsh terrain, and tried to picture in his mind the gangs of sweating navvies, working with pick and shovel, who had brought the plans of the brilliant nineteenth-century railway engineer, Joseph Locke, to fruition. Unlike his contemporaries, who included George Stevenson, Locke was an engineer who wasn't afraid of steep gradients. He said that a railway could be built over Shap Fell, and he proved that he was right. Heinz was disappointed that Harry wasn't in the slightest bit interested in Joseph Locke.

Despite his excitement, Heinz felt his eyelids becoming heavy. The soporific, rocking motion of the train gradually weaned his attention away from the passing scenery and his toothache, and he fell into a fitful sleep.

He was vaguely aware of the train stopping several times and doors slamming, but no one entered their compartment. The next thing he knew was Harry shaking him violently.

'Heinz! Look!'

Heinz blinked and was immediately wide awake. Sandwiched between the railway and a main road was a small grass airfield with Tiger Moths and Magisters lined up at dispersal points around the perimeter. A flight of five Magisters was actually taking off in formation.

'That's it!' cried Harry excitedly.

'My God,' Heinz breathed. 'What a stroke of luck.'

'We're going to have to jump,' Harry decided.

Heinz peered down in alarm at the blur of grass flashing by. 'But, Harry, the train's going much too fast.'

'You've been asleep for an hour,' Harry retorted. 'We're

only about two kilometres out from Carlisle, therefore we can't be far from the Scottish border. If we jump now, we won't have to deal with customs men and border guards.'

Heinz was about to protest his certainty that there was no such thing as Scottish border controls, but Harry had swung the door open.

'Harry,' Heinz moaned. 'We can't jump yet.'

'Listen,' said Harry in a reasoning tone. 'Look upon it as bailing out.'

'That's exactly what I am looking on it as,' Heinz complained. 'Did I ever tell you about my injuries from bailing out?'

Harry ignored Heinz's reply because the train had entered a cutting where there was no one to see them. 'Now!', he yelled over his shoulder, and promptly launched himself off the train.

Heinz gave a moan of despair and threw himself after his comrade. He managed to land on his feet, but his body, possessing the momentum of the train, performed a series of somersaults like a rag doll fired from a gun. He came to rest, lying on his back, fifteen yards from his original point of contact with the ground. He gazed up at the leaden sky and wondered which parts of his body, if any, were still usable. His jaw felt as if it had been dealt with by a team of horses who had first dragged it from his skull and then taken it in turn to kick it.

A shadow crossed his face. Harry was standing over him. The taller airman's face was streaked with mud and there were grass stains on his uniform.

'Get up and stop moaning,' said Harry.

Heinz stood unsteadily. 'I wasn't moaning.'

Harry supported his comrade by the elbow. 'Come on, Heinz. The first thing we've got to do is reconnoitre that airfield.'

Number 15 Elementary Flying Training School at Kingstown, near Carlisle, had started life as a private flying club in southern England before being taken over by the RAF. After a number of incidents during the Battle of Britain, one of which was a pupil on his first solo flight in an unarmed Tiger Moth biplane becoming involved in a dispute with an Me109, the school and all its predominately civilian staff were moved north.

As Harry and Heinz discovered from their vantage point in a section of unused sewer pipe near the unfenced perimeter, the majority of the pupils were Free French. Other nationalities included some Czechs, Dutch and Poles.

Heinz looked at his watch. There were three hours of daylight left and already apprentices were lining up two flights of refuelled Magisters and picketting them before pulling canvas covers over the wings. An hour later the airfield was deserted apart from some coming and going around the flight office, which was among a cluster of hangers and buildings near the main road.

The last movement was an hour before dusk when an apprentice hauled down the windsock.

'I never thought it would be so simple, Harry,' said Heinz gleefully. 'We've got a choice of thirty refuelled aircraft.' He made a move to scramble out of the pipe but Harry put a restraining hand on his arm.

'No. We wait until morning.'

Heinz stared at his friend in surprise. 'But there's an hour's daylight left, Harry. We'll be in southern Ireland before dark.'

'We're not going to southern Ireland,' said Harry firmly. 'There's not enough daylight left for where we're going.'

Heinz gave his comrade a puzzled look. 'What do you mean?'

'We're going to walk up to one of those Magisters in the morning as instructor and pupil. We're going to do it openly – just as everyone else does – and we're flying to France.'

Heinz forgot where he was. He sat bolt upright and clouted his head on the inside of the sewer pipe. The blow started his toothache off again but he ignored it. 'Harry – you're crazy! Those things haven't got the range. We'd have to land and refuel –'

'Listen, Heinz. Our luck has got us this far. I don't know about you but I don't fancy being interned in southern Ireland for the duration. Not when there's a chance that we might make it home.'

Heinz was silent for a moment. 'You mean that it never was your intention that we should try to reach Ireland?'

'That's right,' said Harry. 'We'll head south and refuel at an operational airbase. We'll say that we're on a training flight and that we lost our bearings.'

'Just like that?'

Harry nodded. 'Just the one refuelling stop and then we'll be home.' He punched Heinz playfully 'So let's get some sleep. This time tomorrow we'll be telling our story to Hermann himself.'

At 7.30 the following morning, Alan Graydon and a group of fellow apprentices untied the pickets that secured the eight Magisters of 'A' flight and removed the aircrafts' canvas covers. Unaware that two pairs of eyes were noting their every move, they swung the propellers in turn to warm up the engines and generally prepare the aircraft for another day's work.

'Reckon there'll be any flying today, Alan?' asked one of the younger apprentices.

Alan looked up at the low cloud-base. A light drizzle was falling and the wind was blowing at a moderate 15 knots from the south-west. 'Yes, I think so. It'll take more than this to keep the Poles grounded.'

By 8 am, several pupils and flying instructors of assorted

nationalities were taking their customary early morning stroll around the concrete perimeter track while the flight office decided the day's flying programme.

The windsock was hoisted – signifying that flying was to take place – and the flying school came to life. Aircraft were taxied to the marshalling area; instructors and pupils pored over charts spread out on wings; engines opened up; and formations took off at timed intervals.

Alan was covering the two remaining Magisters in his flight an hour later when an accented but pleasant-sounding voice bade him good morning.

Alan turned round. Two Dutch officers were regarding him – one short and one tall.

'Good morning,' Harry repeated. He nodded to the Magister. 'I am needing this aircraft please for my student.'

'Yes, sirs,' said Alan, pulling the covers off the Magister's twin cockpits and helping the two airmen on to the wing. 'But, sirs – you should be wearing your parachutes. It's against the rules to fly without them.'

Harry looked nonplussed for a moment as he and Heinz lowered themselves into their respective cockpits. Then his face cleared. 'Ah yes, we are not flying. The CO wants my student to have some more taxiing practice.' He gave Alan a conspiratorial wink. 'You know what the CO is like.'

Alan smiled. 'Yes, sir. I do know.'

Harry sat down. His joy at discovering that the Magister's controls were as basic as he had predicted and immediately understandable, gave way to alarm when he realized that he was sitting too low to see over the cockpit coaming. He turned round. There was no sign of Heinz in the rear cockpit. He realized in dismay that there was one thing he had overlooked: the Magisters' seats were designed so that the pilot's parachute pack served as a cushion.

Harry looked up at Alan, who was standing on the wing root, trying hard not to laugh. The apprentice held out two of the folded canvas covers.

'We always sit on these, sirs, when we taxi Maggies.'

Alan obligingly pushed the covers under the two airmen and saw them comfortably settled.

'Thank you,' said Harry. 'I am most grateful. You will now turn the prop please. Magneto switches are off. Brakes on.'

'She's warm, sir. She won't need priming.'

Harry operated the magneto switches correctly.

'Contact, sir?' queried Alan, his hands ready on the propeller.

'Yes, contact,' Harry confirmed.

Alan swung the Magister's propeller. The Gypsy engine fired immediately. He stood clear while Harry tested the engine. The engine settled down to a steady note. Harry gave Alan a thumbs up sign and the youngster dragged the chocks away from the wheels.

He watched the aircraft taxi away from the dispersal point and returned to his task of covering the remaining Magister. He heard the engine open up. He looked across at the aircraft as it turned west into the wind and wondered why the instructor wanted so much power for taxiing. To his amazement, the Magister gathered speed, bumping across the grass. The tail wheel lifted and the monoplane was airborne and gaining height as it flew over the railway track. After two minutes it had disappeared into the low cloud.

Alan groaned inwardly and cursed the two hot-headed Dutchmen who had made him an unwitting accomplice in a serious breach of the rules. He decided that the best thing would be to report the matter immediately to the officer in charge of 'A' flight.

Without flying suits or goggles, Harry and Heinz began to shiver with cold as they flew south. But they didn't care. They were free. They were flying again. For a while all thought of the hazards that lay ahead were set aside.

'Thank you, Graydon,' said Flight-Lieutenant Neads when Alan finished explaining what had happened. 'They'll find themselves on the receiving end of one hell of a rocket when they get back. Were they Poles or Dutch?'

'Dutch, I think, sir.'

Neads nodded and picked up his telephone. 'All right, Graydon. I'll notify the CO. And you had better report the matter to the chief engineer.'

Due to Kruger's careful rehearsals, the morning roll-call ruse to provide cover for two missing airmen succeeded admirably. Kruger had drilled the two prisoners to perfection: they were the shortest POWs in the camp so that the corporal counting the numbers of men in each row did not see them step smartly forward into the row in front as he made a note on his clipboard.

Harry and Heinz took it in turns to fly the Magister. While one held the controls, the other stamped his feet in order to maintain circulation.

After flying south-east for an hour, Harry gradually lost height, so they emerged from the cloud-base. Heinz correctly identified the city to their east as Leeds, and they climbed back into the cloud.

They had flown a hundred miles – just over a third of the Magister's range.

Flight-Lieutenant Neads looked at his watch. 'We'll give them another forty-five minutes,' he told Pat O'Hara, the flying school's chief engineer.

'Long enough for me to think of something particularly horrible to happen to Graydon,' muttered O'Hara.

Neads smiled. 'Don't be too hard on the lad, Pat. Those crazy Dutchmen can be intimidating when they want to be.'

'I'll intimidate them,' O'Hara growled. 'Do we know who they are, sir?'

'The CO's checking "B" and "C" flights now.'

It was inevitable that after two hours blind flying in cloud, with a compass as the Magister's sole navigation instrument, Harry's and Heinz's amazing streak of good luck should begin to run out.

'You take over for bit, Harry,' said Heinz. 'I can hardly feel my feet on the rudder bar.'

'Time we went down and looked for landmarks,' Harry yelled above the roar of the engine as he took control.

The Magister broke through the cloud-base. The two airmen stared aghast at the sea 1000 feet below. They had unknowingly crossed the coast at Skegness and were over the North Sea.

'Our easterly drift must have been –'

'Harry!' Heinz interrupted. 'I think the left-hand fuel gauge must have been stuck – it's just dropped to a quarter!'

Harry looked down at the simple fuel gauge that was set into the port wing root. It was showing a much lower reading than the starboard tank gauge.

'We'll have to fly west,' Harry decided. 'We can't be that far from the coast.'

'And be shot down as a raider?'

'Have you got a better idea?'

Heinz remained silent. The heady feeling of flying again had passed; he was too cold and miserable to care very much what happened, especially now that his tooth was aching again with renewed ferocity.

Flight-Lieutenant Neads replaced his telephone. He brooded for a moment. 'All the school's instructors and pupils have been accounted for,' he informed Pat O'Hara. 'Group are going to check Grizedale Hall and the Shap Fell Hotel camp to see if our two mystery pilots are escaped POWs.'

This time there was no fooling the guards during the snap roll-call. Under Sergeant Finch's hostile eye, each prisoner was required to fall out as his name was called. At the end of forty minutes, when the courtyard had been cleared, the names of two prisoners who had not been ticked off the list were left on his clipboard.

'Three prisoners missing, saar!' he said, crashing to attention in front of Reynolds' desk with such force that a trout rod tumbled from its wall hooks.

'Three?' Reynolds looked surprised. 'I thought it would be two.'

'Wappler – Harold; Schnabel – Heindrich; and Shultz – Herbert. Saar!'

Reynolds sighed. 'Sergeant, there's no need to call Leutnant Shultz's name at every roll-call.'

'Sorry, saar! But he is down on my list as a prisoner!'

Reynolds picked up his telephone and called the commanding officer of No. 15 EFTS. Once through, he gave the RAF officer the names of Harry Wappler and Heinz Schnabel.

The land that Harry and Heinz found and followed south was mile after mile of mist-shrouded Norfolk Broads. It was bleak and desolate, as uninspiring as the sea and the two fuel tank gauges that were showing empty.

'Some sort of marshland,' shouted Heinz.

'Well, at least it's flat,' Harry yelled back.

Heinz made no reply. He was too tired and miserable to care very much about anything, and his tooth was a white hot lance being thrust into his jaw.

At that moment the engine spluttered and picked up again. It fired again for a few seconds and then died for good.

'Don't give up hope yet,' advised Harry as he looked for a suitable field for a forced landing.

The duty engineer at the Horsham St Faith Bomber Command station near Yarmouth took the telephone call from the garage owner because the operations room staff thought that this particular problem ought to be his baby.

He listened incredulously and said, 'Yes, I've got all that, sir. Two Germans have landed in your paddock.' He caught the eye of his sergeant and gave him a despairing look before returning to the unreal telephone conversation. 'Tell me, sir. Are these Germans with you now? . . . I see. What sort of aircraft do they have? . . . Well ask them.'

There was a pause while the garage owner solicited the required information from his visitors.

'A Maggie?' queried the duty engineer in response to the garage owner's reply. 'Well, in that case, sir, they're not Germans. What about their uniforms? . . . Well, describe their buttons.'

The garage owner described the buttons on his visitors' tunics.

'Well, in that case, sir, they're telling the truth – they're definitely Dutch and not German. I'll be with you in fifteen minutes.'

'But you must refuel us,' said Harry with a contrived anger that Heinz could only admire. 'It is important that we are getting back today to our flying school.'

The duty engineer sighed and returned Harry's form Twelve-fifty. 'I'm sorry, gentlemen. But I don't have the authority to order a petrol bowser off the station.'

Harry gestured to the garage owner who was sitting on a workbench swinging his legs and watching the two airmen suspiciously.

'So – you must require this garage to refuel us. It is very simple.'

'Maybe,' said the duty engineer evenly. 'But the work that would have to be done on your engine after running it on MT fuel wouldn't be simple. Look, sirs, come back to Horsham St Faith with me. You can phone your flying school, have a shower and a meal and a bed, and be away first light tomorrow.'

Harry glanced at Heinz and realized that they had no option but to go along with the duty engineer's suggestion. There was a slim, impossible chance that they could continue to brazen it out until the following day.

'What do you fly at Horsham St Faith?' Harry asked.

'We're a bomber station,' said the duty engineer cheerfully.

Harry grinned. With their luck maybe they could steal a bomber. That would give Hermann something to chuckle about.

'Tell you sommat, mate,' said the garage owner sourly, eyeing Harry and Heinz. 'Them's jerries. Came across enough of the bastards on the Somme, I did. I know a jerry when I see one.'

'But maybe not when you see two together, eh?' the duty engineer suggested pointedly.

An operations room officer wandered into the duty engineer's office. 'Where's our two flying Dutchmen, Bill?'

Something about his colleague's tone of voice made the duty engineer suspicious. 'Taking a shower. Why?'

The officer dropped a pink flimsy on the duty engineer's desk. 'Thought you might like to see this, old boy.' He grinned. 'It's an all stations alert from Group. This morning a couple of escaped *Luftwaffe* POWs stole a Maggie from Fifteen EFTS at Carlisle.'

There was a dead silence in the room. The duty engineer's face paled visibly. 'Carlisle?' he choked. 'Carlisle to here? In a Maggie? It's not possible.'

The officer shrugged. 'Could be if they ran their tanks dry, old boy.' He looked levelly at the engineer. 'Which they did.'

Harry turned his naked body blissfully under the shower, enjoying really hot water, an unheard of luxury at

Grizedale Hall. He broke off humming to bang on the partition between his shower stall and the next. 'Heinz. For God's sake cheer up.'

'I'm sorry, Harry,' Heinz's voice replied. 'But this tooth is really giving me hell.'

The duty engineer entered the shower rooms just as Harry resumed humming. He stared at the two stalls and the pair of naked feet visible below each door, before turning his attention to the two uniforms thrown casually over the back of a chair.

'Herr Wappler and Herr Schnabel, I presume?' the duty engineer called out. 'Is there anything else you need before dinner? How about new buttons for your uniforms? These might have woodworm.'

The humming stopped immediately. There was a pause and one of the doors slowly opened. The taller of the two escapees stood naked and dripping under the shower. He grinned amiably at the duty engineer.

'Ah. We are – what is the English expression – rumbled? Yes?' inquired Harry.

'I expect that expression will do,' agreed the duty engineer wearily, without rancour.

The other shower stall door opened. Heinz regarded the RAF officer sheepishly.

'So is there anything you need before dinner?' the duty engineer repeated.

Harry looked puzzled. 'We are to have dinner?'

'Oh yes. In the officers' mess. You're our guests of honour. The CO's refusing to hand you over until he's heard the full story from both of you as to how you did it.'

'There is something I need,' said Heinz, speaking in halting English. 'Could you please take me to a dentist?'

The repercussions of the remarkable escape bid by Harry Wappler and Heinz Schnabel resulted in Pat O'Hara, the chief engineer at Number 15 Elementary Flying Training

School, having to attend two inquiries and fill in endless forms before he got his Miles Magister trainer back.

Alan Graydon received only a 'ticking-off' for handing over a Magister to the POWs, but the RAF came in for harsh criticism about security at their flying schools. At the second inquiry they successfully shoved most of the blame on to the Navy with their assertion that Grizedale Hall's intelligence officer was a certain Commander Ian Lancaster Fleming, RNVR, who was not even present at Grizedale Hall when Wappler and Schnabel must have been planning their audacious escape. The buck, which the Air Ministry passed to the Admiralty, ended up on Admiral Godfrey's desk.

'There's one dickens of a rumpus over all this,' he grumbled to Fleming.

Fleming chuckled. 'So what's going to happen to our intrepid birdmen, sir?'

'They're serving twenty-eight days' solitary at Colchester and will probably stay there. Can't have them going back to Grizedale and gloating. What's more to the point, Fleming, is what are we going to do with you? Grizedale is still our biggest concentration of U-boat officers and I don't want us to lose our toehold there.'

Fleming steeled himself for what was coming. In the summer the Lake District was marvellous – fishing, riding – but he had no wish to spend the winter there.

'Anyway,' Admiral Godfrey continued, 'just to keep everyone happy, I've said that you'll be back there by the end of the week.'

Fleming groaned inwardly. Then he remembered Cathy Standish and his mood brightened.

Part Five

THE PRISONER
IN THE TOWER

Korvettenkapitan Hugo Forster made himself so inconspicuous during his first week at Grizedale Hall that the rumour circulating among the prisoners was that he had discovered a foolproof method of escaping and returning at will, and was therefore only present in the camp for roll-calls and meals.

His diminutive physical appearance made it easy for him to dissolve into the background to the point of invisibility. This unusual, chameleon-like talent was helped by his instantly forgettable face. On those rare occasions when he was spotted in the camp, he was invariably wearing the expression of a man who has just discovered that his mistress was the wife of a world heavyweight boxing champion.

To Willi's dismay, Kruger paused by the vegetable plot that had been allocated to Forster. The U-boat 'ace' lit a cheroot and snapped the match in two with his thumbnail – a sure indication that he was angry.

It was a fine morning in early September. The sun was shining from a clear blue sky and the first delicate, experimental tints of autumn were staining the valley. But the beauty of the surroundings failed to detract from Kruger's temper. He was recovering from a bout of influenza which had led to him finding more faults than usual during his fortnightly inspection tour of all the vegetable plots.

The plot that was the cause of Kruger's extreme irritation

was a wilderness of yard-high weeds that was dominated by a giant thistle and a clump of stinging nettles.

'Willi. You told me that all the plots had been allocated.'

'They have, commander.'

'This one obviously hasn't been allocated.'

Willi consulted his clipboard even though he knew the answer. 'Plot 114. I allocated it to Korvettenkapitan Hugo Forster on his arrival last Monday.'

'He's had six days to clear it. Why has nothing been done?'

'I don't know, commander. He's not been around much.'

Kruger looked sharply at Willi. 'What are you talking about? All the prisoners are around all the time except Leutnant Shultz.'

'He makes himself scarce, commander,' said Willi, wishing that Kruger wouldn't drag Shultz into the conversation.

'I haven't interviewed him, have I?'

'No, commander. Leutnant Shultz escaped before you arrived.'

'I'm talking about Forster!' Kruger snapped. 'Where is he?'

'In the room at the top of the east tower, commander. The one that no one wanted. He said that it suited him.'

'So why haven't I interviewed him?'

'He arrived while you were ill, commander. I thought it best –'

'Well, I'm not ill now. Tell Forster I want to see him in my office in fifteen minutes precisely.'

Kruger turned on his heel and strode towards the hall, leaving Willi cursing the number of steps he would have to climb to find the elusive Hugo Forster.

Alone in his tiny garret room at the top of the spiral staircase in the east tower, Forster read Eva's letter for the hundredth time before carefully folding it and returning it to its envelope. He turned on his side and stared longingly at the photograph on the wall by his bed. It was a picture of his month-old son, Ernst, whom he had never seen. Eva had enclosed the photograph with her last letter. She wrote every week without fail. The news about Ernst in her latest letter had been overshadowed by her excitement at being offered her old job back with the Foreign Ministry as a Spanish translator. Monday's post had also included a letter from his father. He had skimmed through it once. Its contents had made it impossible for him to read it again. His father had enthused about his son's continuation of the family's naval tradition; how his mother would have been proud of him had she been alive; that there was no dishonour in being a prisoner of war; and that there would be a hero's welcome for him in Dortmund when he returned home after the British surrender.

A hero's welcome! Dear God, if only they knew. . . . But soon they would know. They would all know: Eva, his father, all his friends in Dortmund, and one day – his son. It was only a matter of time before the whole sorry story emerged.

In his loneliness and misery, Forster would have wept but for the rap on his door. It was Willi Hartmann, his chest heaving from the climb up the spiral staircase.

'Commander Kruger wants to see you in his office now,' said Willi breathlessly while mopping the sweat from his brow.

Kruger finished reading the questionnaire and asked Willi to leave. As soon as the door closed behind the little Bavarian, Kruger inhaled on his cheroot and stared at Hugo Forster. He was unimpressed by what he saw. The young U-boat commander was clearly ill at ease. He fiddled nervously with his cap while waiting for Kruger to speak.

'This doesn't give much information,' Kruger remarked. 'You say your *U-501* was rammed but you don't say how.'

'We were forced to the surface by two destroyers that had depth-charged us.'

'The names of the warships?'

'One was HMCS *Moose Jaw* and I think the other was *Chambly*.'

Kruger raised his eyebrows. 'They were Canadian?'

'Yes, commander.'

'Were British ships involved in the action?'

'I don't think so, commander.'

'Congratulations,' said Kruger sarcastically. 'You're the first U-boat to be sunk by the Canadians. None of your officers are here, so presumably they all went down with *U-501*?'

Forster nodded unhappily. 'I think so, commander. I was –'

'You only *think* so? Surely you made it your business to find out what had happened to your own crew?'

Forster avoided Kruger's contemptuous gaze. 'No one would tell me what had happened to them.'

'In which case *I* shall find out what happened to them, Forster,' Kruger stated frostily.

'I think I'm the only survivor,' said Forster miserably. 'Why else would the British not tell me what had happened to them?'

'I can think of a thousand and one reasons,' said Kruger, angrily stubbing out his cigar. 'That being so, how is it that you survived and your crew have not?'

'I was first on the bridge after we'd blown our tanks. Both our periscopes and our hydrophone gear had been knocked out by the depth-charges, so I had no idea how close the destroyers were. The *Moose Jaw* rammed as soon as we surfaced.'

'How long did your boat take to sink?'

Forster hesitated. 'I don't know, commander. I was knocked unconscious.'

Kruger stared hard at Forster before returning his

attention to the questionnaire. 'Your boat was sunk on September 10th. Three weeks ago. Show me the injury that knocked you unconscious.'

Forster pointed to his temple. 'Something hit me here, commander.'

Kruger leaned forward and studied the side of Forster's head. 'It has healed remarkably well in three weeks, Forster. In fact, I can't see even a mark.'

'Nevertheless, that's where I was struck,' said Forster doggedly, showing a trace of irritation at the searching questions.

There was a silence while Kruger appeared to be trying to make up his mind about something. 'Very well, korvettenkapitan,' he said at length. 'You may go. I shall expect to see your vegetable plot cleared within the next two days.'

The two men stood, pulled on their caps and exchanged salutes.

Forster opened the door and hesitated. 'There is one thing, commander.'

'Yes?'

'Admiral Doenitz arranged a letter-code for use by captured U-boat captains.'

'What of it?'

'Do you use it, commander?'

'Perhaps,' said Kruger guardedly. 'Why?'

'Oh, it doesn't matter. I merely wondered.'

Willi was standing at the end of the corridor, idly gazing out of a window as Forster brushed passed. He returned to the office.

'What did you think of his story?' Kruger asked.

'I haven't heard it, commander,' Willi replied, his cherubic face a picture of innocence.

'Willi,' Kruger murmured. 'You're as big a liar as Korvettenkapitan Forster. The difference between you and him is that all you've got to hide are the contents of your room.'

*

'Major Reynolds!'

Reynolds jumped guiltily at the sound of the female voice. He didn't know why he felt guilty. It wasn't as if he was having an affair with Nurse Brenda Hobson, however desirable such an involvement would be, even though she was married; it was just that the sound of her voice had that effect on him. He turned and smiled at her as she clip-clopped across the courtyard. As usual, she was in a hurry.

'Good morning, nurse. A beautiful morning.'

'It's about one of the prisoners, sir,' said Brenda, coming straight to the point. 'Korvettenkapitan Hugo Forster. He was supposed to see me for a medical check-up this morning and he didn't show up. I don't have the time to go chasing –'

'I'll speak to Commander Kruger about him,' said Reynolds.

'Personally I don't give a damn if they all die of starvation provided I've got it recorded. You know how I like to keep my record cards up to date.'

'I'll speak to Commander Kruger about it,' Reynolds repeated.

'And while we're on the subject, sir, what do I do about my record card for Leutnant Shultz? Is he still officially a prisoner, or what?'

'I'll ask Sergeant Finch to check with the War Office,' said Reynolds hurriedly. 'Please excuse me. I have to go now.'

Like all Cathy Standish's parties, the one she threw at her spacious farmhouse to celebrate Ian Fleming's return was a great success. There was a plentiful supply of food and drink despite the wartime restrictions, and an even more plentiful supply of unattached young ladies: three commodities which, in reverse order of esteem, had a certain appeal to Fleming.

He disentangled himself from a conversation with Major

Reynolds and a lively little brunette – the daughter of a local landowner – and pushed through the crowd of farmers and their wives who were gathered around Cathy Standish.

'Cathy,' he said, taking her to one side. 'A quick word with you.' He nodded to Mrs Heelis, who was sitting on a sofa wearing an ill-fitting tweed suit, a dishevelled bonnet, and a faintly disapproving expression. 'Major Reynolds tells me that the elderly lady is Beatrix Potter.'

'That's right, Ian,' Cathy replied, smiling mischievously up at Fleming. 'Only you mustn't call her that. She's Mrs Heelis.'

'I thought she was dead. I'd love to be introduced to her. Do you think she'd dance with me?'

Cathy laughed. 'I doubt it, Ian. She never usually goes to parties. I think my invitation to a radio-warming party must've intrigued her.'

'What's happened to your boyfriend?'

Cathy's smile faded for an instant. 'Who?'

'The one togged up in tweeds you always have in tow. I've often seen you riding with him.'

'Oh, him,' said Cathy lightly, steering Fleming towards the sofa. 'He doesn't like parties either.'

'Where do you keep him when he's not at parties?'

'Mrs Heelis,' said Cathy brightly. 'This is Commander Ian Fleming.'

Fleming shook hands with Mrs Heelis. He was surprised by the coarseness of her skin. Obviously she was accustomed to hard, manual work.

'Good evening, commander,' said Mrs Heelis, returning Fleming's greeting. She studied him with sharp, perceptive eyes. 'Ah, navy I see. Well, I've no quarrel with the navy. At least the navy doesn't build prisoner of war camps all over the place and make off with all the vets in the area. The nearest vet lives miles away. It's a serious problem for large sheep breeders such as Cathy and myself. Isn't it, Cathy?'

'Very serious, Mrs Heelis,' agreed Cathy.

'Are you interested in sheep, Mr Fleming?'

'Only when they've taken their coats off and they're served with mint sauce,' Fleming replied.

Mrs Heelis laughed good-naturedly. 'I've nearly doubled the size of my flocks since the war started.'

'You're lucky in one respect, Mrs Heelis,' said Fleming. 'At least the war permits you to continue with your business.'

'Very true. Very true. And what is *your* business, Mr Fleming?'

'Oh, I've dabbled in stockbroking. And journalism.'

'Journalism?' sniffed Mrs Heelis. 'I've had more than my fair share of attention from journalists. They ask the most ridiculous questions about books I wrote over thirty years ago.'

'I'd like to be an author,' Fleming admitted.

'Oh? And what sort of books would you like to write?'

'I've not given it much thought, Mrs Heelis. Thrillers, I suppose.'

'Write for children,' said the old lady firmly. 'A discerning readership, Mr Fleming. And a most rewarding one.'

Cathy laughed. 'I can't see Ian writing for children.'

'I'll make you a promise, Mrs Heelis,' said Fleming, smiling. 'If I do become a thriller writer, I'll write at least one book for children.'

'May I interrupt a minute please, ladies?' said Reynolds. 'I'd like a quick word with Commander Fleming.'

'Oh, I suppose you want to talk about the war,' said Cathy. 'Well, don't be too long.'

Fleming made his excuses and moved to a corner with Reynolds.

'What's the problem, old boy?'

'Will you be visiting the hall tomorrow?'

'I expect so,' said Fleming. 'Why?'

'Kruger's asking a lot of goddamn questions about the whereabouts of a U-boat crew.'

'Hugo Forster's U-boat?'

Reynolds gave Fleming a suspicious look. 'That's right. How did you know?'

Fleming chuckled. 'I guessed.'

'Now look,' said Reynolds. 'Is there something going on that I should know about?'

'Why should you think that, old boy,' asked Fleming blandly.

'Because Kruger's getting tough. He said that no British newspaper has carried a report on the sinking of Forster's U-boat and he wants to know why. He's threatening to complain to the protecting power commission on their next visit if he doesn't get an answer.'

'Oh dear,' murmured Fleming. 'We don't want the Swiss poking their noses into our affairs, do we? I'll deal with it in the morning.'

A guard showed Forster into Reynolds' office. The U-boat commander gave a start of surprise at seeing Fleming sitting at Reynolds' desk.

'Good morning,' said Fleming pleasantly, speaking in German. He offered Forster a cigarette from his gold case and waved him to a seat.

'I thought you'd finished interrogating me in London,' said Forster suspiciously.

'Oh, I just wanted to see how you were settling in,' said Fleming lightly. 'I hear that your senior officer is Otto Kruger of *U-112* fame. You must have a lot to talk over.'

'I've told you everything that I have to,' said Forster nervously, glancing at the window in case any prisoners were in the courtyard. 'Name, rank and number, and names and addresses of my next of kin.'

Fleming chuckled. 'Funny thing, the Geneva Convention. It specifies the information that a prisoner of war may give his captors but it says nothing about what information captors can give their prisoners.'

'I don't understand.'

'So far we've not released any information about the loss of your U-boat.'

'So?'

'And what information we do release is up to us, of course.' Fleming gave a sly smile. 'And you to a certain extent.'

Forster swallowed. 'I still don't understand.'

'Really? Knowing Kruger's record, I rather fancy that he and the other prisoners will make life somewhat uncomfortable for you if the truth emerges.'

There was a silence. Forster raised his head and looked Fleming straight in the eye. 'Commander Fleming, I bitterly regret what happened. But I'm learning to live with the memory of those moments before my boat sank because at least I did what I did in the heat of battle. If I was to tell you the secrets of *U-501*'s equipment, it would be a calculated act on my part and therefore something I could never learn to live with.'

Fleming gave Forster a pleasant smile. 'Very well, old boy,' he said in English. 'It's your decision.'

Admiral Godfrey read through Fleming's proposed press release a second time and made a couple of minor alterations before initialling it as approved. He tossed the typewritten sheet of paper to Fleming.

'Is it true, Fleming?'

'Substantially – yes, sir.'

Admiral Godfrey grunted. 'Well, I only hope to God you know what you're doing.'

'I'm sure it will produce results, sir,' said Fleming, sliding the sheet of paper into his briefcase.

'It's about time, Fleming. As far as intelligence gathering on U-boats goes, one can hardly say that we're outshining MI6.'

'We will be soon, sir,' Fleming promised, patting his

briefcase. 'There will be developments as soon as this gets into print.'

'For Chrissake,' muttered Reynolds when he finished reading the front-page newspaper story. 'Is it too late to stop Kruger seeing this?'

'I'm sorry, sir,' said Sergeant Finch. 'Evans spotted Forster's photograph over the *Daily Mirror* story after he'd handed out yesterday's papers.'

Leutnant zur See Weiner Hertzog had sat his huge frame on a chair outside Kruger's office and was angrily reading the front page of the *Daily Telegraph*. His rudimentary grasp of English was sufficient for him to follow the gist of the story, and his anger mounted with each reading as the words became clearer. He heard footsteps on the stairway. Kruger appeared. Hertzog stood and gave the senior officer a smart salute. His bulk nearly filled the narrow passageway.

'Commander, if I could see you for a minute please.'

'Arrange an appointment with Leutnant Hartmann,' said Kruger curtly. He tried to pass Hertzog but the burly naval officer stood his ground despite Kruger's look of cold disdain. Hertzog was a hardened prisoner. His U-boat, *U-39*, had been sunk after an abortive attack on the *Ark Royal* during the first fortnight of the war against Britain. The long period in captivity had made him taciturn and short-tempered.

'Have you read about the loss of *U-501*, commander?' Hertzog's tone was respectful; it was his eyes that betrayed his anger.

'What about it?' inquired Kruger frostily.

'My brother was *U-501*'s radio officer.'

'I'm sorry to hear that, Hertzog.'

'So I think I've a right to know what's going to happen to that stinking little coward,' said Hertzog bluntly, still undeterred by Kruger's icy stare.

'There will an inquiry into the loss of *U-501* immediately after our liberation,' Kruger replied. 'For the time being, it would be best if we don't allow British propaganda to pre-judge the issue. Now if you will excuse –'

'You mean that you're going to do nothing?' This time Hertzog's tone was insolent but Kruger was a sound judge of men: he could see that Hertzog was simmering with rage and realized that no purpose would be served by getting angry in retaliation. Instead, he said calmly, 'If the newspaper reports about Korvettenkapitan Forster's actions are correct, then you have my word that he will pay the price.'

'And you have my word that Forster will pay the price, commander.'

'Meaning?'

'Meaning just that,' said Hertzog simply. Before Kruger could reply he turned on his heel and clattered his bulk down the stairs.

The *Altestenrat* – literally 'The Council of Elders' – had been convened by Kruger in the music room on the first floor of Grizedale Hall. It was an easy room to cover with sentries to warn of approaching guards, and the thick pile carpet in the elegant room tended to deaden the sound of heated exchanges.

Oberleutnant Karl Shriver of the *Luftwaffe*, a recent arrival at the hall, sat at the head table. He was flanked by Kruger and Hauptmann Paul Ulbrick. The three men had taken considerable pains with their uniforms to ensure that they were correctly turned out. They were all studying several British newspapers that were spread out on the table. Willi was sitting in a chair near the door where he could hear the warning signal from the lookouts. He had a pencil and paper at the ready to make notes of the proceedings. Facing the table were the rest of the council, which consisted of ten of the more senior-ranking officers from among the hall's inmates. To avoid accusations of showing favouritism towards a fellow U-boat officer, Kruger had selected the members of the council so that its naval officers were in the minority, and he had appointed Shriver as the council's president.

Completing the scene – standing rigidly to attention in front of the table – was Korvettenkapitan Hugo Forster. His eyes were fixed on the wall behind Kruger and his two fellow officers of the council.

At 10 am precisely, Kruger looked up from the newspapers piled on the table and made no attempt to conceal his loathing as he regarded Forster. He nodded to Shriver.

Shriver turned to Ulbrick. 'Please proceed, hauptmann.'

'Korvettenkapitan Forster,' said Ulbrick, rising to his feet. 'This is not a court-martial, therefore you are not under oath. The purpose of this *Altestenrat* is to establish the truth concerning the loss of your *U-501* and its crew on September 10th, 1941. The facts will then be reported to your Admiral Doenitz together with any recommendations that the *Altestenrat* feels that it ought to make. Do you understand?'

'Yes, hauptmann,' said Forster woodenly, not taking his eyes off the wall. He was uncomfortably aware that Kruger was staring at him with an icy expression.

'Also, you are not obliged to answer any questions. However, if you do refuse, that will also be reported by Commander Kruger to the Flag Officer, U-boats.'

'I will answer what questions I can,' said Forster.

Shriver nodded to Willi, who started writing.

Ulbrick studied Forster for a few moments and said abruptly, 'Can you read English, korvettenkapitan?'

Forster licked his lips. 'A little, hauptmann.'

Ulbrick contemptuously tossed the *Daily Telegraph* across the table to Forster. 'Read that,' he commanded.

Forster stepped forward and stared down at the newspaper. His fingers shook slightly as he tried to turn the pages.

'It's below the headlines on the front page,' said Ulbrick scathingly. He picked up the other newspapers one by one. 'It's a major story in the entire British press. The *Times*: "U-boat captain abandons his command". The *Daily Mirror*: "U-boat skipper jumps ship".'

'It's not as bad as they make it sound,' Forster protested.

'Forty-three U-boatmen lost,' snapped Ulbrick. 'Tell me how you can make that sound less bad than it is unless the British are lying. Are they lying?'

'Well – no. But –'

'Did you or did you not abandon your boat?'

'Hauptmann,' said Forster desperately. '*U-501* had been cut virtually in two when –'

Ulbrick's scalp went back. 'Did you or did you not abandon your boat!'

'How can I be accused of abandoning my boat when it sank under me?' said Forster defensively.

Ulbrick's eyes opened wide. 'Did I say I was accusing you, korvettenkapitan? I'm sorry, I didn't mean it to sound like that. Obviously I touched a nerve.'

A laugh at the back of the room was silenced by a withering glare from Shriver.

'Let me rephrase the question,' Ulbrick continued. 'Did you leave your boat?'

'It left me when it sank,' said Forster.

Ulbrick picked up a handwritten sheet of paper. 'In your statement –'

'Account,' Kruger corrected.

Ulbrick smiled and bowed to Kruger. He returned to the attack. 'In your account of the action, you said that you were the first man on the bridge as soon as *U-501* surfaced. Why were you so anxious to be the first man out of your submarine?'

Forster looked appealingly at Kruger. 'That's not a fair question, commander. As you well know, it's normal for the commander to be the first through the hatch, especially when there's damage to be assessed.'

Kruger nodded. 'Yes, that's correct, hauptmann.'

'And what was the damage?' Ulbrick queried.

'I didn't get a chance to see the extent of the external damage because the *Moose Jaw* rammed the moment I climbed on to the bridge.'

'Surely you were aware of the warship's proximity?'

Forster shook his head. 'I had no idea the destroyer was so close. We'd been heavily depth-charged. The attack periscope and the sky periscope were useless, and so was our hydrophone equipment. The pressure hull was leaking badly and the boat was filling with chlorine gas. That's why I ordered the chief engineer to blow all tanks and surface.'

'So that you could escape,' Ulbrick remarked.

'Yes, of course.'

Ulbrick paused and glanced at the circle of listening officers. 'So that *you* could escape? What about your crew?'

'I was including my crew,' Forster answered. 'But first I wanted to see if there was a chance of retaliating with our 88-millimetre. There was a gun crew standing by in the control room.'

'Did you order them to action stations?'

'No. I never had the chance. As I said, the *Moose Jaw* rammed immediately – before our deck casings were above water.'

Ulbrick looked up from the note that Kruger had passed him. 'Presumably you realized that all was lost the moment the Canadian destroyer rammed you?'

Forster's unhappy gaze met his inquisitor's eyes for the first time. He nodded.

'Did you order your crew to abandon ship when you realized that all was lost?'

Forster hesitated. 'No,' he said. 'There wasn't time. I was thrown away from the speaking tubes and the klaxon button by the force of the impact. The bows of the destroyer sliced right into the bridge.'

'You were thrown into the water?'

Another hesitation. 'No.'

'So what happened, korvettenkapitan? Why is it that you are here and none of your crew is?'

'Look,' said Forster abruptly. 'The destroyer struck within a metre of where I was standing. The noise was deafening. I hardly knew what was happening. There was this terrible screaming noise – steel smashing into steel. Then the conning tower was keeling over. I remember hanging on to the periscope standard and then I must have climbed onto the conning tower's coaming – I don't know. I saw something in front of me and I jumped.'

'You jumped onto the *Moose Jaw*'s foredeck!' Ulbrick accused.

'I didn't know what it was at the time!'

'You saw a destroyer's deck in front of you? A few metres away? And you expect us to believe that you didn't know what it was?'

Forster began to get angry. 'Look. I couldn't see or hear properly. I knew my boat was going down fast. I saw something in front of me and I jumped.'

Ulbrick regarded his victim in contempt. 'You saw safety?'

'I jumped. It was an instinctive reaction.'

Ulbrick consulted his notes. 'I'm not a U-boatman, korvettenkapitan, but I know enough to know that the foredeck of a destroyer is much higher above water level than the conning tower of a U-boat, especially when the U-boat's conning tower has keeled over. Am I correct?'

'Yes,' said Forster tiredly, knowing what was to follow.

'Therefore your act of jumping from the conning tower on to the destroyer must have been carefully timed and judged. Hardly an instinctive reaction.'

'All I know is that it was an instinctive jump,' Forster asserted.

'You saw safety in front of you and you jumped?'

'I tell you I don't know what I was thinking at the time!' Forster almost shouted. He looked wildly around at the accusing faces. 'Surely you've all been in the same situation before? When you've had to bale out or whatever. Your actions are instinctive. You do things that you can't remember or explain afterwards.'

'I can remember exactly what happened when I was shot down,' said Ulbrick. 'In particular I can remember giving orders to my crew to bale out before doing so myself.'

'A U-boat's different,' said Forster feebly. 'Look, you must understand that I was grabbed by the crew of the destroyer who pulled me on to the foredeck. It wasn't a clean jump if that's what you mean.'

'You jumped off the conning tower's coaming?'

'Yes.'

Ulbrick looked scathing. 'Earlier on you said that your boat had sunk.'

'It did sink.'

'But it was still afloat when you jumped. It would have to have been otherwise how could you have jumped?'

'It was partially afloat.'

Ulbrick arched his eyebrows. 'Earlier you said that the U-boat had sunk when you were rescued, that it had abandoned you. Now we learn that it was afloat.'

'What I said earlier was –'

'What you said earlier was a lie!'

'I didn't lie!' snapped Forster, showing unexpected spirit. 'In the heat of battle –'

'There was no battle!' Ulbrick countered savagely. 'You were depth-charged. You surfaced. You were the first man out of the hatch and on to the bridge. Your boat was rammed and, like the coward you are, you abandoned it by jumping from the conning tower onto the *Moose Jaw*'s foredeck – exactly in accordance with the accounts in these newspapers!'

Forster stared straight back at Ulbrick. 'It is obvious that you are intent on attaching more importance to propaganda stories in the British newspapers than to my account. If I am guilty of anything, it is my inability to convey to you the horror of what it is like to be confronted by the bows of a charging destroyer bearing down on one at distance of a few metres.'

The silence that followed was broken by Kruger. He stood and contemplated Forster. The U-boat captain met the withering stare for a moment and allowed his gaze to drop to the floor.

'The most effective propaganda of all, Korvettenkapitan Forster,' said Kruger, speaking slowly, 'is that which is based on truth. The Canadian crew of the *Moose Jaw* will no doubt be encouraged to relate the story to newsmen so that the whole sorry account will be reported in the world's press – particularly the United States' press. Your cowardly act will serve the British admirably in their campaign to win support in the United States. It will help the American public to believe the lies that the British are circulating about U-boats opening fire on lifeboats crowded with survivors. Do you have anything to say in your defence?'

'I thought that this wasn't a court-martial?' said Forster, a hostile edge in his voice.

'It isn't,' Kruger replied. 'But I will be in touch with Admiral Doenitz and will notify him that we have established that these stories' – he gestured to the newspapers – 'are substantially correct. A court-martial is certain to follow after our liberation and I have no doubt whatsoever that you will be found guilty of abandoning your command and that you will be hanged.'

Forster's face paled noticeably. For a moment it looked as if he was about to collapse.

'Do you have anything to say?' asked Shriver.

Forster shook his head.

'Very well,' said Shriver evenly. 'All that remains now is for us to decide what to do with you until the liberation. Willi, escort Korvettenkapitan Forster outside for a few minutes.'

The discussion among the thirteen members of the *Altestenrat* concerning Forster's fate was opened by Shriver. He said bluntly, 'He'll have to hang, of course. There's no question about that.'

'I agree,' said Kruger. 'But we're here to decide what to do with him until the liberation.'

'Others here might decide for us.'

Kruger frowned. 'I don't understand.'

'He's certain to be punished by the other prisoners,' Ulbrick replied.

'In what way?' asked Kruger.

Ulbrick shrugged. 'I don't have to go into details, but there're a number of your U-boat colleagues who will come up with their own form of punishment for Forster.'

'In which case, those prisoners would face disciplinary proceedings under British military law,' Kruger replied impassively.

'Would you side with the British if such a thing happened?' asked Shriver curiously.

Kruger lit a cheroot. 'I'm not taking any sides but I will not condone officers taking the law into their own hands.'

'Then Forster will have to be transferred to another camp,' said an army major.

'And that means Canada,' remarked another officer.

There was a silence. All the prisoners went in fear at the threat of being transferred to Canada. There was the frightening thought that they would be thousands of kilometres from their homes and loved ones. Also, although most prisoners considered that a British capitulation was imminent, none of them had any doubts that

153

Canada would continue to fight on for years – perhaps even decades. Nothing provoked escape fever in the camp quite as much as rumours of an impending transfer to Canada.

'No,' said Kruger firmly. 'Over forty men died in *U-501*. I'm not having Forster escape justice by being sent to Canada.'

'That only leaves one option,' said Shriver.

'Which is?'

'Forster will have to withdraw from all camp activities.'

'He's never taken part in them anyway,' Kruger observed.

'I was thinking of a withdrawal of *all* privileges,' said Shriver. 'There are the instruction courses, and we control the distribution of mail and food parcels –'

'Stopping his mail and parcels would be illegal,' Kruger pointed out.

'We will be suspending them pending further investigations,' said Shriver smoothly. 'It would certainly hit him hard because he's always first in the mail queue on Mondays.' The *Luftwaffe* officer glanced at Willi. 'Leutnant Hartmann could look after Forster's mail and parcels until the liberation. I understand that the guards never search your room, Willi?'

Willi nodded.

The major laughed and said: 'No one has ever seen the inside of Willi's room.'

'Also, there's a guard who owes me a favour,' said Willi. 'I could ask him to let me have Forster's outgoing mail before it's passed to the censors. That way we'd be stopping all his mail.'

Shriver frowned. 'It's an effective short-term punishment but supposing Forster complains to Reynolds?'

'Reynolds won't listen,' said Kruger. 'Our arrangement is that all prisoners' complaints are channelled through me.'

'Very well,' said Shriver. 'We have a proposal. Is there a seconder?'

'I'll second it,' said the major promptly.

'I'm opposed to it,' Kruger stated. 'The proposed action is illegal.'

'That is not in dispute, Otto,' said Shriver mildly, using Kruger's first name with an easy familiarity that was unheard of among the prisoners.

'In which case, Shriver, you ought to be opposed to the proposal as well.'

'Otto, this isn't your escape committee in which you have the right of veto. You agreed that every member of this council should have a vote. All right, so you're opposed to the proposal. Are you also opposed to me putting it to the vote?'

Kruger tried to outstare Shriver and failed. He shook his head.

'Very well,' said Shriver, well aware that Kruger had failed to get his own way for the first time at Grizedale Hall. 'All those in favour of the total exclusion of Korvettenkapitan Forster from camp activities, including the suspension of his mail and parcels, please raise their right hand.'

The Monday morning mail and parcel distribution system devised by Kruger was an orderly affair – far removed from the noisy throng that used to gather in the courtyard outside Sergeant Finch's office window in the days when Ulbrick had been the camp's senior German officer. The bundles of letters and parcels were stacked in alphabetical order on one of the long, trestle tables in the common room in front of the huge marble fireplace. There were more parcels than usual on this particular Monday morning because the monthly consignment of American Red Cross parcels had arrived – each one about the size of two shoeboxes. They contained tobacco, chocolate, candy, condensed milk, powdered coffee, tea, sugar, and tins of food, in addition to shaving and toilet soap of a quality far superior to that available in the shops in wartime Britain.

Watched by silent, expectant prisoners who were crowding on to the gallery, Willi finished checking the mail against his trusty clipboard. At 10 am exactly, he settled into his chair behind the trestle table and called out: 'Prisoners A to H!'

The twenty or so officers who had been sitting on the stairs scrambled to their feet and swarmed eagerly across the hall to Willi. They formed an orderly line in front of the table with Forster first in the queue. Hertzog was immediately behind him.

'Forster, H. G.,' said Forster excitedly.

'Forster, H. G.,' Willi repeated without looking at his clipboard. 'Sorry. No mail or parcels. Next.'

Forster stared at Willi in astonishment. 'What do you mean? There's a letter from my wife.'

The buzz of conversation in the queue died away to an uneasy silence.

'You know the commander's orders,' said Willi uncomfortably. He pretended to be engrossed in his clipboard so that he didn't have to meet Forster's pleading eyes.

'But the ban doesn't include letters from my wife! It can't. I don't care about the parcels but –'

Willi looked embarrassed. 'I'm sorry, korvettenkapitan. But I'm only obeying orders. Next please.'

Forster's face went white. 'You can't stop my wife's letters!' he whispered. 'It's inhuman!'

'No more inhuman than what you did, Forster,' Hertzog growled. 'Now move.'

For a moment Forster seemed to be paralyzed with shock. Slowly he raised his eyes to the expressionless faces staring down at him from the gallery.

'Move, you stinking little coward!' barked Hertzog, giving Forster a sharp poke in the ribs with a forefinger the diameter of a broomstick.

It was as if the jab had unleashed a coiled spring. Forster spun round and swung his foot with savage force into Hertzog's groin. Hertzog gave a loud cry of pain and doubled up in agony. Willi half-rose to his feet and fell back as Forster lunged at him across the table. One of the trestles collapsed, sending Willi and Forster sprawling on to the floor amid a cascade of parcels. Before anyone had realized what was happening, Forster had snatched up the bundle of letters that had fallen from Willi's hand and was thrusting his way past the prisoners towards the french windows.

'Stop him!' Willi yelled.

An army officer lashed out wildly at Forster and caught him by the sleeve of his jacket. Forster retaliated by swinging a punch into the army officer's face, forcing him to break his grip. Forster recovered his balance. Still clutching the bundle of letters, he darted across the hall to the windows but was brought crashing down in a flying rugger tackle. He fought like a wildcat and managed to break loose from four prisoners who tried to pin him to the floor. Suddenly he was seized from behind by a pair of brawny arms.

The dishevelled prisoners who had attempted to restrain Forster fell back as Hertzog swung him aloft as though he was a sack of hay. The giant U-boatman gave a grunt and hurled Forster across the room. He crashed against a settee which fortunately cushioned his fall. He staggered to his feet. Blood was streaming from a deep cut over his left eye. His expression was one of unbridled fury. He was about to launch himself at Hertzog but was checked by a shrill blast on a whistle.

'Well, gentlemen,' said Sergeant Finch, moving from the french windows into the centre of the room. 'If this is a diversion, you should know by now that they don't work with me.'

'A quarrel,' said Willi, recovering the letters that were

scattered on the rucked carpet. 'An argument over a parcel. It is nothing.'

Finch grinned when he caught sight of Forster's battered face. 'Looks like you lost, mate. Still – your consolation prize is that you get to see Nurse Hobson.' He turned to the two guards who were standing in the doorway. 'Take this gentleman to the sickbay.'

As Forster was led away, he paused in front of Hertzog and wiped the blood from his eyes. The two men stared at each other, their expressions mirroring their mutual hatred.

'I remember your brother on *U-501*, Hertzog,' said Forster bitterly. 'It's a pity that you weren't serving with him. That way the loss of my boat would have meant the end of two pigs instead of one.'

Fleming returned to Grizedale Hall from London that day at 2 pm. He was parking his Bentley in the courtyard when he was accosted by Brenda Hobson with an offer of coffee in her sickbay.

A few minutes later he was appreciatively sipping the best cup of coffee he had tasted since ground coffee had become virtually unobtainable earlier that year.

'My God, nurse, real coffee. How do you do it?'

'It's an American blend. Chalky – er – one of the guards gave it to me,' Brenda replied, smiling. 'He gets a supply from the POWs who don't like coffee. It's funny the way the Americans send them so many food parcels.' She looked worried. 'You won't say anything will you?'

Fleming chuckled. 'It would be impossible to stamp out trading between the guards and the prisoners – and I don't suppose it does any harm.'

'How about Nazi bullying?' said Brenda suddenly. 'Does that do any harm?'

'Ah. Now we're coming to the reason why you've lured me into your sickbay. I had hoped that it was because you either considered me in need of a soft hand on a fevered brow or because you found me irresistible. Tell me more.'

'There's a Korvettenkapitan Forster here – a U-boat captain. I'm sure he's being bullied by the prisoners.'

'Oh?' Fleming queried guardedly. 'Why do you think that?'

'This morning I put three stitches in a cut over his eye. He's a funny bloke. Doesn't say much even though he can speak a bit of English. Keeps himself to himself. He doesn't even work in the gardens and yet Kruger has a strict rule that all POWs have to do some gardening.'

'This is a "white" camp,' Fleming pointed out. 'Any bullying is not likely to be Nazi-inspired.'

'They're all Nazis as far as I'm concerned,' Brenda replied vehemently. 'I don't really care what they do to each other, but I object to them doing it on British soil and getting away with it.'

'Shouldn't you be telling this to Major Reynolds, my precious?'

Brenda gave a contemptuous toss of her head. 'He turns that blind eye of his to a lot of things that go on around here. If you don't believe me, ask him about Leutnant Herbert Shultz's escape or why Willi Hartmann's room is never searched.'

'Why do you think I ought to be interested?'

'You're responsible for camp intelligence, aren't you?'

'Well – sort of,' Fleming murmured guardedly. He glanced around the neat sickbay in a search of something to help change the subject. A framed photograph of a smiling young man in a sub-lieutenant's uniform caught his eye. He picked it up.

'Either you are or you're not,' said Brenda. 'If you're not interested, then I'm sorry to have wasted your time.'

'Is this your husband, Brenda?'

Brenda's expression softened. 'Yes. David.'

'You must introduce me sometime.'

'Oh, I hardly ever see him. But he might be home for Christmas. He said that the *Barham* is due for a refit.'

Fleming smiled. He put the photograph down and stood. 'Well, don't forget that I'd like to meet him. He's a lucky man to have you.'

Brenda was not susceptible to Fleming's charm. 'What are you going to do about Forster?' she persisted.

Fleming made a vague promise to look into the matter. He left Nurse Brenda Hobson a few minutes later feeling very pleased with himself. Things were moving on the Forster front.

Forster stretched out on his hard bed and started reading his prison library book for the fifth time. The ban even covered the loan of library books: he could neither return the book or withdraw a new one. He had avoided the evening meal but the pain from the cut over his eye and his misery made him forget his hunger.

He reached the foot of the first page and realized that not one word had registered because his mind kept returning to the letter from Eva that he knew was somewhere in Willi Hartmann's room. At first he toyed with the idea of creeping into the army officer's room and looking for the letter. After some thought, he abandoned the idea: it was a standing joke at the camp that it was easier to escape from Grizedale Hall than it was to get into Willi Hartmann's room.

By 9.30 that evening, Eva's letter was dominating Forster's thoughts. The more he thought about it, the more angry he became – not only with the attitude of Kruger and the members of the *Altestenrat* but with the whole system that had sent him to war and separated him from his wife and child. Maybe there was another photograph of the baby in Eva's letter? Maybe she had said which she preferred of the second names they had short-listed during his last leave? His last leave. . . . A heady weekend together. They had spent Saturday scouring the shops for baby things. Because of the shortages they had laughingly bought whatever clothes they could find, regardless of whether they were intended for a boy or a girl.

Forster could stand it no longer. He hurled the unread book across the tower room and swung his feet off the bed. He resolved to find Eva's letter whatever the consequences. If necessary, he would threaten Willi Hartmann with a knife. . . .

He emerged from his door and peered down the black, silent well of the spiral staircase. In the distance he could hear the camp choir rehearsing their last song of the evening. As he descended the stone steps, he thought he heard a sound. He turned round and listened. There was nothing. Or was there? He descended a few more steps. Suddenly a flashlight snapped on, its beam stabbing him in the eyes, dazzling him.

'Hallo, Forster,' said Hertzog's voice. 'Guess what I've come for.'

'Well, it won't be for a lesson in good manners,' Forster replied, surprising himself at how steady his voice sounded. 'Most pigs are too stupid to realize that they haven't got any to start with.'

There was a brief silence before Hertzog replied. 'That makes it two apologies I've come for,' he said softly. 'We'll start with the one for what you said about my brother this morning.'

'I meant every word of what I said and furthermore – I'll repeat it. I said that it was a pity that you weren't serving on my boat along with your brother because –' Forster got no further. He didn't see the clenched fist that burst through the light like an express train and slammed into his face. His head snapped back and a pyrotechnique display from a thousand Roman candles exploded in front of his retinas. As the fog closed in he was vaguely aware that he was falling backwards. Either that or it was space around him turning itself inside out.

Whatever it was, he didn't really care. . . .

There were voices. Faraway voices. Near voices. A vague, distant feeling of movement and a curious sense of total detachment from his body. He heard a question asked in a strange language to which someone mumbled an answer using his voice.

'Christ, what a mess,' said one of the voices.

'Sounded like him saying something about falling.'

'Bloody lot of stairs to fall down.'

'Lucky he didn't fall down the middle. Must be a hundred-foot drop down the inside of the tower.'

'You'd think those bloody Jerries would've noticed that he wasn't at breakfast. Okay, report to Major Reynolds and come back with a stretcher.'

The voices disappeared and the darkness returned, bringing with it the pungent smell of fuel oil, the whine of electric motors, and the familiar motion of a U-boat blowing its tanks and surfacing. He clutched the bridge ladder with one hand and released the hatch clips above his head. As he scrambled on to the bridge, he was immediately aware of a new noise, a noise that should not have been there. Barely had he straightened up when the destroyer's charging bows cleaved into the conning tower like a titanic axe. The force of the impact threw him violently against the periscope standard. The tortured, grating scream of steel grinding upon steel deafened and confused him. Through the maelstrom of whirling images, which included the sea reaching up to claw him away from his stricken U-boat, he glimpsed the safety rails that surrounded the U-boat's 'wintergarten' gun deck. He threw himself at the rails and clung to them with a strength fuelled by terror. His body was plunged up to his waist in the near freezing water and then his shoulders were nearly dislocated as the safety rail lifted to the swell. Suddenly there were shouts and the sound of running feet approaching, strong hands closing around his wrists and lifting him over the rails. In that despairing moment he realized to his abject horror that the safety rails belonged to the destroyer. He wanted to release his grip, to let the sea swallow him and his shame, but the brawny arms of the enemy seamen were lifting him on to the destroyer's foredeck. . . .

'Good morning, old boy,' said Fleming breezily, when Brenda showed him into the sickbay.

Forster looked up from the chair where he was sitting by the window and managed to scowl at his visitor despite the bandages that swathed his face.

'Ten minutes and no more, commander,' said Brenda sternly before closing the door behind her.

Fleming listened to Brenda's high heels tapping across the courtyard and sat down opposite Forster. He gave the German a broad grin. 'Well, well. And to think that I thought the war was over for you.'

'I fell down the stairs in the tower,' said Forster sourly.

Fleming chuckled. 'Four cracked ribs. Two teeth knocked out. Six stitches in your cheek. That was some fall.'

'It's a long flight of stairs.'

'Curious how you've become so accident-prone since the story of *U-501*'s loss was released. Now that you're a father, you've got to take care of yourself.' He reached in his pocket and produced an envelope. 'By the way, your wife's doing well for herself.'

'That's Eva's handwriting!' Forster cried. He half-rose from the chair to snatch the letter but Fleming held it out of reach.

'Steady on, old boy,' said Fleming, gently easing Forster back into his chair. 'It may be your wife's handwriting, but it's not addressed to you.'

Forster stared at Fleming in bewilderment. 'I don't understand. She would only write to me.'

'She wrote to the Red Cross in London wanting to know why she hadn't heard from you.'

'But I write to her twice a week!'

Fleming looked speculatively at Forster. 'If you have, your letters aren't reaching the censor's office. Any idea what could be happening to them?'

Forster opened his mouth to say something and changed his mind. He shook his head.

'Did you reply to her last letter?'

'Of course.'

'What do you think of her new address?'

Forster had no idea what Fleming was talking about and made the mistake of attempting to bluff. 'She thought she might find a smaller flat now that I'm stuck here.'

Fleming smiled. 'Nice try, Hugo. Obviously all your mail is being stopped somewhere along the line. Actually, your wife and son are in Lisbon. She's working at the German Embassy there. Is she the Eva Halderene who used to work there before the war?'

'Lisbon?' For a moment Forster looked startled. What was visible of his face relaxed into a smile. 'Oh, yes. Of course. She told me in her last letter that the Foreign Office had offered her her old job back. Lisbon is where we first met in 1936. I was crewing on the *Gorch Fock* – the navy's sail training schooner. We had called in at Lisbon and our embassy laid on a reception for us.'

Fleming regarded the German naval officer thoughtfully. 'How much longer do you expect to be here, Forster? How long before the invasion is supposed to take place?'

Forster gave a wry smile. 'It's no secret that it'll be before Christmas.'

'And when it comes, you'll be in worse trouble than the trouble you're in now.'

'Why should I be in trouble?'

'Let's put it the other way around. If you were a British submarine commander who had abandoned his command during a battle, we'd court-martial you and stand you up before a firing squad.'

Forster said nothing.

'You're a loser whatever happens,' Fleming continued. 'If there's an invasion, you'll be executed. And if the war drags on, the chances of the prisoners here letting you survive are nil. Either way, you'll never see your wife and son again.'

Forster continued to remain silent but the look of misery in his eyes was all the answer Fleming needed. Like the skilled interrogator he was, Fleming had manoeuvred his victim into a position whereby he was wholly dependent on him and listening carefully to every word. He pressed home his attack. 'There is a third course.'

'What's that?' asked Forster, making no attempt to conceal his eagerness.

'It would be easy enough for us to send you out to Lisbon to be reunited with your wife. From there we could send you both to Canada – British Columbia is a beautiful place. We'd give you new identities and money so that you could start a new life together, safe from the war and Adolf and his merry men.'

Forster stared at Fleming in astonishment. 'You could do that?'

'It wouldn't present any problems.'

'There's a catch.'

Fleming laughed. 'Of course there's a catch. We wouldn't do it out of the goodness of our hearts. We would require from you a full account of *U-501*'s radio ranging and location equipment and other gear including her cipher machine.'

Forster slumped back in his chair. 'I don't understand. I read in the papers that *U-570* surrendered to you in August.'

'We had to wait several hours after her surrender for the weather to moderate before we could get a prize crew aboard her,' said Fleming. 'Which meant that her crew had plenty of time to throw all her important equipment over the side.' He paused and studied Forster speculatively. 'Another part of the deal is that we will want you to spend several days with our experts going over *U-570* with them.'

'You're asking me to betray my country. I can't do that, commander.'

'We're asking you to betray a man who's going to destroy your country and the whole of Europe unless he's stopped.'

'In the meantime, the information I give you will be used to help kill thousands of my colleagues in the U-boat arm.'

'We want to bring the war to an end in order to save lives. Including the lives of millions of civilians such as your wife and son.' Fleming paused. 'Listen, Hugo. Our offer to you is the only way that you're ever going to see your wife again, unless, of course, she's allowed to visit you before your execution. A week's co-operation – that's all we ask. In return we'll do everything we can to see that you and Eva and your son start a new life in Canada. Go along with us, and you'll be reunited with her within two weeks.'

'And if I refuse?'

Fleming gave a faint smile. 'You'll be repatriated home to Germany in exchange for a sick Allied prisoner.'

Forster stared at the British officer. 'But I'm not sick!' he protested.

'According to the Red Cross, your OKM aren't quibbling. My guess is that they're keen to get their hands on you.'

There was a long silence before Forster replied. When he spoke, his voice was so quiet that Fleming had to lean forward to hear what he said. 'Nurse Hobson says that I can be returned to my room this evening. I like it there. It's quiet and I can think. Can I give you my answer in the morning?'

166

'Of course,' said Fleming cheerily, standing. He gave Forster Eva's letter. 'No reason why you shouldn't have this. See you in the morning.'

It was 3 am. Forster was back in his room at the top of the tower. He lay wide awake on his bed, agonizing over what to do while his heart ached for his wife and son. To accede to the British demands would be so easy and he would be united with Eva and Ernst. And yet he would have to live with the memory of his treachery for the rest of his life. On top of that, there would the constant, nagging fear that one day his son would discover the truth about his father. But if he refused, he faced disgracing his family and son, and certain death before a *Kriegsmarine* firing squad.

There seemed no way out – no third choice. . . . Or was there?

The pain in his ribs from the beating up Hertzog had given him was forgotten as he crossed to the tiny window and peered down to the courtyard. He estimated that it was twenty metres to the ground. It was a Saturday night when there were few guards on duty. If he made a noise, the chances were that no one would hear him. He came to a single, momentous decision. His mind cleared once he realized exactly what he had to do, but his movements became feverish. He dragged the blankets and sheets from his bed and knotted them together into one long rope. He tested its strength by passing it around the window bars and satisfied himself that it would support his weight.

Kruger's face was hard as he and Major Reynolds strode through the quarry-tiled passageway that led to Forster's tower. Sergeant Finch and two guards trailed along behind.

'I tell you, major, I have not sanctioned an escape by any prisoner,' Kruger was saying. 'There's probably a rational explanation. Maybe the drugs Nurse Hobson gave him have caused him to oversleep.'

'Was he at breakfast?' Reynolds demanded, pushing a door open.

'No,' said Kruger.

'Then goddamn it, why didn't you check then?'

The search party reached the door that opened into the tower. Reynolds was first to mount the spiral staircase, with Kruger close on his heels.

'I'll tell you something, commander,' said Reynolds over his shoulder. 'If he's been beaten up again –'

'He was *not* beaten up,' Kruger insisted. 'He fell. It was an accident.'

Reynolds suddenly stopped without warning, causing Kruger to nearly cannon into him. The Canadian officer was staring up the inside of the stairwell. 'Jesus Christ,' he whispered.

Kruger peered up over Reynolds' shoulder. The only indication of shock he gave was that he failed to draw on his cheroot for some seconds.

A pair of feet hanging down the inside of the stairwell were visible a few yards above Reynolds' head.

The two men silently climbed the stairs until they were level with Forster's hideously distorted face. The knotted sheet noose had cut so deeply into his neck that it was concealed by the discoloured, grossly swollen flesh.

'Jesus Christ,' Reynolds muttered again, unable to think of anything more original or appropriate to say as he stared at Forster's gently swaying body. 'Jesus bloody Christ. What in hell drove him to do a darn fool thing like that?'

Part Six

A GREAT LITTLE ESCAPE

'I've had the visit from the Forestry Commission,' said Major Reynolds, waving Kruger to the chair in front of his desk. 'They've agreed that they're short of able-bodied men for the maintenance of Grizedale Forest and have no objection to clearing work being carried out by POW working parties.'

'Excellent, major,' said Kruger, lighting a cheroot.

'They've laid down a number of conditions.'

'Naturally.'

'Firstly, they insist that only fallen timber can be removed from the forest.'

'Understood,' said Kruger.

'Secondly, there must be no felling of standing timber unless for thinning purposes – and then the felling and coppicing must be under the supervision of the forestry warden.'

'That seems perfectly reasonable,' Kruger commented. 'We're not interested in the standing timber – only the tonnes of fallen timber that is being allowed to rot.'

Reynolds looked curiously at the senior German officer. 'You really think you can get the hall's central heating system working for the winter?'

'My engineering officers are confident of it,' Kruger replied. 'Only a few modifications are necessary to the main boiler to make it run on timber instead of coke.'

Reynolds thought for a moment. 'Well,' he admitted, glancing at the dormant radiator under his window. 'It sure is one helluva temptation after last winter.'

Central heating was rare in England but normal in Reynolds' native Canada. It was Reynolds' guess that Harold Brocklebank knew about central heating from his frequent trips to North America, which was why it had been installed in Grizedale Hall. Unfortunately, the War Office and the Ministry of Fuel and Power had decreed that Grizedale Hall should not receive an allocation of coke.

'The question is whether there's enough fallen timber in the forest to keep the furnace going through the winter,' said Reynolds.

'We have estimated that there's more than enough for us and that there will be plenty for the charcoal burners,' said Kruger. 'Six handcart loads per week will be sufficient provided we shut off the heating to the greenhouses and turn off the radiators in the bedrooms.'

'The administrative offices and the guards' quarters will have to be heated, of course,' said Reynolds craftily.

'Of course,' Kruger agreed levelly.

'Okay,' said Reynolds after a few moments' face-saving consideration. 'I'll authorize a switch from exercise walks to forest working parties.'

'Thank you, major,' Kruger stood, pulled on his cap and returned Reynolds' salute. 'There is one more thing, major. . . .'

'Yeah?'

'There's a rumour going around that we are to be transferred to Canada. Can you enlighten me please?'

'Where the hell did you hear that?'

Kruger gave a thin smile. He could hardly say that Doenitz's last letter had mentioned that a number of captured NCO U-boat crewmen were now writing home from Canada. Instead he said, 'It's just a rumour, major.'

'Well, that's all it is,' said Reynolds. 'As much as I'd like to be sent home, I've heard nothing about it, so I suggest that you forget it.'

The telephone rang. Reynolds picked up the receiver and

listened. 'Okay,' he said, 'I'll tell him.' He replaced the receiver and smiled at Kruger. 'We've got an old prisoner back.'

Kruger looked interested. 'You mean Leutnant Shultz?'

Reynolds' smile changed to a scowl. 'No, I don't mean Leutnant Shultz.'

Kruger was genuinely pleased to welcome Hauptmann Dietrich Berg back to Grizedale Hall. He shook the young officer's right hand, taking care not to jar his left arm because it was in a sling. Willi celebrated Berg's return by opening a prized bottle of whisky and pouring generous measures into three cups.

'And your eyes, Berg?' asked Kruger, concerned. 'They are healed?'

'Oh yes, commander. Perfectly. The British surgeons at St George's were magnificent.' He smiled happily at the two men. 'It is good to be back, commander. Er – the radio transmitter I built. Was any of the transmission heard by a U-boat?'

Kruger shook his head. 'I believe that a part of the transmission may have been heard. But the transmitter failure was before Brunel had a chance to send the important information.'

Berg looked disappointed. 'After all the trouble everyone went to to help me build the radio too.'

'It wasn't your fault, Berg,' assured Kruger. 'You did your best.'

'What have you done to your arm, Berg?' asked Willi, indicating the sling.

Berg glanced ruefully down at his left arm. 'Nurse Hobson said that she will be able to take the plaster off next week.'

'Yes. But how did it happen?' Kruger pressed. 'There was nothing wrong with your arm when you were taken off to hospital.'

'I broke it in hospital,' Berg confessed, tasting the whisky that Willi handed him.

Kruger sighed. Berg's tendency to be accident-prone was legendary but breaking an arm while in hospital was a considerable achievement. He glanced at Willi. The little Bavarian was having a hard time keeping a straight face.

'Tell me, Berg,' said Kruger. 'How does one set about breaking an arm while one's lying in a hospital bed?'

'It happened after I was able to move about. The British allowed me a lot of freedom around the hospital while my eyes were bandaged. I suppose they thought that a blind man didn't stand much chance of escaping.'

'It's a safe assumption,' Kruger agreed impassively.

'I worked out a theory that I could avoid objects by clapping my hands and listening to the echoes,' Berg enthused. 'After a few days I became quite good at moving about the corridors. I soon worked out where walls and obstructions were and how far away they were.'

'So you decided to escape?' Kruger queried.

'Yes.'

'By working out where obstructions were from the echoes when you clapped?'

'Yes, commander. In theory it ought to work. Bats can navigate by sound.'

'Yes, I know. Several million years' research and development has gone into their system. What went wrong with yours?'

'I reached the end of the corridor one night,' said Berg ruefully. 'I knew from my experiments that there was no obstruction and I was right – there wasn't an obstruction but there was a flight of stairs.'

Willi's cherubic face suddenly turned bright pink and he hastily blew his nose. Even Kruger appeared to be having trouble controlling his facial muscles.

'And that's how I broke my arm,' Berg admitted sadly. 'I didn't even know that I was on an upper floor of the hospital until I fell down the stairs.'

'Well, at least you're back in one piece,' said Kruger. 'All your tools and your rock samples have been kept safe in your workshop. You can even have your old bedroom back, but I've re-allocated your vegetable plot.'

Berg pulled on his cap and saluted with his good arm. 'Thank you, commander. You are most kind.' He turned to leave and paused while searching for the right words.

'Commander. . . .'

Kruger raised his eyebrows questioningly. 'Yes?'

'I would like to plan another escape. With proper planning this time.'

Willi made a strange noise into his cup of whisky and even Kruger's voice sounded unnaturally calm when he replied. 'Why, Berg?'

'I heard a rumour that we're all to be transferred to Canada. A British army surgeon told me. He said that it would be a good thing when we're all sent there.'

The smile disappeared from Willi's face.

'Yes, we're always hearing these rumours,' said Kruger with studied casualness. 'But sending prisoners of war to another country is contrary to the Geneva Convention. Somehow I don't think the British would do that.'

'That's exactly what I said. The surgeon pointed out that there's also an article in the convention that requires POWs to be moved out of a war zone. He said that the entire country is a war zone now.'

Willi blinked in alarm. It was perfectly true that the whole of the United Kingdom was now a war zone. On a number of nights *Luftwaffe* raiders had raised the already high morale of the POWs by being heard over the Lake District.

'Well,' said Kruger sceptically, 'I daresay the word of an army surgeon is as reliable a source as any. You have an escape plan of course?'

'Not yet, commander. But I would like your permission to plan a breakout.'

Kruger avoided Willi's eye. 'Really? For how many?'

'Three, commander, Myself, Oberleutnant Max Kluge and Leutnant zur See Brunel. We used to talk about it before I was taken off to hospital.'

Kruger nodded. 'Very well, Berg. Personally, I think that you should stick to your geology and cuckoo clocks, but you have my permission provided that you go no further than making plans and on condition that you say nothing about this ridiculous Canada rumour. Is that understood?'

'Yes, commander,' said Berg gratefully. 'Thank you very much.'

'Canada,' breathed Willi unhappily after Berg had left the room. If we're sent to Canada, we could still be POWs long after the invasion.'

'I shouldn't take any notice of half-baked rumours,' Kruger replied. 'And I'd be grateful if you talked to no one about this.'

'Good afternoon, Ian,' said Reynolds when the operator put him through to Fleming's London number. 'We're all wondering when we're going to see you back here. My phone doesn't stop ringing – inquiries from the local ladies.'

The two men exchanged pleasantries for a few minutes before Reynolds got down to the real reason for the call. 'Ian, I was wondering if you could do me a big favour. You've got some pretty good contacts in Western Command. Do you think you could find out from them if there's anything in these rumours about Number One Camp being transferred to Canada?'

Reynolds listened for a moment before replying to Fleming's query. 'Well, sure, I'd like to know. It's my home, remember. . . . Okay, Ian – if you can find out something, I'd be very grateful. See you next week.'

'*Please*, Fritz,' Berg begged. 'Just one small hole to test my theory.'

'What theory?' Brunel demanded, busily raking over his vegetable plot to remove Berg's footprints.

'That the topsoil is deeper in some places than others.'

'There's no more than about thirty centimetres of soil anywhere,' Brunel declared. 'Go down two spade depths and you hit granite.'

'Max didn't hit granite on the corner of his plot when he dug a hole for me.'

'Well, you get Kluge to dig another hole in his plot. I'm not messing up mine. Not now that it's nice and clear for the winter.'

'Only a small hole,' Berg pleaded. 'I could easily fill it in again with my good arm.'

Brunel proudly surveyed the expanse of neatly raked bare earth that was his plot. Not a trace of weed or vegetable was to be seen. It was the way he liked it. It was easy to keep tidy. Rows of vegetables made life difficult, and luckily the topsoil wasn't deep enough for those winter vegetables such as leeks and parsnips which stayed in the ground for months and always looked a mess. He sighed. 'Where do you want me to dig this hole?'

'Just here,' Berg replied, measuring out ten paces into the middle of the plot and leaving deep footprints where Brunel had just raked. He scratched an 'X' in the soil with a stick.

'Well,' said Brunel grudgingly. 'So long as it's the only hole you want.'

'Oh, it is,' said Berg eagerly.

Brunel looked suspiciously at Berg. 'Is this anything to do with an escape plan?'

'Well, yes. Sort of.'

'I hope it doesn't involve me.'

'But of course it does. Remember how we used to talk about escaping together? Max, you, and me?'

'That was before I discovered just how much of a liability you can be,' Brunel retorted.

'Dig the hole please, Fritz, and we'll talk about it later.'

Brunel grimaced and started digging while Berg cast an

anxious glance at Sergeant Finch who was sitting in his watchtower.

'I won't get much further than this,' Brunel commented when he had reached a depth of about eighteen inches.

Berg urged Brunel to keep digging.

The hole Brunel dug was small – no wider than his spade – but, to his surprise, he succeeded in reaching a depth of two feet without encountering rock. Berg looked eagerly on.

'Give me your rake,' said Berg excitedly.

Brunel handed the gardening tool to Berg, who stood the handle upright in the bottom of the hole. He held it awkwardly with his good hand and pushed down. To Brunel's astonishment, two feet of the rake's wooden handle disappeared into the ground before it encountered rock.

'You see?' said Berg, looking very pleased with himself as he withdrew the rake and started kicking soil into the hole. 'There's more than a metre of topsoil on this part of your plot.'

'I don't want to attempt an escape with you,' Brunel warned.

Berg chuckled. 'All right then. But there's no reason why you shouldn't grow root vegetables here next year.'

Brunel looked pained. 'There're two very good reasons why I shouldn't grow root vegetables anywhere next year. Firstly, we'll be liberated before next year. Secondly, I can't stand root vegetables – either to eat or look at.'

Kruger's expression was inscrutable as he studied the neatly drawn map of the camp and grounds that Berg had proudly spread out on his desk. 'Very pretty,' he remarked. 'Do I hang it on my wall or what?'

'I shouldn't do that, commander,' said Berg worriedly. 'The fault line might give the game away if the British saw it.'

'What game? What fault line?'

Berg traced his finger along a finely shaded pencil line

178

that started at the eastern end of the hall and ran south-wards across the vegetable plots and under the perimeter fence. 'I'm certain that there's a fault in the granite stratum, commander. By that I mean a step in the layer of rock. It's now filled in with soil. My guess is that the step runs beneath the hall and out across the grounds.'

'A step?'

'It's where the entire stratum has fractured and lifted about two metres on one side. It probably happened during an earthquake shortly after the last ice age when the land recovered from the weight of the ice. It's quite a common phenomenon where land has been covered by ice. Norway is still lifting a few centimetres each century.'

'All very interesting for one of your geology instruction courses,' Kruger murmured politely. 'Let me know when you'll be bringing the subject up and I shall make a point of attending.'

Berg stared at Kruger in surprise. 'Oh, I wasn't thinking of that, commander.'

'Then what is the purpose of this drawing?'

'I'm sorry, commander, but I thought that was obvious. If the fault is continuous, it means that we can dig a tunnel along it.'

Kruger looked sharply at Berg and saw that the young officer was serious. 'I think, Berg,' he said slowly, 'that you had better show me what you're talking about.'

Kruger and Berg reached the eastern end of the terrace and leaned on the stone-balled parapet. They watched the activity on the vegetable plots as the prisoners took advantage of the mild November afternoon to finish preparing the ground for the winter. To the left of the two men, a party of prisoners were busily sawing and chopping broken branches into three-foot lengths for burning in the boiler. Each piece was added to the growing mountain of timber stacked against the wall of the servants' quarters. Two guards were patrolling the southern perimeter fence, and Sergeant Finch was sitting in his favourite position on the rickety firewatching tower where he could see everything that was going on and translate every innocent activity into an element of the mass breakout which he knew was imminent.

'We're standing right over the fault now,' said Berg, speaking in a conspiratorial whisper even though there was no one nearby.

'*If* it extends under the hall,' Kruger pointed out.

'I'm positive that it does, commander. It stretches for a long way. I don't want to point, but you see that outcrop of rock on the skyline in the field just beyond the watchtower? I think that's part of the fault where the wind has eroded away the topsoil.'

'All right,' said Kruger. 'Assuming that you're right, why isn't the fault visible across the grounds of the hall?'

'That's simple,' Berg replied. 'Over the centuries, rain has washed soil down from the hills which has silted up against the side of the fault. Also, it's a safe bet that Harold Brocklebank had any visible outcrops earthed over when the grounds were landscaped.'

Kruger lit a cheroot and inhaled slowly while staring thoughtfully across the grounds. 'How deep could the tunnel be?' he asked at length.

'No deeper than the lower stratum of rock, of course,' said Berg. 'Which is about two metres below the surface. That won't be a problem because ninety per cent of the tunnel's length will be underneath the vegetable plots, which the British never inspect, of course. Ventilation ducts can be easily arranged at intervals, disguised as compost heaps with straw over them – that sort of thing.' He glanced sideways at Kruger's face in the hope of seeing a flicker of enthusiasm for the project, but the U-boat commander maintained his usual disinterested expression as he studied the line the tunnel would follow.

'It wouldn't be enough to end the tunnel on the other side of the wire,' Kruger pointed out. 'You would have to continue under the road and come up on the other side of that dry-stone wall.'

Sensing approval of his scheme, Berg nodded enthusiastically. 'Also, the wall would hide the opening from the camp, commander.'

'Which means that the tunnel will have to be at least two hundred metres long. Correct?'

'About that,' Berg agreed.

'How much soil would have to be removed?'

'About one hundred cubic metres, commander. Spread over all the vegetable plots, it would add no more than five centimetres to their overall level – which will never show because winter digging raises the level of the soil by aeration anyway.'

Kruger dropped his cheroot and ground the butt with his heel. 'All right, Berg. I'll convene a meeting of the escape committee for tomorrow. I shall want you, Brunel and Kluge to attend as well.'

Berg watched apprehensively as Brenda nibbled away at his plaster cast with a pair of sharp scissors. She managed to slice away two inches of plaster, exposing pallid and puckered skin.

'Did you see Grizedale Hall being built?' asked Berg. It was a question he had been carefully rehearsing since he had learned that Brenda was a local girl. He winced as she thrust cold steel between his tender forearm skin and the unyielding plaster cast.

'Certainly not,' said Brenda sharply. 'It was built around the turn of the century. Do I look that old?'

'I'm sorry,' said Berg apologetically.

'God, this is tough. What did they mix into it? Cement?'

'I don't know. I was unconscious when it was put on.'

'Usually it goes soft in water.'

A large piece of plaster fell away and landed painfully on Berg's toe. He made no complaint.

'Of course,' said Brenda, working the scissors vigorously back and forth under the plaster and against Berg's newly healed bone, 'I used to come here a lot when I was going out with old Brocklebank's chauffeur.'

'That must seem like a long time ago,' said Berg. He suddenly realized that he had said the wrong thing again and added hastily, 'I mean – there have been many changes. The war and such things.'

'Oh gosh, yes,' said Brenda, wrenching away some more plaster and returning to the attack with her scissors. 'The parties that old Brocklebank used to throw!' She giggled. 'Harry and me used to get quite tiddly on the wine that was left over.'

'Tiddly?'

'Drunk. You know.'

'Ah yes.'

Brenda gave an extra hard push with the scissors. The remains of the plaster cast suddenly split without warning. The scissors slipped and she stabbed Berg so hard that one blade sank an inch into his delicate skin. He gave a loud yell of pain and yanked his arm away with the scissors still embedded in his flesh. He clamped his hand over the wound and the action slashed the scissors' free blade across his knuckles. What was left of the plaster around his arm began staining red with blood.

'Oh hell!' Brenda exclaimed, snatching the scissors out of the wound. 'I'm terribly sorry, hauptmann, really I am. You must think I'm an awful clot.'

'It is nothing,' said Berg calmly, as though being stabbed was an everyday occurrence. 'You must not worry please.'

Brenda continued to apologize profusely while she bathed the stab wound in a dish of saline solution. Berg watched woodenly as tendrils of blood gradually stopped oozing out of his arm.

'I'm afraid it'll need at least four stitches,' said Brenda, still red with embarrassment as she examined her handiwork.

Berg left the sickbay ten minutes later. His arm felt curiously light without the plastercast, but the pleasure of being free of its weight was offset by the dull ache from the stab wound and the stitches.

As he crossed the courtyard, something started nagging at the back of his mind. Perhaps it was something that Nurse Hobson had said? But he wasn't sure.

The three members of the escape committee, Kruger, Hauptmann Paul Ulbrick, and Hauptmann Karl Shriver, watched intently as Brunel and Kluge helped Berg stand a table on its side on the floor of the music room. Brunel's expression suggested that he disapproved of the demonstration.

'What happened to your arm, Berg?' inquired Kruger, noticing Berg's bandage.

'Nurse Hobson stabbed me when she —'

'Well, I'm pleased to see that you managed to ward off the blow with your arm. Continue with your demonstration.'

Berg cleared his throat and pointed to the table's now vertical top. 'This is the side of the fault in the granite stratum, gentlemen, and the floor is the base of the fault. That will give us a stable floor and side to the tunnel.'

'The fault is filled in with topsoil, I presume?' Shriver queried, glancing at the sketch plan in front of him.

'Yes, hauptmann.'

'How do you propose shoring-up the tunnel?'

'That's simple,' Berg replied. He nodded to Brunel.

The diminutive naval officer sighed. He leaned a four-feet-long piece of floorboarding against the table and crawled through the triangular-shaped arch formed by the table and the floorboard. He scrambled to his feet and pointedly brushed the dust off his trousers.

'I estimate that we will need two boards or lengths of straight branch for every metre of the tunnel,' said Berg. 'We'll be just below the surface so there won't be much weight of soil to support.'

Ulbrick broke the brief silence that followed. 'It all seems too simple,' he observed.

Brunel's nod of agreement earned him a scowl from Berg.

'I hardly think two hundred metres of tunnel could be described as simple,' said Kruger drily. 'What we have to decide is whether or not Hauptmann Berg's proposal is worth pursuing.'

'It's an interesting idea,' said Shriver, studying the plan again. 'But I see many problems. The plan doesn't show the entrance to the tunnel. Presumably, you intend cutting down through the floor of a room in the servants' quarters? Sergeant Finch's snap searches are extremely thorough. Concealing an opening from him over a long period is going to be impossible. Also, how does one transfer one hundred cubic metres of soil from the tunnel to the vegetable plots?'

'Not all the minor details have been worked out,' said Berg.

Shriver looked frosty. 'The location of the tunnel's entrance is hardly a minor detail, Berg.'

Brunel suppressed a snigger.

'Berg has proved that a tunnel is possible,' Kruger intervened. 'For the moment I propose instructing all prisoners to provide him with whatever co-operation he needs to complete his planning. Are we all in agreement with that?'

The escape committee remained silent. Kruger turned to Berg, Brunel and Kluge. 'So it's up to you and your two comrades now, Hauptmann Berg. We agree in principle with the tunnel, but that's all for the time being. Dismissed.'

Kruger waited until the door had closed behind the three men before speaking again.

'As you know, gentlemen, the old rumour about our transfer to Canada has started circulating again. But this time I have evidence that a number of our men have been sent there.'

The other members of the escape committee remained silent but Kruger saw the momentary flicker of apprehension in their eyes.

'This may be wishful thinking on my part,' Kruger continued. 'But I have a suspicion that the British may not be too keen to transfer this camp if we establish a reputation for habitual escaping – not when there's a neutral, unguarded border for us to cross into the United States. We will let Berg continue with his planning. If he comes up with a practical scheme, we will take it over and organize a mass breakout.'

For the next three days Berg wrestled with the question of where to start the tunnel. But no matter how many rough sketches he made of the hall's ground-floor plan, or how many times he and Kluge strolled around the grounds making mental notes of their paces, a solution to the problem eluded him. Also, his concentration was spoilt because, for some unaccountable reason, his thoughts kept returning to his conversation with Nurse Hobson when she had stabbed him.

'I've decided that I want nothing to do with your damned tunnel,' said Brunel the following Monday morning as he, Kluge, and Berg joined the dozen or so prisoners in the common room who were excitedly opening their letters and parcels. 'It sounds too dangerous for me.'

'Nothing much has been decided yet,' Kluge pointed out.

'That's what is worrying me.'

'Surely you want to escape?' said Berg.

'Not by digging a tunnel, I don't,' Brunel replied, ripping the wrapping paper off his parcel. 'And certainly not with an accident-prone liability like you.'

A prisoner clapped Berg on the back. 'Hey, Berg. We hear you're planning a mass escape. Any chance of Dormitory Six joining in?'

'My God!' Brunel yelped. 'Look what my sister's sent me!' He produced a bottle of Reisling from his food parcel and held it proudly aloft.

'You're lucky it didn't break,' a prisoner commented. 'Do we have a party tonight?'

'How about now?' another prisoner suggested.

'At 11 am?'

Berg stared at the bottle of wine. His eyes seemed to glaze over with shock. He suddenly grabbed Brunel by the arm. 'Fritz! I need your help!'

'You're not having my wine.'

'I don't want it. But I need your help downstairs.'

'In a minute.'

'No, now . . . ,' Berg insisted. '*Please*, Fritz.'

Brunel sighed. 'Very well then. Just so long as you don't expect me to start digging a tunnel.'

Berg excitedly clattered down the stairs with Brunel in tow.

'We'll need some tools from my workshop first,' said Berg breathlessly. 'It was crazy of me not to have noticed it before. Crazy.'

'What was?' Brunel demanded, having to break into a trot to keep up with Berg.

'What's the one thing that's missing from this place, Fritz?'

'Women?'

'No. No. Much more important than women.'

'What could be more important than women?'

The two men entered Berg's workshop.

'Nothing is more important than women,' Brunel declared, as Berg rummaged among his tools and produced a home-made cold chisel. 'Except wine maybe.'

Berg beamed delightedly. 'That's right, Fritz – wine.'

'What?'

'Grizedale Hall hasn't got any wine cellars! And yet a mansion like this *must* have been built with them!'

Berg kept watch while Brunel knelt down and worked the cold chisel into a joint in the quarry-tiled floor. The room they were in had been part of the butler's parlour in the days when Grizedale Hall had been a stately home.

'Try lifting now,' Berg urged.

'I haven't got the chisel right in yet!' Brunel hissed in reply. 'Just you keep your eyes and ears open! God knows why I get myself involved in your lunatic schemes.'

Brunel prised upwards, slipped his fingertips under the edge of the tile and eased it up. Underneath was the hall's original subfloor consisting of a layer of sand over a bed of rammed hardcore.

'Try one of the tiles in the centre,' Berg suggested, hiding his disappointment.

'I tell you, it's a waste of time.'

'*Please*, Fritz. Only, I can't do much with this arm since Nurse Hobson stabbed me.'

Brunel replaced the tile and went to work on one that Brunel pointed out. It lifted easily to reveal fresh, white concrete beneath. He stared at it in amazement.

'You see!' said Berg triumphantly.

Brunel made no answer but set to work to lift a neighbouring quarry tile. It took him less than five minutes to expose a rectangle of concrete set into the hardcore subfloor. The concrete was a metre square and it emitted a hollow ring when Brunel rapped it with the cold chisel.

'Will it lift in one piece?' asked Berg.

'I don't know,' Brunel replied, tapping the concrete again. 'It sounds thin enough. We ought to report this to the commander.'

'Try lifting it,' Berg begged.

By now Brunel was curious to see what was under the

concrete. He levered upwards very carefully and was able to lift the thin slab of concrete in one piece to reveal a wooden trapdoor complete with brass lifting ring. He grinned up at Berg. 'Sorry, Dietrich. Looks like you were right. This has to lead to the wine cellar. The British made a lousy job of concreting it over.'

Berg forgot about his lookout duties. He knelt down beside Brunel and helped him lift the trapdoor. It opened easily on oiled hinges, releasing a musty smell of dry rot. Berg nearly dropped his matches in his excitement but he eventually managed to strike one. The light flickered on a steep flight of timber steps that disappeared into the darkness.

Before Brunel could counsel caution, Berg lowered himself feet first through the opening and started to descend the stairs. As his head reached floor level, there was the sound of collapsing, rotten timber. Berg looked at Brunel in panic. The sudden grab he made at the edge of the hatchway was a fraction of a second too late. Brunel was also too late trying to seize Berg's wrist. The army officer gave a cry of terror and dropped with a sickening thud on to the stone floor of the cellar ten feet below.

'Amazing,' said Ulbrick, holding his candle high and peering the length of the cellar between the rows of wine bottle racks that were stacked high with empty bottles. 'To think that this has been here all the time.'

'It's lined with lead but I don't believe it will be difficult to cut through,' said Kruger. 'Most important, its volume is double the volume of the soil from the tunnel. And those racks will make excellent shoring boards.'

Ulbrick nodded. 'Will there be enough air to seal a digging party in here for an entire shift?'

Kruger nodded. 'Possibly. While Berg was waiting for the plaster cast on his ankle to set, he told me that it ought to be possible to dig four metres per day. I hope that can be bettered.'

The two men climbed the ladder out of the cellar and watched while Brunel and two prisoners concealed the trap-door. Brunel had bonded the original quarry tiles to a square piece of plywood which dropped neatly into place. He checked that the quarry tiles over the trap were flush with the floor and quickly rubbed some wood ash into the joints. The operation took less than thirty seconds. There was no sign that the floor had been disturbed when he stood up.

'Excellent, Brunel,' said Kruger approvingly. 'Incidentally, you did a good job lifting Berg out of the cellar. The British accepted his story that he fell over the step outside his workshop.'

'Thank you, commander.'

Kruger nodded. 'This evening we shall draw up the lookout rotas and the digging party shifts. We start cutting the tunnel tomorrow.'

Brunel was surprised. 'Surely we'll be waiting for Haupt-mann Berg to come out of hospital before starting work, commander?'

Kruger shook his head. 'Major Reynolds told me that with a septic arm and a broken ankle, Berg isn't expected out of Barrow General for at least four days. That's provid-ing he doesn't come to any more harm in hospital. I want forty metres of tunnel excavated for him by then. You'll be in charge of the digging parties.'

Brunel looked nervously from Kruger to Ulbrick and tried to read some meaning into their impassive ex-pressions. 'It's very kind of you, commander, but I'm sure Berg would prefer to make the first cut himself. He worked hard on planning –'

'What Berg would or would not prefer is of little conse-quence,' said Kruger crisply. 'Work on the tunnel starts tomorrow.'

Berg hopped slowly and painfully down the ladder into the cellar by taking most of his weight on his good arm. His left foot was completely swathed in a bulbous plaster cast that was about as big as a bucket and roughly the same shape. It meant that it was too large to fit between the rungs of the ladder. Fortunately, Nurse Hobson's stab wound was healing satisfactorily. Brunel handed him down his crutch and Kruger steadied his elbow as he tucked it under his armpit and pivotted around to survey his surroundings.

Two naked light bulbs illuminated the cellar. The wine bottle racks had been dismantled and their component timber planks stacked neatly against one wall. At the far end two prisoners were treading down a heap of soil. But it was the triangular hole cut in the wall three feet above the floor that held Berg's attention. It was over three feet wide at its base and of about the same height on one side. A prisoner was hauling on a cord that led into the opening.

Without saying a word, Berg hobbled forward and stooped to peer along the tunnel. It had only the one vertical wall which, as he had predicted, consisted of a cross-section through a fractured granite stratum. The tunnel ran straight for fifteen metres before curving to the left. It was lit at five-metre intervals by low wattage light bulbs that were recessed into the roof. The shoring boards were cut to the right length and precisely positioned. Two parallel timber planks with raised sides served as rails to guide the truckle-mounted box that the prisoner working at the tunnel entrance was hauling towards the cellar.

'You're to be congratulated, Berg,' said Kruger. 'We found the fault exactly where your measurements said it was. We've dug twenty-five metres. I had hoped to have dug more by now. The first ten metres was no problem, but now we're running into shale and small rocks.'

'Thank you, commander,' said Berg, straightening up. Above the opening was a noticeboard bearing the names of the prisoners working the four-hour shifts. Everything was well organized and functioning efficiently.

'Well?' Kruger inquired. 'What do you think?'

Berg did his best to hide his disappointment. The tunnel project had been his pet scheme and one that he had looked forward to starting.

'Well?' Kruger repeated.

'Twenty-five meters is a remarkable achievement,' said Berg. 'I'm very grateful to you.'

The box laden with soil trundled to a standstill in the tunnel opening. The prisoner unhooked its cords and connected them up to an empty box. He rapped twice on the rails and the box disappeared down the tunnel.

'The railway is the only modification we've made to your original design,' said Kruger. 'It makes removing the debris that much easier.'

'Yes, of course,' Berg replied, hoping that he didn't sound disappointed. 'How many men are working at the face?'

'Two – just as you suggested. There is one cutting the soil away and another loading it into the box.'

The two men watched the prisoner add the contents of the box to the heap of soil and debris that was being trodden down.

'My name isn't on the rota, commander,' said Berg respectfully.

'That's correct,' Kruger replied.

Berg peered at the noticeboard again. 'It says that Brunel is the engineer in charge of the tunnel, commander. Yet Brunel was against an escape.'

'He's not now that I've discussed the matter with him,' said Kruger cryptically.

'But the tunnel was my idea, commander, therefore I thought that –'

'I can understand your disappointment, Berg,' said Kruger. 'But you are in no state to go crawling along tunnels just yet, whereas Brunel is very fit and very small. Besides, I have some much more important work for you. I will visit you in your workshop after lunch.'

'This is an odd request from Kruger, sir,' Sergeant Finch commented, dropping a letter in Reynolds' in-tray. 'He wants to redesign the layout of the allotments.'

'*Commander* Kruger,' Reynolds stressed, picking up the letter and reading it. 'He may be the enemy, but I guess we should stick to the formalities. It's warm in here, huh?'

'Very pleasant, sir. I wish there was a radiator in my office.'

'Have a word with Commander Kruger. I guess it wouldn't be any trouble for his engineering officers to fix you up with one of the unused radiators from the dormitories.' Reynolds finished reading the letter. 'What's so odd about this?'

Finch shrugged. 'It just struck me as odd, sir.'

'It would be odd if he wanted to do it during the growing season. November is about the best time.' Reynolds wrote 'OK' at the foot of letter, signed it, and tossed it into his out-tray. He looked up and saw Finch's disapproving expression. 'What's the matter, sergeant?'

'Nothing, sir.'

'Aw, come on. I know that look. You have my permission to speak freely.'

'I think you give in far too easily to that Jerr- to Commander Kruger, sir.'

'I don't give in to anyone,' Reynolds corrected. 'Either I agree with a request or I don't agree.'

'You always agree to his requests.'

'He's never made an unreasonable one. Okay, so maybe I shouldn't've let him take over the distribution of mail and food parcels, and maybe there is too much prisoner control in the kitchens – but it's taken a load off our shoulders. And yours in particular.'

'I wasn't thinking of that, sir. I think he's planning something.'

'Sure he's planning something,' Reynolds retorted irritably. 'He's always planning something. And it's your job to find out what it is – which you won't find out in here talking to me.'

Kruger picked up the unfinished miniature pendulum clock. It was barely the size of a matchbox. The tiny Gothic numerals on the varnished clock face were a work of art in themselves. 'Very clever, Berg,' he admired. 'Some of these parts must have been virtually impossible to carve, especially with your arm and two missing fingers.'

'Oh, I manage, commander,' Berg replied self-effacingly. Kruger's presence in his workshop made him ill at ease. He talked to conceal his nervousness. 'I learned to manage without those two fingers years ago, and I did most of the work on that clock before Nurse Hobson stabbed me. I used floorboard knots for the parts that have to take wear because they're hard. It took me three weeks to make –'

'I'm sorry that you won't be able to work on the tunnel,' Kruger interrupted.

Berg smiled apologetically. 'Oh, please don't worry, commander. I could never have made that sort of progress by myself.'

Kruger hesitated. 'Tell me, Berg. Just how keen are you on escaping?'

Berg looked surprised. 'Very keen, commander. Kluge, Brunel and I used to talk about nothing else. And now with these Canada rumours. Why do you ask?'

Kruger shrugged. 'I'm sorry, Berg. I misjudged you. I had formed the opinion that you really prefer solving problems, that escaping was just another problem to be solved and that you wouldn't be so interested in escaping once you had solved the problem.'

Berg shook his head. 'All three of us want to escape more than anything else in the world, commander.'

'In that case, you will need three of these,' said Kruger, placing a civilian identity card on Berg's workbench.

'That's our last one. You'll have to make replicas because I don't want that one to leave the camp.'

Berg opened the card and was relieved to see that it did not have to bear a photograph of the owner. He opened a drawer and took out a magnifying glass, which he used to examine the identity card. 'It's poor quality paper. I don't think that will be too much trouble. But the printing. . . .' He peered closely at the card. 'Well . . . I suppose it will be possible to make three copies.'

'How?'

'Well, there's only one method and that's hand-lettering with Indian ink. Kluge is brilliant at lettering. He does all my clock faces.'

'I want you to carve printing blocks, Berg. All three cards must be identical.'

Berg blinked in surprise. 'Blocks, commander? But that would take weeks!'

'You won't be escaping until the spring.'

'But I thought –'

'That I would permit a winter escape? An individual escape with the officer provided with the necessary travel warrants, perhaps – but not three of you. You would attract too much attention and be forced to sleep rough. I can't allow that in the winter. Besides, your arm and ankle won't be strong enough for at least another three months.'

Berg was so shocked that he momentarily forgot who he was arguing with. 'But my arm and ankle are healing nicely. They'll be perfectly –'

'I don't like having my orders questioned,' Kruger observed mildly. 'Now, about your identity cards. You're a genius at wood-carving, Berg, therefore I do not think that making blocks will present you with problems that you can't overcome.'

Berg examined the identity card and made a conscious effort to focus his mind on the problem. 'I suppose it might be possible to carve founts of different print styles,' he said.

Quite suddenly he became absorbed as his fertile brain raced ahead, anticipating problems and seeking solutions. 'Yes, that's it, commander. I could make a wooden *forme* to hold the individual founts and set one line at a time. It might even be possible to make a proper platen and ink the *forme* with a hand-roller. In fact, making a wooden printing press wouldn't be that difficult. We could print all sorts of documents. A camp newspaper?'

Kruger smiled. 'Let's not get too far ahead of our immediate objectives, Berg.'

'And with a printing press, commander, we'd be able to print dozens of identity cards – not just three.'

Kruger nodded and picked up the identity card. 'Yes, I had thought of that, Berg.' He moved to the door. 'I'll get Willi to check the questionnaires. I believe there are two ex-printers among the prisoners.'

'Yes, commander. Also it would be a great help if Konig and Endelmann could help make the founts. They're fantastic wood-carvers.'

'I'll have a word with them,' Kruger promised as he left the workshop.

Berg made no reply: he was already deeply absorbed, preparing a preliminary sketch of a home-made printing press.

Finch sat in his rickety firewatching tower with Corporal White and glowered suspiciously down on the whirl of activity taking place on the reorganized vegetable plots. Over fifty prisoners, working to string lines, were busily treading new paths between the plots and moving wheel-barrow loads of rotting compost around. Even the toolshed that the prisoners had built for their gardening implements was being dismantled and moved to a new position.

'Bloody odd, the whole thing,' Finch muttered to Chalky.

'What's that, sarge?'

'All that work.'

'What about it?'

'It's all so bloody pointless.'

Corporal White glanced down at the vegetable plots. 'Looks a lot tidier than the old layout. All them compost heaps in a straight line. Funny how the Jerries like everything all neat and tidy.' He lowered his voice. 'I expect you've heard the little whisper that I've heard, sarge?'

Finch wasn't particularly interested; Corporal White was always hearing little whispers. 'Oh?' he said boredly, watching a prisoner position a compost heap so that it was perfectly aligned with all the other compost heaps. 'What sort of whisper?'

'It's only a rumour of course, sarge.'

Finch began to get angry. 'Okay, so let's have it.'

'That they're planning a mass escape.'

There was a pause before Finch replied. 'Are you certain?'

Corporal White nodded sagely and glanced over the side of the watchtower. 'It seems that they're going to grow giant runner beans and use them to pole-vault over the wire, sarge.'

While Sergeant Finch was threatening Corporal White with extreme physical violence, Kruger – grim-faced and silent – was striding along the corridors towards the servants' quarters. There was no indication which of the loafing prisoners were lookouts – none gave any obvious signal – but Kluge was already waiting expectantly for him by the wine cellar's open trapdoor when he appeared in the butler's parlour.

'More shale?' queried Kruger.

'Worse,' said Kluge tiredly, wiping the grime from his sweat-streaked face. 'Brunel thinks it's solid rock.'

Kruger went quickly down the ladder into the cellar. The evidence of the problems that the digging shifts had encountered was the large heap of rocks – some were small boulders – that had been removed from the tunnel.

A prisoner helped Kruger change out of his uniform into a pair of working trousers and a muddy sweater. He also slipped out of his shoes and socks because he wouldn't be needing them – there was nowhere to stand up in the tunnel.

'Brunel's waiting for you at the face, commander,' said Kluge as his commanding officer carefully laid himself chest down on the wooden passenger trolley. 'Don't forget to keep your feet tucked in.'

'Ready,' said Kruger cryptically.

Kluge jabbed an electric bell-push button three times. The cord attached to Kruger's trolley tightened. Helped by a push from Kluge, the trolley began rumbling jerkily along the tunnel, bumping over the joints in the wood track.

Kruger instinctively lowered his head and pulled his shoulders in. He was by no means a broadly built man yet there was barely enough room for his body to clear the shoring timbers. Despite the ventilator pipes whose openings were concealed by the compost heaps, the air in the fifty-metre length of tunnel was dank and humid: it stank of sweat from the men who had laboured in it for the past two weeks and reminded Kruger of the smell of a U-boat's interior after several weeks on patrol. He chanced a brief glance ahead and saw Brunel's face illuminated in the pool of electric light at the tunnel's face. The tiny naval officer was sweating as he hauled on the cord, pulling Kruger towards him. He stopped work when the trolley drew level with his feet.

Kruger lifted himself off the trolley and discovered that there was enough headroom for him to kneel. 'What's the trouble, Brunel?'

'This is the trouble,' said Brunel savagely. He gave the face an angry blow with his palm and made room for Kruger to squeeze alongside him. 'A boulder. God knows how far down it goes.'

Kruger ran his fingertips over the rock's surface. It was a slab of delicately shaded pink Coniston granite. Massive and immovable. 'How about going round it?' he suggested.

'It'll be impossible,' Brunel replied. 'We're only half a metre beneath the surface here anyway and the ground above is Werner Leyden's plot – the steepest part of the slope. If we dig to one side, we're certain to break through above ground level. And trying to go round it will mean putting a junction in the track and excavating enough room for someone to transfer the trollies from one track to the other. It'll double the time taken to empty just one box, which is taking long enough as the tunnel gets longer.'

Kruger rarely resorted to cursing, but he felt that an expletive was justified on this occasion. After that both men were silent for some moments.

'So that's it,' Kruger murmured phlegmatically. 'Well . . . at least it's kept our minds occupied.'

Brunel swore and ineffectually punched the rock face. 'So what do we do now? Fill it all in to keep our minds occupied?'

Kruger thought for a moment. 'How about getting Berg to take a look?'

'You think he's capable of shifting half a dozen tons of granite boulder?'

'I think he's capable of coming up with a suggestion,' Kruger replied equitably.

'Explosives would shift it,' said Berg brightly, steadying himself on his crutch while a prisoner brushed the dirt from the tunnel off his clothes.

Kruger groaned. 'I had hoped for a practical suggestion from you.'

Berg looked hurt. 'But that is a practical suggestion, commander.'

'Even if we could get hold of explosives,' said Kruger icily, 'has it occurred to you that even Sergeant Finch could hardly fail to notice an explosion right in the middle of Werner Leyden's cabbage patch?'

Berg thought for a moment. 'There are a number of difficulties with using explosives,' he admitted. 'But it still remains the quickest and easiest way of breaking up that boulder.' He smiled at the circle of faces that were staring at him in the cellar. 'I made the study of explosives my hobby when I was at school and college.'

'Is that how you lost your fingers?' Kruger inquired.

'Yes, commander. Would you like to hear about some of the various explosions I have been responsible for?'

Not only had Leutnant Walter Hilgard served on the *Bismarck*, but he was built like it as well. Unlike the *Bismarck*, he was a survivor – helped to a considerable extent by his 220 pounds of bone and muscle. Before the war he had been a chef at the Kaiserhof Hotel in Berlin and often boasted about the times when he had cooked for Hitler. The Fuehrer's diet and that of the prisoners had much in common in that it was largely vegetarian. For that reason, Kruger had appointed Hilgard as Grizedale Hall's officer-in-charge of catering. Complaints about Hilgard's cooking were rare but that was due more to his fiery temper and dexterity with a meat cleaver than to his culinary talents.

It was his meat cleaver that he rested a massive arm on when he saw Berg hobble into his domain. 'If you're another complaint about my *crêpe suzettes*, I'll cut your bloody head off and boil it for brawn,' he threatened.

'No, I haven't come about that, Hilgard.'

'You try making *crêpe suzettes* with dried eggs. It's not easy.'

'They were delicious,' Berg enthused, saying the first thing that came into his head. 'Nice and crunchy.'

'So what do you want?'

'You've got a bag of potassium nitrate in here which I –'

'I've got what!' Hilgard boomed in astonishment, his

voice rattling the saucepans hanging on the wall of the kitchen.

'Shh!' said Berg, glancing nervously at the open door where two guards were talking. He swung his weight forward on his crutch so that he could whisper in Hilgard's ear. 'You've got a large bag of potassium nitrate. I need it please.'

'I've got no such thing in my kitchen! I never use chemicals in my cooking.'

'Listen,' said Berg patiently. 'When I did my stint in here, I remember that there was a ten-pound bag of saltpetre in –'

'You can't have that!' said Hilgard indignantly. 'I need that for curing the rabbits.'

'But you don't need it. We hardly ever snare rabbits any more – we've wiped them all out.'

Neither Berg or Hilgard saw Kruger approaching.

'I'm not parting with my saltpetre,' the naval officer declared. 'If you've snared any rabbits, then you should bring them to me for curing and not try to do it yourself.'

'What's the trouble, leutnant?' Kruger inquired.

'This idiot wants my saltpetre, commander.'

'That's correct, leutnant,' said Kruger. 'I would be grateful if you would kindly let him have it sometime today when it's quiet.'

Hilgard gaped at Kruger. He was about to argue but changed his mind. 'All right,' he said sulkily. 'I'll bring it over. But there's no one in the camp as good as me at curing rabbits.'

Kruger nodded his thanks and left.

'By the way, Hilgard,' said Berg. 'Do you ever use sodium chloride in your cooking?'

Hilgard scowled angrily. 'Of course not. No chemicals – that's my rule – even if I could get them.'

'Just as I thought,' Berg murmured. 'Sodium chloride is common salt.'

Sergeant Finch stopped wheeling his bicycle. He was standing directly over the spot where the troublesome granite boulder lay. He sniffed deeply and looked suspiciously at Leyden and Willi. 'I can't smell a thing,' he declared. 'It's all your bloody imagination.'

'I'm sorry, sergeant,' said Leyden. 'I've been working this vegetable plot for two weeks now. Every time I come out here, I can smell gas.'

'I can smell it too,' Willi chipped in.

Finch sniffed again. 'There's nothing. Just clean Lake District air. Which you lot don't deserve, I might add.'

'I know gas when I smell it,' said Leyden.

Finch looked exasperated. 'How can there be a smell of gas out here? We're a hundred yards from the kitchens.'

'Maybe the gas pipe goes under the garden?' Willi suggested.

'But the road is up there!' said Finch, gesturing in the direction of the hall. 'Why would the gas company route their main this way, for God's sake?'

'Maybe Harold Brocklebank insisted that the pipe was laid this way?' Willi observed. 'After all, he didn't allow the kitchens to be built in the main hall, did he? Perhaps he was scared of the fire risk.'

'All right. All right,' said Finch impatiently, wheeling his bicycle back to the drive. 'I'll report it, but I still say that it's your imagination.'

Berg peered through the boiler's mica inspection port. 'All right,' he said, straightening up and hobbling out of the way. 'It's ready.'

The prisoner in charge of the boiler swung the furnace door open and used a pair of long-handled stoker's tongs to drag several blazing baulks of timber on to the boiler room floor. 'How much do you need?' he asked Berg.

'About two kilos.'

The prisoner grunted and busied himself with a shovel,

scraping lumps of smouldering charcoal off the burning timbers.

'That's fine,' said Berg when there was enough charcoal scattered on the floor to fill a bucket.

The two men broke some of the larger lumps to make sure that they were blackened right through and spent five minutes pounding the charcoal to a fine dust with coal hammers.

Berg had a bag of good-quality charcoal powder tied under the armrest of his crutch when he hobbled out of the boiler room. He was also looking very pleased with himself. All he needed now was sulphur. He knew where to find that: there were several sticks of it in the greenhouses where it was used for fumigation purposes.

The chill, cutting edge of the November wind sweeping across the fells from the north-east brought with it the first flurries of snow.

Reynolds stood with Kruger and Willi in the middle of the vegetable plots. He turned up the collar of his greatcoat and sniffed while Kruger looked questioningly at him.

'Nothing,' said Reynolds. He sniffed again. 'No. Nothing at all.'

'I can't smell it so strongly today,' Willi admitted.

'Yeah,' said Reynolds, anxious to get back to his office. 'I guess the wind is too strong, huh, commander?'

'I expect so,' Kruger replied. 'The smell was certainly more noticeable yesterday.'

Reynolds thrust his hands in his pockets and thought for a moment. 'Okay. I'll report it to the gas company. Let's see what they say.'

Kruger, Ulbrick and Brunel watched intently as Berg sprinkled two tablespoonfuls of saltpetre on to a brick. He made a hollow in the centre of the heap of white powder and mixed in smaller quantities of the sulphur and the charcoal dust. The concoction turned black as he stirred the ingredients together.

'There we are,' said Berg proudly. 'Twenty grammes of black powder – or gunpowder as it's better known. Stand back please, gentlemen. Oh, please don't worry – it only explodes when it's ignited in a confined space such as the breech of a musket or cannon.' He grinned and added, 'Or underground.'

The three officers took a step backwards. Berg remained seated but leaned back in his chair. His plaster-encased ankle stuck out awkwardly from under his workbench. He struck a match and plunged the burning head into the powder. There was a loud whoosh and a burst of brilliant white light that lasted for less than a second. Sparks and lumps of burning gunpowder splattered across Berg's workbench. He extinguished them by deftly flicking them with a handkerchief. The draught from an open window quickly cleared the acrid fumes from the workshop.

Berg proudly examined the blackened patch on the brick. 'You see, gentlemen? Not a trace of the powder left. I've got enough ingredients for five kilos of gunpowder which I've calculated is just the right amount to shatter the rock. Of course, we'll have to remove the railway track and shoring boards from at least ten metres of the tunnel – and fill it in. We don't want any traces around for the British to find when they inspect the crater.'

Brunel thought he could smell something burning.

'How will you ignite the charge?' Kruger asked.

'That's simple, commander. I'll imbed an exposed torch bulb filament in a priming charge. Apply a battery to the wires, the filament glows, sets off the priming charge – and bang – no more rock.'

Brunel became convinced that he could smell something burning.

'Yes,' Kruger persisted. 'But where will you operate the charge from?'

'The tool shed.'

'Is that safe?'

'Fifty metres?' said Berg confidently. 'Oh yes. It won't be that big an explosion.'

'Just enough to shatter a twenty-tonne chunk of granite,' Ulbrick observed scathingly.

'That's right,' said Berg animatedly. 'Granite is brittle. The shock will probably shatter it into a dozen pieces, possibly more. When we fill in the crater, all we have to do is make sure that the fragments are buried where they won't be in the way.'

Ulbrick shook his head doubtfully. 'I still think it's the most lunatic idea –'

'I agree wholeheartedly,' Kruger interrupted. 'But right now it's the only one we've got. Either we try Berg's scheme or we abandon the tunnel.'

'Something's burning,' said Brunel, but no one took any notice of him.

'That's what's worrying me: that it *is* Berg's scheme,' said Ulbrick. 'They have a habit of going wrong.'

'Nothing can go wrong with this plan,' Berg declared. He twitched his nose and wondered if the burning smell was his imagination. 'I'm always extremely careful with explosives and take all the necessary precautions.'

'Berg,' said Brunel quietly.

'Yes?'

'I think some of that black powder went astray just now.'

'Really? Where?'

'Your plaster cast is on fire.'

The gas company engineer frowned over his maps, which he had unrolled on Major Reynolds' desk. 'I'll be honest with you, major, we just don't understand it. Maybe there's an old main down there that Harold Brocklebank had installed by the old Furness Gas Company. If so, we don't know anything about it. Their records were destroyed before the Great War, and there's nothing on our maps.'

'The pressure test showed that there's a leakage,' Reynolds pointed out.

'The loss was very slight,' said the engineer patiently. 'Well within tolerance. Personally, I think your POWs are playing a practical joke on you.'

'Not very practical if we can't see the point of it,' Reynolds observed. 'Okay, Mr Williams. Thank you for coming. We're sorry to have wasted your time.'

Willi's timing was perfect: he opened Kruger's door just as Corporal White was passing.

'Ah, Chalky. Do you have time for a drop of whisky?'

It was an offer Corporal White could not refuse, not even at eleven o'clock in the morning.

'This gas leak is annoying us,' Willi remarked as his guest tasted his drink.

'Why's that, Willi?'

'It's making us prisoners look such fools. The commander is very angry with us. We can smell gas and yet you British cannot. I have tried telling him that it's only to be expected, but he won't listen.'

The NCO was puzzled. 'Why should you be able to smell it and not us?'

'But it is only natural,' said Willi. 'We eat plenty of chocolate and you eat none.' He opened a drawer and produced a monster one-kilogramme bar of Swiss Toblerone. 'Surely you know that chocolate sharpens the sense of smell?'

Chalky shook his head numbly while goggling at the huge bar.

'It is true,' said Willi. 'My brother is a doctor. He told me. Chocolate improves your sense of smell, he said. You have heard that the Swiss keep their country very clean?'

Chalky nodded.

'They have to because they have a heightened sense of smell from eating so much chocolate,' said Willi, holding the bar out to Chalky. 'Try it if you don't believe me. You eat that chocolate and I am sure that you will be able to smell that gas leak.'

The bar disappeared inside Chalky's battledress blouse before Willi could blink. 'Perhaps I should try two bars?' Chalky suggested. 'Just in case one doesn't work.'

Willi opened his drawer again and produced a second bar which vanished as quickly as the first one.

'How long do you think it'll take to work?' Chalky queried.

'Oh, by about noon tomorrow.'

'And if I do smell gas, should I report it?'

'Oh definitely,' Willi murmured. 'It will be your duty to do so.'

Chalky fidgetted.

'Problem?'

'Well,' said Chalky reasonably. 'I'm going to feel a bit of a chump if I'm the only guard that smells this gas leak. Maybe if you let me have another couple of bars for me mates. . . .'

Willi sighed and opened his drawer for the third time.

Berg's bomb weighed nearly ten pounds and completely filled a wooden case the size of a shoebox.

To install it, Berg had to work at the tunnel face while lying flat on his stomach on the trolley. Ignoring the ache in his arm and ankle, he cut the string that secured the bomb to the trolley and slid it into the hole that Brunel had excavated beneath the slab of granite. He took special care not to damage the two lengths of fine enamelled copper wire that were connected to the bomb's firing charge. A final push with a board and the bomb was in position. He backed the trolley a few metres along the track while playing out the wires until one of the ventilation openings was above his head.

'Leyden!' he called softly.

'Ready,' Leyden's voice answered from the ventilation hole.

'I'm pushing the wires up now.'

Berg threaded the ends of the wires into the tube.

'Okay,' said Leyden. 'I've got them.'

There was a gentle tug on the wires. It took a minute for Berg to uncoil the sixty-metre lengths of wire and feed them through the ventilation tube. He rapped three times on one of the rails when he had finished, which was the signal for Brunel to haul him back into the cellar.

'All ready, commander,' he reported to Kruger as Brunel and one of his assistants helped him off the trolley.

'Excellent, Berg,' said Kruger. He turned to Brunel. 'All right. You had better start filling in. Ten metres back from the face should be more than enough. Correct, Berg?'

'Correct, commander.'

Kruger nodded. He looked regretfully at the glowing butt of his cheroot before dropping it and grinding it underfoot. 'All right, Berg,' he said. 'Get the wires connected up to the shed ready for tomorrow. After that I want to see what progress you've made with the printing press.'

'I think it's working, Willi,' said Chalky as he mounted the terrace steps. 'I ate half a bar this morning and I'm certain I could smell gas just now.'

'Yes,' said Willi drily. 'Your sense of smell will be at its best at noon tomorrow.'

'Will it fade when the chocolate's finished.'

'I suppose it will,' said Willi cautiously.

'A pity. I shall miss it.'

As Willi returned Chalky's bland smile, he had an uncomfortable feeling that he had met a fellow expert in the useful arts of bribery and blackmail.

At eleven the next morning, an hour and ten minutes before Berg's bomb was due to be detonated, Brunel reported to Kruger that the filling in of ten-metres of tunnel had been completed. Also, Berg had wired up the bomb and was sitting in the shed awaiting the signal. Kruger thanked him and glanced at his watch. The timing of his visit to Reynolds was critical.

Berg crouched in the toolshed and peered through the grimy window. From his vantage point he could see the terrace steps. Nearer to the shed, about fifty metres away, was Leyden's vegetable plot. A light drizzle was falling and the only activity was a few prisoners tending their reorganized plots. Berg checked the two wires that disappeared through a crack in the shed floor and carried out a final test on the toggle switch and battery. Everything was in working order.

A movement outside caught Berg's eye. Exactly on time, two prisoners appeared. One was carrying a bundle of short wooden stakes and a length of ribbon made from bits of rag. The other was armed with a hammer. They worked steadily for ten minutes, knocking a circle of stakes into the ground around Leyden's vegetable plot. They strung the ribbon from the stakes and returned to the main hall.

Berg slid his plaster-encased ankle under the tiny workbench and sat down on a box to wait.

Reynolds had just finished speaking on the telephone to Fleming in London when Kruger was shown into his office.

'This gas leak is getting serious, major,' said Kruger, coming straight to the point. 'I demand that something is done about it before any of my officers are injured. I've closed off an area of the vegetable plots and I must say that I'm disappointed to note that you are not treating the matter as seriously as I am.'

Reynolds tried not to look too exasperated. 'For God's

sake, commander, the gas company experts are convinced that there's nothing there and, if there is, that there's no danger.'

'That smell is now so strong that it *must* be dangerous,' Kruger stated firmly. 'Come out and see for yourself if you don't believe me.'

At a minute to noon, Berg saw Corporal White and Private Jones appear. The two guards strolled along one of the paths between the vegetable plots. They reached the circle of wooden stakes, which they proceeded to investigate with great interest. Something appeared to distract Chalky. He looked around in surprise and sniffed the air. He said something to Private Jones. Both men sniffed hard and seemed to agree on something. They abandoned their inspection of the staked-off area and hurried off in the direction of the hall.

Berg started worrying about the bomb. Had he got the ratios of the three ingredients right? Would it be big enough? Would the detonating charge work? A minute passed. He told himself that it was too late to change anything now, and to stop worrying.

Reynolds forgot Kruger's presence and looked sharply at Chalky. 'Are you certain of this?'

'Positive, sir. So's Private Jones, sir. We could both smell it. Plain as anything it was.'

'Perhaps we should both investigate?' Kruger suggested.

Reynolds nodded. He stood and pulled on his cap. 'All right, Corporal White – you and Jones go on ahead.'

Chalky saluted and left the office.

As Reynolds was putting his greatcoat on, he said to Kruger, 'I have something to tell you outside which I want you to treat as confidential, commander.'

Kruger made no reply. He followed Reynolds out into the courtyard and fell in step beside him.

'It's about these goddamn Canada rumours,' said Reynolds. 'I've heard from a reliable source that there are no plans to move the Number One camp for the time being.'

'How sure are you of this, major?' asked Kruger expressionlessly.

'Like I said, it came from a reliable source. I can't go further than that.'

At five minutes past noon, Berg saw a prisoner up-end his spade and start cleaning it. It was the warning signal that told him to get ready. He moved the toggle switch into the centre of the toolshed's workbench and connected its two wires to the battery's terminals.

Willi stepped through the french windows on to the terrace at seven minutes past noon, just as Kruger and Reynolds rounded the corner of the building and headed towards the vegetable plots. A hundred yards away in the toolshed, Berg reached for the toggle switch while keeping his eyes fixed on Willi.

Kruger and Reynolds reached the first vegetable plot. They were approximately seventy yards from Leyden's plot with its fluttering ribbons tied to a circle of stakes.

Berg's fingers were posed expectantly on the toggle switch. He didn't take his eyes off Willi for a second.

Willi whipped out a large, spotted handkerchief and blew his nose.

'When is Commander Fleming returning, major?' Kruger asked Reynolds.

'In his own good time. Why?'

'Oh, nothing.'

Reynolds glanced sideways at Kruger and realized that there was something different about the U-boat ace. He was about to speak when Berg's bomb went off with a tremendous WHUUMPH!

A shock wave punched through the ground and hammered into Reynolds' body with what seemed like enough force to ram his feet into his groin. The blast followed through an instant later, hitting him like an express train and making him stagger backwards. He recovered his balance and stared in dumbfounded horror as a column of rocks, soil and flame erupted out of the ground and roared high into the air like the by-products of Mount Vesuvius on a bad day.

One particular small boulder climbed higher than its neighbours. Reynolds watched in stunned disbelief as it soared like a brick albatross into the grey sky It reached the top of its trajectory and curved gracefully over. The rest of its journey consisted of a rapid downwards acceleration that ended with it plummeting with unerring accuracy straight into the toolshed, which it successfully reduced in an instant to a heap of splinters and firewood.

The spectacle's finale was a mighty howl of anguish from Berg.

That evening Kruger called an emergency meeting of the escape committee. His opening remarks dealt with the amazing success of Berg's gas leak and bomb ruse. The gas board engineers had been baffled by the explosion but had decided that it must have been due to a freak seepage of natural gas through the rocks. Whatever the cause, they had decided that it was most unlikely to happen again. Best of all, the troublesome boulder had been shattered into over forty fragments, all of which had been recovered by the prisoners with Reynolds' consent because Kruger had told him he was keen to rebuild one of Grizedale Hall's rockeries.

'It means,' Kruger finished, 'that we should have no more major problems when work is resumed on the tunnel.'

Shriver was puzzled. 'I don't follow you, commander. Surely the work is to continue.'

'I propose resting the tunnel project until the spring,' Kruger replied.

There was a chorus of groans. 'We might be in Canada by then!' Ulbrick protested.

'I doubt it very much.'

Shriver smiled. 'Or we might be liberated by then.'

'I doubt that very much too,' said Kruger coldly.

Shriver was about to dispute Kruger's views but was interrupted by a rap on the door. Willi entered and handed Kruger an envelope. It was still slightly limp from when he had steamed it open.

'With Major Reynolds' compliments,' said Willi.

'You've read it, of course, Willi?'

Willi knew better than to lie to Kruger. He nodded guiltily.

'Then perhaps you would be good enough to tell us what it contains.'

Willi swallowed. 'Some good news, commander. Major Reynolds says that he has heard from Barrow General Hospital. The compound fracture of Hauptmann Berg's leg isn't as bad as was first thought. And if he gets over his concussion, he should be back with us in time for Christmas.'

The brief silence that followed was broken by Ulbrick. 'You said "good news", Willi,' he said accusingly.

The next day Reynolds had a sudden thought. 'You know something, sergeant?' he said to Finch, who was filling in some requisition forms. 'I do believe that Kruger has run out of those poisonous goddamn cigars. I didn't see him smoking one yesterday.'

Part Seven

BOMBERS' MOON

For the third night in succession the eerie wail of Ambleside's solitary air raid siren, echoing across the fells, was heard at the camp. The floodlighting and perimeter fence wire lighting were extinguished almost immediately so that the hall did not provide the marauding bombers with a landmark.

Kruger signalled to Willi to turn off the light in the office before he cautiously drew the blackout curtain aside and peered out. The ghostly light of a full moon shining from a clear sky bathed the frost-covered grounds. The spidery silhouette of the firewatching tower was visible above the conifers of Grizedale Forest. He heard whistles blowing from the direction of the guards' quarters.

'Molde! Braun!' he snapped. 'Get a move on! They're turning out the blackout guard!'

There was enough moonlight in the room for Leutnant Victor Molde and Oberleutnant Klaus Braun to finish blacking-up their faces with shoe polish. They knew from timings made during the previous raids that they had less than three minutes before the number of soldiers patrolling the grounds was doubled.

The two bomber pilots were each wearing seamen's black trousers and jumpers. Willi helped them into their kitbag harnesses and ensured that the bags were settled comfortably on their shoulders. Berg's home-made wire cutters were pushed securely into a sling around Molde's waist. Kruger checked that the terrace thirty feet below was clear before hurling the knotted blanket rope out of the window. One end of the rope was tied to the radiator.

The two would-be escapers exchanged hurried handshakes with Willi. Kruger shook hands with Braun as the *Luftwaffe* officer swung his leg over the windowsill and grasped the rope.

'Good luck, oberleutnant.'

Braun gave Kruger a broad grin. 'Thank you, commander. I'll write.' He realized his mistake before he had finished the sentence. 'Commander, it was a slip of the tongue.'

'A slip that could get you shot!' Kruger snapped. 'From the moment you put those clothes on you were Dutch seaman Hans Menckin on your way to Londonderry via Liverpool. I'm sorry, Braun, but your escape is out of the question.'

'Oh, for God's sake!' Braun protested, almost shouting. 'You can't stop –'

'Molde!' Kruger interrupted. 'Don't stand there gawping. Get down that rope!'

After an uncertain glance at Kruger and Braun, Molde climbed over the windowsill and went hand over hand down the rope. He dropped the last ten feet, landing lightly on his feet, and vaulted over the terrace's parapet before Kruger started hauling the rope up. Luckily the two guards who appeared on the terrace at that moment did not see the last few feet of rope disappearing into Kruger's office.

'This is absurd!' Braun protested. 'We've worked hard planning this escape.'

'Not hard enough.'

'But you're crazy! You can't let Molde go alone.'

'Molde will manage perfectly well without you,' said Kruger curtly. 'Take off that kitbag please, and return to your dormitory.'

Braun returned Kruger's icy stare. 'After this, commander, you will find that you have lost the respect of the *Luftwaffe* officers here.'

'Oh, I don't know, Braun. I rather imagine that the *Luftwaffe* football team will be pleased to discover that they haven't lost their centre forward.'

Braun slipped the kitbag off his back and nearly threw it at Willi before storming out of the office.

Willi said nothing. He was about to turn the light on when the anti-aircraft battery to the east near Windermere suddenly started pouring a steady stream of shells into the sky. Kruger was tempted to peer out of the window but he knew from his experience of the previous two nights that he would be unable to see anything out of the south-facing window.

'Odd,' he commented to Willi. 'That's the third night in succession that that battery has opened up. If the target is Barrow-in-Furness, it doesn't say much for the *Luftwaffe*'s navigation.'

After a hundred-yard dash from the hall across the grounds, taking advantage of the shadows thrown by shrubs, Molde threw himself down between two wheelbarrows that were standing side by side on the open expanse of the vegetable plots. They had been strategically positioned earlier that day to provide the necessary cover for an escape bid should there be yet another bombing raid. Once he had allowed three minutes after the first two-man patrol had passed the point where he intended to cut through the wire, he had five minutes before the next patrol were within fifty metres. He kept very still and waited.

Molde was relieved that Braun was not accompanying him. During the twenty-four hours planning that had gone into the impromptu escape, Braun had adopted a carefree attitude. He had preferred to spend the day telling his circle of prisoners about how he would be fooling the British rather than getting down to serious study of maps and routes.

The reason why Kruger had sanctioned the winter escape was because Braun spoke perfect English without an accent and because Molde had often camped in the Lake District before the war. Both men were athletic, which would stand them in good stead when it came to stowing-away on a neutral ship in Liverpool. Also, the finds of litter clearing parties and Willi's bribery of the guards meant that both men were well-equipped with identification and travel documents.

The anti-aircraft guns started firing just as he decided to make the final sprint to the fence. He twisted his head round and watched the probing beams of the searchlights and the points of tracer fire climbing with deceptive laziness into the sky.

Molde knew all about British flak. There was the curious, unreal feeling of watching the tracer reaching up with what seemed unbelieveable slowness and then appearing to accelerate madly as it neared its target; the dull shocks of shells passing right through an aircraft without exploding and then the nightmare kaleidoscope of flying instrument glass as had happened when one exploded in the nose and another a second later in the tail, killing his gunners and toppling his Junkers into a spin.

The young pilot offered a prayer of deliverance for the aircrews of the unseen aircraft and wondered if they were from his *gruppe*.

The first patrol were more interested in the battle raging in the east than the barbed wire fence they were supposed to be guarding. Molde watched them until they were out of sight. As he began the final dash for the wire, he heard the unmistakable sound of an over-revving engine of an aircraft in an uncontrolled dive.

*

'Bloody hell,' breathed Private Jones. 'It sounds like they got one!'

He and Chalky paused near the firewatching tower and stared eastwards towards the sound of the diving aircraft. The searchlight beams swung southwards about their axis like the spokes of a celestial wheel as they hunted for their lost quarry. One beam momentarily illuminated a cluster of white specks and immediately swept back to pinpoint five parachute canopies hanging in the sky.

Chalky gave an exclamation of annoyance and dropped his cigarette. 'Come on, Jonesy, they'll be wanting us to go and hunt for the bastards. On a bloody freezing night like this too. Bleedin' Jerries.'

'Parachutes!' Kruger exclaimed angrily, drawing his head back into the office. To Willi's amazement, he grabbed the bundle of knotted blankets and dropped it out of the window. 'Willi! Go after Molde and bring him back!'

Willi's portly frame stood rooted to the floor in terror. 'I'm to what, commander?' he queried faintly.

'Go down the rope and bring Molde back. There'll be search parties combing the fells for that aircrew – he doesn't stand a chance of getting away. Go on, man! Move!'

'But, commander –'

'Don't argue with me, Willi. I ordered you to attend Ulbrick's keep fit sessions for an occasion such as this – now get down that rope!'

Willi knew better than to argue, especially as Kruger's temper had not been good of late since he had either run out of the toxic little cheroots or had given up smoking. He moved trance-like to the window and lifted a plump leg over the windowsill.

'You'll need this,' said Kruger, putting the rope in Willi's virtually lifeless hands. 'Good luck.'

*

Molde was working the wire-cutters through the last strand of barbed wire when he heard someone running towards him. He looked over his shoulder and gazed in amazement at the apparition charging across the wide strip of grass that was used for sports practice. Willi paused uncertainly at the trip wire, uncomfortably aware that the guards wouldn't hesitate to take pot shots at him if he was seen. He stepped over the low wire and flopped down beside Molde like a wounded sea elephant.

'What the hell do you want?'

Willi's heaving chest continued hoovering air in and out of his lungs for some moments before he could gasp out Kruger's order.

'Don't be bloody crazy!' Molde hissed in reply, returning to the attack on the wire.

'*Please*, Molde,' Willi begged. 'You must come back. He'll kill me if you don't.'

'Tell him I was gone by the time you'd reached the fence!'

The last strand parted. Molde bent it out of the way and started wriggling through the hole. Willi grabbed hold of his ankle.

'You stupid bastard!' Molde hissed angrily. 'Leggo!' He tried kicking himself free but Willi hung on to his leg with a grim determination born of fear.

'Molde, I beg of you. You must come back. Please!'

Molde replied by planting his free foot on Willi's face and shoving with all his strength. He broke free, wormed the rest of his body through the wire, and scrambled to his feet.

'Oh God,' Willi wailed to himself as he watched Molde running towards the trees. 'He'll kill me. He'll kill me.'

'Tut tut,' said Fleming sympathetically, wandering up behind Reynolds and Finch, who were ruefully examining the hole in the wire. 'Never mind, gentlemen. You've got me back. Who have we lost?'

'Victor Molde, *Luftwaffe*,' said Reynolds bitterly.

'Ah,' said Fleming knowingly. 'In that case there's no chance that the hole was made by Leutnant Shultz trying to get back in?'

Reynolds was clearly not amused by Fleming's joke. 'Good morning, Ian,' he said stiffly. 'Good to have you back.'

Fleming nodded. 'I knew there'd been an escape. I was stopped at two road blocks.'

'It's this stupid single fence,' said Finch angrily. 'We need two fences with the outer one electrified.'

'Not a bad idea,' Fleming observed.

'Try telling the War Office,' said Reynolds. 'They say that every yard of barbed wire is needed for beach defences.' He nodded to the firewatching tower. 'I only managed to get that thing by scrounging it from the Forestry Commission.'

'How's Kruger been keeping?'

Reynolds scowled. 'That guy's been impossible just lately.'

'I think I can guess why,' said Fleming, chuckling.

Fleming tapped on Kruger's door and entered. 'Good morning, Otto. Long time no see.'

Kruger's expression as he looked up from his desk was the nearest that Fleming had ever seen to hope on the U-boat commander's face.

'Good morning, commander.'

'I expect your lookout system told you that I was coming?'

Kruger smiled wryly. 'I knew someone was coming who was not German. That is all.'

'Your security system is better than ours,' Fleming observed, unbuckling his briefcase. 'Prisoners breaking out by the score; people smuggling stuff into the camp. Look what I managed to get past the guards yet again.'

Kruger took the huge box of German cheroots that

Fleming held out. 'I am very grateful to you, commander,' he said, unwrapping one of the cigars and lighting it.

Fleming grinned. 'An early Christmas present, old boy. I've found you another supplier. He said that he's only too glad to get rid of them. No one else can stand them. I think his stocks will last you until the end of the war.'

Kruger exhaled slowly, releasing a cloud of acrid fumes. 'And how long will that be, commander?'

With ten minutes to go before the Wehrmacht referee blew the final whistle, the noisy, aggressive football match between the *Luftwaffe* and the *Kreigsmarine* was still a goal-less draw. If results were according to number of supporters, the *Kreigsmarine* would have been well ahead because their representatives at Grizedale Hall outnumbered both the other services – a reflection on the intensity of the Battle of the Atlantic that was now being fought.

After a foul that was blatant, even by the standards of Grizedale Hall, the referee awarded a penalty kick to the *Luftwaffe*. The supporters crowding along the touchline fell silent as Braun squared up to the ball. He was about to begin his run-up when his attention was distracted by the sight of Sergeant Finch climbing the ladder to his favourite perch on the firewatching tower.

The combination of a target, still air and his frustration at being denied the chance to escape decided Sergeant Finch's fate. As Braun's foot slammed into the ball, he knew instinctively that the kick was a good one.

Sergeant Finch settled down on his seat. He bent down and started unscrewing the searchlight's rusting switchbox that was screwed to the watchtower's boarded surround. Of all the problems in his life, the searchlight and its ancient wiring was the most persistent; it was for ever blowing fuses. Requisitions for new equipment were just a waste of time and paper – they disappeared into the War Office machine and were never heard of again. He was about to pull the front off the switchbox when a splintering crash right by his ear caused his heart to catapult into his throat and try to crawl out of his ears.

'My God,' Ulbrick whispered to Braun as Sergeant Finch's infuriated face appeared at the hole that the football had punched in the rotten boards. 'I think there's going to be trouble.'

Ulbrick was right. Finch almost slid down the ladder with the football clutched under his arm and stormed across to the prisoners.

'Who kicked this?'

'I did, sergeant,' Braun answered 'Did it scare you?'

Finch calmed down and his manner became calculating. 'I find it very strange, Oberleutnant Braun.'

'You find what strange, sergeant?'

No one noticed Kruger appear. He regarded the crowd of prisoners for a moment before stepping over the trip wire and picking up a piece of timber that Braun's football had dislodged from the tower.

'I find it strange how your talent with a football has suddenly deserted you,' Finch replied.

Braun smiled. 'It comes and goes like your sense of humour, sergeant.'

'Really, oberleutnant? Well let's see how *your* sense of humour survives a ten-year sentence for sabotaging a War Office installation.'

A silence fell as the prisoners sensed that Finch was not joking.

Braun forced a laugh. 'You are not serious?'

'Aren't I? You're under arrest, oberleutnant. How much more serious would you like me to be?'

'What's the trouble?' inquired Kruger from the back of the crowd. The prisoners made a path for him through their midst. In his hand was the piece of timber from the tower. 'Good afternoon, Sergeant Finch. Do you have a problem?'

'Oberleutnant Braun is the one with the problem, commander. He's under arrest for sabotaging a War Office installation. That kick was deliberate.'

Kruger crumbled a piece of the tower's timber in his fingers. 'But the tower is still standing, sergeant. Just. As you can see – it is rotten.'

'That's not the point –'

'But it is the point,' Kruger insisted. 'I saw what happened. It was an accident.'

'I can fight my own battles, commander,' said Braun in German.

'It was a deliberate act of sabotage,' Finch declared.

Kruger shook his head. 'It would only be sabotage if Oberleutnant Braun knew that the timber was in this condition, sergeant. Timber this thick would normally withstand a football hitting it. Oberleutnant Braun has never been up the tower. Therefore, if he's charged, the question is certain to arise: how did he know of the tower's condition? Did a guard tell him? Passing information to the enemy? There may have to be a separate inquiry.'

Finch glowered at Kruger. 'What the hell are you talking about, commander?'

'I expect I am making as much sense as you with your talk of sabotage,' said Kruger evenly. 'It was an unfortunate accident which I am certain Oberleutnant Braun is anxious to apologize for.' He turned to Braun. 'Is that not so, oberleutnant?'

For a moment it looked as if Braun was prepared to continue the argument, but he thought better of it and muttered a grudging apology to Sergeant Finch, which the British NCO accepted in the same spirit in which it was offered.

'Let it happen again, oberleutnant,' Finch warned, tossing the football to the referee, 'and you'll find yourself in serious trouble.'

Kruger nodded his approval. 'Thank you, Braun.'

Braun acknowledged and rejoined his team mates as play resumed. Kruger pointedly ignored Finch and turned to watch the match for a few minutes, inhaling on the last inch of his cheroot. He dropped the butt, ground it into the grass and walked away. Finch pounced on the butt immediately and examined it with an expression that was a mixture of bewilderment and frustrated rage.

Kruger was sitting writing at his desk when he heard the warning whistle. He looked up expectantly just as there was a rap on the door.

'Come!'

The door was opened by Braun.

'You wanted to see me, commander?'

'Come in, Braun. Close the door. Take a seat.'

Braun did as he was told. He lounged languidly in his chair while regarding Kruger with undisguised hostility. 'Thank you for dealing with Sergeant Finch, commander.'

'That was a remarkably stupid thing to do, Braun. But that's not what I wanted to see you about. It would seem that Molde is still free.'

Braun remained silent.

'When the bomber was shot down during the raid, I tried to cancel his escape as well, in case there would be search parties out on the fells hunting for parachutists. Willi claimed that he was too late and that Molde had already got through the wire.'

Braun shrugged. 'So Willi told me. What has it got to do with me? Or are you going to admit that you were wrong in stopping me from escaping?'

Kruger gave a thin smile. 'I doubt if you'd be interested if I said that my reasons arose out of concern for your safety.'

'For once, commander, your judgment is not at fault. Thank you for telling me about Molde.' Braun stood. 'Now if you would excuse me, I have a coaching session with my reserve team.'

'I've not finished, Braun. Please sit down.'

Braun sat and contrived to look suitably bored.

'As a U-boatman,' said Kruger, ignoring Braun's insolent expression, 'I know very little about flying problems. I wish to pick your brains. I hope you have no objection?'

'Go ahead,' said the pilot disinterestedly.

'For the past two nights there have been abortive *Luftwaffe* raids on Barrow-in-Furness. At least I'm assuming that the target has been Barrow. Why have the bombers been going off course?'

Braun flushed angrily. 'Commander, am I here to listen to your criticism of the *Luftwaffe*?'

'No, Braun. You're here for me to listen to you. I recall that you were shot down on a Barrow raid. Am I correct?'

Braun nodded. 'Yes. Despite the difficulties, Barrow was a priority target for my group. It probably still is in view of the raid two nights ago.'

Kruger looked interested. 'Was the target the Vickers submarine construction yard?'

'Yes.'

'Well there's hope for us yet, even if the *Luftwaffe* are unloading their bombs all over the Lake District.'

'I'm sorry, commander, but I don't follow you.'

'Co-operation between the *Luftwaffe* and the *Kriegsmarine*,' Kruger commented. 'It used to be non-existent. U-boats returning across the Bay of Biscay to our bases at Lorient and St Narzaire were never provided with air cover. The result was that the RAF threw anything that could fly at us. Sunderlands, biplanes – even lumbering old Walrus amphibians. These raids on Barrow would suggest that some co-operation lessons have been learned. Why else would the *Luftwaffe* bomb submarine yards?'

'I was opposed to the raids.'

Kruger raised an eyebrow. 'Oh? May I ask why?'

'I couldn't see the point in risking aircraft on such a difficult target when there are juicier targets nearer to home. The war will be over soon. What difference will the production of a few submarines a month at Barrow make to the British war effort?'

Kruger gazed thoughtfully at Braun for a moment before opening a desk drawer and removing its contents. He pulled the emptied drawer right out from the desk and turned it over. He placed it in front of Braun. Drawn on the underside of the drawer's plywood bottom was a detailed Indian ink map of the Lake District and nearby coast, showing roads, railways, towns and villages. Also included was Barrow-in-Furness.

'Neat, commander,' Braun observed.

'All escapees' maps are copied from this master.'

'Including the one I wasn't given a chance to use?'

'Why is Barrow a difficult target?' asked Kruger.

'Is this some sort of trial that the *Luftwaffe* is on, commander?'

'Not unless you know of something that the *Luftwaffe* should be on trial for, Braun,' said Kruger acidly. He gestured to the map. 'I would like to know what the problems are with Barrow.'

Braun studied the map. 'Well, firstly, there's the distance. It's over a thousand kilometres from our base. It's even further than Liverpool. Which means that we have to sacrifice some of our bomb payload for extra fuel – which also means, when we find Barrow, our bombing has to be that much more accurate.'

'That's understood,' said Kruger. 'But why do your bombers always seem to end up here over the Lake District, several kilometres north of Barrow?'

Braun smiled ruefully. 'That's what happened to me when I was shot down. Barrow's at the extreme effective range of our radio navigation beams. The tendency to drift north could be due to distortion of the beam caused by the high ground around here, or – as we believe – that the British have found a way of interfering with the beam. No one was ever one hundred per cent certain. What we were certain of was that Barrow was a swine to find.'

'But the lakes are such obvious landmarks. Surely it would be not be difficult to correct one's course for Barrow from them?'

'It's not that simple, commander,' said Braun, his hostility towards Kruger forgotten for the time being. He pointed to Barrow and to nearby Walney Island. 'A glimpse of a lake through a break in the cloud can easily be mistaken for the channel between Barrow and Walney Island. You see the similarities? Also the lakes are roughly the same width as the channel.'

Kruger studied the map in silence for a moment. What Braun said was true: there were remarkable similarities between Barrow's topography and that of the lakes. He sat back in his chair and steepled his fingers. 'So what would you say is the solution, oberleutnant?'

Braun shook his head. He added jokingly, 'What's needed in this area is a distinctive landmark.'

Kruger's expression remained serious. 'What would you call a distinctive landmark?'

'I'm sorry, commander, I'm not sure I understand you.'

'What detail is visible from the air during a full moon?'

Braun thought for a moment. 'Well . . . virtually everything that's visible during the day. Houses, gardens – even the white rings the British have painted round tree trunks.'

'The white rings around trees? You surprise me, oberleutnant.'

'The difficulty isn't so much spotting landmarks,' said Braun. 'It's identifying them correctly to obtain an accurate bearing.'

'The white rings round trees. . . .' Kruger mused. 'Fascinating. I had no idea.'

Braun looked puzzled. 'Why are you asking these questions, commander?'

Kruger was lost in thought before he replied. 'What are

the chances of your group taking another crack at Barrow during next month's bombers' moon?'

Braun smiled. 'Well . . . our *Geschwader* doesn't give up that easily. And as I said, Barrow is a priority target for my group. Yes, they'll be back.'

'Good,' said Kruger. 'In that case, we'd better make sure that we are ready for them. I shall need your help, oberleutnant. I hope you are in agreement?'

'That depends on what you want,' said Braun cautiously.

Molde thought he heard a seal bark. After three attempts to engage his sleep-drugged mental gears, he succeeded in co-ordinating the various facial muscles that were required to open an eye. He thought he saw something that looked vaguely like a grey, uninviting sky viewed through the neglected roof of a broken-down barn. Upon opening both eyes, he discovered that what he was looking at was in fact a grey, uninviting sky viewed through the neglected roof of a broken-down barn.

As reason returned like an unwelcome black tide, he realized that he was cold, bitterly cold despite the layer of straw covering his body. But there was an exception: the small of his back was surprisingly warm. After a minute's contemplation, the reason for his warm back became apparent: someone was breathing down it. It wasn't ordinary breathing. As the gusts of warm humid air blasted down his spine like clouds of steam, he reasoned that it just wasn't possible for anyone to breathe like that unless they were on the verge of a catastrophic failure of their bodily systems. He reached out a cautious hand and his fingertips encountered a bristly chin. Above the chin were soft, sensual lips and a pair of flaring nostrils.

Molde twisted his body around and found himself staring a horse in the eye. The horse took grave exception to the liberties that his hand was taking and promptly bit it.

*

Sergeant Finch was sitting morosely in his firewatching tower like a khaki vulture. All was not well within his well-ordered little world. He treated the absence of Leutnant Molde as a personal insult. If he hadn't been so intent on his brooding, there was a faint chance that he might have spotted certain surreptitious activities going on under his nose. On the other hand the prisoners were masters at disguising their nefarious deeds, so burying a long length of rope under a few inches of top soil hardly tested their undoubted talents. The rope led across the vegetable plots and disappeared in the general direction of the drive. Some prisoners were covering the rope with soil that they were excavating from bean trenches and others were raking soil over the rope. Where it ran across open grass, it was being covered with heaps of dead leaves.

The working party filling in potholes in the drive were so preoccupied that they appeared not to notice the laundry van until the driver hooted at them. He rested his arms impatiently across the steering wheel while the prisoners unhurriedly gathered up their tools.

One prisoner distracted the driver's attention for a crucial moment with an obscene gesture to ensure that he did not glance in his mirror. While the driver was leaning out of his window, trading insults with the prisoner, Brunel darted out of the rhododendrons beside the van, rolled underneath the vehicle, and lashed the end of the rope to its rear axle.

As soon as the road was clear, the driver angrily slammed the van into gear and accelerated towards the hall. The prisoners watched, fascinated, as the rope snaked after the speeding vehicle. All the prisoners who had been working in the grounds to cover the rope moved clear as soon as they saw the van move off. Their movements were unhurried but purposeful. Suddenly the rope leapt three feet into the air, showering soil and leaves in all directions, and snapped taut with a loud twang. The firewatching tower's timber leg that had the other end of the rope looped around it snapped like a matchstick and was yanked out of place as though it had been struck by a giant, invisible sledgehammer.

The driver of the van leapt from his seat to find out what it was that had jerked his vehicle to a standstill, nearly hurling him through the windscreen in the process. His attention was immediately rivetted by the sight of the tottering firewatching tower and therefore he didn't see Brunel quickly untie the offending rope and drag it out of sight.

Unable to withstand the increased load, the tower's three remaining legs bowed inwards. A six-inch diameter cross-brace – about the only sound timber in the tower – hung on grimly for as long as it could. When it finally gave up the unequal struggle, it emitted a tremendous crack like a pistol shot and fell away in two pieces. For some seconds nothing but habit kept the tower upright as it swayed drunkenly in the breeze, defying gravity for several moments before the entire structure crashed down on itself like a pole-axed giraffe.

It wasn't only the welter of collapsing, splintering boards and struts that every prisoner who witnessed the scene would remember for the rest of his life, or the pyrotechnique display of blue sparks when the searchlight power cable shorted out; what would be indelibly etched on every man's memory was the expression of abject terror on Sergeant Finch's face in those few seconds before he was unceremoniously buried under a huge pile of rotten timber that had once been his beloved firewatching tower.

As soon as he heard the sound of a car start, Molde climbed down from the bales of straw and, taking care to avoid Caligula – as he had named the horse – because its hobby was collecting bits of his anatomy, he tiptoed to the door and peered through a crack.

He was just in time to see Fleming's Bentley swing into

the farmyard and swerve sharply to avoid ramming a
Morris as it backed out of a garage.

'Ian,' said Cathy delightedly, winding down the window
of her car. 'I didn't know you were back from London. This
is a lovely surprise.'

'Surprise being the operative word,' said Fleming, stepping down from the Bentley's running board and leaning
on the Morris's driver's door. 'Actually, I only got back
yesterday. I thought I'd pop over to see if you were all right.
You heard about last night's escape?'

'Oh yes,' said Cathy, giving Fleming a dazzling smile.
'Ambleside police rang me up this morning. I got John to
check all the outhouses.'

'John?'

'The son of one of my tenants. You've seen him. He
often goes riding with me.'

Fleming remembered the young man in the smart tweed
suit. 'Oh, yes.'

'It's sweet of you to come over, Ian, it really is. I've left
all my livestock in the care of a tenant because I'm just off
to spend a few days with my sister at Kendal to help her with
her early lambs.'

'I wish I could join you.'

Cathy laughed. 'I can just see you chasing ewes all over
the fells.'

'I'll have you know that I'm an expert at chasing women.'

Cathy laughed again. 'Don't I know it. Anyway, if you're
around after three o'clock next Friday afternoon, do drop
in for a cup of tea, won't you? Must fly now. Byee!'

Fleming said goodbye and watched the Morris drive off.
He returned to his own car and followed Cathy out of the
farmyard. Had he glanced back at the farmhouse, he would
have seen a young man wearing an immaculate, expertly
cut tweed suit watching his departure from an upstairs
window.

Molde straightened up and turned round in time to avoid

Caligula who was stretching a long neck and bared teeth in his direction. Luckily the beast was tethered. He climbed up to his bed on top of the bales of straw and considered his next move while eating quarter of a bar of chocolate from his kitbag. He was ravenously hungry and he needed all his self-control to prevent himself from wolfing down the entire bar. He decided that it would be best to stay in the barn until nightfall. By then the British were certain to have rounded up the aircrew of the crashed bomber, and the soldiers and police looking for him would probably think that he was a long way from the camp by then. In the meantime there was nothing to do except sleep and try to keep warm.

Before curling up in the straw, Molde helped himself to a drink from Caligula's water trough when he thought the belligerent beast wasn't looking. It was looking and it did its best to take a lump out of his rear as he dived for safety.

Reynolds was particularly annoyed by the disruption of the camp's routine caused by the collapse of the tower. His fishing tackle was in need of attention; he had been looking forward to revarnishing his favourite pike rod.

'It was sabotage,' he declared angrily to Kruger, having summoned the German officer to his office. 'There is no other word to describe it!'

'I would dispute that,' Kruger replied. 'There are other words such as accident, and —'

'That was no accident, commander, and you know it wasn't.'

'I might've been killed,' Sergeant Finch chimed in, much aggrieved.

'Sergeant Finch might've been killed,' said Reynolds, picking up a fly and examining its bedraggled feathers.

'I suggest you ask the forestry warden about the condition of that tower,' said Kruger evenly. 'It is common knowledge that it was rotten before it was moved here, and that was over a year ago. He once told prisoners on a working party that he was surprised that it had stood for so long.'

'The state of the tower is immaterial,' said Reynolds testily. 'What matters is that it was deliberately destroyed by your officers.'

'Can you prove that?' Kruger countered.

'That's for a court-martial to decide.'

Kruger looked exasperated. 'Who are you going to charge? The entire camp or just me? If it does go that far, then I shall insist on calling the forestry warden to testify as to the tower's condition.'

'The matter's out of my hands once I submit a report.'

Kruger decided that it was time to bring the conversation around to the subject that was uppermost in his mind. 'Major Reynolds,' he said, being deliberately hesitant. 'I have a suggestion to make which may offer a way out of this dilemma.'

'Oh yes?'

'Without prejudging the question as to why or how the tower collapsed, I suggest that we build you a new watch-tower.'

Reynolds blinked and dropped the fly he had been playing with. He stared incredulously at Kruger. 'You mean the prisoners to build a new tower?'

'Precisely.'

'You're crazy. I could never permit that.'

'Why not? There's plenty of timber available in the forest which the working parties are clearing. Hauptmann Shriver was a civil engineer before he joined the army. I'm sure he could design an excellent tower, complete with a proper ladder and a decent observation platform with sides and a roof to protect the guards from the wind and rain. Also I need a project to keep my men occupied, if only for a few weeks. There's not much gardening to be done at this time of year.'

Reynolds glanced at Sergeant Finch for support but his NCO was staring at Kruger with an expression that was a curious mixture of hostility and suspicion.

'There's a very good reason why I can't permit it,' said Reynolds. 'The Geneva Convention prohibits the employment of POWs on construction work of a military nature. Clearing the forest and gardening – that's fine, but I can't allow you to go building prison camp watchtowers. Thank you for the offer, commander, but it's out of the question.'

'But a firewatching tower is *not* a military structure,' Kruger pointed out. 'It is no more military than the drive that we are for ever rebuilding.' He saw the uncertainty on Reynolds' face and pressed home his argument. 'What you use a firewatching tower for is entirely up to you. And because we will most likely be salvaging timbers from the wreckage of the old tower, our rebuilding work can be classed as maintenance.'

'Well . . .' said Reynolds doubtfully. 'I guess there's no harm in –'

'I have a suggestion,' said Kruger resolutely. 'You defer submitting a report until we have rebuilt the tower. Is it a deal?'

Molde opened an eye and promptly closed it. His brain was messing him about again. He kept his eyes tightly closed and decided that his brain could work a smart hallucination when it felt like it. This particular one was brilliant. For one thing it had got rid of Caligula. For another it was in colour – the lights glinting on the silver tureen cover were in glorious, living Technicolor. But the crowning achievement was the inclusion of smells – real smells – smells you could set to music: coffee, fried eggs, bacon and toast, and home-made blackcurrant jam like his mother used to make.

Molde sat up, picked the straw out of his hair, and avoided looking in the direction on the door where the hallucination was lurking. And yet the mouth-watering odours were as persistent as a Hamburg prostitute. Slowly, he looked up. He was now wide-awake but the hallucination refused to go away: the folding table was still there and so were the pieces of bone china, together with the silver tureen cover over a dinner plate, and a coffeepot. He lowered himself to the floor and approached the table. He lifted the tureen cover and solemnly regarded the fried eggs, ham, and sausages that were gently sizzling on the over-heated plate. He picked up the coffeepot. It was hot to the touch and felt full.

Molde's first inclination was to grab his kitbag and run but he realized that whoever had provided the meal was probably covering the barn with a shotgun until the police or army arrived. There was only one sensible thing to do: he dumped a bale of straw in front of the table and sat down to eat the best meal he had had since his capture.

Hauptmann Karl Shriver was already making some preliminary sketches as he listened to Kruger outlining his plans for a new watchtower.

'It needs to be the same height as the old tower,' Kruger was saying. 'About fifteen metres high, I imagine. I'm particularly anxious that we show the British just how good our civil engineering can be, and it must be finished before the next full moon.'

Shriver gave Kruger a questioning look. 'That gives us about twenty-five days. Not very long.'

'It's imperative that it's finished by then.'

'Why, commander?'

'That's when the camp is due to be inspected by a high-ranking British army officer,' said Kruger smoothly. 'If there's no tower, questions are likely to be asked.'

Shriver continued with his drawing. 'Have you spoken to Braun about the tower?'

'Why should I?'

'He was the one that organized the tower's demise.'

Kruger gave a rare smile. 'I'm very grateful to Ober-leutnant Braun. He has given us a problem to test our resourcefulness.'

'It'll be tested all right,' said Shriver dolefully, shading the watchtower's pitched roof on his drawing. 'The biggest problem is going to be getting hold of long enough lengths of timber for the legs.'

'Can it be built using short lengths?'

Shriver considered and made some amendments to the drawing. 'I suppose it would be possible to build the tower up as a series of arches, with the arches getting progressively smaller – yes – that would be the best approach.' He showed the drawing to Kruger.

'Very neat, hauptmann. It looks right.'

Shriver nodded. 'There's an old adage about something being right if it looks right. This would make quite a sturdy structure. I haven't worked out the exact dimensions, but there need not be any timbers in it over three metres long.'

'Will we be able to salvage any of the timbers from the old tower?'

'I doubt it,' said Shriver, smiling. 'Most of them are fit only for burning in the boiler. Maybe some of the nails and spikes could be reused.'

'There's only one thing wrong. The observation platform must have a flat roof.'

'But that's absurd,' the army officer protested. 'A pitched roof made from split pine will not only look attractive, but it will be easier to make weatherproof.'

'It must have a flat roof,' Kruger insisted.

'And where do we get roofing felt from?'

'How about some of the linoleum from one of the unused dormitories?'

'Well I suppose it will do,' said Shriver doubtfully. 'But it won't be as effective as a pitched roof.'

'A flat roof please, hauptmann. As large as possible to

provide plenty of overhang protection for the tower's occupants. I would be grateful if you have the final drawing ready by this evening so that I can show it to Major Reynolds in case he disappears on a fishing trip tomorrow.'

As soon as Molde heard footsteps approaching the barn, he jumped down from the bales of straw. In case his would-be captor was nervous with a shotgun, he held his hands high above his head and mentally rehearsed the English phrase 'don't shoot' several times.

The latch was lifted and the door pulled open. Light streamed into the barn, making it difficult for Molde to see the man standing against the light. But there was no mistaking the silhouette of a shotgun draped over the man's forearm. The barrels were pointing at the ground.

The door swung closed. Molde saw that the man was about his own age. He was very English-looking and wearing an immaculate, expertly cut tweed suit.

'Don't shoot. I am unarmed,' Molde blurted out.

'I'm very pleased to hear it,' the young man answered. 'Please don't worry – there's no ammunition in this thing.'

Molde gaped in amazement at the young man. There was nothing very extraordinary about what he had said. What was extraordinary was that he had said it in German; not German as an Englishman would speak it, but with a distinct Saxony accent.

'You must be Leutnant Molde,' said the young man pleasantly, 'Correct?'

Molde nodded dumbly, his mind racing.

'I hope you enjoyed your meal?'

'Oh, yes, fine,' said Molde.

'I'm glad,' the young man smiled beguilingly. 'They mentioned your name on the radio this morning. I knew you were in here because you left a foot sticking out of the straw when you tried to hide. I moved the horse to another outhouse. He can be a bit touchy about sharing his accommodation.'

'Who the hell are you?' Molde eventually managed to stammer out.

The young man smiled disarmingly and gave a little bow. 'Leutnant Herbert Shultz of the *Kriegsmarine*. I used to be a prisoner of war at Grizedale Hall.'

Willi was armed with his trusty clipboard when he finally tracked Ulbrick down in the common room.

'No,' Ulbrick declared empathically when he had heard what Willi had to say. 'I refuse to have anything to do with Kruger's latest hare-brained scheme. It's bad enough having to do gardening, but I draw the line at collaborating with the enemy.'

'It's not collaborating,' said Willi.

'Building the British a new watchtower? If that's not collaborating, then I would like to know what is.'

'A number of officers will be in serious trouble with the British if a new tower isn't built,' Willi pointed out.

Ulbrick grunted. 'That's their problem. I had nothing to do with pulling the bloody thing down.'

'Everyone's got to help,' said Willi. 'And besides, it'll be something to do.'

'There's plenty to do. There's newspapers to be read. Chess games to be played. Radiators to be sat on. I lead a full life.'

'I'll put you down for tomorrow's forest working party,' said Willi, writing on his clipboard. 'Everyone has a job. Any officer refusing to co-operate will lose their privileges. Commander Kruger's orders.'

'And what will our commanding officer be doing? Nothing as usual. After the liberation there's going to be lot of embarrassing questions asked about Commander Kruger, and a lot of prisoners here are going to supply a lot of embarrassing answers.'

'That's where you're wrong,' said Willi, consulting his clipboard. 'He's got himself down for the last job of all on the tower.'

Ulbrick looked surprised. 'What's that?'

'He hasn't said on the work schedule,' said Willi. 'But according to the list he's drawn up, he will be driving in the final nails. Do I tell him that you're refusing to co-operate?'

Ulbrick muttered a curse under his breath. 'What do I have to do?'

'Report in the courtyard tomorrow morning immediately after roll-call.'

Work on the watchtower started the following day as soon as the forest working party returned with a handcart laden with lengths of pine. Shriver personally examined each timber. Those suitable for use in the tower were handed over to a working party to have the bark stripped off, and the rejected timbers were loaded on to the woodpile outside the hall's central heating boilerhouse.

The first stage of the operation – the digging of four deep trenches for the leg stays – was completed on the first day. During the rest of the week, the leg stays were set upright into the ground like piles. They provided a firm base for the legs to be positioned with temporary supports until the cross-bracing members were spiked permanently into place.

Shriver's design approach was to opt for cross-halfing joints wherever possible because they were simple to cut and stake. Only where strength was paramount did he insist on the more complex tusk tenon joints. Tools such as tree saws, sledgehammers, augers and chisels were loaned by the forestry warden.

By the end of the week, the tower was fifteen feet high. Progress slowed down for two days after that because a derrick – used for lifting heavy timbers – had to be designed and built, and positioned securely on top of the tower.

*

Cathy folded her table napkin and poured coffee for herself and her guests. She smiled warmly across the dinner table at Molde and Shultz in turn. 'Well,' she said. 'This is a lovely surprise. Two men to look after me. I'm going to be thoroughly spoilt, I know it.'

Shultz took her hand in his. 'Cathy,' he said gently. 'I have had a wonderful time with you. I do not think I will ever be able to repay you for your hospitality.'

Cathy's smile faded. 'But . . .' she prompted.

'It is time I moved on.'

'But, Bertie, you can't leave me. Where would you go? Back to the hall?'

Shultz looked faintly embarrassed. 'I do not know. Perhaps I will be able to find a ship at Liverpool to take me to southern Ireland – or even Sweden.'

Cathy stared down at the table and toyed absentmindedly with her napkin ring. 'When do you want to leave?'

'Tomorrow. Cathy, I am sorry, really I am –'

Suddenly Cathy brightened up as though she had made a determined effort to push the inevitable out of her mind. 'Let's worry about that tomorrow. Tonight we'll have a party. Just the three of us.'

'You're seeing Nurse Hobson tomorrow for your check-up, aren't you, commander?' Willi queried apprehensively, looking up from his newspaper.

Kruger glanced at his home-made wall calendar. 'That's correct, Willi. What of it?'

'Can you remember the name of the ship her husband was transferred to?'

The anxious note in Willi's voice alerted Kruger. 'The *Barham*. Why?'

'That's what I thought.' The little Bavarian continued reading, his face drawn and pale.

Kruger began to get annoyed. 'Willi, do you mind telling me what's the matter?'

Willi passed Kruger the newspaper he was reading. 'It's on the front page, commander. HMS *Barham* was torpedoed in the Mediterranean three days ago.'

Kruger read the news item in silence. It was terse, and to the point: on 25 November 1941, the battleship *Barham*, a veteran of the Battle of Jutland during the Great War, had been torn apart by a cataclysmic explosion following a torpedo attack by a U-boat. The mighty ship had sunk almost immediately, taking over eight hundred men to the bottom.

'Hell,' breathed Kruger softly.

'Maybe she won't come in to work tomorrow?'

'She will,' said Kruger emphatically.

The following day Cathy crammed Leutnant Herbert Shultz's kitbag with food. She tried hard not to cry but when Shultz appeared in the kitchen, wearing his original dark trousers and rollneck pullover instead of one of her late husband's tweed suits, she finally broke down and wept.

'Please, Bertie,' she pleaded between her tears. 'Stay just a few more days.'

'I have to go now, Cathy. I have been free for a year and I have only got five miles from the camp. Someone at home might start asking questions.'

'But there'll be police and the army still out looking for Victor.'

'But I am not Victor.' Shultz kissed the inside of her palms. 'We have had some lovely times together, Cathy. I do not know how I will ever be able to repay you.'

'You will write, won't you, Bertie? You promise?'

'Of course I will. And I will be back as soon as this stupid war is over.'

'That could be years,' Cathy sobbed. 'What am I going to do in the meantime?'

'Victor will look after you.'

Cathy struggled to bring her tears under control. She clung to Shultz. 'I don't want Victor, I want you.'

'I will be back, Cathy,' said Shultz, gently disengaging Cathy's fingers. 'I promise.' He picked up a wallet that was lying on the kitchen table. 'Is this the money?'

Cathy nodded. 'Thirty pounds. I hope it's enough. And the identity card is in the kitbag.'

Shultz kissed her. He pulled on a greatcoat and buttoned it up. 'It is more than enough. God bless you, Cathy. Thank you for everything.' He swung the kitbag on to his shoulder, opened the kitchen door and left the farmhouse. Cathy watched him walking across the farmyard. He reached the gate, turned around and waved, and then was gone.

She stood at the window for several minutes, gazing with unseeing eyes at the farmyard gate where Shultz had vanished. She felt in her apron pocket and took out the identity card that she had stolen during a visit to a tenant's house. Perhaps leaving it out of the kitbag had been selfish but she had been unable to think of anything else that would bring Bertie back to her.

A polite cough behind prompted her to hurriedly stuff the incriminating identity card back in her pocket and turn around.

Molde was standing in the doorway, looking uncomfortable in an expertly cut tweed suit, despite the fact that the suit was a perfect fit. Cathy stared at him.

'Er . . . Does it look all right?' asked Molde, embarrassed by Cathy's silence.

'All right?' Cathy echoed hollowly, taking a trance-like step towards Molde. 'All right?' There was a dazed look in her eyes.

'I thought that perhaps the waistcoat needs altering. Not too much. Perhaps it is a little loose at the front, do you think?'

'You're perfect!' said Cathy abruptly. 'You're stunningly, marvellously perfect!'

Suddenly, to Molde's surprise and alarm, she launched herself across the kitchen, threw her arms around his neck, and held him in a powerful grip. 'Victor!' she cried. 'You're perfect! Absolutely perfect! You won't ever leave me, will you? Promise me. *Please, please* promise me.'

As Molde steadied himself by circling his arms involuntarily around Cathy's waist, he couldn't help wondering what he had let himself in for.

'Get undressed and get on the scales,' Brenda told Kruger. There were dark shadows under her eyes and her voice lacked its usual briskness. She checked Kruger's weight and entered the information on her record card.

'You can get dressed now.'

Even Kruger was deterred by the ice in her voice. He tightened his tie and said. 'Nurse, we were all very upset to hear about what happened to your husband.'

'Thank you, commander,' Brenda replied calmly, without looking up from her desk.

Kruger's eyes went to the photograph of the smiling young man and the child. 'Is that your son?'

Brenda slipped the card back into the index drawer and slammed it shut. 'Yes.'

'He looks like his father. You must be very proud.'

'Yes, I am.' She looked at Kruger for the first time and he was immediately aware of the hatred in her eyes. 'What's it to you?'

'What is his name?'

'Stephen.'

'How old is he?'

'He's seven on New Year's Eve . . . Commander, I would appreciate it if you would leave now before I say something that both of us might regret.'

Kruger pulled his cap on and turned to the door. 'It will be Christmas soon, nurse. If there's anything that I can do, or any of the prisoners can do –'

244

Brenda suddenly flared up. 'Haven't you done enough? You and all the other bastards like you in your cowardly U-boats? Or have you come in here to gloat?'

'I want you to know –'

'I don't care what you want me to know. All I want from you right now is for you to get out!'

Fleming finished his monthly report to Admiral Godfrey and read it through. Something in his nature revolted against using padding, with the result that the report – his eighth – only covered a single side of a foolscap sheet. In general, his appearances at Grizedale Hall had not produced a flood of intelligence, and his efforts to learn about German radio ranging and location development from Kruger and other prisoners had got nowhere. There had been exceptions in other fields of technical development, such as the time in September when he had helped a captured U-boat officer with his divorce papers. From that officer, Fleming had learned about an anti-Asdic device called *Pillenwertha* that was being fitted to all U-boats. Apart from that, his posting had been a disappointment, although Admiral Godfrey had generously commented after one particularly meagre report that what intelligence had been obtained was providing valuable corroborative evidence.

Fleming sighed and decided that it was time for him to return to London for a spell. He was sealing the report in an envelope when Kruger tapped on his door and entered.

'Otto,' said Fleming, genuinely pleased. 'This is a pleasure. Please take a seat.'

'I would prefer to stand,' said Kruger stiffly. 'This won't take a minute.'

'Fire away, old boy.'

'I'm sure you are aware that some prisoners have been in the habit of selling unwanted items in their parcels to the guards – shaving soap, that sort of thing.'

Fleming chuckled. 'I know it goes on,' he replied, wondering where the conversation was leading. 'Why?'

Kruger seemed lost for words for a moment. He reached into his pocket and laid an envelope on Fleming's desk. 'I know that this is unorthodox, commander, but the prisoners have organized a collection to buy some Christmas toys for Nurse Hobson's son. There's fifteen pounds in this envelope. Perhaps on your next trip to London, you would be kind enough to spend it for us?'

Fleming was too taken back to reply immediately. When he did, it was to shake his head and push the envelope back across his desk. 'I'm sorry, commander. Tell the prisoners concerned that it is a generous thought, but I can't do it.'

'Then perhaps Major Reynolds will be willing to help?'

'It's not because I'm not willing, Otto,' said Fleming hastily. 'It's simply because there are hardly any toys to be had in the shops right now. What toys there are disappear on to the black market right away. I'm sorry.'

Kruger nodded and pocketed the envelope. 'I would be grateful if you said nothing about this to Nurse Hobson.'

'Understood,' Fleming replied.

By the end of the first week in December, the watchtower was nearly up to its full height, and lacked only the covered observation platform.

It held the promise of being a magnificent structure. All the timbers were carefully varnished before they were fixed in position, and Shriver's attention to detail was such that he had a special team of five men at work whose sole responsibility was to build the spiral staircase that wound its way up through the centre of the gracefully tiered timber arches.

Even Sergeant Finch, who still mistrusted Kruger's motives in wanting to build the tower, found himself grudgingly looking forward to when it would be finished.

'It's going to be a fine Christmas present, sergeant,'

Major Reynolds had observed when they had inspected the unfinished structure.

Sergeant Finch had cautiously agreed with him.

The prisoners organized a rapturous welcome for Berg when he arrived back at the camp. He eased himself down from the back of the truck and looked around in surprise as the cheering prisoners swarmed around him. He barely had time to exchange handshakes with Kruger and Willi when two prisoners scooped him on to their shoulders and carried him around the grounds at the head of a cheering mob.

Those prisoners who had arrived at the hall after Berg had been carted off to hospital stared in amazement at the curious spectacle. One even plucked up the courage to ask Kruger who the new arrival was, and why wasn't he being put in solitary confinement?

After the months of soft living with Cathy, Shultz was having a miserable time on the run. A day's walk had taken him to Windermere railway station but he had turned away into a side street because the station forecourt was swarming with civilian and military police who were meticulously checking every passenger's identity card. The next day he discovered that it was exactly the same at the smaller stations of Staveley and Burneside.

He spent two shivering, thoroughly miserable nights in a shepherd's stone shelter high up on Wansfell Pike overlooking Lake Windermere. On the third night he lit a small fire in the fireplace. He decided that he didn't care if someone came to investigate the smoke. As luck would have it, the wood stacked up in the shelter was tinder dry and burned without smoke. As he sat staring into the flames, the same questions kept running through his mind. Why had Cathy left the identity card out of his kitbag? Had she left it out accidently? Or had she done so deliberately? And if so, why?

'It certainly is good to have you back with us, Berg,' said Kruger during the evening meal.

Berg beamed around the crowded common room. 'It's great to be back, commander. In three months my leg should be back to its former strength.'

'And your concussion? Its after-effects can be most unpleasant,' Kruger observed.

'Sometimes I get a ringing in my ears,' said Berg dismissively. 'But I've got used to it now.'

'Well, let's hope you haven't brought back any more rumours from hospital about our transfer to Canada.'

Berg chuckled and sliced up the extra sausages he had been given. 'I heard nothing this time, commander. Only the ringing noise in my ears.'

Kruger watched Berg's knife expertly slitting the sausages open. 'I see that your skill with your hands hasn't deserted you, Berg.'

'Oh, not at all, commander. I kept my hand in at the hospital by making all sorts of things.'

'Good. Because I've got some work for you.'

Berg looked interested. 'On the tower? I'd enjoy that – it's a fascinating project.'

'No,' said Kruger, shaking his head. 'Not on the tower, but on something almost as important.' He went on to briefly outline what he wanted Berg to do.

'I'll be delighted to help,' said Berg, smiling warmly. 'I can't think of anything else I'd rather do.'

Molde surprised himself at how easy he found it to slip into a routine at Cathy's farmhouse. When the weather was fine, he went riding with her on the high fells. At other times she found innumerable small jobs for him to do in and around the farmhouse and its outhouses. Caligula soon learned to accept him as part of the household and an uneasy truce was agreed between them which the cantankerous horse was inclined to forget. The only irksome aspect of living with Cathy was having to make himself scarce whenever she had visitors. But, on the whole, the life was agreeable and the occasional moments of daytime boredom were more than offset by the tempestuous night-time events that Cathy loved to stage in her bedroom.

Berg was kept frantically busy from the day after his return and was rarely seen outside his workshop. Brunel was press-ganged into helping him and, after some initial objections, soon become absorbed in acquiring the skills necessary to operate Berg's home-made woodturning lathe with a reasonable degree of proficiency. After two days he surprised himself by making a matching set of four wheels out of a fruit packing case. That they had to be made again because Berg's first experiment with home-made axles went badly wrong was hardly his fault.

It took Shultz five minutes to smash a hole in the layer of ice that covered the tarn. He dipped his fingers in the freezing water and hurriedly withdrew them. He decided to remain dirty. Anyway, there was always a wind blowing so he could never really smell himself. The water in the ice pool became still. Shultz looked at his reflection and was shocked by the appearance of the fearful, unshaven apparition that stared back at him. It was hard to believe that five days living rough could do that to a man. He was cold, miserable and hungry, and had had enough. He stood up and was dismayed to discover that he now had diarrhoea to add to his problems. He decided to give himself up at the nearest police station.

At 10 am on 8 December, Shriver reported to Kruger's office. He gave his senior officer a smart salute and said, 'The tower is finished except for the work you said that you wanted to do on it, commander.'

'Excellent, hauptmann,' said Kruger, lighting a cheroot.

'You've done an excellent job. My congratulations. I will need a hammer and some clout nails.'

'They're ready on the platform for you, commander. Everyone is waiting,' Shriver replied, eyeing the ten-feet high roll of black linoleum that was standing in the corner of the office.

'Thank you, hauptmann. Give Major Reynolds my compliments and tell him I'll be along in five minutes.'

Shriver saluted and left.

The hall sounded curiously empty and quiet as Kruger went down the main staircase with the roll of linoleum tucked under his arm. He paused at the french windows to gaze across the grounds at the watchtower, rising solid and dependable above the trees. Shriver had gone to considerable pains shaping the timbers to ensure that the tower was symmetrical. The result was that from a distance it looked as though it was of steel girder construction.

All the prisoners were standing at ease in parade formation near the foot of the tower. Shriver, Braun and a few other senior German officers were standing in the front row. They were flanked by all the guards on duty. Major Reynolds and Sergeant Finch were standing side by side facing the parade. Even Fleming was watching from a distance.

Kruger made his way around the vegetable plots and walked to the head of the parade. He stood the roll of linoleum on end and shook hands with Reynolds and Sergeant Finch.

'I guess this is a great day, commander,' Reynolds observed. 'I've just delivered a little speech congratulating everyone who has worked on the tower.'

'We have all worked on it, major,' Kruger replied. He gestured at the roll of linoleum. 'Even I have a job to do. I have to waterproof the observation platform's canopy. The final task of all.' He caught Braun's eye and correctly guessed that the young pilot was having to work hard at preventing himself from bursting out laughing. He picked up the roll of linoleum. 'Am I correct in assuming that the question of a report concerning the collapse of the old tower is forgotten?'

Reynolds grinned. 'What report, commander?'

Kruger nodded. 'Thank you, major. If you will forgive me, the tower will be ready for handing over in about fifteen minutes.'

With that, Kruger walked beneath the structure and tied the roll of black linoleum to a rope that was hanging down from the observation platform. As he climbed the spiral staircase, he noticed minor constructional details such as the fact that the balustrade had been sanded smooth so that there were no splinters waiting for an unwary hand. He reached the spacious observation platform and glanced down at the sea of faces looking up at him. It took him a few seconds to haul the linoleum up to the platform and push it through the trapdoor on to the flat roof. He pocketed the hammer and a box of nails and climbed through the trapdoor.

Unrolling the linoleum in the strong breeze posed an expected problem, which he solved by placing the linoleum in its approximate position and temporarily tacking it down at the corners. The orientation of the roof covering was vital. He used a pocket compass to confirm that it was correctly aligned before he started nailing it down in its final position. It took him ten minutes to make sure that the linoleum was securely fastened to the canopy. He trimmed off the surplus linoleum with his pocket knife and stood up to study his handiwork with a dispassionate eye.

Painted across the linoleum in three-feet high white letters was the single word: **BARROW**. Beneath the solitary word was a broad arrow, over six-feet long, that was pointing south-west towards Barrow-in-Furness.

Kruger had used poster paint for the giant sign, which

meant that it would not survive many Lake District downpours. He prayed that it would last until the bombers came that night or the night after.

The one thing Berg enjoyed doing most in his workshop was painting. There was a particular satisfaction to be derived from sanding a carefully worked piece of timber to a mirror finish before applying successive coats of lacquer and rubbing down each coat when it had hardened. Provided it was done carefully, what was originally a rough lump of wood could be made into something that looked like polished steel.

He and Brunel made a good team, and the results of their labours – lined up on the shelves – were a testament to their painstaking craftmanship.

Shultz dithered outside the tiny police house at Hawkshead, uncertain what to do. A woman passed by and wrinkled her nose in disgust. She made up Shultz's mind for him. He pushed the door open and shuffled into the house. A uniformed police constable was reading a newspaper while resting his feet on a pot-bellied boiler. He lowered the paper and gazed suspiciously at the thing confronting him. His nose gave an experimental twitch.

'Good evening,' said Shultz politely. 'I am an escaped German prisoner of war and I wish to give myself up.'

Police Constable Harry Tinker was Hawkshead's acting village policeman while Sergeant Webb was on leave. The last advice Sergeant Webb had given Harry before leaving was to tell him to watch out for a tramp named Soapy Sam who would do anything during the winter months to get himself in a police cell for the night. Under no circumstances was Soapy to be allowed into the police house because it had to be fumigated afterwards.

'Clear off,' said Harry curtly.

'But I'm an escaped –'

252

'I said – clear off!'

'But –'

'OUT!' Harry lent emphasis to his request by threatening Shultz with a truncheon which he clutched in his right hand while he used his left hand to hold his nose.

Shultz wandered forlornly out into the cold and wondered what to do next.

Brunel and Berg waited until 11 pm before they decided it was safe to make a move. They had remained in the workshop after lights out, crouching in the dark behind the workbench, hardly daring to breathe as the guards checked that the place was empty.

They carefully wrapped the smaller items in rags and placed them in a sack which Berg tied across Brunel's shoulders. Brunel checked that he had some suitable lengths of wire in his pocket and pulled on a pair of thick woollen socks while Berg opened the door and peered cautiously across the courtyard. He waited until two guards strolled by and then signalled to Brunel.

The diminutive officer raced cat-like across the courtyard and crouched under the window of Brenda's sickbay. He carefully slipped a length of bent piano wire under the sash catch and teased it into position. After a while he managed to slide the catch back and open the window. He disappeared into the sickbay and emerged a minute later clutching the now empty sack in his hand. He raced back to the workshop, grinning triumphantly.

'Nothing to it,' he whispered to Berg.

'Fine,' said Berg. 'Now for the rest. Can you manage the car as it is or shall we wrap it up?'

'I'll take it as it is,' Brunel answered.

'Well, mind you don't scratch it.'

By midnight all the results of Berg's and Brunel's labours had been safely transferred to the sickbay.

Unknown to the two men, another prisoner was also out

and about that night when he should have been locked up in the main hall.

'Schumann, John, Leutnant!' Sergeant Finch yelled, calling out the names from his roll-call list that he knew virtually by heart.

'Present!'

'Shulke, Jacob, Oberleutnant!'

'Present!'

'Shultz, Herbert, Leutnant!'

'Present!'

'Siemens, Wolfgang, Hauptmann!'

'Present!'

Sergeant Finch suddenly froze. His eyes narrowed. Someone was playing silly buggers. 'Who answered to Herbert Shultz's name?' he bawled indignantly.

'I did, sergeant!' answered a voice from the back of the parade.

All the prisoners turned their heads.

'Eyes front!' Kruger ordered.

'Who said "I did"?' Finch roared, his face puce with anger as he strained to look over the heads of the prisoners.

'Me, sergeant.'

'Who's me? What's your name? Where are you?'

'Leutnant Herbert Shultz. I am here.'

'Step forward that man,' Kruger called out.

A bedraggled, miserable looking creature shuffled forward. The prisoners quickly and willingly made a path for him through the parade.

'Who the hell are you!' Finch demanded, taking an involuntary step back when he caught a whiff of the new arrival.

'I'm Leutnant Herbert Shultz,' said Shultz, managing to muster a smile through his unkempt beard. 'It looks like we are all one big unhappy family again.'

*

Brenda unlocked the door of her sickbay, pushed it open and gave a gasp of surprise at the spectacle that confronted her.

There were toys everywhere. They were on her desk, on the filing cabinet, on the scales, and even on the couch. There were brightly painted little tanks, a glove puppet, a wooden soldier with a drum slung across his chest, a model train sitting on a circular track with a clockwork key sticking out of the top of the locomotive, and even a clock with toyland scenes painted on its face. The largest toy of all was a magnificent child's pedal-car that looked like a miniature version of Fleming's Bentley.

Hardly able to credit her senses, Brenda entered her Aladdin's Cave sickbay and picked up one of the toys. Four gaily coloured wooden chickens mounted on a table-tennis bat immediately started banging their beaks on the bat in time with a swinging weight suspended beneath the bat. She put the toy down and picked up a hand-painted Christmas card. It bore the inscription: 'To Stephen – wishing you a happy Christmas, a happy birthday, and a happy 1942. From all the prisoners at Grizedale Hall '

Brenda felt her legs threatening to collapse under her. She sat hurriedly down on her chair. Suddenly she was trembling violently and then she broke into a flood of anguished tears.

Fleming fell into step beside Kruger as the senior officer took his customary stroll around the grounds. 'That was a decent gesture, Otto,' he remarked. 'Making all those toys for Brenda's son.'

'Don't thank me, commander,' Kruger replied. 'Thank the officers who made them.'

'But you instigated it, Otto.'

'Perhaps.'

'I'm off back to London until the new year,' said

Fleming. 'I thought I'd wish you a happy Christmas before I left.'

'Thank you, commander. I wish you the same.'

The two men walked in silence for a few minutes. They reached the southern barbed wire perimeter fence. 'Have you thought about how much longer this war is going to last?' Fleming asked.

'I think of nothing else,' said Kruger. 'Four months? Six months perhaps? I don't know.'

'I think it will be longer than that, Otto. A lot longer.'

'What makes you so sure?'

'Everything has changed,' said Fleming. 'Hitler has just declared war on the United States.'

Kruger stopped walking and stared at Fleming. 'Are you sure?'

Fleming nodded. 'It'll be on the news within the hour.'

Kruger remained silent. He lit a cheroot and inhaled deeply. 'So . . . what will happen to us now?'

'Well . . . it looks as if you'll be here for at least another year.'

Kruger turned to face the wire.

Fleming waited for a minute but Kruger gave no indication that he was going to speak or that he wished for Fleming's company to continue. The British officer decided that there was no point in staying. He turned and walked away. Only when he reached the terrace steps did he look back.

Kruger had not moved. He was standing motionless, staring at the high barbed-wire fence. His greatcoat flapped in the wind and the flurries of driving snow sweeping down from the fells offered a bleak promise of a long, bitter winter to come.